The Black Opal

By Victoria Holt

VICTORIA HOLT

*The Black
Opal*

DOUBLEDAY
New York   London   Toronto   Sydney   Auckland

PUBLISHED BY DOUBLEDAY
a division of Bantam Doubleday Dell Publishing Group, Inc.
1540 Broadway, New York, New York 10036

DOUBLEDAY and the portrayal of an anchor with a dolphin are
trademarks of Doubleday, a division of Bantam Doubleday Dell
Publishing Group, Inc.

Library of Congress Cataloging-in-Publication Data

Holt, Victoria, 1906–
The black opal/Victoria Holt.—1st ed.
p.   cm.
I. Title.
PR6015.I3B55   1993
823'.914—dc20   92-33830
CIP

ISBN 0-385-47024-X
Printed in the United States of America
September 1993
First Edition

1   3   5   7   9   10   8   6   4   2

Contents

The Black Opal

Discovery
in the Garden

ONE EARLY MARCH MORNING when Tom Yardley was strolling round the garden to see how the newly-planted roses were coming along, he made a startling discovery.

Tom was gardener to Dr. Marline at Commonwood House and, as he said, he was not much of a sleeper. He would often rise as soon as it was light and go into the garden, which provided his main interest in life.

He could not believe his eyes, but there it was. He heard it cry first and, looking under the azalea bush—the one which had given him all that trouble last year—what should he see wrapped up in a woollen shawl, but a baby.

I was that baby.

The doctor had lived in Commonwood House ever since he had taken over the practice from old Dr. Freeman. He had bought it with his wife's money, so it was said, and people in small country places always knew such details about their neighbours. The doctor and Mrs. Marline kept a comfortable house—on her money, of course—and it was Mrs. Marline who was master as well as mistress of the house.

At the time when I made my appearance there were three children in the family. Adeline was ten and simple. The servants whispered about her and I learned that her birth had been a "difficult" one. She had never been quite "all there." Mrs. Marline, who could not believe that anything she produced could not be perfect, had been most upset and there had been a long gap before Henry was born. He was four years old at the time of my arrival, and there was nothing wrong with him, nor with Estella, who was two years younger.

Nanny Gilroy was in charge of the nursery and Sally Green, who was thirteen at the time, had just come to the house to be trained by Nanny, which was fortunate for me, for she told me, when I was of an age to understand, of my coming and the effect it had had on the household.

"Well, nobody might have found you," she said. "You could have stayed under that bush till you died, poor mite. But I reckon you would have made yourself heard. A proper little bawler, you was. Tom Yardley come up them nursery stairs holding you as if he thought you was going to bite him. Nanny wasn't up. She come out of her bedroom in that old red flannel dressing-gown and her hair in curlers. I'd heard too, so I came out. Tom Yardley said, 'Look what I found . . . under that azalea bush—the one I had all that trouble with last year.'

"Nanny Gilroy stared at him. Then she said, 'My patience me. Here's a nice how do you do, I must say.'

"I took to you straightaway. I love babies, especially when they're little and helpless, before they start getting into everything. Nanny said, 'It belongs to one of them gypsies, I'll be bound. Come here, making a nuisance of themselves, and then go off, leaving messes for other people to clear up.' "

I did not like hearing myself referred to as "a mess," but I loved the story and kept silent. The gypsies, it seemed, had been camping in the woods not far from Commonwood House. One could see the woods from the back windows; and it was clear why the house was called Commonwood House, because there were views of the common from the front.

Sally went on to tell me that Nanny Gilroy had thought the sensible thing would have been to send me off to an orphanage or the workhouse, which were the places for babies left under bushes.

"Well, there was a regular to-do," she explained. "Mrs. Marline came up to the nursery to take a look at you. She didn't much like what she saw. She gave you that funny look of hers with her mouth turned down and her eyes half-closed, and she said the blanket must be burned on the rubbish heap and you cleaned up.

Then the authorities could be consulted and could come and take you away.

"The doctor came up then. He looked at you for a bit without saying anything. He was all the doctor then. He said, 'The child is hungry. Give her some milk, Nanny, and clean her.'

"There was this thing hanging round your neck."

I said, "I know. I have always kept it—a pendant. It's on a chain and it's got markings on it."

"The doctor looked at it and said, 'They're Romany signs . . . or something like that. She must have come from the gypsies.'

"Nanny was ever so pleased, because that was what she'd thought. 'I knew it,' she said. 'Coming here in them woods. It ought not to be allowed.' The doctor held up his hand. You know the way he has . . . as though he didn't want to hear her, but you know Nanny. She thought she was right and she said the sooner the baby was on its way to the orphanage the better. It was the proper place for you.

"The doctor said, 'Can you be sure of that, Nanny?'

" 'Well,' said Nanny, 'she's a regular little gypsy, sir. It should be the poorhouse or the orphanage for that sort.'

" 'Can you be sure what sort she is?' His voice was all cold like, and Nanny should have noticed, but she was so sure she was right. She said, 'There's no doubt in my mind.'

" 'Then you are very discerning,' he said. 'But to me this child's origins are not obvious as yet.'

"You started to bawl at the top of your voice and I was dying to tell you to stop, 'cos, with your face all red and screwed up, you wasn't the prettiest sight, and I thought, 'They'll get rid of you, you silly baby, if you go on like that, and how are you going to like that orphanage?'

" 'I think, sir,' Nanny started to say, but the doctor stopped her.

" 'Don't make the effort, Nanny,' he said, which was a polite way of saying 'shut up.' 'Mrs. Marline and I will decide what is to be done.'

"Well, Nanny had to do what the doctor ordered, so she washed you and put you into some of Miss Estella's clothes, and you looked like a proper baby then. We heard that you were to stay at Commonwood for a while because someone might claim you—which seemed unlikely since whoever you belonged to had just left you under that azalea bush.

3

"Nanny said, 'The doctor's soft, but it won't be him who has the last word. Mistress will be the one who has that. He can't see that it's better for that baby to go now, before she gets to know the ways of gentlefolk.'

"Nanny was wrong. She could have sworn Mistress would have had that baby out of the house in next to no time. But, for some reason, she had to do what the doctor wanted."

So I stayed in Commonwood House and what was most extraordinary was that I was to share the nursery with the Marline children.

"You was more my little baby than anyone else's," Sally said. "I took to you and you took to me. Nanny couldn't forget how you'd come. You didn't belong here, she said. She couldn't bring herself to treat you like the others, never had and never would."

I knew that well enough. As for Mrs. Marline, she scarcely ever glanced at me, though once or twice, when I caught her doing so, she looked quickly away. The doctor was aloof on the rare occasions when I encountered him, but he always gave me a vacant smile and sometimes patted my head and said, "All right?" to which I would nod nervously and he would nod in return and quickly pass on, as though eager to get away from me.

Adeline was always gentle. She liked babies and helped me when I was small. She used to hold my hand when I was learning to walk; she showed me pictures in the nursery books and seemed to delight in them as much as I did.

Estella was in turn friendly and hostile. It seemed that she sometimes remembered Nanny's contempt for me and shared it. At other times she treated me like a sister.

As for Henry, he took little notice of me, but, as he appeared to have no time for any girls or people younger than himself—and that included his sister—it was not hurtful in the least.

It was some time before they decided I must have a name. I had always been referred to as "the child," or by Nanny as "that gypsy."

Sally told me how it had come about. Sally was interested in names. "Ever since I heard mine meant 'Princess.' That's Sarah, see? Well, they was going to call you Rose. Tom Yardley was always telling how he'd gone out to look at the roses he'd just planted when he found you under the azalea bush. So they thought

4

Rose would be a good name for you. I didn't like it. You wasn't a Rose to me. There are lots of Roses. You were somehow different. I thought you had something of the look of a little gypsy. Once I'd heard of somebody who was a gypsy called Carmen . . . no, it was Carmel, I think. And, do you know, when I found out Carmel meant a garden, well, it was right, wasn't it? You couldn't be anything else but Carmel. Wasn't you found in the garden? 'Carmel,' I said. 'That's her name. Couldn't be anything else.' Nobody minded much and they all started calling you Carmel. Then March . . . it was March when Tom Yardley found you. So, you could say I named you."

"Thank you, Sally," I said. "There *are* a lot of Roses."

So there I was. Carmel March, origins unknown, living in Commonwood House by the grace of Dr. Marline and suffered with something less than grace by his masterful wife and Nanny Gilroy.

It was perhaps not surprising that I grew up to be what Nanny Gilroy called "pushing." In that household, where I had to fend for myself in a way, I had constantly to make people understand that I did not intend to be treated as a person of no importance. I had to make them understand that, although my origins might be obscure, I was as good as any of them.

In those early days, my domain was mostly the nursery where Nanny Gilroy made a distinct difference in her treatment between me and the others. I was the outsider, and although I had to admit the truth of this, at the same time I had to show them that there was something rather special about being a person of mystery. I was there under sufferance because of a strange idea the doctor had got into his head about orphan children, and for an even stranger reason that Mrs. Marline had let it pass, so I was defiant. I told myself I was as good as any of them. This made me assertive.

"Gypsy blood!" commented Nanny. "Weren't they always pushing in with their clothes pegs and trying to tempt you into crossing their hands with silver in return for their telling you some trumped-up tale about the great fortune that would be yours?"

I wondered a good deal about the gypsies and tried to find out all I could. I discovered they lived in caravans and travelled from place to place. To me they were mysterious and romantic people. And it was almost certain that I was one of them.

Miss Mary Harley used to come to the house to teach us.

She was the vicar's daughter—very tall, angular with untidy, wispy hair which kept escaping from the hairpins which were intended to control it. She was nervous and self-effacing, and, I know now, not very effectual. But she was kind and, as I was very appreciative of any kindness which came my way, I was fond of her.

She came because Mrs. Marline had said the children were too young to go away to school and Miss Harley would do very well until that time came.

Miss Harley was very pleased to come. I had heard Nanny Gilroy comment to Mrs. Barton, the cook, that she would be glad of the money. There wasn't much of that to spare at the vicarage, and not surprising with that barn of a place to keep up and three daughters to marry off and none of them much to look at. Everyone said the vicarage family was as poor as their church mice, and the money would come in handy.

Miss Harley taught me my letters and I used to sit with Adeline, whom I soon overtook—and I was very contented during these sessions.

Outstanding in all my childhood memories was my first meeting with Uncle Toby.

I liked to go into the garden alone and my steps often took me in the direction of the azalea bush. I would imagine that March morning when I was placed there. I would picture a hazy figure stealing into the garden, creeping silently so as not to be heard. And there was I, wrapped up in a shawl. Carefully, lovingly, I should have been placed under the bushes and whoever had left me would kiss me tenderly, because she—it must have been a she, for it was women who were concerned with babies—must have been very unhappy at leaving me.

Who was she? A gypsy, Nanny had said. She would have big earrings in her ears and her hair would be black and curly, hanging down over her shoulders.

And while I stood there, someone came very close to me. He said, "Hello! Who are you?"

I turned sharply. He seemed enormous. He was indeed very tall. He had fair hair—bleached by the sun, I discovered later—and his skin was golden brown. He had the bluest eyes I had ever seen and he was smiling.

6

"I'm Carmel," I said with that dignity I had learned to assume.

"Well, that's fine," he said. "Now, I knew there was something special about you. What are you doing here?"

"I'm looking at the azalea bush."

"It's a very nice one."

"It gave Tom Yardley a lot of trouble once."

"Did it then? But you like it?"

"I was found under it."

"Oh, so it was there, was it? Do you come here often to look at it?"

I nodded.

"Well, I suppose you would. It's not everyone who's found under an azalea bush, is it?"

I hunched my shoulders and laughed. He joined in my laughter.

"How old are you, Carmel?"

I held up four fingers.

He counted them solemnly.

"Four years old? My word! That's a fine age to be! How long have you been it?"

"I came in March. That's why I'm Carmel March."

"I'm Uncle Toby."

"Whose Uncle Toby?"

"Henry's, Estella's, Adeline's. Yours too, if you'll have me."

I laughed again. I was apt to laugh without any definite reason when I was happy; and there was something about him which made me so.

"Will you?" he went on.

I nodded. "You don't live here," I said.

"I'm visiting. I came last night."

"Will you stay here?"

"For a while. Then I'll be off."

"Where?"

"To sea . . . I live at sea."

"That's fishes," I said disbelievingly.

"And sailors," he added.

"Uncle Toby! Uncle Toby!" Estella was running towards us. She flung herself at him.

"Hello, hello!" He picked her up and held her up above him while they laughed together. I was jealous. Then Henry came up.

"Uncle Toby!"

7

He put Estella down and he and Henry started talking together.

"When did you come? How long will you stay? Where have you been?"

"All will be revealed," he said. "I came last night after you were in bed. I've been hearing all about you, what you've been doing when I wasn't here. And I've made the acquaintance of Carmel."

Estella glanced rather derisively in my direction, but Uncle Toby's smile was warm.

"Let's go in," he said. "I've got lots to tell you and lots to show you."

"Yes, yes," cried Estella.

"Come on then," said Henry.

Estella clung to Uncle Toby's hand and pulled him towards the house. I felt suddenly left alone, and then Uncle Toby turned to me and held out his hand.

"Come along, Carmel," he said.

And I was happy again.

Uncle Toby's visits were the happiest times of my early days. They were not very frequent but all the more cherished for that. He was Mrs. Marline's brother, which never ceased to amaze me. There could not be two people less like each other. There was none of her austerity about him. He gave the impression that nothing in the world ever bothered him. Whatever it was, he would overcome it, and he made one feel that one could do the same. Perhaps that was at the root of his charm.

The household was quite different when he was there. Even Nanny Gilroy softened. He used to say things to them all which he could not have meant. Lies, I thought? Surely that was not very good. But whatever Uncle Toby did was right in my eyes.

"Nanny," he would say, "you grow more beautiful every time I see you."

"You get along with you, Captain Sinclair," she would say, pursing her lips and bridling. I think she really believed it.

Even Mrs. Marline changed. Her face softened when she looked at him and I continued to marvel that he could be *her* brother. The doctor was also affected. He laughed more. As for Estella and Henry, they were always hanging round him. He was kind and especially gentle with Adeline. She would sit smiling at him so that she really looked quite beautiful in a strange way.

What enchanted me was that he always made a point of including me. I fancied he liked me more than the others—but perhaps that was what I wanted to believe.

He would say, "Come along, Carmel." And he would take my hand and press it. "You keep close to Uncle Toby." As if I needed to be asked to do that!

"He is *my* Uncle Toby," Estella reminded me. "He's not yours."

"He says he will be my uncle if I want him to, and I do."

"Gypsies don't have uncles like Uncle Toby."

That saddened me, because I knew it was true. But I refused to accept it. He never showed any difference between me and the others. In fact, I think he made a very special point of showing that he wanted to be *my* uncle.

When he did come to the house, he always spent a great deal of time with the children. Estella and Henry were having riding lessons and he said I ought to have them too. He set me on a pony with a leading rein attached to it and led us round and round a field. That was the height of bliss to me.

He used to tell us stories of what he did at sea. He took his ship to countries all round the world. He spoke of places of which I had never heard: the mysterious East, the wonders of Egypt, colourful India, France, Italy, and Spain.

I would stand by the globe in the schoolroom, turning it round, and would cry out to Miss Harley, "Where is India? Where is Egypt?" I wanted to know more about those wonderful places which had been visited by the even more wonderful Uncle Toby.

He brought presents for the children and—wonder of wonders—for me, too. It was useless for Estella to tell me that he was not my Uncle Toby. He was mine . . . more than theirs.

My present was a box in sandalwood on which sat three little monkeys. He told me they were saying, "See no evil, Speak no evil, Hear no evil," and when the lid of the box was lifted, it played "God Save the Queen." I had never possessed anything so beautiful. I would not let it out of my sight. I kept it by my bed so that in the night I could stretch out my hand and feel it was there, and the first thing I did on waking was to play that tune.

Commonwood House was enchanted territory when he was there; and when he went away it became dull and ordinary again. Yet still it was touched with the hope that he would come again.

When he said good-bye I clung to him; he seemed to like that.

"Will you come back again soon?" I always asked.

And his reply was always the same: "As soon as I am able."

"You will, you will?" I demanded earnestly, knowing the inclination of grown-ups to make promises they never intended to carry out.

And to my almost unbearable joy, he replied, "Nothing would keep me away, now that I have made the acquaintance of Miss Carmel March."

I stood listening to the sound of the horses' hooves and the wheels of the carriage which was taking him away. Then, as we went into the house, Estella said, "He's not *your* Uncle Toby."

But nothing would convince me that he was not.

One day, during the spring following Uncle Toby's visit, Henry came in and announced, "The gypsies are in the woods. I saw their caravans as I came past."

My heart began to pound. It was years since they had been this way—not since the time of my birth.

"My patience me," said Nanny Gilroy. "Something ought to be done about that lot. Why should they come here and pester honest folk?"

She looked at me as she spoke, as though I were responsible for their coming.

I said, "They've got a right. The woods are for everybody if they want to go there."

"Don't give me any of your sauce, Miss, if you please," said Nanny. "*You* might have your reasons for being fond of such like. I—and there are thousands like me—feel different. It's not right to let them come here and something should be done about it. If they come here with their clothes pegs and their bits of heather, you can give them the rough side of your tongue, Sally, and that's what they'll get from me."

Sally wisely said nothing and I put on my sullen look, which was silly really because it did not help.

There was a good deal of talk about the gypsies. People were suspicious of them. They would pester, it was said, try to steal things and in their way threaten with sly hints of misfortune for those who would not buy their wares or have their fortunes told.

They made fires in the woods at night and sat round them singing. From the garden we could hear them. I thought they sounded quite melodious. Several of the young girls in the neighbourhood had their fortunes told.

Nanny cautioned Estella to be careful.

"They get up to all sorts of tricks. They kidnap children, starve them, and make them go out selling clothes pegs. People are sorry for starving children."

I said to Estella, "That's not true! They don't go round stealing children."

"No," agreed Estella. "They leave them under bushes for other people to look after. Of course, *you* would stand up for them."

She was jealous of me, I told myself. She was two years older than I and I could read as well as she could. Besides, Uncle Toby liked me specially.

She chanted:

> "My mother said that I never should
> Play with the gypsies in the wood."

"And why not?" she went on. "Because they kidnap you, steal your shoes and stockings, and send you out selling clothes pegs."

I walked away and tried to look haughty, but I was disturbed. I wished Uncle Toby were here. I should have liked to talk to him about the gypsies.

I was very interested in them and found it difficult to keep away from the encampment.

I was six years old at this time, but I think I might have been taken for more. I was as tall as Estella and that trait in me for asserting myself was stronger than ever. After all, I was made constantly aware that, although I was fed and clothed and shared lessons and the nursery with the children of the household, I was only there because of the charity of the doctor and his wife. So I had to show them constantly that I was as good as, if not better than, the rest of them.

I loved Sally; I was fond of Adeline and Miss Harley. I was fond of anyone who showed me kindness and, of course, I adored Uncle Toby. I seized with great eagerness on any affection which came my way because I was so very much aware of the lack of it in some quarters.

It was easy for me to slip away and I invariably made my way to the encampment. From the shelter of the trees I could look out on the caravans drawn up there without anyone's being aware of my presence.

There were several children, brown-skinned and barefooted, who played there together, and young women squatting about weaving wicker baskets and cutting wood with knives. They sang quietly and chattered as they worked.

There was one woman in particular who interested me. She was by no means young. She had thick black hair streaked with grey. She always sat on the steps of a particular caravan and worked away with the rest of them. She talked a great deal. I was too far away to hear what she said, but I did hear her singing now and then. She was plump and laughed frequently. I wished I knew what it was all about.

I often wondered what would have happened to me if I had not been left under the azalea bush. Should I have been one of those barefooted children? I shuddered at the thought. Even though I was not really wanted, I was glad that I had gone to Commonwood House. I was doubly grateful to the doctor for insisting that they keep me. He didn't really want me, of course, but perhaps he thought it was a good idea and he might not go to Heaven if he sent me away. Well, I was glad that they had kept me, whatever the reason.

It was a hot afternoon. I sat among the trees and watched the gypsies, the children shouting to each other. The plump lady was on the caravan steps as usual. The basket she was weaving was on her lap and she looked as if she might be dropping off to sleep at any moment.

I thought they were less aware than usual because of the heat and that I might venture closer. I stood up abruptly and did not see the stone which was protruding from the ground. I tripped and went sprawling into the clearing.

It happened so quickly that I could not stop myself from calling out. There was a sudden pain in my foot and I saw that there was blood on my stocking.

The children were watching me and I tried to scramble up. I gave a cry of pain, for my left foot would not support me and I fell.

The plump woman started to descend the caravan steps.

"What is it?" she cried. "Why! It's a little girl! Oh my! What have you done? You've hurt yourself, have you?"

I looked down at the blood on my stocking. Then she was kneeling beside me while the children gathered round to look.

"Hurt there, dearie?"

She was touching my ankle and I nodded.

She grunted and turned to the children. "Go and get Uncle Jake. Tell him to come here . . . quick."

Two of the children ran off.

"Cut yourself a bit, lovey. Your leg. Not much. Still, we'll stop it bleeding. Jake'll be here in a minute. He's over there . . . cutting wood."

In spite of the pain in my foot and my inability to walk, I was excited. I always enjoyed escaping from the dull routine of the Uncle-Toby-less days and I was glad of a diversion of any sort. This was particularly intriguing because it was bringing me closer to the gypsies.

The two children came running back followed by a tall man with dark curly hair and gold rings in his ears. He had a very brown face, white teeth displayed by his pleasant smile.

"Oh, Jake," said the plump woman. "This little Miss has had a bit of a mishap." She laughed in a silent way and one only knew she was laughing by the way in which her shoulders shook. It seemed a clever thing to have said and I smiled my appreciation of her choice of words.

"Better get her into the 'van, Jake. I'll put something on that wound."

Jake picked me up and carried me across the clearing. He mounted the steps of the caravan on which the woman had been sitting, and we went inside. There was a bench on one side of the caravan and a kind of divan on the other. He laid me on this. I looked round. It was like a little room, very untidy, and on the bench were some mugs and bottles.

"Here we are," said the woman. "I'll just put something on that leg. Then we'll see about getting you home. Where do you come from, dearie?"

"I live at Commonwood House with Dr. Marline and his family."

"Oh," she said. "Well, fancy that!" She shook as though with secret laughter. "They'll be worried about you, dearie, so we'd better get a message to them."

"They won't worry about me . . . not yet."

"Oh . . . all right then. We'll get that stocking off, shall we?"

"You all right?" said Jake.

The woman nodded. "Call you when we want you."

"Right you are," said Jake, grinning at me in a friendly way.

"Now then," said the woman. I had taken off my stocking and was gazing ruefully at the blood which was oozing out of the wound.

"Wash it first," she said. "Here." She indicated one of the children who had followed us into the caravan. "Get me a basin of water."

The child ran to do her bidding and half-filled a basin, which stood on the overcrowded bench, with water from an enamel jug which also stood there.

The woman had a piece of cloth and began bathing my leg. I looked in horror at the blood-soaked rag and the reddening water in the basin.

"That's nothing to worry about, dearie," she said. "That'll soon heal. I've got something to put on it. Made it myself. Gypsies know these things. You can trust the gypsy."

"Oh, I do," I said.

She smiled at me, flashing her magnificent teeth.

"Now, this might hurt a bit at first. But the more it hurts the quicker it'll get better, see?"

I said I did.

"Ready?"

I winced.

"All right? You the doctor's little girl, are you?"

"No. Not exactly. I'm just there."

"Staying there, are you?"

"No. I live there. I'm Carmel March."

"That's a nice name, dearie."

"Carmel means garden, and that's where they found me, and because it was March, they called me that."

"In a garden!"

"Everyone round here knows. I was left under the azalea bush. The one that gave Tom Yardley a lot of trouble one year."

The woman was staring at me in amazement and kept nodding her head slowly.

"And you live there now, do you?"

"Yes."

"And they're good to you?"

I hesitated. "Sally is and Miss Harley and Adeline . . . and, of course, Uncle Toby, but . . ."

"Not the doctor and his wife?"

"I don't know. They don't take much notice, but Nanny Gilroy always tells me I don't belong there."

"She's not very nice, is she?"

"She just thinks I ought not to be there."

"That don't sound very nice to me, lovey. Now I'm going to wrap this up."

"It's very kind of you."

"We're nice people, gypsies. Don't you believe all the things you hear people say about us."

"Oh, I don't."

"I can see you don't. You're not a bit scared of me, are you?"

I shook my head.

"You're a brave little girl, you are. What we're going to do is take you back. Jake will have to carry you because you can't walk. But what we're going to do first is give you a nice toddy, and we can have a little chat while you rest a bit. Your ankle will be all right. It's only a sprain. It'll hurt a bit but soon it will be well. Mustn't walk on it yet, though. This is a drink of herbs . . . soothing after a shock . . . and you've had one of them, dearie."

The toddy was rather pleasant. She watched me closely while I drank it.

"There now," she said. "You and me, we'll have a little chat. You tell me about the doctor and his wife, and Nanny, and all of them. They feed you well, do they?"

"Oh yes."

"That's a good thing."

She listened with great interest while I told her about Commonwood House.

"I don't like the sound of that nanny," she said.

"She is supposed to be a good nanny, really. It's just that she thinks I'm not good enough to be brought up with the others."

"And you let her know different from that, I'll be bound."

Her shoulders shook with laughter and I joined in. Then she said seriously, "Do you mind about that nanny?"

"Well . . . yes . . . a bit . . . sometimes."

Then I told her about Uncle Toby and her eyes shone with secret mirth.

"And he gave you the box with the monkeys. My word, he seems a nice man."

"Oh, he is . . . he is."

"And you like him and he likes you?"

"I think he likes me better than the others."

She nodded her head and again her shoulders heaved.

"Well, dearie," she said, "that does not surprise me one little bit."

It was a wonderful adventure. I liked her. She told me her name was Rosie . . . Rosie Perrin. Then I explained that I might have been called Rose and why.

"Fancy that!" she said. "We should have been two blooming Rosies, shouldn't we?"

I was rather sorry to be taken back to Commonwood House.

There was some consternation when Jake arrived with me in his arms.

"Little Miss have had a fall," he explained to Janet, the house-maid who opened the door to him.

Janet didn't know what to do, so Jake stepped into the hall.

"She can't walk," said Jake. "I'd best take her to her bed."

He followed Janet up the stairs to the nursery quarters. Nanny was horrified.

"My patience me!" she said. "What next?"

"Little maid's had a fall in the woods," Jake explained. "Can't stand on her feet. I'll put her on her bed."

Sally was there, round-eyed and curious, watching while I was laid on my bed. Then Janet conducted Jake downstairs and the storm broke.

"What on earth did you think you was up to . . . bringing gypsies into the house?" demanded Nanny.

"She couldn't walk," said Sally. "He had to carry her."

"I never heard the like. What were you up to? In the woods, were you? With the gypsies?"

I said, "They found me when I fell over. They were very kind to me."

"Kind, my foot! They're always out to get what they can from gentlefolk."

"They didn't get anything. They gave me a toddy."

"What next? What next? I shall go straight down to the mistress and tell her what's happened."

The result was a visit from the doctor. Nanny was standing there, her lips tight, her eyes accusing me. The doctor scarcely spoke to her. I had the idea he did not like Nanny very much. He smiled at me rather nicely, I thought.

"Well," he said, "what have you been doing?"

"I fell over in the woods," I told him. "The gypsies found me. One of them gave me a toddy and put stuff on my leg with a bandage."

"Well, let's have a look at it, shall we? Does it hurt?"

"Not now. It did."

He touched my ankle.

"You've strained it," he said. "Twisted it a bit. No real damage done. You must let it rest for a few days." He took off the bandage and said, "H'm. That's all right." He went on: "Let's keep the bandage on for a while. This will do for now." He tied it up deftly and gave me that nice gentle smile. "Not much harm done," he added reassuringly.

"She shouldn't have been in the woods," said Nanny. "Bringing those people into the house."

He gave Nanny that rather cool look which confirmed my belief that he did not like her at all.

He said, "Carmel could not have walked back herself. It was good of them to take care of her. I daresay Mrs. Marline will want to write a note thanking them for their kindness."

He turned to me and his smile was gentle again.

"I don't suppose they mentioned their names?"

"Oh yes," I cried. "One did. The one who gave me the toddy and bandaged it. She is Rosie Perrin."

"I shall remember that," he said, nodded and went out.

Nanny muttered, "Writing to gypsies, my foot! What next? Mistress will know better than that. A nice thing you've done. Falling about in woods and bringing that sort into the house!"

Sally wanted to hear all about my adventure, and I think Estella wished it had happened to her. Sally said it was very nice of the gypsies to look after me.

The doctor came every day to look at the wound on my leg and to test my ankle. He was always kind and gentle to me and cool to Nanny. I liked him more for both of these reasons. Mrs. Marline did not come to see me. I wondered whether she wrote that note to Rosie Perrin.

That incident marked a turning point in my relationship with the doctor. He noticed me now and then and would say, "Ankle feeling all right now?" and after a while, just, "All right?"

I was getting quite fond of him. He gave me the impression that he really cared that I was "all right," even though I was left under the azalea bush and had brought gypsies into the house.

The big house in the neighbourhood was The Grange. It was owned by Sir Grant Crompton, who was regarded as the "lord of the manor." Sir Grant and Lady Crompton were the benefactors of the neighbourhood and employed quite a number of the local population; they let their farms to tenant farmers and sent a goose to the poor every Christmas.

It was all very traditional. Lady Crompton officiated at fêtes, bazaars, and such affairs which raised money for good causes. The family always appeared at church if they were in residence, sitting in those pews which had been occupied by the family for two hundred years. The servants sat immediately behind them. Sir Grant contributed generously to funds for the church's needs and he was greatly revered by us all.

There were two children of the household—Lucian and Camilla. I used to see them riding with a groom. They seemed a very handsome and haughty pair who rarely looked our way when we passed them in the lanes—they on magnificent steeds, we on foot. Estella sighed and wished she lived at The Grange and rode a white horse with her brother, equally splendidly mounted, beside her. Lucian, moreover, was much bigger and more handsome than Henry.

Well, of course, they were "Grange folk," and although the doctor was not exactly despised in social circles, and had on occasion even been invited to The Grange, it was suspected that it was only to make up numbers or due to the last-minute cancellation of some more worthy guest.

Mrs. Marline was a little disgruntled about it, and had been heard to ask who the Cromptons thought they were, but when an opportunity came to extend the connection between The Grange and Commonwood House, she was delighted.

Mrs. Marline had been engaged on some charitable work which

entailed a visit to The Grange, where she had been graciously received by Lady Crompton, and during the interview it had transpired that both ladies were concerned about their sons' education.

Lady Crompton was proposing to engage a tutor for Lucian because she felt it was not quite time for him to go away to school, and, as the same problem concerned Mrs. Marline, the two ladies had a great deal to talk about. The outcome was that Lady Crompton suggested that the boys share the tutor who was to come to The Grange.

Mrs. Marline was delighted with the idea.

I presumed that she would share the cost of the tutor, for I heard Nanny Gilroy say that, in spite of their grandeur, the Cromptons were not ones to "throw their money about" and she reckoned they were rather "near." And, of course, we all knew that Mrs. Marline had the money and she would be ready to pay for what she would consider such a privilege.

So it was arranged and every morning, except Sundays, Henry used to set off for The Grange and he would return in the mid-afternoon with books and work to be done in preparation for the next day's session.

It was a very satisfactory arrangement in Mrs. Marline's eyes, for it meant that the families met more frequently than they had before. Estella, Henry and Adeline were invited to The Grange to tea with Lucian and Camilla. Estella was delighted, but it made her very dissatisfied with Commonwood House, which was humble in comparison with The Grange.

I was never asked to go. I believe Nanny Gilroy had something to do with that, and Mrs. Marline would, of course, have been in agreement with her. But I was sure the doctor would not have been if he had had any say in the matter.

Then it changed.

Uncle Toby paid us a visit while his ship was in port for minor repairs.

It was, as usual, a wonderful visit. He brought me a present from Hong Kong. It was a jade pendant on a slender gold chain, and the pendant was decorated with signs which he told me meant "good luck" in Chinese.

I had in my possession that other pendant, which had been round my neck when I was found under the azalea bush. I often looked at it, but I never wore it. I think I felt it would remind people of my arrival and that I did not really belong here.

Uncle Toby's gift was different. I was enchanted—not only for its promise of good fortune, but because Uncle Toby had given it to me. Nanny Gilroy would have said it was unsuitable for a child of my age to wear jewellery and would have ordered me to take it off, so I used to wear it hidden under my dress when she was around. I was never without it, even during the night, and the first thing I did, on waking, was to touch it and murmur, "Good luck," while I stretched out my other hand to the musical box and listened to "God Save the Queen."

Estella was very excited because she and Henry had been invited to take tea at The Grange. If the weather was fine—and we were in the middle of a heat wave—it was to take place on the lawn in front of the house.

Nanny had told Sally to press Estella's blue dress with a satin sash and the puffed sleeves. Estella must look just as well-dressed as that Camilla. "And prettier, too," added Nanny.

I watched Sally carefully pressing the dress.

"It's a shame they don't ask you," she said. "You'd like to go, wouldn't you? You'd look as good as any of them."

"I don't want to go," I lied. "I'd rather be here."

"It would be nice for you," persisted Sally. "And they ought to ask you. I reckon they might well . . . but for Nanny. I wouldn't mind taking a bet on that. And then there's Her, too."

By Her, she meant Mrs. Marline; and I was sure her conjecture was correct.

Estella was duly garbed in the dress and I had to admit, though rather reluctantly, that she looked very pretty.

I watched them from my window as they set out for The Grange, and a wild idea came to me. I had not been invited but that was no reason why I should not go.

I had on one occasion been inside the grounds of The Grange. Curiosity had overcome me. It had been one afternoon when I guessed the house would be at its quietest. If I were discovered, I told myself, I could say I was lost. There was a way in through a hedge round the paddock and beyond that was the shrubbery which bordered the lawn in front of the house. I had crept through the hedge and sped across the paddock to this shrubbery from where I had a good view of the lawns and the house.

Very fine it was—of grey stone and ancient, with a turret at either end and a big gateway which I could see led into a court-yard. From the shrubbery I could have a good view of the tea party without any one of them being aware that I was there.

Well, if I could not be a guest, there was no reason why I should not look in on the party. So when they had left, I slipped out after them, fingering my good luck pendant to assure myself that I had that with me and that while I had, no matter what reckless action I took, I was safe.

I made my way to the shrubbery undetected. I had a clear view over the lawn. A white table with white chairs had been set up in readiness for the *al fresco* party. Estella and Henry had arrived and had first been taken into the house. I guessed they would come out very soon, accompanied by Lucian and Camilla, and possibly the pale-faced young man who was the tutor.

I crouched under the bushes. On no account must I be seen, and I must choose the right moment to slip away. I would creep through the shrubbery and then negotiate the dangerous part, which was running across the paddock to the hedge. Once I had crawled through that, I would be safe.

All would be well because I had my good luck pendant with me. I put my hands up to touch it and horror swept over me. It was not there.

For a few moments I was so numb with horror that I could not move. Only a short while before I had touched it. It must be there. I was dreaming. This was a nightmare. I stood up, risking being seen. Again I put my hands to my neck. No pendant. No chain. What could have happened? I had fastened it securely when I put it on. I always did. I shook my dress. I stared at the brown earth. There was no sign of the pendant.

It could not be far, I comforted myself. It had been round my neck only a few minutes ago. I was on my hands and knees search-ing. It must have fallen off. I had lost my precious gift—Uncle Toby's gift—and all my luck.

I felt desolate. There were tears on my cheeks. I must find it, I must. I crawled around . . . searching . . . searching. I must go back the way I had come. Could I be sure of the exact path I had taken across the paddock? My despair overcame me. I sat down, covered my face with my hands and wept.

Suddenly I was aware of someone close to me.

"What's wrong?" asked Lucian Crompton.

I forgot that I had no right to be there. There was no other thought in my mind than that I had lost my most treasured possession.

I stammered, "I've lost my good luck pendant."

"Your what?" he cried. "And who are you? What are you doing here?"

I answered the questions in order. "The pendant my Uncle Toby brought home from Hong Kong. It says 'good luck' on it. I'm Carmel and they didn't ask me to the party, so I came to have a look."

"Where do you come from?"

"From Commonwood House."

"They're here today."

"Yes . . . but not me. I was just going to watch."

"Oh, I know. You're the little girl who . . ."

I nodded. "I was found under the azalea bush which gave Tom Yardley a lot of trouble one year. I'm Carmel, which means garden. It's where I was found, you see."

"And you've lost this pendant?"

"It was there after I'd crawled under the hedge."

"Which hedge?"

I pointed across the paddock.

"That was the way you came in, was it?"

I nodded.

"And you had it then. Well, it can't be far off, can it? It must be round here somewhere."

I felt a little happier. He spoke so confidently.

"Well, let's have a look for it. Which way did you come?"

I pointed.

"Well, here we go. You show me. Two pairs of eyes are better than one. You keep yours open. This way. Watch your step. Don't want to tread on it, do you? What does it look like?"

"It's green and it's got 'good luck' on it in Chinese letters."

"Right. It shouldn't be hard to find."

We came to the edge of the shrubbery without success.

"Now," he said. "You crossed the paddock. I see where you got through the hedge. There's a little opening there, isn't there? That's where it was."

I nodded.

"Then we'll make for that space. Keep your eyes open and we'll cross the paddock. Try to remember the exact way you came."

We walked across, a little apart and arrived at the hedge. He knelt down and gave a cry of triumph.

"Is this it?"

I could have wept with joy.

He held it up and said, "Ah, I see. Look. The clasp is broken. That's why it dropped off."

"Broken," I said in dismay, my joy evaporating.

He studied it intently.

"Oh, I see. A link has come off. All it needs is to fix it back. The clasp itself is all right. It's a job for the jeweller, though. Old Higgs in the High Street will fix it in a few minutes."

He handed it to me. I clutched it, half joyful, half tearful. I had not lost it, but I had to get it to old Higgs in the High Street. Nanny would not allow that. I should have to get Estella or Henry to help me. Perhaps Sally could.

He was watching. Then he smiled.

"I tell you what we'll do," he said. "After tea I'll take it to Higgs and he'll do it right away."

"Would you?" I cried.

"I don't see why not."

"After . . ."

"Well, we ought to be there now, you know. Let's go."

"But I'm not supposed to be there."

"I've invited you. This will be my house one day and I can ask whom I like."

"Nanny . . ."

"Nanny who?"

"Nanny Gilroy. She'd say it wasn't right for you to ask me. You see, I was found under the azalea bush. Nanny would say I didn't belong . . ."

"If I say you belong, you belong," he said in a swaggering way which made me laugh.

I was hugging my pendant. Good luck had returned.

So I went back with him to The Grange. Estella was amazed, and so was Henry. Lucian told them about the pendant and Camilla wanted to see it and hear about the Chinese letters which meant "good luck."

"It's lovely," she said. "I wish I had one."

I glowed with pleasure and was very happy.

Estella looked alarmed. She said, "You know Carmel is . . . not really one of us."

"Oh yes," said Lucian. "She was found under the bush. She told me. Why wasn't she asked?"

"Well . . . she's a foundling," said Estella.

"What fun!" cried Camilla. "It sounds exciting. Like something out of Shakespeare or a romance . . ."

"She was left under an azalea bush."

"Yes!" said Lucian. "The one that gave poor old Tom Yardley a lot of trouble one year."

He and Camilla looked at each other and laughed.

I liked them. They were very friendly. I guessed it was because they were rich and important and did not have to keep reminding people that they were really better than they seemed. They behaved to me as though I were just another guest. The cake was delicious. It was sprinkled with coconut and I had two pieces.

"Do you like it?" asked Lucian, smiling at me as I took my second piece.

"It's lovely."

"This is better than crouching in the shrubbery, eh?"

He and Camilla laughed and I said, "It's a lot better."

They both seemed to like me and as soon as tea was over Lucian went to the stables and told the groom that he was going to take the dog cart into the town and we were all going. Lucian seemed to be very important, for all of them did what he said without question; and we all crowded into the dog cart, which was fun. Lucian drove and I sat beside him.

Then we went into Mr. Higgs's shop and Mr. Higgs himself came out and said, "Good afternoon, Mr. Lucian. What can I do for you?"

"Just a little job," said Lucian. "It's a link on this chain. It just needs fixing, I think."

Mr. Higgs looked at it and nodded.

"Jim will do it," he said. "It won't take more than a minute or two. Just needs fixing on the ring. Jim! Here's Mr. Lucian. Wants this fixing. See what's happened?"

Jim nodded and went off.

"Little girl's pendant, is it?" said Mr. Higgs.

"Yes, her uncle brought it from Hong Kong for her."

"Chinese, yes. Good craftsmen. They turn out some interesting stuff. And how's everyone up at The Grange?"

Lucian assured Mr. Higgs that they were all in excellent health, and I listened in admiration to his easy manner of conversation while I waited impatiently for the return of my pendant.

And there it was . . . just as it had been . . . and no one would know that there had been any trouble with the link.

Lucian was going to pay for it, but Mr. Higgs said, "Oh, that's nothing, Mr. Lucian. Just a matter of fixing it. Glad to oblige."

Lucian fastened the pendant round my neck.

"There," he said. "Safe as houses."

And I loved him from that moment.

Nanny Gilroy did not like what she heard from Estella about my being at the party.

"Pushing," she commented. "Didn't I always say?"

Estella said, "Lucian brought her in. He saw her in the shrubbery when she lost her pendant."

"Pendants! What's a child of her age doing with pendants?"

"Uncle Toby gave it to her."

She smiled in that way she did when Uncle Toby's name was mentioned, and clicked her tongue. But clearly she thought it was not quite so bad if he had been responsible for it.

The next time Estella and Henry were invited to tea, I was too. I began to grow accustomed to going there. I liked Camilla. She never showed in any way that she thought I was not the equal of the others. As for Lucian, I felt there was a special friendship between us because of the pendant.

So the friendship between Commonwood and The Grange was growing. The shared tutor had been the beginning and then there was Mrs. Marline's determination to return to the sort of society she had enjoyed before she married beneath her; and she did everything she could to win the approval of Lady Crompton—by devoting herself to charitable works—particularly those in which her Ladyship was involved. Consequently she was a frequent visitor to The Grange.

Henry could be a friend of Lucian and Estella of Camilla. How fortunate that the sexes fitted so well in the families! I was not excluded. In fact, Lucian always had a special smile for me. At least, I imagined it was special. He would glance at the pendant which I always wore outside my dress when I was out of Nanny Gilroy's range, and I knew he was recalling our first encounter with some amusement. Life was very pleasant.

Mrs. Marline had always been a keen horsewoman and we all had riding lessons. Estella and Henry had their ponies and Uncle Toby had provided me with one so that I could join them. What a wonderful uncle he was to me! And I attributed the change in my fortunes to him.

I had begun to realise how important Mrs. Marline was in the household. Even Nanny Gilroy was subdued in her presence. Everyone was in considerable awe of her—even the doctor. Perhaps it would be more accurate to say, especially the doctor.

I heard Nanny Gilroy talking about her to Mrs. Barton, the cook.

"She's a holy terror," she said. "She goes on and on and never lets the doctor forget whose money pays most of the bills. She's the boss all right."

"He's good, the doctor," said Mrs. Barton. "His patients think the world of him. Mrs. Gardiner said she was in agony with her leg until she went to him. He's really a nice gentleman . . . in his way."

"Mild as milk, if you ask me. Can't seem to stand up for himself. Well, she's got the money . . . and money talks."

"Money talks all right," replied Mrs. Barton. "Poor doctor. I reckon he don't have much of a life."

Mrs. Marline took little notice of me. She seemed as though she did not want to know I was there. I did not mind that. Indeed, I was rather glad of it. I had Uncle Toby and now Lucian, Camilla and Sally; and Estella and Henry were not bad and Adeline had always liked me.

At the end of the summer, the gypsy encampment was no longer in the woods.

"There one day and gone the next," said Nanny. "Well, good riddance to bad rubbish."

I wanted to defend them and remind her of how Rosie Perrin had dressed my leg and Jake had carried me home. But of course I said nothing.

Then there was talk of Henry's going to school.

"That Lucian from The Grange is going, so Master Henry must do the same. Some grand school, I expect it will be. Well, they're

Grange people and where Lucian goes, mark my words, Henry will go too. That's if I know anything about Madam."

"Who else, if you don't?" added Mrs. Barton sycophantically. She was eager to be on good terms with Nanny, who was reckoned to be a power in the household—second only to Mrs. Marline herself.

I should be very sorry when Lucian went away. He and Camilla came to tea at Commonwood now and then. They were very special occasions and I never enjoyed them as much as going to The Grange. Mrs. Marline was not actually present at tea but she hovered. She was so anxious that everything should be in order and that tea at Commonwood should be in every degree as good as that taken at The Grange.

I believe she would really have liked to exclude me, but in view of the fact that Lucian had insisted that I join them at The Grange, she could hardly keep me out of these.

She was intruding more and more on my notice. She had a shrill and penetrating voice and a very domineering manner; and she was usually complaining about something which had or had not been done. She was such a contrast to the mild-mannered doctor. I wondered if it was because of her that he had become as he was—resigned. I imagined she would have that effect on someone like the doctor, who seemed to be a man who would avoid trouble at all cost.

It has always amazed me how our lives can go along in a sort of groove for a long time and then some incident changes the entire pattern and what happens after is the result of that one detail without which nothing that follows would have taken place.

This is what happened at Commonwood House.

Mrs. Marline was eager to join the Hunt, an enthusiasm which she shared with the Cromptons.

Henry, Estella, Adeline and I would often assemble to see the start of it. It would set out from The Grange and Mrs. Marline, looking very much the horsewoman, and as completely in command of her steed as she was of the doctor and her household, would be in the centre of it, exchanging pleasantries with the gentry who had come in from the surrounding neighbourhood.

The men looked splendid in their pink coats. The dogs were barking and there was general excitement in the air.

The doctor did not hunt. He would have been quite out of place among such people.

However, we would watch them ride off after the poor little fox until they were all out of sight. Then we would return home.

It was a cold day, I remember, and we ran all the way. Henry was sighing for the day when he would be able to join the Hunt. Estella was not sure whether she wanted to. She was not all that happy on her pony and even contemplating the frisky mounts of the riders made her nervous.

The day went on as usual. How could we know what an important day it was going to prove to be to us all at Commonwood House?

It was due to the stump of a tree which sometime before had been uprooted. The recent rains had exposed it apparently and it lay in the path taken by the hunted fox.

The first I heard of what had happened was when I was in the garden with Estella. The household was quiet. It was amazing what a difference the absence of Mrs. Marline made.

We saw Fred Carton, the policeman, wheeling his bicycle up to the gate. He came walking up the path.

"Mr. Carton," cried Estella, "what's happened?"

"Is Doctor in?" he asked. "I want to see him at once."

"Yes. He's here," said Estella.

Jenny the parlourmaid came out. She was startled at the sight of Mr. Carton.

"I want to see Doctor now," said Mr. Carton, rather curtly for him. He was usually affable and inclined to joke.

Estella and I looked at each other with mounting excitement. Something was wrong and Mr. Carton had come to tell us what it was.

We followed Mr. Carton into the house and Jenny went upstairs to call the doctor.

He came immediately and there was consternation in his voice as he said, "What is it? What is it?"

Estella and I hovered.

"It's Mrs. Marline, sir. Her horse took a toss. They've got her in the hospital. Reckon you ought to get there right away."

"I'll go at once," said the doctor.

The Governess

THE DOCTOR WAS AWAY a long time. The news spread through the house. The mistress had had an accident on the hunting field. It must be bad because they had not brought her home on a stretcher, which was what had happened when Mr. Carteret of Letch Manor had broken his leg on the hunting field. They had taken her to the hospital, and that seemed significant.

It is only natural that people's first thoughts are of how such events will affect them. Was she going to die? To the servants this might present a threat of losing their jobs. Everyone knew that she had the money. Nobody in the house liked her. The servants avoided her whenever possible.

However, there was no talk of Mrs. Marline's being a "holy terror." In fact, she was rapidly turning into a saint, which, I had long realised, was what death did for people. So they had decided that Mrs. Marline was going to die.

The doctor returned at last. He talked to the servants and then sent for Estella, Henry and me.

When we were assembled, he said to us, "I have to tell you that your mother has been badly hurt. Her horse tripped over an exposed tree root just as she was about to jump over a fence. As a result, the horse was so badly hurt that it has already been destroyed. Your mother will be in the hospital for a few days. There are fears that she may not be able to walk. We must pray that something can be done and that she will be restored to full health. In the meantime, we can only wait . . . and hope.''

We were all very solemn. Nanny was closeted with Mrs. Barton and they discussed the future. Estella and I did not know what to say. We were shocked and expectant. As for myself, she had never played a big part in my life, and her presence or absence made very little difference to me. But I suspected that from now on nothing was going to be quite the same again.

And how right I was.

Two rooms on the ground floor had been prepared for Mrs. Marline. They both had french windows opening onto the garden— one was her bedroom, the other her sitting-room. There was a wheelchair in which she could propel herself from room to room, but she needed help to get through the french windows to the garden. She had bells, by which she could summon the servants to her, and their imperious clanging was often heard throughout the house.

Each morning Annie Logan called to help her wash and dress. Annie Logan was the district nurse. She would arrive promptly on her bicycle at nine o'clock and spend an hour or so with Mrs. Marline. Then she would go to the kitchen and drink a cup of tea with Nanny Gilroy and Mrs. Barton. They would chat and after a while Annie would cycle off to the next poor creature who needed her attention.

It was obvious that Mrs. Marline was in intermittent pain. Dr. Everest, from the next village, called on her. That seemed to me rather odd since we had a doctor in the house. I said so.

"Silly!" retorted Henry. "A doctor can't attend his own wife."

"Why not?" I demanded.

"Because they think he might finish her off."

"Finish her off? What do you mean?"

"Murder her, stupid!"

"Murder her!"

"Husbands do murder wives."

I thought then that it was a reasonable arrangement, for Dr. Marline might well want to do that.

She was more vociferous than ever. She continually raged against everything and everyone. Nothing was right for her. We often heard her haranguing the poor doctor. We would hear her loud voice and his meek replies. "Yes, my love. Of course, my love."

"My love" seemed incongruous. How could Mrs. Marline be anyone's "love"?

The poor doctor was looking gaunt and haggard. I understood very well then why it was necessary for Dr. Everest to look after her.

It was a very unhappy household. I was one of the more fortunate ones, because I could keep out of her way.

When Uncle Toby came life brightened. Even Mrs. Marline seemed a little happier, for she was clearly pleased to see him. He sat with her, talking to her and making her smile now and then.

I had a long talk with him. It was in the garden.

"Nice to get out of the house," he said. "Poor old Doc. Things not too bright for him. And you have to be sorry for Grace. She's always wanted her own way. She ought to have married someone more like herself, someone who could put a curb on her. Doc's all for a comfortable life." He raised his eyes to the sky. "And he married Grace! Some people do have bad luck. Their own fault, I suppose. 'Not in our stars but in ourselves,' and all that. And what about you, little Carmel? How does all this affect you?"

"She doesn't take much notice of me . . . she never did . . . so I'm lucky."

"Ah, there's good in everything, eh? You're growing up now. How old is it? Eight?"

"Eight in March," I told him.

He patted my hand. "Not much fun, is it? I wish it could be better."

"It's nice when you come."

He put his arm round me and held me tightly.

"One day," he went on, "perhaps I'll take you to sea with me. We'll sail round the world. How would you like that?"

I clasped my hands together in ecstasy. There was no need for words.

"We'll sit on the deck in the moonlight," he said, "and we'll look up at the Southern Cross."

"What's that?" I asked.

"It's the stars you see on the other side of the world. On hot days we'll watch for the whales and we'll see the dolphins jumping out of the sea. We'll watch the flying fishes skimming across the water . . ."

"And mermaids?" I asked.

"Who knows? We might even produce one of those for you."

"They sing songs and lure sailors to destruction."

"We won't be lured. We'll go on sailing."

"When?" I asked.

"One day . . . perhaps."

"I'll pray every night."

"You do. I believe those up there occasionally answer prayers."

I thought about those words for a long time afterwards, and I dreamed of the day when Uncle Toby kept his promise and took me away with him.

Uncle Toby left soon after that and uneasiness settled on the house. Dr. Marline looked lost and exhausted. Nanny Gilroy and Mrs. Barton had long conversations in the kitchen with the district nurse.

I overheard some of them.

"Nothing pleases Madam," complained Nanny Gilroy.

"She's in pain," said Annie Logan. "Not all the time . . . but it's there, threatening. That's why she's got those rather strong pills, for when it's specially bad. Morphine in them. It helps her. She wouldn't be as well as she is without them."

"She was bad enough before," said Mrs. Barton. "Nothing pleased her then, but it's ten times worse now. There's no pleasing her."

The weeks began to pass. My eighth birthday came. It was set on the first of March, though nobody knew the exact day. Tom Yardley had found me on the sixteenth, and they reckoned I was a few weeks old at that time, so the first seemed about right. Uncle Toby had given orders that I was to have a fine dress. Sally had bought the material and had given Mrs. Grey, the local seamstress, one of my old dresses to copy for size. It was the finest dress Mrs. Grey had ever made and I was not to see it until the morning of the first. Sally had given me a book of children's rhymes which I had seen in the bookshop and coveted; Estella's gift was a blue sash which she no longer liked, and Adeline's a bar of chocolate. No one else remembered it, but I did not care because I had my wonderful dress.

Then there occurred that event which was to shape the future for us all at Commonwood House. Mrs. Harley, the vicar's wife, had a slight stroke and Miss Harley was unable to continue teaching us because she had to look after her mother. A governess had to be engaged, and so Miss Kitty Carson came to Commonwood House.

When we heard that we were to have a governess, Estella and I shared mixed feelings. There was excitement and apprehension. We discussed her constantly between the times of her appointment and her arrival at Commonwood House.

What would she be like? She would be old and ugly, declared Estella. She would have hairs on her chin like old Mrs. Cram in the village who, some people said, was a witch.

"She can't be very old," I protested. "If she were, she'd be too old to teach."

"She'll give us hard sums and make us sit at the table until we finish them."

"She might be all right."

"Governesses never are. Nanny says they're neither one thing nor the other. They don't belong anywhere. Think they're above the servants and they are not good enough for the others. They give themselves airs downstairs and crawl to the family. I'm going to hate her anyway. I shall be so horrid to her that she'll go away."

"You might wait and see what she's like first."

"I know," said Estella. She had made up her mind.

On the day of the governess's arrival, we were at an upstairs window, watching as the station fly brought her to the house. We gazed intently as she stepped out and made her way to the gate and up the path with Tom Fellows, who drove the fly, carrying her bags.

She was tall and slender. I noticed with relief that she was not in the least like old Mrs. Cram. In fact, she looked very pleasant—not exactly handsome, but with such a gentle and attractive expression that I thought she would be easy to get on with. She might have been in her late twenties. In fact, just what I thought a governess ought to be.

As soon as she entered the house, Estella and I left the window and crept to the top of the stairs. We saw that she was taken into Mrs. Marline's room. The door was shut, so we could not hear what was said. Then Mrs. Marline's bell rang and Nanny, who was hovering, went into the room.

She came out with the governess. Nanny was rather tight-lipped. She did not like the idea of a governess in the house. She might have felt she threatened her authority in some way, and I knew that she was preparing to find fault with Miss Kitty Carson.

We dodged back as they came upstairs and we hid in one of the rooms, leaving the door slightly open, so that we could hear.

"It's this way," said Nanny coldly; and then suddenly Dr. Marline appeared.

I peeped round the door and saw them as they were just passing.

The doctor smiled very pleasantly and said, "You must be Miss Carson?"

"Yes," said the governess.

"Welcome to Commonwood House."

"Thank you."

"I hope you will be happy here. You haven't met the girls yet, I suppose?"

"No," she said.

"Nanny will send for them," he told her.

Suppressing our giggles, Estella and I remained very quiet until they had passed on to the room which had been prepared for Miss Carson on the second floor. Then we came into the corridor and walked sedately up the stairs.

"Oh, here they are," said Nanny Gilroy.

"And Adeline?" said the doctor.

"She will be in her room," replied Nanny. "Carmel, run up and bring her down."

"But first, Miss Carson," put in the doctor, "here are your two pupils, Estella and Carmel."

She had a lovely smile which lighted her face into something like beauty.

"Hello," she said easily. "I do hope we shall get on well together. I feel sure we shall." Her eyes rested on me. Estella might have been scowling slightly. I had taken an immediate liking to Miss Carson and I felt sure she had to me.

I went off to get Adeline. She was in her room, looking rather bewildered and frightened. I guessed she had heard Estella giving her version of what the new governess would be like.

I said, "You are to come and meet Miss Carson, Adeline. I think

34

she is very nice. There is nothing frightening about her. I feel sure you are going to like her."

Adeline was easily influenced one way or another. She brightened and looked relieved.

I was so pleased by the way in which Miss Carson greeted Adeline. She had obviously heard of her disabilities. She took both her hands and smiled warmly.

"I am sure you and I are going to get along very well, Adeline," she said.

Adeline nodded cheerfully, and I noticed how pleased the doctor was looking.

"Well, we'll leave you to unpack, Miss Carson," said Nanny briskly. "Then, as the doctor says, the girls can show you the schoolroom."

"Say in half an hour?" said Miss Carson.

"Yes, they can come to you then. Would you like a cup of tea? I will get Mrs. Barton to send one up to your room."

"That would be very welcome, thank you," said Miss Carson, and we left her then.

"I think she's all right," I said.

Estella's eyes narrowed. "There are such things as wolves in sheep's clothing," she said.

"She's not a wolf," cried Adeline. "I like her."

Estella put on a look of worldly impatience. "It means she might not be what she seems," she said darkly.

Estella was determined to resent her. She had not wanted a governess. She would have liked to go away to school, where girls could have lots of fun. They slept in dormitories and had midnight feasts, and here we were with a silly old governess.

But I felt differently. Miss Carson was high on my list of favourite people. She was warmhearted and showed a particular kindness to those who most needed it. Miss Carson knew exactly how to treat Adeline. She was very patient with her, and instead of dreading lessons, Adeline looked forward to them. She was developing a slavish devotion to Miss Carson: she constantly contrived to be where the governess was, and when we went for walks, she insisted on holding Miss Carson's hand and was happiest when she was near her.

Adeline had quite blossomed since her arrival.

I knew the doctor was aware of this and it made him very happy. He now made a habit of coming in to listen to lessons and took far more interest in them than he had when Miss Harley was in control.

On one occasion, when I was in the garden, Miss Carson was there too and we sat together and talked. Miss Carson always seemed so interested in other people that it was easy to talk to her. I was able to explain how I had never felt like a member of the family—except when Uncle Toby was there—and the reason why was that I did not really belong. I explained how Tom Yardley had found me under the azalea bush.

"You see," I said, "my mother didn't want me, so she left me there. Most mothers love their babies."

"I am sure your mother loved you," she said. "I think she probably left you there because she loved you so much and wanted you to have a better life than she could give you. In Commonwood House, there would be people to look after you, to feed you well, to care for you. And there was a doctor in the house too."

I was surprised that my mother should have left me because she loved me. It was an idea which hadn't occurred to me before.

"But I always felt they didn't really want me," I explained. "Nanny thought I should have been sent to an orphanage or the workhouse. They might have sent me there, but for the doctor. Mrs. Marline didn't want me either, and she is the one who counts."

"The doctor is a very good and understanding man. *He* wanted you and that was what mattered. Your mother made a great sacrifice because she wanted the best for you, and you must not feel inferior in any way. You are going to show them all that you may have been found under that azalea bush, but you can do as well as any of them."

"I will, I will," I said. And I felt as I did when Uncle Toby was there.

And, like Adeline, I loved her.

Nanny did not like the governess, of course. She was prejudiced against her from the start. She did not like governesses in households interfering with the children, and she was not going to change her mind. They gave themselves airs; they had too high an opinion of themselves; they thought themselves "a cut above" the servants. So even the gentle-mannered Miss Carson could do nothing right for her.

And, of course, Mrs. Barton was her staunch ally in this. Governesses were a nuisance. They had to have meals sent up to their rooms. Couldn't eat with the servants, and, of course, they were not acceptable in the family. In any case, what was the family now, with Her in her room, demanding this and that, and Him sitting there alone . . . and not a man to take much notice of what was put before him, in any case. It was a funny setup, if you asked Mrs. Barton—and not helped by having a governess in the house.

Then there was always the overpowering presence of Mrs. Marline. The constant clanging of bells and the maids run off their feet.

"Grumble, grumble," said Mrs. Barton. "Morning, noon and night."

"She'd find fault with the Angel Gabriel himself," declared Nanny.

We used to hear the rumble of Mrs. Marline's voice behind the closed doors when the doctor was with her. She was, of course, complaining. On and on it went, and then there would be a brief pause. We knew then that the doctor was trying to placate her, speaking in his soft, gentle voice.

"Poor man," said Sally. "Worn out, that's what he is. Nag, nag nag, and between you and me and the gatepost, he'd be better off without her. She's going to be an invalid all her life . . . and her going on like that, well, he'll be the first in the grave, if you ask me. And don't you dare mention what I've said."

I was sorry for the doctor. He was so gentle, and he looked very tired when he emerged from that room. He stayed in his own room as much as he could, I was sure; and he seemed eager to get off to his surgery, and he stayed there longer than he did before, which I guessed was because he hated coming home to Mrs. Marline. As soon as he did come in, she would call out for him; and then the rumbling of the voices would begin.

Annie Logan continued to come in the mornings and evenings, and she always stayed for a chat and tea; then there would be a lot of whispering in the kitchen with Nanny and Mrs. Barton. I tried to listen when I could, and it all seemed to be about Her and Him.

I felt—or perhaps I imagined I did afterwards—that there was an uneasy tension in the house. Sometimes when Mrs. Marline had taken her pills because the pain was worse than usual, a stillness would descend on the house as though it were waiting for something to happen.

Then it would change again, and we would hear the wheelchair going from one room to another, or Tom Yardley or the doctor wheeling it into the garden. We would all avoid going there when the chair was there.

It was easy for me, because she had always ignored me. Not so her Estella, Henry and Adeline. She found continual fault with them, and particularly Adeline. She could not hide her contempt for the poor girl. She could not forget that she had borne a child who was not normal and, I imagined, she had always seen herself as a woman who achieved perfection in all she did.

Poor Adeline would invariably resort to tears as soon as she escaped from those sessions with her mother, for she dared not let her mother see them. It was very pathetic to realise how she had to hold back her misery. But Miss Carson was always there when she emerged from that dreaded room. She knew exactly how to comfort her; and soon Adeline would forget her mother and accept Miss Carson's assurances that all was well because she had her dear Miss Carson, who said she was quite clever after all.

In the summer, the gypsies came to the woods again.

One morning I awoke to find them there. They often came late at night and settled in the woods.

Their presence was always a source of excitement to me. I suppose because of my connection with them; and I should never forget my encounter with Rosie Perrin and Jake.

Soon we were seeing them around with their baskets of clothes pegs and sprays of dried heather and lavender.

"Buy a little posy for luck," they said. They went round the houses in the neighbourhood and some of the girls went to Rosie Perrin and had their fortunes told.

She would look at their hands and tell them what the future held for them. It did not cost a great deal and Sally told me that, if you wanted to have a really big glimpse into the future, you could pay more and go into Rosie's caravan where she had a crystal ball. That, said Sally, was the "real thing."

I could not resist watching them from the shelter of the trees, just as I had on that occasion when I had hurt my ankle. And one day, when I crouched there, looking at the barefooted children and, among them, Rosie Perrin on the steps of her caravan, I heard footsteps behind me and I turned and saw Jake grinning at me.

"Hello, little girl," he said. "Taking a look at the gypsies?"

I didn't know how to reply, so I said, "Well . . . er, yes."

"You've got a fancy for us, I'd say. Not like the folk you're accustomed to, are we?"

"No," I replied frankly.

"Well, change is a fine thing. Don't you agree?"

"Oh yes."

"You remember me, don't you?"

"Oh yes. You carried me back."

"Ankle all right now?"

"Yes, thank you."

"Rosie took quite a shine to you."

I was pleased. "She was very nice to me," I said.

"So you liked her, did you? Didn't take against her because she was a gypsy and all that?"

"I liked her very much."

"I'll tell you something. She'd like it if you went to see her."

"Would she?"

"You can bet on that."

"She might not remember me. It was a long time ago."

"Rosie remembers everything, so she'd remember you all right. Come along and say hello to her."

He started towards the encampment and I followed. The children stopped in their play to stare at me, and Rosie Perrin cried out in pleasure when she saw me.

"Why! It's little Miss Carmel! Come up, dearie. Well, who'd 'a thought it!"

I mounted the steps of the caravan, followed by Jake, and stepped inside.

Rosie said, "Sit down, dearie. Well, well, it's some time since you were here. How's that ankle and the leg? All nice and healthy now? I knew it would be. Tell me all about it. How is it at the house now? Still treat you all right, do they?"

"Oh yes. We have a governess now."

"That's grand, that is. Is she good to you?"

"She is very nice and I like her a lot."

She nodded. "And what about the lady and the gentleman . . . Dr. . . . Dr. . . . I beg his pardon?"

"She had a riding accident. She can't walk. There's a wheelchair and she's in pain a lot of the time."

"Poor soul. That little nurse goes there, don't she . . . morning and evening. One of our little 'uns fell over in the road. She came by on her bike and looked after the child. Did a good job and brought her back to us. She had a little chat with me."

"That was Annie Logan. Yes, she comes in to help Mrs. Marline."

"A bit of a tartar, that lady, eh?"

"Yes . . . I suppose so."

"All right with you, is she?"

"She doesn't notice me much. She never did. I think she doesn't like to be reminded I'm there."

"Well, that's not such a bad thing, eh?" She nudged me and laughed. I laughed with her.

"As long as they treat you right."

Jake slipped away and left us, and she went on to ask questions about the house and its inhabitants. I found myself telling her about Mrs. Marline's rooms on the ground floor, the wheelchair, the bells that rang all the time, and how the servants grumbled and said there was no pleasing her.

Then I heard someone singing. It was a beautiful clear voice with a lilt in it.

> "Three gypsies stood at the castle gate,
>   They sang so high, they sang so low,
>   The lady sat in her chamber late,
>   Her heart it melted away like snow."

I had stopped talking to listen.

"That's Zingara," said Rosie, and at that moment the door of the caravan opened and the most beautiful woman I had ever seen came in. Creole earrings dangled from her ears and her thick, shining black hair was piled high on her head; her dark eyes sparkled and Rosie looked at her with great pride.

"Zingara!" she cried.

"Who else!" said the woman. Then she smiled at me and said, "This is . . . ?"

"Little Carmel March, who comes from Commonwood House."

"I know about you," said Zingara, looking at me as though she was very pleased to see me. "And how you came to visit the rag-gle-taggle gypsies."

I did not know what to say, so I gave a little giggle. She came close to me and put her hands on my shoulders, studying me intently and giving me the impression that she liked me very much. Then she put a hand under my chin and turned my face up to hers.

"Little Carmel March," she said slowly. "I'd like to talk to you."

"Sit beside her then," said Rosie. "I tell you what. I'll make you some herb tea. Then you two can have a little chat."

She rose and went to the back of the caravan where there was a small alcove. I was more or less alone with Zingara. She kept looking at me; she touched my cheek lightly with her finger.

"Tell me," she said earnestly. "Are they kind to you at that house?"

"Well, yes . . . I think so. The doctor always smiles, and Mrs. Marline doesn't notice me, and Miss Carson is very nice."

She wanted to hear about Miss Carson and listened intently while I talked. I thought it was very kind of her to seem to care so much. I repeated what I had told Rosie a short time before.

"You're being educated, and there's a great deal to be said for education," said Zingara. "I wouldn't mind a bit more of it my-self. Still, I get along."

"Do you live here with the gypsies?" I asked.

She shook her head. "No, this is a visit. I was brought up with them. I used to run about like those little boys and girls you saw down there. I'd sing and dance a lot. I couldn't stop myself, and then, one day, one of those gentlemen who write books was going to write one about gypsies and he came and stayed with us in the camp. He heard me sing and saw me dance and he said I ought to do something about it. He was the one who did it. I was sent away to a school where they trained people for the stage—and that's what I did. I sing and dance and travel round the country. Zin-gara, the singing gypsy dancer."

"But you've come back."

"Now and then I do. I can't tear myself away, you see. It's all in the song about the raggle-taggle gypsies. Oh, you can never forget where you belong."

"But you like being Zingara the dancing, singing gypsy."

"Yes, I like it. But every now and then I am drawn back."

Rosie arrived from the alcove with three mugs.

"You'll like this," she said to me. "It's my own special brew. And how are you two getting on together? Like a house on fire, I see."

"Just like that," said Zingara.

"Lucky you were here when Miss Carmel came visiting," said Rosie with a pronounced wink.

"It was the luckiest thing," Zingara agreed.

"Now, what do you think of my tea?" asked Rosie. "Is it as good as that served by the doctor's servants?"

"It's different," I replied.

"Well, *we* are different, aren't we?" said Rosie. "We can't all be alike. Did Carmel tell you about the governess?"

"Yes," answered Zingara. "She seems to be a very good governess."

I nodded vigorously.

"I reckon," said Zingara, "that one day they'll send you away to school."

"Henry is going with Lucian Crompton," I told them.

"That's good," said Rosie. "You'll be going with the young man's sister. That'll make a real lady of you."

How I enjoyed sitting in the caravan, talking to them. Zingara fascinated me. She had been a gypsy child, running about the encampment, and had been taken away by the man who liked her singing and dancing to go on the stage. It was a wonderful story. I should have loved to see her dance. We talked and talked and then I suddenly realised how long I had stayed and that Estella and Miss Carson would be wondering what had happened to me.

I said, "I must go. I ought to be back by now."

"They'll miss you, will they?" said Zingara.

"They will begin to," I answered.

"They'll think you've been stolen by the gypsies," put in Rosie with a laugh.

"They wouldn't think that," I protested.

"You never know," said Rosie.

"I shall see you again," Zingara told me.

"Oh, I do hope so," I said.

She took my hands and gripped them firmly. "It has been lovely to be with you." She gave me her dazzling smile, and Rosie's expression was tender and loving. I felt a glow of happiness and wished I need not leave them.

Then I thanked Rosie for the drink and told them how much I had enjoyed being with them.

Zingara suddenly put her arms round me and held me tightly. She kissed me, and Rosie sat very still, smiling.

"She must go," she said at last. "They'll be waiting for her."

"Yes," Zingara said and came to the door of the caravan with me.

"Better not go with her," said Rosie. "Better to let her go on her own."

Zingara nodded.

I came down the steps and looked back. They were both standing, watching me.

I waved and then sped across the clearing and into the trees.

I had not gone far when I heard the sound of voices. I pulled up sharply and listened. That sounded like the doctor. It could not be. What would he be doing in the woods at this time?

Quietly I went forward. I did not want to be seen by anyone, for I did not want to talk of my visit to the gypsy encampment. I was not sure why, except that I thought there might be objections, and I did not want to be told I must not go there. I wanted to think about it. Zingara had made a deep impression on me, as Rosie Perrin had before her. But this was different. I wanted to think about our meeting just by myself. I did not want Estella's scornful comments. She would say that they had flattered me because they wanted to tell my fortune—or something like that.

I wanted to remember every moment clearly, from that one when Jake had stood beside me and said Rosie Perrin would like to see me, to the time when I had left.

So, I must not be seen.

But, yes . . . that was the doctor's voice, and then . . . Miss Carson's.

Then I saw them. They were sitting together on the trunk of a fallen tree. I knew the spot well. I had often sat on that tree trunk myself.

I had approached them from behind. Otherwise I should have

been seen. I stood for a few moments watching them. They were talking earnestly. I could not hear what was said, but every now and then one of them laughed, so it must have been amusing. The doctor's manner was quite different from usual. I had never seen him like that before. As for Miss Carson, she seemed very merry. It struck me how happy she appeared to be.

It was rather strange, because they both seemed like two different people.

I congratulated myself on hearing them before they could have seen me. I should have had to explain, and I did not want to do that, even to Miss Carson, that I had been visiting the gypsies.

I turned away and silently made my way back to the house through the trees.

I did go again to the gypsies after that. Rosie Perrin was sitting on the steps of her caravan weaving a basket, as she had been when I had first seen her.

She told me Zingara had gone away. She had to fulfil a contract. People thought highly of her in the theatres, she said, and she danced and sang a lot in the big towns, even London.

We talked a while. She asked me how I had liked Zingara.

I told her, "Very much," and she pressed my hand and said, "She liked you, too."

There was a subtle change in Commonwood House. Not in Mrs. Marline so much. She was just as demanding as ever, though Mrs. Barton said she grew worse every day. She never bothered to wait until the door was closed before she started criticising Dr. Marline again and again, and we heard her reminding him that it was her money which had bought the house, and how he owed everything to her. She seemed to want to hurt everybody, and, perhaps because Adeline was most easily hurt, she seemed to single her out for especially harsh treatment.

She would send for her and ply her with questions to test her progress with the new governess and, as Adeline was reduced to a state of terror, she seemed to lose what wits she had. Mrs. Marline would bewail the fact that she had given birth to such a poor creature, and implied it was all due to some inadequacy in the doctor, and the blame could not be laid at her door.

Miss Carson would be waiting for Adeline to emerge, shaking and demoralised. She would take her upstairs to the schoolroom where she would put her arms around her, hold her tightly, wipe away her tears and murmur words of comfort. She would assure Adeline that she was not a poor creature by any means, she was doing very well with her lessons, and she must take no notice of anything anyone said to the contrary. Nobody was going to hurt her while Miss Carson was there. They would have to face Miss Carson first.

I would follow them up and join in the comforting. Adeline would smile and listen. She would put her arms round Miss Carson's neck and cling to her.

Fortunately, Adeline's moods were transient and Miss Carson could soon convince her that all was well—until the next dreaded summons came.

When it did, instead of Adeline, it was Miss Carson who faced Mrs. Marline. Estella, Adeline and I knew that she had gone to Mrs. Marline, and we were all hanging about round the door to discover what would happen.

We heard Mrs. Marline's raised voice and the low murmur which was Miss Carson's; and after a while Miss Carson came out, her face red, her eyes blazing. She looked frustrated and angry. I was afraid then that she had been given notice to leave, and the thought of her going filled me with dismay. Adeline and I loved her, and even Estella admitted that she was "not bad."

Miss Carson went to her room and shut herself in. Overcome with fearful suspense, I could not stop myself going to her.

She was sitting on her bed, staring ahead of her. I threw myself into her arms and she held me tightly.

"You are not going to leave us?" I cried fearfully.

She did not answer. She just looked miserable, and I feared that she had been ordered to leave.

Then she said sadly, "I could be happy here . . . so happy," as though she were speaking to herself.

"Don't go," I said. "Don't leave us. Adeline couldn't bear it . . . nor could I. We love you."

"You dear child," she said. "I love you, too. I love this house. I love . . ."

Her lips were trembling, and she went on: "She said I am to go away. She is wicked. She cares for no one but herself. The poor doctor . . . what, what am I saying? There is nothing . . . nothing to be done, but accept what is . . ."

I thought: If Mrs. Marline has given her notice to leave, there is nothing to be done. Mrs. Marline always gets what she wants.

I thought of how dreary it would be here without Miss Carson. There would be nothing to look forward to except Uncle Toby's visits, and they were so infrequent. There would perhaps be Zingara the gypsy, but she had contracts. She would come very rarely.

When the doctor came home, we were all waiting, for what would happen when he went to his wife's room, as he did every day on his return.

There was a great deal of shouting on Mrs. Marline's part. There was no doubt that she was very angry. The doctor came out of the room. His face was white. He went straight to Miss Carson's room and was there a long time.

I never learned exactly what happened, but Miss Carson did not go. The doctor had his way, by some means, as he had had before when Mrs. Marline would have sent me to an orphanage and he had wanted me to stay.

There was a mood of uncertainty in the house. No one was sure what would happen next, and there was a lot of talk behind closed doors. It seemed that Miss Carson had a reprieve. In any event, she stayed.

She did not go to Mrs. Marline's room after that. Nor did Adeline. The poor girl was spared those terrifying interludes and she knew that Miss Carson had saved her from them.

Adeline was of a loving nature, and more than anyone she had ever known she adored Miss Carson. Her face would light up with joy when she set eyes on her, and she would watch her all the time, smiling to herself. I had the notion that Adeline only felt safe and happy when Miss Carson was there.

The doctor was intruding more on my notice. I saw him more frequently. He had changed so much. He had become more and more interested in our work, which had never seemed to interest him until Miss Carson came. He would come to the schoolroom often and ask how we were getting on.

His visits were not in the least alarming. He was always smiling. Miss Carson was proud of Adeline's progress, for she could read a little now, which she had not been able to do before Miss Carson came.

Adeline would flush with pleasure when Miss Carson said she

must read to her papa to show him how clever she had become. And Adeline, a frown of concentration on her face, would open the book and run her finger along the line as she read:

> "Three idle ducklings,
>   They played beside the pool.
>   The naughty little idle things,
>   They ought to have been at school."

Miss Carson clapped her hands when Adeline lifted her eyes, full of pride in her achievement, and waited to see the wonder on the faces of the onlookers. The doctor joined in the applause; and Adeline was very pleased with herself, and so happy.

I wondered whether the doctor was thinking what I was, which was how different Miss Carson was from Mrs. Marline.

Then he would ask how Estella and I were getting on, and Miss Carson would show him our work.

"Good. Good. This is excellent," he would say, looking at Miss Carson.

"I thought of starting them in French," she said one day.

"What a capital idea!"

"I could do my best . . ."

"Which I am sure would be very good indeed," said the doctor, and he smiled benignly at us all, including Miss Carson.

There was no doubt that he at least approved of her, and I often thought how happy the household would be if it were not for Mrs. Marline.

Henry came home from school. He had become very friendly with Lucian Crompton and often went to The Grange. Camilla was at school, too, and when she came home, we were invited to tea. She told us hair-raising stories of school life which made Estella envious, but I would not have changed Miss Carson for any excitement and reckless adventure.

A new year had come, and the atmosphere at Commonwood House seemed to be changing further. I often heard the doctor laughing. Even when he emerged from Mrs. Marline's room, and she had been upbraiding him fiercely, he did not have that depressed and frustrated look which I remembered from the past. Often I heard him humming a tune from one of the Gilbert and Sullivan operas which lots of people were singing at that time. That was something he would never have done in the past.

Then Mrs. Marline was having more bad days. We could not help welcoming these, because Dr. Everest came and gave her a sedative which made her drowsy and silence reigned on the ground floor and the servants did not have to listen for those perpetually clanging bells.

Miss Carson seemed happy. Her pleasant face was radiant and she looked quite beautiful. Not as Zingara was, but with what I can only say was some inner light.

Adeline was happy. She went round singing to herself:

> "Twinkle, twinkle little star,
> How I wonder what you are . . ."

Whenever I hear that, I am transported back to those days, and I realise, of course, that they were the prelude to the storm which was about to break and submerge us all.

But we were all very happy during that time. Even Estella did not sigh for school.

I noticed that the servants were constantly whispering together, and that the whispering stopped abruptly when any of us children appeared.

Something was happening. Vaguely I wondered what.

The top floor of Commonwood House consisted of attics—odd-shaped rooms with sloping ceilings. That was where the servants slept. The nursery was just below on the third floor. Here was the schoolroom and our bedrooms—mine, Adeline's, Estella's, Henry's, and Nanny's and Sally's, of course. Miss Carson's was on the second floor, and on the first floor was the master bedroom which had once been occupied by Dr. and Mrs. Marline and which was now the doctor's alone.

I don't know why I should have awakened on that night, but I did. Perhaps it was due to the gibbous moon which was shining right through my window onto my bed. I opened my eyes and looked at it. It seemed very near.

Then suddenly I heard something. It was like a door being shut. I immediately thought of Adeline. Her room was close to mine. Miss Carson had said we must be watchful of Adeline and always make her feel she was just like we were . . . never imply that she was different in any way.

I got out of bed and quietly opened my door. All was silent, and there was no sign of Adeline. I saw that her door was shut. I told myself I had imagined that I had heard something. Perhaps I had been dreaming. Then I heard a sound from below. I looked over the banisters and saw Miss Carson. She was walking stealthily along the corridor towards the stairs, as though she were eager to make as little noise as possible. She descended to the next floor and walked along the corridor until she came to the master bedroom.

Then, quietly, she turned the handle and went in.

I was amazed. Why did she want to see the doctor at such a time? Could there be something wrong with Adeline? But she must have come out of her bedroom and gone straight down to him. I could not think she had been to Adeline's room.

I waited a while. Nothing happened. Minutes went by and the door of the master bedroom remained shut.

I was very young and I did not fully understand what this must mean. Of course, later, so much became clear to me.

There was something different about Miss Carson. At times she would sit staring into space as though she could see something which was invisible to the rest of us. Her face would be gentle and beautiful and touched with a kind of wonder. Then one of us would say something which would bring her out of her dream. She was as kind to us as ever.

Moreover, there was something secretive going on in the house. It seemed to please and amuse Nanny Gilroy, although it was something she disapproved of. But then, I had discovered that she was often pleased about certain things, particularly if they were what she called shocking, as when the baker's wife ran off with a travelling salesman, which she declared was downright wicked as she sat and smirked and said the baker's wife would come to a bad end, which was no more than she deserved. She seemed highly gratified about that. I had never been the least bit fond of her, but now I disliked her more than ever.

One day Miss Carson told us that she had to go away to see someone and she would be away for a few days. When she left, Adeline was in a panic. She was terribly afraid that her mother would send for her, and whenever we were on the ground floor she would keep close to me and hold my hand.

When Miss Carson returned after a week's absence, Adeline clung to her more than ever.

"Don't go away," she kept saying.

Miss Carson looked as though she were going to cry. She hugged Adeline tightly, and said, "I never want to go away, darling. I want to stay here forever with you and Carmel, Estella and . . . Forever and ever I want to stay."

It was September. Lucian and Camilla, who had been home for the holidays, would soon be going back to their schools. Lucian was still kind to me, although he was so much older. He always took notice of me and would chat with me. Estella was not very pleased about that, which made me doubly appreciative of his attention. She was fond of Lucian and always trying to get him to talk to her.

The weather had turned hot and sultry. Tom Yardley said there was thunder in the air. In fact, we heard the occasional rumble of it now and then. Looking back, I think of that as being symbolic of what was about to happen in Commonwood House.

Mrs. Marline had been a little better, and for the last few days Tom Yardley had wheeled her chair out through the french windows to a shady spot in the garden where she would sit reading or dozing.

On that particular day, Lucian and Camilla came to Commonwood and we all had tea in the drawing-room on the ground floor. As Mrs. Marline was in the garden, we did not have to worry about making too much noise.

Lucian always led the conversation; he was older than Henry, and seemed mature to all of us, so we respected him and when he talked we listened without interrupting.

He had been reading a book about opal mining in Australia, which had clearly fascinated him, and he was telling us about the stone. Adeline was present. She always wanted to take part in whatever was going on, and Lucian always included her.

"They are fantastic," he was saying with that enthusiasm which he always showed for something which interested him and which made one share his pleasure in it.

"Just imagine searching for them and then coming across some wonderful specimen. The colours are magnificent. They glow in reds and blues and greens. That's why they call them black opals. There are the milky sort, too. They are found somewhere else. My mother has a black opal. She doesn't wear it much. She keeps it with other jewellery in the bank."

"People say they are unlucky," said Camilla. "That's why our mother keeps hers in the bank. She thinks the bank will get the bad luck instead of her."

Lucian laughed. "She does not! She keeps it there for safety. It's very valuable."

"My mother has an opal," said Henry. "It's in a ring. She wears it sometimes."

"Perhaps that's why she had an accident," said Camilla, determined to pursue her bad luck theory.

"Nonsense," said Lucian lightly. "How could a stone be unlucky? People just say they are unlucky because they chip easily. You know how these stories start. People exaggerate and then you get superstitions. I'd like to see your mother's ring."

"It's been in the family for a long time," said Henry. "It's in her jewel case."

"She doesn't wear it very often," said Estella. "Of course, it will be mine one day. The opal has little diamonds round it."

Lucian went on to tell us how they mined for opals, sorting them out and cutting them to the shapes they wanted. He said how strange it was that they were only found in certain places.

When we had finished tea, Henry said he wanted to go into the village to get something for his bicycle and Lucian was going with him.

Adeline said, "Will you come back here?"

"I expect so," said Lucian.

We took Camilla up to the schoolroom and played guessing games which Camilla said the girls played in the dormitory after lights out.

Just before the boys had left, Mrs. Marline had come in from the garden. But after a while she had apparently decided that, as it was such a fine day and she was feeling better, she would like to go out there again, so Tom Yardley wheeled her out and the house was peaceful once more.

Lucian and Henry had not returned. I expected they had gone off somewhere. We all walked back to The Grange with Camilla. Mrs. Marline was still in the garden.

I went up to my room and, soon after, the trouble started.

It was on the ground floor and I went down to see what it was all about.

Adeline was in great distress. She was seated on the floor in her mother's bedroom with the drawer of the bureau upside down beside her and its contents scattered around. Apparently she had opened it and it had come right out. She had dropped it and it now lay upturned on the carpet. Finding herself in such a position, Adeline could think of nothing to do but cry for help, hoping that one of us, preferably Miss Carson, would come in and help her emerge from this situation before her mother discovered she had been in her bedroom and meddled with her bureau.

Unfortunately, her cries were heard by Mrs. Marline. Tom Yardley happened to be nearby and Mrs. Marline ordered him to wheel in her chair, and in her bedroom she found Adeline seated on the floor with the contents of the drawer around her. By this time Nanny Gilroy had arrived. There followed a heartrending scene which, being in the hall, I was able to observe through the open door. Mrs. Marline was looking at the sobbing Adeline with disgust.

"I only wanted to show Lucian," cried Adeline between her sobs. "Just a look. I didn't mean . . . It all came out when I pulled . . ."

"Stop snivelling, child," said Mrs. Marline. "You look ridiculous. Yardley, pick up those things and put them back."

Tom Yardley did as he was bidden.

"Come here," snapped Mrs. Marline to the cowering Adeline. "You stupid child, when will you learn a little sense?"

"I only wanted Lucian to see the opal ring. I only wanted . . ."

"Be silent! How dare you go into my bedroom and open drawers!"

"I only wanted . . ."

Miss Carson had come down.

"What has happened?" she asked me.

"I think Adeline went in and opened a drawer which came right out," I said. "Lucian was talking about opals and Adeline wanted to show him her mother's ring."

"Poor child. That's not the way to treat her; it won't help at all."

"You shall be punished," said Mrs. Marline. "You shall go to your room and stay there without a light when it is dark."

Adeline let out a wail of terror. Then Miss Carson went into the room. Adeline gave a cry of joy and ran to her, clinging to her.

"It's all right," said Miss Carson to Adeline. "Nobody's going to hurt you."

Adeline went on sobbing and clinging to Miss Carson.

"How dare you interfere!" cried Mrs. Marline. "What impertinence! This is really too much. You are to leave this house at once."

"No, no, no!" screamed Adeline.

"I can't believe my ears," said Mrs. Marline. "Has everyone taken leave of their senses? Miss Carson, how dare you come in here!"

"Adeline meant no harm and has done none," said Miss Carson firmly. "Come along, Adeline."

Adeline gripped Miss Carson's hand while Mrs. Marline stared at them in amazement. Miss Carson walked to the door with Adeline and into the hall. Then suddenly she gave a little cry. She stumbled and would have fallen if Nanny Gilroy had not stepped forward and caught her. As it was, she slipped to the floor and lay on the carpet. Her eyes were shut and she looked very pale.

"She's fainted," said Nanny, with a look of grim satisfaction on her face. "She's fainted clean away."

"What on earth is happening?" demanded Mrs. Marline from her bedroom.

"The governess has fainted, Madam," said Nanny Gilroy. "I'll see to her."

Adeline was staring in dismay at Miss Carson. I was horrified. It seemed so unreal.

Mrs. Barton ran out and said, "What's up?"

"The governess has fainted clean away," said Nanny, and there was something significant in her manner of which I was faintly aware. It was almost as though she were saying to Mrs. Barton, "I told you so."

The next minutes were like something from a nightmare, touched with unreality. I heard Adeline sobbing and crying, "Wake up! Wake up! And don't let her hurt me!"

Nanny was whispering to Mrs. Barton: "Annie will be here soon. Might be a good idea to let her have a look at her." She nudged Mrs. Barton, who smirked. It was as though they shared some secret joke.

Then, to my relief, and Adeline's, Miss Carson opened her eyes.

"What . . . What . . . ?" she began.

"You fainted, dear," said Mrs. Barton.

Miss Carson looked about her in a bewildered, frightened way. Adeline was kneeling beside her, clinging to her hand.

"Don't faint," she pleaded. "Stay here . . . with me."

"I'll help you up, dear," said Mrs. Barton. "Best go and have a lie down."

"That's it," said Nanny. "You go and lie down. You've had a nasty turn."

Miss Carson went to her room. Nanny and Mrs. Barton went with her, and Adeline and I followed in their wake.

I was very shaken by the scene which I had witnessed. I even went into Miss Carson's bedroom. She lay on the bed, staring at the ceiling, and there was fear in her eyes.

"Now, you lie there for a bit," said Mrs. Barton. "Mustn't upset yourself, you know."

I saw Nanny's lips turn up at the corners in that familiar smirk. Then her eyes fell on me and Adeline.

"What are you doing here?" she demanded. "You get along with you."

I took Adeline's hand and we went out.

"Miss Carson is not ill, is she?" asked Adeline anxiously.

"She'll be all right," I told her.

"They won't send her away, will they?"

I pressed her hand. "Oh no, no," I said, without conviction. I had to soothe Adeline. I could not bear to see her face so distorted by fear.

Nanny Gilroy had come up behind us. She seized Adeline's hand and drew her away from me.

I went to my room. I knew something dramatic was going to happen. I believed Miss Carson would be told to pack her bags and go. Mrs. Marline would never allow anyone she employed to talk to her as Miss Carson had. She had come near to dismissal once before. She could not escape again. Like Adeline, I was wretched, contemplating what the house would be like without her.

When Annie Logan came at half past six to settle Mrs. Marline, Nanny Gilroy took her up to Miss Carson's room. I opened my door and peered over the banisters. I saw them in the corridor.

"It would be best for you to have a look at her, Annie. Fainted clean away, she did. I mean, it's not natural for a young woman to faint like that. There could be something wrong."

Then they went in and the door shut.

I hung about, waiting, and in due course they came out and went down to the kitchen to have the customary cup of tea. I watched and I waited. They were there for some time with Mrs. Barton. I wished I could hear what they were saying.

Then the door opened and I heard Nanny say, "It's only right and proper. Madam will have to be told. I ask you! To think of it! Mind you, I've had my suspicions all along. And I know you have too."

Annie Logan, with Nanny and Mrs. Barton in attendance, went into Mrs. Marline's room. I could not hear what was said. For once, Mrs. Marline was not shouting. Then they came out and Annie Logan went off on her bicycle, and Nanny and Mrs. Barton went back to the kitchen for more talk.

When the doctor came home, Mrs. Barton told him that the mistress wished to see him without delay. I knew there was going to be a discussion about Miss Carson's future, and, as I had become a skilled eavesdropper, I managed to hear some of it.

Because it was a hot day, the french windows leading from the garden to Mrs. Marline's room were open. I went as close as I dared and managed to hide myself in some measure behind a bush, and, although I could not hear all, I did hear some, particularly when Mrs. Marline raised her voice, as she did when she was incensed; and she was very angry.

"The insolence of the woman! Telling me how I was to treat my own daughter!"

Then there was a rumble from the doctor which was indecipherable.

"You would stand up for the slut! This is the last straw. She is going now. It would be a disgrace to keep her. You'll dismiss her . . . or . . . will you leave it to me? I want her out of this house. Let her stay the night, and then . . . out."

The doctor must have left then, for there was silence.

I crept into the house and, on impulse, went to Miss Carson's room. I knocked and, when she heard my voice, she said, "Come in."

I went in. Adeline was lying on the bed with her, her arms round

Miss Carson. She was crying, and Miss Carson was comforting her.

I felt such a rush of emotion that I went to Miss Carson, and the three of us were lying on the bed, our arms round each other, when the doctor came in.

He looked pale and unhappy.

"Oh, Papa," sobbed Adeline, "don't let Miss Carson go."

"We must do our best to make her stay," he said.

"Yes, yes, yes," cried Adeline.

"And now, children, I have something important to say to Miss Carson. Carmel, will you take Adeline away?"

We rose from the bed and Adeline ran to her father. She took his hand.

"Please . . . please . . . make her stay."

"Dear child," he said, and he stooped and kissed her. It was something I had never seen him do before. "I shall do all in my power," he said.

Then he smiled kindly at me, and, taking Adeline's hand, I led her away.

It was a strange night. I slept little. When I awoke to daylight, it was with a sense of deep foreboding. I knew it was going to be an important day.

Of course, it was the day when Henry was going back to school. He was to leave at ten in the morning, as he had done before. Previously everything else had been forgotten in Henry's departure and it seemed much the same today.

Henry had spent the evening with Lucian at The Grange and seemed to know nothing of the events of the night before, but then Henry was rarely interested in anything that was not of immediate concern to himself and, as Miss Carson had played a very small part in his existence, he would not realise—or care—what a tragedy her departure would be.

The doctor drove him to the station, as he always had. There Henry would meet Lucian, and the two of them would travel together. Having said good-bye to them, the doctor would go to his surgery and not return until late afternoon. It was strange, after last night's drama, that everything should seem to have returned to normal. But of course things were far from normal; this quiet was what people called the lull before the storm. Mrs. Marline would insist on Miss Carson's departure. Would the doctor be able to prevent it?

Miss Carson was not feeling well enough to take lessons. Estella was pleased about this. She knew that there had been trouble between Miss Carson and her mother, and she gave me the impression that she knew something which she then refused to tell me. She went over to see Camilla, who was not going back to school for a few more days.

I did not go with her. I did not want to leave the house, for I did not know when the next momentous event might occur.

Mrs. Marline stayed very quietly in her room.

I heard Nanny say to Mrs. Barton, "The mistress is upset. Who wouldn't be? Wait till *he* comes back, then the fireworks will start."

There was something ominous about the silence that afternoon. It pervaded the house. It would break when the doctor returned, as that would be time for the "fireworks."

But it happened before his return. It was when Tom Yardley went into Mrs. Marline's room to see if she would like the chair taken into the garden. Tom Yardley seemed destined to make momentous discoveries.

The french windows were open, so he rapped on them and called out. There was no answer, and he looked into the room. Mrs. Marline was in bed. He thought she was fast asleep and was about to turn away when he heard a strange gurgling noise, which didn't sound quite right to Tom Yardley. He thought he'd better mention it, so he went round to the kitchen. Mrs. Barton was there and he told her.

Together they went to Mrs. Marline's room. Mrs. Marline was silent and there was no gurgling sound; but they both thought she looked different somehow, and Mrs. Barton said there was no harm in sending for Dr. Everest.

Tom went off to get him, but Dr. Everest was with a patient and it was a good hour before he arrived at Commonwood House. When he did come, it was to find that Mrs. Marline was dead.

A Sea Voyage

IT IS HARD FOR ME to remember exactly what happened on that day. There were so many comings and goings, so much whispering and heavy silences.

The news that Mrs. Marline was dead was a great shock to everyone. Dr. Everest must have sent for Dr. Marline, for he came home, in a state of disbelief and horror.

The doctors were together for a long time and then Dr. Everest left. Nanny Gilroy and Mrs. Barton whispered together and when Annie Logan came, she stayed with them and they shut the door in case anyone heard what they were saying.

The doctor and Miss Carson were in the drawing-room together. They both seemed in a state of shock.

Estella and I talked about what had happened. Neither of us could pretend to mourn Mrs. Marline. I had many times heard the term "happy release" applied to death, and I often thought how well it fitted in this case. It was certainly a release for us, and, since Mrs. Marline had been in such pain, for her also.

I heard Nanny say ominously, "There'll have to be an inquest, and then we shall see what's what."

The house was different. There seemed to be menacing shadows everywhere. I felt that something tremendous was about to burst on us, but I told myself that it would be very pleasant when it was all settled, for we should be without Mrs. Marline and we could all be happy.

But life does not work out like that.

There was the inquest to come, and that ominous word seemed to crop up in every overheard conversation.

The blinds were drawn throughout the house so that the place was darkened. The doors of those rooms which had been occupied by Mrs. Marline were locked and no one was allowed to go into them.

Estella said that when people died suddenly they were cut up to see what had killed them, and, with my talent for eavesdropping, I sensed from Nanny and Mrs. Barton that, when this was done, something important would be revealed.

It was about three days after Mrs. Marline's death when a visitor arrived at Cottonwood House. She was a tall, thin, important-looking lady and I was struck by her resemblance to Mrs. Marline. She was greeted with some surprise by the doctor.

From my vantage point, I heard her say, "I thought it was time I came. Something should be done about the children."

She went into the drawing-room with the doctor and there was a long pause during which I could hear nothing. After a while Estella was summoned to the drawing-room. She was there for a long time and then she emerged, looking bewildered. She ran up to her room and I followed her.

"Who's that and what does she want?" I asked. "I haven't seen her before."

"She's my Aunt Florence. Adeline and I are going to stay with her."

I looked at her blankly.

"When?"

"Now," she said. "I've got to get Nanny to help me get some things together."

"Where are you going?"

"I told you. To stay with her. She's come to fetch us."

"Is it a holiday?"

Estella shrugged. "She says it's best for us not to be here."

"Do you mean you're going . . . *now?*"

"That's what I said, wasn't it?"

Estella was always irritable when she was worried, and I could see she was not very eager to go with Aunt Florence, who, to my knowledge, had never come to Commonwood before.

"How long for?" I asked.

"I think until this inquest is over. She thinks that's best. She says we shouldn't be involved."

"What about me?"

Estella shrugged again. "She didn't say anything about you . . . only Adeline and me. And Henry's all right because he's at school."

I felt more deserted and alone than I had since the days before Uncle Toby came into my life.

Aunt Florence went away, taking Estella and Adeline with her. I shall never forget Adeline's face as she got into the station fly, with Estella, Aunt Florence and the luggage. She looked as though she were too bewildered and miserable even to cry.

Then I was alone.

It was strange without Estella and Adeline, but at least Miss Carson had not gone with them. She seemed very nervous. She told me that Aunt Florence was Mrs. Marline's sister. They had not seen each other for years because they could not get on with each other. That did not surprise me, as I could not imagine anyone's getting on well with Mrs. Marline; and her sister, Aunt Florence, seemed very like her.

Miss Carson said, "There was some upset in the family when Mrs. Marline married the doctor. They thought she married beneath her by marrying a country doctor when she should have married into the peerage." Miss Carson added, in a bitter voice which did not fit her somehow, "What a pity she didn't."

I wondered what would happen to me when the inquest was over. I was aware of a feeling of doom in the house. Once I heard Nanny Gilroy say to Mrs. Barton, "We shall be called, I don't doubt. I shall tell all I know. You can't hold things back at a time like this. They'll find out anyway. There's nothing much they miss."

"*He's* not going to like it," replied Mrs. Barton. "People prying into his affairs."

"People should think of these things before they get caught."

I was beginning to wonder what would happen at this dreaded inquest.

Then Uncle Toby appeared and I forgot everything else. I flung myself into his arms. I was joyful and tearful all at once.

I said, "They've gone . . . Estella and Adeline."

"I know. To my sister Florence. Poor little things. And they left you, did they?"

I nodded.

"Just as well, because I've come to take you away with me for a while."

I could not believe that I was hearing correctly.

"Away with you?" I repeated.

"Just a little while. Till things settle down. Didn't we say we'd sail together one day?"

"Sail?" I cried.

He looked at me and smiled. "It seemed a good idea."

I could not believe this was really happening. Life had taken a strange turn since Mrs. Marline's death, but this was more fantastic than anything so far. To go away from this gloomy house, with its secrets which I could not understand, to be with Uncle Toby! To sail, he had said. It was too much to be taken in all at once. It was like a dream from which I feared I would wake at any moment.

I just stared blankly at him as I realised he meant what he said, joyous relief beginning to flood through me.

I have to admit that I was too excited to think much about poor Adeline, parted from her beloved Miss Carson. Estella would not mind so much. She might even feel excited to have a change. It had not been very pleasant lately at Commonwood House. And now I was presented with this most exciting prospect, beyond everything I could have imagined.

Uncle Toby laid his plans before me. "We have just over a week before we board *The Lady of the Seas,*" he told me. "There is much to be done. Not only will you require certain garments, but there are some formalities to be seen to. I'll arrange all that. You and Mrs. Q. can settle the other."

"Who is Mrs. Q.?" I asked.

"She's my landlady. Polly Quinton. Bless Polly! What should we do without her? Well, the fact is, I rent some rooms in her house. Very convenient, really. Well, that's why, of course. We usually dock in Southampton and it's my *pied à terre*. You know what that is, because I heard you've been learning French. It's a little place to step into when the need arises. One day, when I've finished with the sea, I'll settle. But in the meantime it's a *pied à terre* with Mrs. Q. She's a real sport. You'll love her. She looks after those she calls her sailor boys. Oh, I'm not the only one. One of a crowd, actually. They come and go. It suits me and it suits Mrs. Q. I've got four rooms at the top of the house with a view over the harbour. Not far from the old vessel, you see. Well, you know, the ship becomes part of you. Ships are wonderful. They're temperamental . . . they've a life of their own. Funny little tricks they get up to—and each one's different. Capricious, that's what they are. Just like women, they say. Did you know they always call a ship 'she' . . . never 'he.' No, there's nothing of a man about a ship. That's why you get to love them, you know."

I revelled in these conversations. He had always been loquacious and had a jaunty way of speaking, and everything that had happened in Commonwood House during those last months began to fade into a memory and I was entering a new and enthralling world, and with this exciting project ahead and the company of Uncle Toby, I was completely absorbed.

As Uncle Toby had said, the house was near the docks and Polly Quinton greeted me as though she had known me all my life. She was very plump, with a rosy face and eyes which almost disappeared when she laughed, which was frequently. Everything seemed amusing to her. She had a habit of folding her hands across her large bosom and shaking with mirth.

The house was on five floors and all the rooms except those in the basement were let to sailors.

Mrs. Quinton had a special feeling for sailors, I soon discovered, for one never had to lure Mrs. Quinton into talking of herself. She would do so for as long as one cared to listen.

"My Charley was a sailor boy," she told me, her eyes wide open and misty for once. "He was a real man, he was. The times we had!" She shook on recollection. "He'd come home hell bent on making the most of his leave. He was like that. They get a lot out of life, dear, that sort. Those were the days! And then that was it. He went down with his ship off South America." She was silent for a moment, her face sad. Then she was merry again.

"Yes, we had some good times together, and he left me comfortable. He always used to say, 'You'll be all right, Poll, when I've gone. You've got this house. There's a living in it.' And so there has been. I'd stop him talking like that. It upset me. Well, he was right. I let this place off to my sailors. They remind me of my Charley. Your Uncle Toby has been with me for a number of years.

He's a real gentleman. I don't mind telling you, dear, I've got a special soft spot for him. You're a lucky girl, you are. He's taking you off to sea with him. Well, I reckon that's something, I do. I wish I'd been with my Charley when . . . Well, it's not good, is it? I always felt I'd have found some way of looking after him. But that's me. Charley always used to say, 'You think you can do everything better than everyone else.' It's true. That's why I'd have found some way of getting him out of that sea. Well, dear, we're going to do some shopping tomorrow. To tell you the truth, there's nothing I like better than spending a bit of money."

She was laughing, her temporary sadness gone.

We shopped together. We bought the garments which Uncle Toby said I should need for shipboard life—sturdy shoes with soles that would not slip on wet decks, some summer dresses for a hot climate. Mrs. Quinton thoroughly enjoyed these expeditions, and so did I.

Uncle Toby was away for long periods during the day, since he had business to attend to. The ship was in port and certain repairs were being done. He took me over her. And what a thrill that was! I was to have a cabin on the deck just below the bridge where Uncle Toby's own cabin was situated.

"You'll be a passenger," he told me, "a very special person. I have to look after the passengers, but for the most part the cargo looks after itself. So I shall be able to keep my eyes on you."

He showed me the dining-room with its long tables. There were a smoking-room and a music room, as well as public rooms where people could indulge in all sorts of activities, and stretches of deck where one could sit and contemplate the sea. I felt I had skipped into a fantastic new world.

And then we were sailing and this was like the realisation of a long-cherished dream. My pride in Uncle Toby was excessive. He looked splendid in his captain's uniform and everyone deferred to him. He was the Master of *The Lady of the Seas* and all who sailed in her.

He had changed subtly. He was god-like and alert for the safety of all who depended on him. He was usually very occupied, but we did have moments together, and I was gratified and honoured because I believe he enjoyed them as much as I did.

He would say, "I'll be on the bridge for some time, so I shan't be able to be with you—but just as soon as it is possible . . ."

I would nod, delighted that he should explain to me, which was something grown-ups rarely did. I often thought how lucky I was to have him, for he was not really my uncle, though he always spoke and acted as though he were. I would never forget that I was the one he had taken to sea with him—not Henry, Estella or Adeline. One would have thought he would have taken Henry, because boys were usually chosen for adventures like this. Secretly I thought Uncle Toby did not like Henry—or even Estella or Adeline —as well as me. And that was where the miracle came in.

Occasionally, I would think of the old life, though I did not want to, but it would force itself into my mind. How were they getting on with Aunt Florence, I wondered? Perhaps they would be home by now. They would have the inquest and the house would settle down to its old routine. Lessons and walks with Miss Carson; and Mrs. Marline safely buried and unable to spoil anything again. Adeline would be pleased. She might miss me a little, but Miss Carson would make up for that.

So it would be a happy ending for them as well as for me? Now and then the thought came to me of what would happen when this voyage was over. I should go back to Commonwood, I supposed, and then everything would be settled.

But I did not want to think of that. I was going to enjoy every moment of this wonderful adventure first.

Shipboard life was absorbing. At meal times we sat at a long table, which was jolly. Everyone was friendly towards me because I was the Captain's protégée, and they told me how lucky I was to have an uncle who took me on his ship for a long sea voyage. Sometimes Uncle Toby joined us. People all wanted to talk to him. They asked questions about the ship and he talked to them in his jolly, jaunty way which they all seemed to like.

At night I would lie in my berth in the cabin just below the bridge and think of Uncle Toby up there, looking at his charts and the stars as he drove the ship along.

I shared a cabin with a girl who was more or less my own age. Gertie Forman was going to Australia with her family—father, mother and brother Jimmy—to settle there.

There were two berths, one above the other, and I climbed into mine—the top one—by means of a ladder which could be pulled down when one needed it. It was great fun lying up there, particularly when the ship rocked.

Gertie and I soon became friendly. We explored the ship together. It was her first time on a ship too, so we had a lot in common. We discovered the public rooms and the best places to sit on deck. Not that we did a great deal of sitting; we always seemed to be dashing around. Sometimes we would talk to the sailors— dark men, a number of them, who could not speak much English. But some of them were English and they often referred to me as "the Captain's little 'un."

It was wonderful to have a companion at such times when I could not be with Uncle Toby, and Gertie and I spent a great deal of time together. Then we would lie in our berths at night and talk to each other.

I learned that the Formans used to live on a farm in Wiltshire. Gertie told me how she and her brother always had daily tasks to perform . . . like bringing in the cows for milking, collecting eggs from the fowls, making the pigs' food. There was always something which had to be done on a farm. They were going to buy a property in Australia where land was cheaper than at home.

The family had left because "they"—Gertie was not sure who— were planning to build a road right through the farm, which would have finished it off as a paying proposition. They were anxious about it for a long time and the Formans had hoped it would never come to pass, but, when they had known it was inevitable, they made the decision to buy a property in Australia.

I told her a little about myself, but I was guarded. I did not want her to know that I had been found under the azalea bush. She would certainly have asked how the splendid Captain Sinclair could be uncle to such a waif. I wondered what I should say if her probing became awkward. But Gertie, like most people, I have discovered, was far more interested in their own affairs than those of others, and it was not difficult to steer her away from asking awkward questions.

In spite of all his responsibilities, Uncle Toby often found time to be with me. He would take me up to the bridge and show me the charts and instruments, and then we would sit in his cabin and talk. I enjoyed every moment on board ship, but to be with Uncle Toby was the highlight of the day.

He talked to me as though I were a grown-up—one of the most endearing aspects of our relationship—and when I considered the insults I had been subjected to from Estella, Henry and Nanny

65

Gilroy, it seemed miraculous that the mighty Captain could treat me as though I were important and interesting.

He asked me how I liked shipboard life, and did not wait for me to reply. "Wonderful, isn't it?" he said. "To feel the fresh sea breeze coming to you . . . the rise and fall of the waves . . . and the sea . . . the ever-changing sea that can be so soft and gentle and then suddenly rages. You haven't seen it in a fury, and I hope you never will."

He talked about the places we should visit. We were right at the start now and had yet to go through the Bay of Biscay.

It had a reputation for being perverse, he told me, and we had to look out for squalls. There were currents and winds to be watched. Sometimes the elements were benign and sometimes the reverse. Then we should go through the Mediterranean and call at Naples and Suez.

"We shall pass through the Canal. That will be very interesting for you, Carmel. A little while ago you would have had to go round the Cape, but now we have this convenient Canal. You'll like Naples. Italy is one of the most beautiful countries in the world, in my opinion—Egypt one of the most mysterious. You are going to see a great deal of the world, Carmel. Do you miss your lessons? Perhaps that is not good. But a journey like this . . . well, you will learn more from it than you will find in your school-books . . . perhaps. In any case, we will tell ourselves so. It salves the conscience and that is usually a good thing to do."

He used to talk about the ancient explorers, Christopher Columbus, Sir Francis Drake. How brave they had been, going off in their ships—not in the least like *The Lady of the Seas*—before the seas were charted . . . not knowing what hazards they would face.

"Imagine the storms . . . the lack of equipment! What men! Doesn't it make you proud? Voyages of discovery! What days they were! What adventurers!"

I loved to hear him talk like that. I caught his enthusiasm. In my eyes, he was as great as Christopher Columbus and Sir Francis Drake.

He mentioned remote countries and I was transported back to the schoolroom in Commonwood House, and in my mind's eye I saw Miss Carson pointing out places on the revolving globe.

A feeling of depression came to me then with a sense of guilt. I had forgotten them all so quickly, and I had a sudden qualm that all might not be well. I recalled the sly looks and the smirks I had seen so often on Nanny's face, and the poor, sad lost look on Miss Carson's.

They had been such a part of my life, and now they seemed like shadows . . . puppets belonging to another world—a world of nightmares and secrets from which I had been miraculously saved by Uncle Toby.

There were times when I awoke and thought I was in my bedroom at Commonwood House and that something terrible which I did not understand was happening. I would be filled with foreboding, then I would be aware of the movement of the ship and in the early morning light I would see above me the bulkhead and know that I had been dreaming and I was actually in my bunk with Gertie sleeping below me in this wonderful world to which Uncle Toby had brought me.

Then Gertie would call out, "You awake?" and I would joyfully answer, "Yes."

"What shall we do today?"

What an ideal way for a day to begin for a girl who was not yet eleven years old—though she would be in March, which was not very far away.

The Forman family had more or less adopted me because Gertie and I were such close companions. I would join them for tea or sit with them on deck, and I seemed part of the family. Jimmy Forman was not often with us. Gertie and I were younger than he was and he considered us too immature for his company. In any case, we were girls, and as such he had not much respect for us. He spent a lot of time with the sailors, seeking information about the ship.

Mr. and Mrs. Forman were delighted that Gertie had found a companion, and it really was amazing how quickly people became close friends on a ship. I suppose it was because we saw so much of each other.

We had passed through the Bay without much discomfort and we were sailing along the Mediterranean. Uncle Toby told me that there was a party going to Pompeii and Herculaneum, and it would be good for me to join it.

"Alas," he said, "I shall be completely tied up with business, but I don't see why you shouldn't go with the Formans."

Gertie and I had already discussed it.

"We must go," she said, and her family would be pleased for me to go with them.

The Formans were quite happy to concede, apart from Jimmy, who did not want to go with the family but with Timothy Lees, with whom he shared a cabin.

It was a wonderful day. In my imagination I was transported to that time long ago when the disaster had happened. There, looking above me, was the menacing mountain. It was not difficult to conjure up in one's mind the panic that ensued when the hot ash spurted from its summit, covering the city and destroying it with its inhabitants.

We had an excellent guide and, as we picked our way through the ravaged byways of the ancient city, I was seeing it all as it must have happened.

When we returned to the ship, I was in an ecstatic state. As soon as I saw Uncle Toby, I told him what a wonderful day it had been.

He listened intently and suddenly he put his arm round me and, holding me tightly against him, said, "Yes. We need not worry about missing a few lessons. It's all right for a while at any rate."

I felt suddenly sombre. I did not want to think of the future. I was living in an enchanted present and I wanted it to go on forever.

I said, "I expect Estella and Adeline are back from their Aunt Florence now and they'll be having lessons again. I shall have to catch up when I get home."

Home, I thought? Commonwood House. I had never really thought that I really belonged, and now I could not bear to contemplate going back.

Uncle Toby said lightly, "Oh, you'll catch up. I've always maintained that seeing the world is an education in itself."

He changed the subject abruptly. "Gertie is a nice girl, isn't she? You were lucky to get with her. It doesn't always work out so neatly."

Then he began to tell some funny stories about ill-assorted people who had shared cabins in the past.

"Ports are fun, aren't they?" he went on. "The next is Suez. We are staying there only a very short time, and there isn't an excursion planned. We don't get in until eight in the morning and we must leave at four-thirty. Not much time for sight-seeing. It's too far from the pyramids, and you can't really get a taste of the allure of Egypt. I am sure the Formans will be glad if you join them. We have to go in on tenders, which takes a little time. It's too shallow for us to get right in. You'll enjoy it. We use the lifeboats and, of course, have to let them down, as we do if we had to abandon ship. It's a good exercise. You'll see. Smaller ships can get in without trouble, but we have to anchor some little way out in the bay."

I enjoyed having such details explained to me. I was proud and happy that he considered me capable of understanding, and I forgot about the earlier references to the education I was missing, which had brought home the transience of the life I was now experiencing. I determined to enjoy every moment that I might carry it forever in my memory.

The Formans said they would be delighted if I joined them for the day we were in Suez. Gertie told me that Jimmy and Tim Lees were going off on their own. They thought they were too old to be in family parties.

The days were balmy, and when we were at sea Uncle Toby had more free time. Often I would sit on deck with him. One day, when we were talking, the ship's doctor came by. Dr. Emmerson was a pleasant young man, in his mid-twenties, I imagined.

Uncle Toby said, "We are just enjoying a quiet *tête-à-tête*. We don't have them as frequently as I'd like, but Carmel is a very resourceful young lady and she manages to get along very well without my interference."

"I am sure she does," said Dr. Emmerson. "May I sit down for a moment?"

"Please do. Are you ready to leave?"

"Still one or two things to do," said the doctor.

Uncle Toby turned to me and said, "Dr. Emmerson is leaving us at Suez and another doctor will be joining us there. We can't sail without a doctor, you know, so Dr. Kelso will take Dr. Emmerson's place. We shall miss you, Lawrence."

"You'll get along well with Kelso."

"Dr. Emmerson is going to spend some time in a hospital in Suez," said Uncle Toby. "He's very interested in the ailments of the skin, and he's making some special studies of it there."

"Shall you be able to get ashore, Captain?" asked Dr. Emmerson.

"Alas, no, but the Formans—you know, the family who are going to Australia—are taking Carmel."

"That's good," said Dr. Emmerson.

We chatted for a while about Suez, which Dr. Emmerson seemed to know very well, and then the doctor mentioned that he still had quite a few things to do in preparation for his departure, and he left us.

Uncle Toby said, "A nice fellow, Lawrence Emmerson. Ambitious, too. He'll do well. I think his family wanted him to go into the Church, but he knew what he wanted. Now he's doing this course in Suez, but I expect he'll be back specialising in London. Good luck to him. His family will be proud of him then. You know, my family didn't want me to go to sea. But, like Lawrence Emmerson, I'd made up my mind. When I was seventeen, I ran away and joined the Merchant Navy. We used to do the Indian run, taking soldiers and civil servants to India and bringing them back home. It was a wonderful life and I've never regretted it. That's one of the great secrets of life. Never regret. If it's good, it's wonderful. If it's bad, it's experience. That is well worth having. It warns you not to do it again."

I wanted to ask about the family, but remembered that Mrs. Marline had been his sister, and I was afraid of getting onto something unpleasant.

He went on, however: "I was forgiven in time, and taken back into the bosom of the family. But I was always a bit of an outsider. I did not conform, you see. I'm not a conformer."

We laughed together, and he made no further mention of the family, but he went on to tell me more of his experiences at sea. I was going to be exactly like him, I told myself. I was going to enjoy the good things as they came and not let others disturb me.

In two days we were to reach Suez, and Gertie and I talked constantly of what we would do. I loved getting into my berth and snuggling down and talking to Gertie until one of us dropped off to sleep.

The morning before we were due to arrive at Suez, Gertie told me that her father had been quite ill during the night.

"It's one of his bad turns, Mum thinks," she said. "He gets them really bad. It's his chest."

During the day Mr. Forman's cold grew worse and Dr. Emmerson said he must not go out the next day. Mrs. Forman felt that she must stay with him, for these chest colds of his could turn nasty.

Gertie was woeful. "You know what this means, don't you?" she said. "We shall have to stay on board."

Mrs. Forman was distressed. She knew how much we had looked forward to going ashore, but she could not possibly leave Mr. Forman.

Gertie was so upset that finally Mrs. Forman said that, if the boys were with us, she thought we might go.

Gertie rather gloomily told me of the boys' reaction to the suggestion. Jimmy had said they didn't want a lot of kids trailing round with them.

"I told them it was not a lot, only two, and we're not kids anyway. Then my mother got angry and told Jimmy not to be so selfish, and how upset our father would be if he knew he'd refused to keep an eye on his sister and her friend so that the poor little things had to stay on board. Then Jimmy said, all right, they'd take us. But they don't want us."

"Perhaps we'd better not go then," I suggested.

"Not go! Stay on board! Not likely! We'll have to go with them, or they won't let us go at all."

So the prospect was not as bright as it might have been, and, much as we resented the boys' ungracious resignation, we decided that it was better to force our unwanted company on them than not go at all.

It was fun getting into the launch which was to take us ashore. First we must descend the gangway to the landing stage, which was bobbing about in the swell; then we must step from that to the launch, which was drawn up at the side of the ship. This was not an easy matter, and there were two stalwart sailors, standing like sentinels, waiting on the swaying platform to help people into the launch.

They lifted Gertie and me and placed us in the boat, which was rocking rather roughly on the sea. We clutched at each other to steady ourselves, laughing immoderately as we did so while the two boys—our reluctant guardians—looked at us with contempt.

It was well into the morning before we had boarded the launch, as many people were going ashore and the boats only took a certain number at a time and we had to wait for our turn. We had been warned that we must be back on board at the latest by four o'clock, as the ship was sailing at four-thirty and the last launch would leave Suez at half past three.

Then we were on dry land. I glanced over the water to *The Lady of the Seas,* and I thought how majestic she looked, but Jimmy and Timothy were impatient to be off and we followed in their wake. After a time we came upon a market. The cobbled streets were narrow and lined with shops, like caves with stalls in front of them. There was a great deal of noise, for everyone seemed to be shouting excitedly. Many of the men wore long robes and turbans, which looked very exotic. Everything was different from anything I had seen before. We listened to the people chattering at the stalls. They appeared to be bargaining, but, of course, we could not understand what was said; they seemed to be very fierce and at times looked as though they were about to strike each other. Then the bargain would be concluded, which must have been satisfactory, for they smiled benignly on each other and in one case kissed.

The boys had paused by a stall on which were a variety of necklaces, rings and bracelets. This was because of the two dusky girls there who had called to them. The girls had long black hair and laughing black eyes; earrings hung from their ears and necklaces round their necks—all similar to those displayed on the stall. Then one of them threw a necklace round Jimmy's neck. He looked embarrassed and the girls appeared to think it a great joke.

"Nice, nice," said one of them. "You buy?"

The boys laughed and the girls giggled.

A necklace was thrown round Timothy's neck by the other girl.

The boys clearly did not know what to do, which by no means displeased Gertie and me, who were amused to witness their discomfiture. The girl who had put the necklace round Jimmy's neck started to pull the necklace slowly towards her, and with it Jimmy.

"You come," she said.

Then the other girl drew Timothy towards her in the same way.

"This is getting silly," said Gertie to me. "Let's go and look at those leather things on that stall over there."

We moved over to the one indicated by Gertie. Among the goods were wallets in different coloured soft leather with a pattern in gold embossed on them.

"It's my father's birthday next week," said Gertie. "I might buy one of those for him." She picked up one and the salesman was immediately beside her.

"You like? Very nice."

"How much?" said Gertie in the grown-up voice she often assumed.

"You tell me . . . what you pay?"

"I have no idea," said Gertie. "Tell me what you are asking."

The man picked up a writing pad and scribbled a figure on it.

"I haven't enough," said Gertie and, turning to me, "Let's go."

She put down the wallet and attempted to move away, but the salesman held her by the arm.

"How much? How much?"

His hands were on the little bag she carried. "How much? How much?" he kept saying.

We were both wishing heartily that we had not become involved in this, and I was sure the wallet was becoming less and less attractive in Gertie's eyes.

But the salesman had a firm grasp on her arm and would not release her. He looked lovingly at the wallet and then turned his tragic gaze on us, as though to imply that the sale was of the utmost importance to him. He must have noticed that he aroused our interest and compassion, for he went on: "Poor man. Me very poor man."

He released Gertie momentarily and held his arms as though he were rocking a baby. Then he held up eight fingers.

"Babies," he said. "Starving . . ."

Gertie and I exchanged glances. She shrugged her shoulders and took all the money from her purse. The man smiled, took the money and wrapped up the wallet.

We had freed ourselves, but I was not quite sure whether it was done out of compassion or the need to escape from this embarrassing transaction.

We saw then that, while this had been going on, the boys had disappeared. So had the girls with the necklaces.

"Never mind," said Gertie. "We'll be better on our own. They didn't want us and we didn't want them."

We went along the narrow street, glancing sideways at the stalls, determined not to get involved in any more bargaining.

There was a maze of streets, one very like another, and we must have wandered for half an hour before we emerged from them.

We had thought we would come out at the point where we had come in and then we would have known our way back to the launch; but the scene was quite different.

Gertie looked at the watch which she wore pinned to the bodice of her dress. It was half past two.

"Let's get one of those little donkey carts to take us back to the ship," she said.

"Don't you think the boys will be looking for us?"

"No. They'll be glad to be rid of us. Besides, we'll show them we don't need them. Look, there's one."

We hailed it. The driver—a boy who could not have been more than fourteen years old—came up to us.

"We want to go back to the launch which takes us to our ship, *The Lady of the Seas*. Do you know?"

The boy nodded vigorously. "I know. I know. You come."

We climbed into the carriage, which was a sort of cart. We were sorry for the two little donkeys who were going to pull us along. They looked pathetically frail, but we were soon laughing and clinging together in our glee, for it was not the smoothest of rides. It seemed long and, after a while, we were soon waiting rather impatiently for a glimpse of the sea.

Gertie called to the driver.

"We should be there now. Why don't we see the sea?"

"Sea here," cried the boy, waving his whip vaguely, but we could not see any sign of it.

What followed was like a nightmare. I dreamed of it for a long time afterwards. The vehicle was brought to a standstill and we clambered out.

"Where are we?" cried Gertie.

"This sea," was the reply. "Ship here."

"I can't see them," we said.

"Here. You pay."

"But you haven't taken us there," wailed Gertie in exasperation.

"No," I agreed. "This isn't the right place."

I was beginning to feel nervous. We had been caught once over the wallet. It was just about three o'clock and the last launch left at three-thirty.

Gertie clearly was thinking the same.

"You *must* take us there at once," she said.

The young boy nodded. "You pay," he said.

"But you haven't taken us there. We will pay when you do."

"You pay. You pay."

"What for?" cried Gertie indignantly.

"We didn't ask to come here," I added. "You must take us to the launch."

We had very little money. Gertie had lost all hers to the wallet salesman, and there was only what I had, which I knew was not a great deal. But we had to get back to the launch which would take us to the ship.

I tried to explain. I opened my purse.

I said, "All this is yours if you take us back to the launch."

He looked contemptuously at the money.

Then he nodded. "You pay. I take."

He took all the money and, still nodding, turned and leaped into the driver's seat and drove off.

We looked at each other in dismay. We were far from the ship, without money, bewildered and more and more alarmed with every passing moment. The awful realisation came to us. We were alone in an alien country. The people were unfamiliar: recent experiences had taught us that we must be wary; it was difficult to communicate with them, for we did not speak their language. We were helpless, numb with fear, too scared to think clearly, and we were old enough to guess a little of the horrors which might befall us, but not old enough to have a notion of how we could cope with the situation.

The thought flashed into my mind that only a miracle could save us.

"Only God could help us." I had spoken my thoughts aloud.

Gertie was staring at me.

"What can we do?" she said in a whisper.

"We can pray to God," I said.

I suppose faith grows strong when we are in desperate situations from which there appears to be no escape except through Divine help. I knew mine was the faith of desperation. I believed because I had to—the alternative was too awful to contemplate. And I think Gertie felt the same.

We stood very still, closed our eyes and put the palms of our hands together. "Please, God," we whispered, "help us to get back to the ship."

We opened our eyes. What had we expected? To see the dock and the launching place materialise before our eyes?

Everything was exactly the same. Nothing had changed . . . except ourselves. We had faith. The panic had left us. We would find our way back somehow. God would show us the way.

Gertie had taken my hand.

"Let's go along there. I am sure we came past that place."

I noticed the big white building which stood a little apart from the others.

I said, "We'll ask in there. That's it. Someone will be able to speak English. They'll help us."

Gertie nodded and we hurried towards the building.

And then . . . the miracle happened. A man came out of the building and there was something familiar about him. I saw that it was Dr. Emmerson. I was exultant. God had answered our prayer.

"Dr. Emmerson!" I called.

He stopped. He stared and then he hurried towards us.

"Carmel! What are you doing here? The ship sails at four."

"Dr. Emmerson," I panted, "we're lost. A man brought us here and left us. He said it was the dock."

Dr. Emmerson looked puzzled for a second or so. Then he hesitated no longer. He hustled us away from the building. One of the donkey-driven carriages was approaching. He hailed it and said something to the driver. He could speak the language and there was a moment of excited talk. Then we got into the carriage and drove off at great speed.

We somewhat incoherently told Dr. Emmerson what had happened.

"I can't think why you two young girls were allowed out on your own!"

"We weren't," said Gertie.

"We lost the boys," I explained.

Dr. Emmerson looked shocked.

"I only hope we can make it," he said. "Time's running short."

"The last launch goes at . . ." I said.

"Yes, I know." He looked at his watch and was clearly worried.

I was silently giving prayers of thanks all the time while Dr. Emmerson was urging the driver to go faster. I could see by his gestures that the man was getting the utmost speed out of the poor donkeys.

The joy of seeing the dock was great, but dismay followed. The last launch had left a few minutes before we had arrived and was on its way out to *The Lady of the Seas*.

We got out of the carriage. Dr. Emmerson gave the driver money and we stood for a few seconds, staring at the departing launch, which seemed to be rapidly reducing the distance between itself and the ship.

Dr. Emmerson looked very dismayed.

There were a few rowing boats on the water. He shouted to one of them.

He was pointing to *The Lady of the Seas* and to us. I guessed what he was saying. They came to a hasty agreement and the next moment we were all climbing into a rowing boat.

It was slow progress. We saw that the launch had reached the ship and the passengers were already on board. The launch was, in fact, being drawn to the deck from which it usually hung. The ship was preparing to sail.

There were some men standing on the landing stage, which was in the process of being dismantled. Dr. Emmerson shouted to them. It was not easy to get their attention, but at last he did.

He shouted, "Two little girls. Passengers. The Captain's niece."

He had their attention. We were tremendously relieved. We were going to be all right—but we had known we would be when our prayers were answered.

There was some time to wait. Several people had come out onto the deck and were leaning over the rail, looking at us.

Dr. Emmerson was clearly greatly relieved. He was confident that he would get us back on board now. He must have been wondering what he would do with two girls on his hands.

He said, "They can't set up the landing stage again. I expect they'll let down a rope ladder."

"A rope ladder!" I cried, looking at Gertie.

"That'll be fun," she said, with more apprehension than conviction.

She was right to be concerned. It was no easy matter.

We were bobbing about in our little boat, which seemed very tiny and frail beside *The Lady of the Seas*.

The people from the deck watched while the ladder was being lowered.

"You'll have to be careful," said Dr. Emmerson. "This can be a tricky business. They'll be waiting up there to catch you, and I'll help from here below . . . but there's a little distance when you'll be on your own. Understand?"

"Yes," I said.

He caught the end of the ladder as it descended.

"You first, Carmel," he said. "Ready? Go carefully. On no account lose your grip on the rope. Hang on to it at all cost. And don't look down at the sea. Keep your eyes straight ahead. Ready?"

I was off. He was holding me until I got beyond his reach. Then for a short time I was alone, clinging to the ladder as Dr. Emmerson had advised. I took one cautious step after another. Then I felt hands from above. Two strong sailors had hauled me onto the deck.

Then it was Gertie's turn.

We stood beside each other. We were safe. We had seen our miracle and felt exalted. I knew Gertie felt as I did.

We looked down at Dr. Emmerson, who was smiling very happily. The look of anxiety had completely disappeared from his face.

"Thank you. Thank you, Dr. Emmerson," we shouted.

"Good-bye," he replied. "And don't do it again!"

People were surrounding us, among them Jimmy and Timothy.

"Idiots!" said Jimmy. "What did you think you were doing?"

Mrs. Forman was hugging us, half-laughing, half-crying.

"We were so worried," she said. "But, thank God, you are safe."

"Yes," I said. "Let us thank God."

There was a great deal of fuss about the adventure. Uncle Toby had heard nothing of it until we were safe on board. It was the law of the ship that he was not to be disturbed at such times except with emergencies, and our failure to return on board in time would not be considered a disaster in nautical terms.

He was very disturbed when he learned what had happened, and I realised even more what potential dangers we might have faced.

He sent for me to go to his cabin an hour or so after sailing.

"Never, never let a thing like that happen again!" he said sternly.

"We wouldn't have let it happen then if we could have helped it," I told him.

"You could have helped it. You should have stayed with the boys."

"We didn't mean to leave them. They just disappeared."

"You shall never go ashore again unless you are with a reliable person."

He had never been angry with me before, and I could not stop my tears. I had been so elated to be safe, and to have incurred his anger made me more unhappy than anything else could.

He relented at once and took me into his arms.

He said, "It's only because you mean so much to me. When I think what could have happened . . ."

We were silent for a while, clinging to each other.

"Never . . . never . . ." he began.

"No, I won't. I won't, I promise."

After a few moments, he was his old self again.

"All's well that ends well. I can't be grateful enough to Emmerson. It was a miracle that he happened to be there."

"Yes," I said with conviction. "It *was* a miracle."

"He's a good fellow. I'll write to him and you and Gertie can enclose a note."

"Oh, we will, we will. I'm so happy to be back with you, and you're not really angry."

"As long as you don't do anything so foolish again."

"Oh, I won't. I'll be careful. I promise."

So all was well. I was back and Uncle Toby was only cross with me because he loved me so much.

He sent for Jimmy and Timothy. He must have talked to them very severely, for they emerged from his cabin red-faced and solemn. They were subdued for several days afterwards.

Mrs. Forman blamed herself. She should never have allowed us to go, she said. But she was assured that she must not blame herself, and in any case she had been so worried at the time about Mr. Forman, who was now making satisfactory progress and would be recovered completely in a few days.

That incident had an effect on Uncle Toby. He was a little quiet at times and sometimes absentminded, as though preoccupied in some way.

We were together as often as before, and I believed that, whenever it was possible, he wanted to be with me and what he enjoyed most was sitting in a quiet spot on deck and talking to me.

There were occasions, though, when he would lapse into silence —rare with him in the past—and he would begin to say something, then change his mind.

This change in him had come about since our dramatic adventure, and I believed it had something to do with that.

Then I learned what it was all about.

We had dined, and it was one of those occasions when Uncle Toby had an hour or so to spare. It was a beautiful night. The sea was calm and a full moon was making a path of light across the water. There was no sound but the gentle swishing of the waves against the sides of the ship.

Uncle Toby said suddenly, "You're not a child anymore, Carmel. I've been thinking that perhaps it is about time you began to learn a few things."

"Yes?" I said eagerly.

"About me," he said. "About yourself."

I was tensely, eagerly waiting. "Please tell me, Uncle Toby. More than anything, I want to know."

"Well, in the first place, I'm not your Uncle Toby."

"I know. You're Estella, Henry and Adeline's, of course."

"Yes. I'm that all right. Perhaps I'd better start from the beginning."

"Oh yes, please."

"I told you that my family didn't want me to go to sea, didn't I? I wasn't like the rest of them. Well, you knew my sister, the doctor's wife. You wouldn't say I was like her, would you?"

I shook my head vigorously.

"I wasn't like my sister Florence, either."

"The one Estella and Adeline went to . . . Oh, no!"

"That's the one. You see, I am most unlike them all. They all conformed, except perhaps Grace herself, who married the country doctor who was considered unworthy by the family. But then, it was probably that he was the only one who had ever showed any desire to join forces with Grace, so it was the doctor or no one. I'm being unkind. The fact is, I was never close to any of them. You can understand why I went to sea."

I nodded. Certainly I could understand anyone's wanting to get away from Mrs. Marline, not counting the rest of them.

"You were so different," I said.

"Chalk from cheese, as they say."

"But you were reconciled afterwards."

"Let me tell you how it was. When I was a young officer, my ship was stationed in Australia. In Sydney, actually. It's a fine place and the harbour is grand. One of the finest in the world. Didn't Cook say that when he discovered it? And he was right. Well, there we were based and there we took on our passengers and cargo and sailed round the world . . . just like *The Lady of the Seas* . . . to places in the vicinity mostly. Hong Kong, Singapore, New Guinea, New Zealand. I was twenty when I met Elsie. I was young, hot-headed, romantic you might say. We were married."

"You have a wife?"

"Kind of."

"How can you have a wife . . . kind of?"

"You were always a very logical young lady, and you are right. You either have a wife or you don't. What I mean is that ours was not like most marriages. We don't share our lives anymore. We both decided it was best that way."

"But she is your wife."

"Marriage vows are binding. You're either married or you're not. So we are."

"Shall I see her?"

"Yes. You'll meet Elsie, when we get to Sydney. She and I are the best of friends. We don't see each other very often. Perhaps that's why."

"You don't really like her."

"Oh, but I do. I like her very much. We get on well for a time. She's a good sort."

"Then why . . . ?"

"There are things you'll understand later. Human beings are complicated creatures. They rarely do what they're expected to. She couldn't leave her country, and I'm a wanderer. She's got a comfortable little place near the harbour. She was born there. Native heath and all that. But I want to talk about us . . . you and me."

"Yes," I said excitedly.

"We took to each other from the start, didn't we? There was something special, wasn't there?"

"Yes, there was."

"We were drawn to each other. Carmel, I am your father."

There was a deep silence while joy flooded over me.

"You are pleased?" he asked at length.

"It's the best thing that's ever happened to me."

He took my hand and kissed it tenderly. "It's the best thing that ever happened to me, too," he said.

I sat in wonder. If I could have been granted my dearest wish, it would have been just this.

He said, "You must be wondering how it all came about."

I nodded blissfully.

"When I heard you had been left behind in Suez, it gave me such a shock. I could only be thankful that I did not hear until you were safe. I should have been frantic. I should have left the ship and gone in search of you. And that would have been the end of my career at sea."

"Oh, I'm sorry . . . so sorry."

"I know. It wasn't your fault. Those stupid boys should have taken more care of you. The idea came to me that you were growing up and it was time you knew the truth. It was then that I decided to tell you, Carmel. I did not know. I had not an inkling until the doctor wrote to me. I was in New Zealand when I received the letter. Posts are often delayed, as you can imagine. Dear old Doctor Edward. His heart was in the right place. You see, he knew. Thank God he did."

"They would have sent me to an orphanage. I should never have known you . . . or who I was."

That prospect seemed doubly gloomy now that I could compare it with what I should have missed.

"Even Grace had to relent and look after you when she knew you were one of the family. But let me tell you. Your mother was a gypsy girl."

"Zingara!" I cried.

He looked at me in amazement.

"She became that. She was Rosaleen Perrin. You knew?"

"I saw her once." I told him how I had become acquainted with Rosie Perrin when she had bandaged my leg, and how later I had met Zingara.

"She must have come there to see you. What did you think of her?"

"That she was the most beautiful person I had ever seen."

"She was unlike everyone else in every way." He smiled reminiscently. "I was at Commonwood House for all of three months. I had a long leave due to me, and the ship was going into dock for a thorough overhaul and refit. It was during that time that I met Rosaleen. I was deeply attracted by her."

"And she by you."

"It was a wild and deep attraction while it lasted."

"It did not last?"

"It did not have a chance to. There had been someone who came to the encampment . . . something about material he was collecting for a book he intended to write about the gypsies' way of life. He had been interested in her ever since then. That was not surprising. She and I used to meet at night in the woods. I have travelled a great deal and known many people, but never one like Rosaleen. She was having tuition for a stage career and she was bent on that. I would not be there forever. We both knew that it could not last, and we were the sort of people to accept that. I knew nothing of your existence until Edward wrote and told me. I'll explain all that. She left you at Commonwood House because she thought it was the best for you. She was full of her own sort of wisdom. She was a great one with the cards and that sort of thing. She reckoned she had special insight; she would have worked it out that it would be best for you. She would never have let them send you to an orphanage. You were her child and mine and the best place for you was not with her . . . or the gypsies. It was Commonwood House."

"And you knew I was there."

"That's what I'm going to tell you. Edward—Dr. Marline—knew of my passion for Rosaleen. He deplored it, naturally, but he knew. Poor man. He was caught with Grace, and a nice dance she led him. He did not approve of my way of life. A wife in Sydney and wandering fancy-free around the world. Yes, he knew about Rosaleen. He remonstrated with me. 'Grace must never know,' he said. As if I would have thought of confiding in Grace!

"There was a little shop in the High Street in those days. 'The Old Curiosity Shop,' it was called. It's not there now. I don't suppose it paid, but it was a pleasant little place. A Miss Dowling ran it; a nice little lady, but with no head for business.

"She had all sorts of curios in the window, and one day I saw this pendant. It had an unusual inscription on it and I went in to see it. Miss Dowling was delighted when people were interested in her goods, and she immediately brought the pendant out of the window to show me.

" 'I think it's of Romany origin,' she said. 'That's what I was told. These signs mean something. Good luck, something like that. It usually is.' Well, I decided to give it to Rosaleen, so I bought it. She loved trinkets, and the gypsy association would amuse her.

"As I was coming out of the shop, I saw Edward. He was just going in because he was interested in an old book Miss Dowling had. We found the book and we chatted with Miss Dowling, who mentioned the pendant.

"As we walked back to Commonwood House, the doctor asked me about it, and I showed it to him and told him about the Romany designs which had some meaning—and which the gypsies might understand. He was always intrigued by anything like that and he was immediately interested in the pendant. I felt he was rather reluctant to hand it back to me. Then he went on to give me a lecture on this gypsy association of mine. Gypsies were a wild and reckless people, he warned me.

"I answered him in my flippant way and told him that life was littered with pitfalls and, if one watched out for them all the time, one would fail to see all the blessings which were undoubtedly there.

"I'm fond of the doctor, and I think he is of me. Moreover, I was desperately sorry for anyone who had married Grace. I think he was aware of my sympathy and grateful for it and, although he deplored what he called my attitude to life, I think he was a little envious of it.

"I used to talk of him to Rosaleen. She was very interested in everything at Commonwood. She knew about Adeline's deficiencies and said it was a punishment for Mrs. Marline's arrogance and pride. I pointed out that it was a pity poor Adeline should suffer for her mother's sins.

"Well, the point of all this is that, when you were found, the pendant was round your neck, and Edward immediately knew whose child you were—and he told Grace. Her brother's child was a Sinclair and that must not be forgotten. So she agreed that you should be brought up in the Marline household.

"And Rosaleen, satisfied that her child was in the best place, went away and pursued her career. The doctor wrote to me and told me that my daughter was at Commonwood House, being brought up with his children.

"You can imagine how excited I was. A daughter of my own! There had been no question of children for Elsie and me. Elsie couldn't have them. It was one of the reasons why things went wrong between us, I believe. Elsie's the motherly kind. You'll see when you meet her.

"I longed to see this daughter of mine. It was unfortunate that I was so far away. You were three or four months old when Edward's letter reached me. I wanted so much to come home. But there I was, on the other side of the world, and it was four years before we met.

"Meeting you was wonderful."

I clasped my hands together, remembering. "Everything changed when you came," I said. "Everything was different."

He turned and kissed me. "And that, my daughter, is exactly as it should be."

I was in an ecstatic mood. Life was wonderful! At last I belonged, and there was no one I could have wanted to belong to more than to this wonderful man who was my father.

It was not surprising that I believed in miracles.

Each day seemed full of pleasure. I would awake with a feeling of intense delight. I was afraid to go to sleep in case I dreamed that this wonderful thing had not happened. When I was wide awake I could assure myself that it was really true, and then I would be completely content.

I wanted to shout to everyone, "I am the Captain's daughter," but I could not do that. It would be too complicated to explain. I could not even tell Gertie. No, I must remain Carmel March, and he must be Uncle Toby until we reached Sydney and I met Elsie.

Uncle Toby—I still called him Uncle Toby—and I would sit on deck, whenever he could spare the time, and talk of the future.

We agreed that he would remain Uncle Toby until we reached Sydney. Then we should say good-bye to the people with whom we were travelling. It was unlikely that we should see any of them again. Then, should I call him Father? Papa? They didn't seem to fit. For so long, I had called him Uncle Toby, so he suggested it should be just Toby. Why not? We must drop the Uncle. So we decided on that.

I should, of course, have to go back to Commonwood House and be educated. He reckoned it would be a good idea for me to go away to school. Estella would certainly go. It would be different now that I was known to be her cousin—not the gypsy foundling.

I grimaced, thinking of school.

"It has to be," said Toby dolefully. "Education is something you can't do without, and you won't get the right sort roaming the seven seas with your newly found father. Time passes. We shall meet whenever we can, and when an opportunity comes along I may take you to sea with me. In the meantime, we have the rest of this voyage to enjoy. I am so glad you know the truth. I've wanted to tell you for a long time. I thought you were too young, and then the moment seemed to come."

"I am so glad to know."

"Well, now we'll go on from there."

"It will be different at Commonwood House now."

"Without Grace," he said.

"I hope Miss Carson will be there."

"It won't be so bad, you know. And there will be those times when we can see each other."

"I wish you were not so often away."

"Life is never perfect. It's better to accept that and not crave the impossible. It is not so bad now, is it?"

I said with fervour, "It's wonderful!"

The days were passing too quickly. I wanted to hold back time. We should soon be in Sydney. I looked forward to seeing that great city of which I had heard so much, but I was beginning to think of it as the first stage of my great adventure, and when we left it, I should be on my way back to England. There was some time ahead yet, but everything must come to an end; I should be back to the old life. I should have to go to school. The halcyon days would not last forever. That was why I could not bear them to pass so quickly.

The Indian Ocean would always have a special place in my dreams. Those balmy days when I walked on deck with my father, or sat with him looking out over that benign and beautiful sea, and those nights in the cool of the evening when we talked of the future and the glorious present. He would point out the stars to me and speak of the mystery of the universe and the wonder of living on this floating ball which was our planet.

"There is so little we know," he said. "Anything could happen at any moment . . . and the lesson of that is that, if we are wise, we should enjoy every one of them as they pass."

I can appreciate those days now, and I can smile at the innocent child who believed that she had found the perfect way to live.

However, it is good to know such happiness, and perhaps one is fortunate not to know that it cannot last forever.

We had rounded the north coast of Australia and had come down the east to Queensland. We spent a day in Brisbane and, as Toby had much to keep him in port, I went off for the day with the Formans.

They had changed. They had been so eager to reach Sydney and begin to take up their new life, but now that they were almost there, I sensed a certain apprehension. They had been full of hope; land was cheap in Sydney, they had said, and if people worked hard, they could not fail to succeed. It all seemed so simple to talk of, but when it was near at hand, the doubts began to appear. It must be a wrench to leave one's native land, even though "they" were planning to make a road through your property and destroy its prosperity.

Gertie was a little withdrawn, and it was not the same as our first shore excursion. I remembered Naples with nostalgia. But, of course, I did not then know who my father was. I was in good spirits, of course, but that did not prevent my feeling for the Formans.

We explored the city stretched out on either side of the River Brisbane. We visited Moreton Bay and the slopes of the Taylor Range on which the buildings which comprised the city had been erected. We listened to our guide's account of how, in the early part of the century, it had been a penal colony; but we were all a little absentminded.

Gertie and I talked in our berths that night. Neither of us was tired—or if we were, we were disinclined for sleep.

"It will be different there," Gertie was saying. "I suppose I'll have to go to school. It's such a bore being young."

I agreed.

"It's funny," went on Gertie. "All these weeks, we've been seeing each other every day, and when we get to Sydney, we'll say good-bye and perhaps never see each other again."

"We might. I might come out to Sydney."

Gertie was silent for a while.

"Before we go, you ought to give me your address. I can't give you mine because I won't have one. I can give you the place we'll be staying at, though. It's a boarding house run by a friend of someone we knew at home. She's fixed us up there and we'll be staying till we find a property."

"I'm glad you thought of it," I replied. "We'll write to each other. That'll be good."

We both fell silent, a little comforted at the thought of not losing this link with a part of our lives which we should always remember with pleasure.

In two days, we should be in Sydney. Toby had said that the ship would be in port for a whole week, and we could leave it and stay with Elsie. He often did this in such circumstances, he told me. All the passengers would leave then and, before we sailed on, we should embark others and in due course begin the journey back to England. It was necessary to stay that time as the ship was having an overhaul and needed some repairs.

"You'll enjoy getting to know Elsie," he said. "Elsie's a good sport."

I was eager to see Sydney. In his graphic manner, Toby had told me a great deal about the place. He loved to talk of the old days. We sat on deck in the evening after dinner, and he explained how the First Fleet had come out in 1788 with its shipload of prisoners.

"Imagine those men and women, cramped up in the hold . . . very different from a nice cosy berth in a cabin shared with Gertie Forman on *The Lady of the Seas*, I can tell you. Sailing out from a home which most of them would never see again . . . to a new country and they knew not what."

I shivered as I listened. I saw those men and women, taken from their homes . . . some of them little more than children . . . my age perhaps . . . wondering what would become of them.

"Captain Arthur Phillips . . . he was the one who brought them out, and you'll see his name here and there about the city. Sydney itself is the name of one of our politicians. And that of another, Macquarie, that's a name you'll see. He was a governor of New South Wales. He was a clever man. He did a lot of good to the colony. He wanted them to feel they were not so much convicts expelled from their own land, as colonists making a new one good to live in. He was the one who encouraged them to explore the land around them. It was in his time that they found a way across the Blue Mountains. Before that there was a feeling among the aborigines that the mountains could never be crossed because they were full of evil spirits who would destroy those who attempted to get to the other side. But they got across . . . and what was on the other side? Some of the best grazing land in the world."

"Tell me more about the Blue Mountains," I begged.

"Magnificent. We'll go there one day. We won't be afraid of spirits, eh?"

That was how he talked, and I was all eagerness to see this land, but at the same time my pleasure must be tinged with sadness, because I hated to say good-bye to Gertie.

We had arrived. The ship had become oddly unfamiliar. I made my farewells to Gertie and her family. Mrs. Forman embraced me warmly and said, "We won't lose each other, dear. We'll be in touch."

Mr. Forman had shaken my hand, and Jimmy had said a rather embarrassed good-bye. He had been somewhat shamefaced since our Suez adventure, when Toby had reprimanded him so sternly. Gertie had given me a brusque good-bye, which I knew meant she was deeply moved by our parting. And now all the passengers had gone.

I was waiting for the summons to Toby's cabin, and then he and I would leave the ship—but only temporarily, of course.

He had said, "This happens now and then. We have a longer stay in port than usual and I'll have a night or two at Elsie's. It makes a change. Of course, I'm back and forth to the ship all the time, but it's good to be on land for a spell."

So, I was going to Elsie's. I had not thought a great deal about her until now. His wife! They couldn't get on as married people, but they liked each other otherwise. Surely it was very unusual for husbands who had left their wives to go back and stay with them for a friendly visit? But then, most such things were usual with Toby.

I walked round the ship, into those deserted public rooms. How different people make places! I went on deck. I leaned over the rail, looking at that magnificent view. I imagined coming in with the First Fleet and that I was a poor prisoner who had been sent away from home.

And I thought how fortunate I was. I might have been sent away to an orphanage. But my beloved father would never have allowed any harm to come to me. And that was how it would always be.

Elsie's house was set in grounds of about three acres. It was built in the old Colonial style with a platform round the front and six steps leading up to a porch before the main door.

We were about to mount these when a little dark man came running from some outbuildings which were obviously stables.

"Captain! Captain!" he cried.

"Why," said Toby, "if it isn't Aglo! How are you, Aglo? It's good to see you."

The little man stood before Toby, grinning. They shook hands.

"Missus waiting, Miss Mabel, work hard. All clean. All waiting for Captain."

"I'm glad of that," said Toby. "Polishing for me, is that it?" He winked at Aglo to show he was joking as he went on: "I should have been heartbroken if they hadn't put on a bit of polish to greet me."

He turned to me and, at that moment, a door opened and a woman came onto the porch.

"Captain!" she cried, and flung herself at him.

"Mabel, Mabel . . . wonderful to see you. This is Carmel."

He was smiling at me, and, before Mabel had time to speak, another woman came out of the house.

"Well, here you are at last, Toby," she said. "What's been keeping you? I saw the ship come in early this morning."

"Duty, Elsie. What else could keep me?"

She kissed him on both cheeks and he said, "This is Carmel."

She turned to me. She was tall, with reddish brown hair—a good deal of it—coiled about her head. Her eyes were decidedly green. They sparkled and her teeth were very white against her suntanned skin. There was an openness about her. I knew at once that she was the sort who would say exactly what she meant. There would be no subterfuge about her. I liked her immediately. She was a person one could trust.

"Carmel," she was saying. "Well, now. I've heard about you

and now here you are. Come to Sydney, eh? Had a good trip, have you?"

She took my hands and looked intently into my face. I wondered fleetingly what a wife would think of a daughter her husband had had, who was not hers. But not for long. Elsie would have said what she thought of it and she did not appear at this stage to think it was so very odd.

"A pity you're only staying a week," she said to me. "Can't see a lot of the place in that time. And there's something to see, I can tell you. Well, we'll make the most of what we have. And what are we doing standing about here? Come on in, you two. Now, I reckon you're hungry. Don't suppose they fed you very well on board that old thing, did they?"

She threw a glance at Toby which showed she was teasing, and he said immediately, "Our food was excellent, wasn't it, Carmel?"

"Oh yes," I said. "It was very good."

"You wait until you see what we can give you, love. Why, at the end of the week, you'll be wanting to stay here. I'll take a bet on that."

She took my arm as we went in, and I could see that Toby was very pleased by this reception.

"You know where to go, Tobe," said Elsie. It sounded strange to hear his name pronounced thus, but I had to learn that Elsie had a habit of shortening people's names. She turned to me.

"Always the same room when he stays here, which isn't as often as I'd like. But we have to make the best of what we can get, don't we? And you, love. I'll show you where you are. You've got a lovely view of the harbour. We're proud of our harbour. Show it off when we've got the chance. You'll find a bit of mail in your room, Tobe. Letters from home. I've been storing them up, but don't start on them yet, because you've got a meal waiting for you."

Toby stretched himself and looked up at the sky and at the house. "Good to be here," he said.

"Good to have you," said Elsie. "Isn't that so, Mabe?"

"I'd say," said Mabel.

"And Aglo agrees with us," said Elsie.

The aborigine grinned.

"He's a good boy, Aglo. He wouldn't go walkabout when the Captain's coming."

Aglo shook his head and grinned.

When I asked later what was meant by this, Toby told me that the aborigines were good workers when they worked, but it had to be remembered that they were unused to living in houses or being confined in any way, and now and then the urge came to them to "go walkabout," which meant going off. Sometimes they came back, sometimes not. One could never be sure. Even the most devoted ones could take it into their heads to go walkabout.

"Now come on in," Elsie was saying.

It was undoubtedly a warm welcome. I thought of Mrs. Marline greeting Lady Crompton on the rare occasions when she had come to Commonwood House. How different that had been!

My room was large and, as Elsie had said, had a good view of the harbour. There was a bed, wardrobe and washbasin, a dressing-table and a few chairs. The floor was wooden blocks with a few mats on it. The room had been furnished with the essentials, and again Commonwood was brought to my mind by its very difference.

I had been told to come to the dining-room as soon as I was ready, and when I opened my door Toby was just coming out of his room.

"All right?" he asked, with a touch of anxiety in his voice.

"Yes. It's fun."

"I knew you'd get along with Elsie. Most people do."

"Except you," I said.

"Oh, that's different. We get along well in most things, but not in marriage." He took my arm and pressed it. "Pity," he went on, "but that's how it is. You'll like it here. There's lots to see. Elsie couldn't wait to meet you. Come and look at my room."

It was very like mine—wooden floor, rugs and essential furniture.

"Not much like Commonwood," said Toby.

"No . . . I was thinking that."

"Different atmosphere. No formality here. It's all open and honest."

"Yes," I agreed. "I feel that."

He ruffled my hair and kissed me.

"I've just combed it!" I said.

"Never mind. Elsie won't scold."

I looked round his room. "There are a lot of letters waiting for you," I said.

"Yes. I didn't want to delve into them yet. They can wait. Nothing important, I guess. Come on, let's go down. Otherwise there'll be trouble."

It was a good meal. We were joined by Mabel, who seemed to be a kind of housekeeper/friend. There was a young girl of about fifteen who waited at table. She was Jane, and again I was struck by the lack of formality. And because it was all so different from Commonwood, I found myself yet again wondering what was happening there. It would all be changed now Mrs. Marline had gone. Miss Carson would be there and Adeline would have nothing to fear.

Elsie talked a great deal in a bantering sort of way to Toby, but her conversation was directed mainly at me. She told me what we must do while we were in Sydney. There was so much she wanted to show me. We could take a boat trip across the harbour. That's if I wasn't a bit tired of boats! But this would be a little rowing boat perhaps. Though there was a ferry. Did I ride?

"Oh, goodo. You need a horse out here. You'd be lost without one." We'd have some meals outside. "The weather's good, you see. You can rely on it more than you can at home."

I discovered that she often talked of England with a kind of affectionate contempt. Things were always done better "down under," which was Australia. I learned afterwards that she had been born in Australia and had never been to England, yet she called it "home."

Toby said that some people did that here. Their roots were in England, he supposed, because their parents or grandparents had come out and settled, looking for a better life. Some may have found it, but whether they had or not, the Old Country was "home" even to those who had never seen it.

It was all very interesting to me—a different phase of that wonderful life to which Toby had introduced me.

I slept deeply that night, and when I awoke, I got out of bed, opened the glass doors and stepped onto the balcony with the iron railing. It was a very pleasant sight. I could look out to the harbour, its bays bordered by green shrubs which grew down to the water. There were tall trees, which I learned later were of the eucalyptus family, and yellow blossom which they called wattle.

I liked Elsie very much already. She was warm and friendly, even though she could not get on with Toby in marriage. But they did otherwise well enough, I supposed, since he called on her whenever he came to Sydney. And standing there, looking out across that most majestic of harbours, I was thinking once more of this happy turn in my fortunes, when I was suddenly startled by a burst of mocking laughter. It was as though some satanic creature was jeering at me for my complacent acceptance of the good life which had miraculously become mine. I looked around. There was no one near.

When I saw Toby and Elsie, I felt tremendously relieved. They must have heard it too. They did not seem to be in the least surprised; they were engaged in deep and clearly serious conversation. It was all very strange, for they were not quite like the lighthearted people they had been the night before. If I had not been wide-awake, I should have thought I was dreaming.

Suddenly they looked up. Their expressions changed as they saw me. They were smiling now.

"Good morning," cried Toby.

"Had a good night?" added Elsie.

"Good morning. Yes, thank you."

"Goodo," said Elsie.

Then there was that mocking laugh again.

Elsie made a clucking noise with her tongue.

"Those old kookaburras are at it again." And as she spoke, a bird about seventeen inches long, in a grey-brown colour, flew past and settled in a branch. Then another flew out to perch beside it.

The laughter rang out again and I realised that it came from the birds.

"They want their breakfast," said Elsie. "I feed them with the others; that's why they come here. Funny noise they make, but you get used to it. Laughing Jackass, they call them, and you can see why. Sounds as though they're jeering at you. Perhaps they think I'm a silly old woman to bother with them. It's time we had our breakfast too, I'm thinking."

I joined them and we sat down to coffee, bacon and eggs and freshly baked bread.

"The way they do things at home," said Elsie. "We stick to the old customs. That's right, eh, Tobe?"

He said it was, and we talked about what we would do that day. He would be going down to the docks to the ship and he was not sure how long he would be away. Elsie was going to take me round the house and gardens and show me how they lived "down under."

We were all very merry again. Toby left us as arranged, and I watched Elsie feed the birds. It was a wonderful sight as they fluttered round her—beautiful creatures of many colours. They looked like parrots and budgerigars—the sort we kept in cages at home. These were all about, chattering with satisfaction as they flew round her. There was something essentially peaceful about the scene.

I saw the kookaburras there, taking their share. Then I heard their mocking laughter. It was no longer disturbing.

Elsie told me I should enjoy meeting people.

"People are different in Australia," she said. "Different from where you come from, I mean. None of this high and mighty 'I'm better than you are.' We're all equal here—although some are more equal than others, as they say." She added with a nod: "As long as they remember that I'm in charge and they do as I say— then that's all right."

"Well, that's just the same . . ." I was beginning to say, but she grinned.

"You'll see what I mean, love," she said. "We've got two maids, Adelaide and Jane. You've seen Jane. Then, of course, there's Mabel. That's the household. Mabe's a treasure—cooks and keeps everything going as it should be. Jem and his wife and son Hal live over the stables, but they're in and out of the house all the time. And Aglo's there too. Sometimes he goes off, but we're never sure whether he's coming back. I don't think he'll ever go altogether. He certainly won't while Tobe's here. He's got a special feeling for Tobe. Well, most people have. There's something about him. Well, let's make our tour of the house."

We did. It was spacious and wood was very much in evidence. It was furnished with simplicity and with an eye to necessity rather than adornment. There was a washhouse, large pantry and storing rooms, a still room and a large kitchen with a huge range, ovens and a long wooden table.

I met all the inhabitants and I knew what Elsie meant when she said there was no formality as we had at home. Everyone was free and easy and, as Elsie said, that was fine as long as they did the work they were there to do.

"Who wants caps and aprons and 'call me Madam'? Mrs. Sinclair is good enough for me."

She said that a little wistfully, and I wondered if she would like to be Toby's wife in all ways instead of his just calling when his ship was in Sydney.

During that first morning, she told me that her grandfather had been sent over to Sydney in the early days of the settlement. He was no criminal—he had aired his views too openly. He had been working in one of the mills and trying to get rights for his fellow workers.

"Like one of those Tolpuddle Martyrs. Well, he never forgot what they had done, but he wasn't the sort to wear himself out railing about something that could never be put right. So he set about doing his seven years, and then he found a piece of land. He worked hard and did well for himself. Then he went gold-mining out Melbourne way. My father followed in his footsteps, and they made quite a fortune. So there we were, in a country which seemed good to us, and there was never any talk of our going back."

I found it all absorbing and wanted to hear more.

"You will, love," said Elsie. "I was never one for keeping my mouth shut."

"You must tell me. I shan't be here long, you know."

"Oh, we'll find plenty of time to talk, you'll see."

And so the morning passed, and in the afternoon Toby came back. I was in my room hanging up some of my things in the wardrobe when I heard the sound of his horse.

I went to the window. Elsie had apparently heard it too. She came out of the house and ran to meet Toby. They were walking back to the house together. There was about them an unaccustomed seriousness—like that I had noticed early that morning when the sound of the kookaburras had disturbed me.

They stopped for a moment and stood still, talking earnestly. I called to them. They looked up and their expressions changed. They smiled at me. Oddly enough, I fancied there was something forced about their smiles; and the uneasy feeling that all was not as well as they wanted me to believe came to me. I almost expected to hear the mocking laugh of the birds, but, having been fed, they had moved off.

I went downstairs to meet Toby and Elsie.

"You've had a good morning, I gather, looking round the place," said Toby.

"Oh yes, it was very interesting."

Elsie said, "Tobe wants to talk to you, love." She looked almost appealingly at Toby, and went on: "Look, why don't you do it now? Go into the sitting-room . . . just the two of you."

I was not sure, but I fancied Toby looked reluctant, and that she was urging him, but he said, "All right, then. Come on, Carmel."

So we went into the sitting-room and Elsie went out and left us alone.

I looked in consternation at Toby. I was certain now that all was not well.

"There's something I have to tell you, Carmel," he began, and hesitated.

I looked at him questioningly. It was unlike him to be at a loss for words.

"I thought there was something," I said. "You are different."

"It's a big decision."

"About what?"

"Well, you see, Carmel, things have been happening at home."

"At home?"

"At Commonwood House. It's the doctor."

"What about him?"

"He's not expected to live."

"You mean, he's dying?" I said stupidly.

"He's had a lot of worry . . . and that's how it is. Estella and Adeline are going to live with Florence, and Henry too, of course. So you see . . ."

"You mean, they won't go back to Commonwood House?"

"Yes, that's about it."

"And the doctor is very ill? How can they be sure he's going to die? Mightn't he get better?"

Toby was looking over my head. I had never seen him like this before.

"You see," he said, "we have to think of what is going to happen to *you*."

"Is Miss Carson going with Estella and Adeline?"

"I don't know about Miss Carson. I should not think so. I only know that Adeline and her sister are going to Florence. She will look after them."

"You mean there is no place for me?"

He looked relieved. "The problem is," he went on, "that I haven't a home there, just a lodging, and then I must be away most of the time. You see what this is all about?"

I felt very uneasy, for Toby was obviously very worried.

He must have sensed my fear, for he put an arm about me.

"There's no need to worry. Not while I'm around," he said.

I clung to him. "I know."

"You're my little girl and I'm here to look after you, so there is really nothing for you to worry about. You won't have to go to Florence."

"Oh, I know that. She wouldn't want me."

"But this is something that has to be considered very seriously."

"Yes. Elsie knows, doesn't she?"

He nodded. "She's helping to figure it out. She thought you shouldn't be left in the dark but should be told as soon as possible."

"What should I be told?"

"I can't take you back to England with me because there would be nowhere suitable for you to go when you got there. You're only eleven years old. That's too young to be alone when I'm miles away at sea. Besides . . . after this trip, I shall be away from England for a year at a time. *The Lady of the Seas* is more often on this side of the world. In fact, she's reckoned to be based in Sydney more than any other port. I shall be calling here fairly frequently. Elsie had this idea, and I must say it seems a good one—the best we can come up with at short notice. When I sail next week for home, you stay here with Elsie. In about four months' time I'll be back in Sydney."

I looked at him in utter dismay, and he went on quickly: "I know your voyage is only halfway through. I did not think this could possibly happen. I thought things would be straightened out at Commonwood by the time we got back and then it would all be more or less as it was before, and when Estella went to school you would go with her. What is most important is for us to be together as much as we can. Is that not what we want?"

I nodded vigorously.

"I know what a blow this is. We have been wondering how we could tell you. Elsie thought there was no point in pulling wool over your eyes. You should at least know what had to be. She said you were too smart to be bamboozled. This is our plan . . . Elsie's and mine . . . and yours now. You can trust Elsie. She is one of the best. She says you should stay here. You can live with her. There's a good school not too far away—a boarding school where you can get a good education. You'll go there, and in the holidays you'd be with Elsie, and when my ship comes in, you and I will be together."

He drew back and looked at me searchingly. Then suddenly he put his arms round me and held me tightly.

"It's the best thing, Carmel, my darling child. I assure you, in the circumstances, it is the only way."

I was too bewildered to take it in. I could only cling to him and assure myself that he was still there, that he was my father and he would love me forever. But the wonderful journey home would not take place. He would go away in a very short time, and it would be a long time before I saw him again. This new country was to be my home.

It was too sudden and too bewildering to take in all at once. I was in a way like one of those people who had been taken from England and sent to a new land—uncertain, disbelieving that this could really be happening to me. But I was not like those people. They had had no one, and I had Toby to love me, even if he had to leave me. And there was Elsie at hand, and I was already fond of her.

My thoughts went back to that early morning when I had suddenly heard the mocking laughter of the kookaburras. I had thought that the laughter sounded like a warning. Perhaps it had been, in a way.

Life had seemed too good, and perhaps life is not like that.

Then I thought: "But Toby is my father. Nothing can change that. I may not see him for a long time, but he will come back. He is truly my father and he will always be there."

The Sundowner

GERTIE AND I had said good-bye to all our old school friends, to the school itself, and the way of life which had come to an end after more than six years. The long end-of-term holiday was before us—only it was more than the end-of-term for us. I should probably spend some time at the Formans' property in Yomaloo, and Gertie would come to stay with me for a time at Elsie's. It was a pattern we had followed over the last years.

In March of next year I should be eighteen years old, and it seemed a long time since Toby had told me I should not be returning to England.

It had all happened so quickly then. Long-term arrangements had been brushed aside and in a few days a new way of life had been established. I had been so bewildered in the beginning that I seemed to have been caught up in a whirlwind and suddenly deposited in a new home, in a new country. But I never forgot how lucky I was to have two people such as Toby and Elsie caring for me.

When Toby had taken me away from England on that fantastic trip, I had escaped into a wonderland and thought that I had found happiness forever after. Now, from the wisdom of my maturer years, I could look back on the child I had been then and smile. Happiness is not like that. It cannot be there forever. It has to be waited for, and that is why it is so precious when it comes.

How grateful I should be to Elsie! She was my stepmother, but she was more like an older, and so much wiser, sister. She told me, in a rare sentimental moment, that she had always wanted a daughter. I had filled that need.

It had been February of that year, just before I was eleven years old, when Toby had sailed off in *The Lady of the Seas,* leaving me alone with Elsie, whom I had known for about one week.

I shall always remember going on board and saying farewell, and that lost, empty feeling because I was not going to see him for a long time. But Elsie understood my grief and helped me to bear it. Toby had tried to be merry, and succeeded to a certain extent. He kept assuring me it would not be so long before he would be back, and then we would make some exciting plans.

Afterwards, we had stood on the dock and watched the ship sail. Toby could not be visible because he had to be on the bridge, and so we watched her glide away, and I was comforted to see that Elsie was crying too. She had put her arm round me and said, "We'll get along all right, love, and next time we'll be standing here watching the ship sail in and bringing him with her."

Then we went back to the house and drank cocoa and talked of him.

Elsie had been wonderful in the weeks that followed. I know now that she turned all her attention to me. She understood absolutely how I was feeling, and determined to assure me that I was safe with her. Toby may have momentarily disappeared, but she had stepped into his place.

We were constantly together. Elsie had several friends in Sydney, and we visited them and they came to us quite often. Mabel, who did the cooking and ran the household, became a good friend of mine; so did all the others in and around the house. I would go to the kitchen and watch Mabel, kneading dough, stirring puddings while she told me about her childhood in a little township west of Sydney on the way to Melbourne. There were seven children in the family, and she was the eldest. She wanted to get out and about a bit, she said, so she came to the city. She took one or two jobs. She was a dab hand at cooking and finally ended up with Elsie, "one of the best," and that was good enough for her. She'd been here ever since.

There was Adelaide, who was several years older than Mabel, and Jane, and they did the housework between them. There was no standing on ceremony, no one more important than another, really, and they all seemed to be happy.

Then there were Jem and Mary, living over the stables with their son, Hal. They did odd jobs about the house when necessary, and the garden as well. And Aglo lived there too. He always had a grin for me when he saw me. It was a happy household.

I was constantly reminded of Commonwood House by the very difference of this place. How strange it would be there now! The doctor very ill and the children with Aunt Florence. What of Miss Carson? I expected she had gone to Aunt Florence's house to be with the children. But perhaps the doctor had recovered and they had all gone back to Commonwood House.

I tried to talk to Elsie about them, but she did not seem to be interested. That surprised me, because she was usually eager to know about everyone. But I did notice that, when I spoke of anything to do with Commonwood House, she took the first opportunity to change the subject.

People called at the house all the time. Some of them gave no warning of their coming and would join us at meals if they were about to be served. Some came from a long way off and stayed for a night or two.

There was one special friend. His name was Joe Lester. He was a big man, rather quiet and serious. He was very friendly to me and told me of the early days when Australia had become a penal settlement, much as Toby had done.

Joe had property some miles out of Sydney. He had a nephew living with him who helped run the property. Elsie and I used to visit them now and then.

About two weeks after Toby had left me with her, Elsie broached the subject of schools.

"Everyone has to go to school," she said, "and that includes you, love. We don't have the schools here that you do in England, but there is one I've heard of which seems pretty good. It's some miles off, between Sydney and Melbourne, and I was wondering . . ."

"I was going to school with Estella when she went, I believe, but then she went to Aunt Florence."

Elsie said quickly, "Well, yes, but you'll make friends here. People are very friendly. I tell you what we'll do. We'll go and see it and if we think it's all right, you might go. Toby thinks you should go on just the same, as though you were at home. Everything here is done like at home. You'll be eating a hot Christmas dinner in midsummer. You wouldn't have to go to school until September, because that's when the school year starts at home, and so it has to start then here. There's no desperate haste about it, really."

I was very excited when a letter came from Gertie. The Formans had found a property in Yomaloo. It was some ten or twelve miles north of Sydney.

I wrote at once. They were astounded to hear that I was still in Sydney. They had not expected to hear from me for some time because they had thought the letter would have to be forwarded on to England. The outcome was that, when Gertie and her mother came into Sydney, they called to see us.

I explained that circumstances had changed and I was staying in Sydney. Gertie was delighted, and her mother said that we must come to stay with them when they were settled in. We laughed a great deal talking about the voyage out. I met Jimmy again—he had become James—who was still a little shamefaced about the part he had played in the Suez adventure.

It was a very happy reunion.

There was talk of my going to school and, as the Formans wanted Gertie to go too, it was decided that we should go together.

Then came the day when Toby returned to Sydney. I shall never forget waiting on the dock for the ship to come in, and that moment when he came down the gangway and embraced me, holding me as though he would never let me go.

Later he told me that Dr. Marline had died and he was very sad about it. I guessed it upset him to talk of it, so I did not ask all the questions I wanted to.

He did tell me that Adeline and Estella were still with Aunt Florence and would stay with her. He did not know what had happened to Miss Carson.

It would be best for me to stay in Australia, he said, for there he could be sure of seeing me more often than if I were anywhere else; and Elsie and I had become such good friends.

Everything sounded better when Toby spoke of it. What a piece of luck that the Formans were not too far away! Gertie and I had been such good friends during the voyage out. Everything was turning out well.

I did go for a short voyage with him to New Guinea from Sydney and then back again. It lasted only three weeks, but there was hope of another; and during those years I only went once more with him, because it had to fit in with my school holidays.

School absorbed me, and so the years passed.

And now we were grown up. We felt very mature and excited about that. School days were over. Gertie and I were adults.

That homecoming was different from all the others. There was a certain amount of ceremony about it. The coach brought us back with several other girls who lived in the Sydney area, and Gertie was dropped at Yomaloo. There were the usual assurances between us that we should be meeting soon. I should be going to stay at the Forman property as I always had done, and she would be coming to Sydney.

Elsie was waiting for my arrival.

"My word!" she cried, looking sentimental. "You're quite the young lady now."

And there, in the porch, were Mabel, Adelaide and Jane, with Aglo standing by.

I was taken into the house and Mabel announced that there was schnapper for lunch, which was my special favourite, and she didn't want it getting cold while a lot of chatter went on. There was time enough for that afterwards.

During the meal, as I had always done, I told them what had been happening during the last term at school, and they recounted how life had gone on there.

Later, when I talked to Elsie alone, she said, "I thought I'd be giving a party—say at Christmas—for you and perhaps Gertie. We'd turn the sitting-room into a sort of ballroom. It would be quite big with the chairs and all the clutter taken out. I'd get some fiddlers in. It would be a sort of coming-out party for you and Gertie—rather like that nonsense they do at home, though without all that silly business of wearing feathers and bowing to the Queen. We'd want some young men around. Joe's not so young, but there's his nephew, and the McGill boys are all right. Then there are the Barnums and the Culvers, and, of course, James Forman. I reckon I could pull in quite a number."

I was silent for a moment, and she went on: "Well, you're getting on, you know. It's time you saw a bit of life. You want to 'come out,' as they say. That's what you'd be doing if you were at home."

My thoughts went fleetingly to Estella and Adeline. Estella would be nineteen now, Adeline much older. Henry would be twenty-one. What were they doing now? It was only occasionally that I thought of them now. How strange it was that people who had once been so much a part of one's life could become like shadowy figures in a dream.

Elsie was saying, "I reckon you'll want a rather special dress. Something in red or blue or that mauve shade you like so much . . . something bright. We'll give ourselves plenty of time, choose the material and get old Sally Cadell to make it. She's always looking for work. I suppose in a week or so you'll be wanting to go over to the Formans. When you come back we'll start getting the party in motion. It'll take a bit of planning."

She paused and lowered her eyes. Then, after a few seconds, she raised them and smiled at me.

"I kept the best bit of news till now, because I thought that, if you heard it, you wouldn't give your mind to anything else. Tobe's due in December. Christmas Eve, in fact."

I stared at her and we were in each other's arms.

"Wouldn't you call that good news, eh? It's going to be a special Christmas for us, I can tell you."

"It's wonderful!" I cried. "Quite wonderful."

We were speechless after that, eyes shining, contemplating what lay in store for us. How good Elsie was to me! Another fleeting memory of Commonwood came. How different it was here where Elsie and Toby did everything to make life good for me. I was overcome with emotion.

I would be free now. If it were possible to take a trip with him, there would be no school to prevent it. This was perfect bliss.

We could talk of little else after that but the good fortune which would bring Toby to Sydney at such a time. But any time, of course, would be wonderful. We chattered excitedly.

The following day I went to the stables and made sure my particular mount, Starlight, was well. He showed his appreciation of my return. Hal said he had missed me, but he knew I had to go away to school and didn't hold it against me that I'd deserted him all that time.

Starlight confirmed this by nuzzling against me.

"He's telling you how pleased he is you're back," went on Hal. "I reckon he knows school days are over and you're back for good now."

Elsie and I sat in our favourite spot in the garden and talked over trifles, although our minds were perpetually on Toby's return. I told her how Sarah Minster had only just beaten me at the horse jumping competition, how I'd come top in English and just barely scraped through in maths. She told me how one of the horses had gone lame when she was eight miles from home, and how she'd spent the night at the Jennings property.

Then she said suddenly, "I reckon you'll settle here, Carmel. You'll be one of us. Do you ever think of going home?"

Again there came those flashes of memory. Dr. Marline in the schoolroom, Adeline crying in her mother's bedroom, Miss Carson coming out of the room and fainting.

I said, "Gertie talks of it often. She has an Aunt Beatrice in London. She says she's going home one day."

"It's always home to some of them," said Elsie. "They can't seem to forget it. Others don't want to see the place again."

"I expect it depends on what happened to you there."

She looked a little perplexed. "You've been happy here, haven't you?"

"Wonderfully happy. You're here . . . and Toby, sometimes."

She nodded. "Perhaps you'll marry and settle here."

"Marry? Marry whom?"

"That's in the lap of the gods, as they say. There are one or two young men round about. Some very nice ones. Joe's nephew, William. He's a bit bashful, but since he's been out here with Joe, he's coming out of his shell a bit. Joe says he's a great help on the property, and he'll have the money to set up a place of his own when he's learned a bit more. Well, he's here on the spot. We shall see a lot of him. He'll be coming over with Joe."

"But you don't marry people just because they are 'on the spot'!"

"I reckon that comes into it. How are you going to meet them if they're not? And I think James Forman likes you."

"James Forman! You're forgetting all that trouble in Suez when he left us there. I don't think he's ever got over that."

"He was only a boy. You're not going to hold that against him."

"No. But I think he holds it against himself. He's always a bit shamefaced with me."

She smiled. "Poor lad. He'd like you to see him as a sort of hero —dashing up and getting you to the ship and climbing by that rope ladder."

"But that was Dr. Emmerson."

"He's a nice boy, James. I like him and, what's more, I think he likes you."

After that, I began to think more often of James Forman.

We were all stretched out on the grass, our horses tethered nearby. We had come to the stream known as Wanda's Creek which was on the edge of the Yomaloo property. We had been riding out to the Jensens, who were the Formans' nearest neighbours.

It was an unwritten law that neighbours came to the aid of each other when it was needed. Jack Jensen had hurt his leg while he was fixing some fencing, and, as soon as the news had reached Yomaloo, James had immediately set out to offer assistance.

Gertie and I accompanied him, in case we could help in the house, as there was only one daughter, Mildred, her mother and no servant.

James had fixed the fence and we were on our way back, having had a meal with the Jensens. We had ridden some way, but there were still a few miles to go, and we decided to rest and take a little refreshment. So there we were. James had taken from his saddle-bag a bottle of Mrs. Forman's homemade wine and was pouring it into beakers and handing them round. He always carried the wine with him, for often during his journeys he felt in need of refreshment and places for finding it were few and far between. It was on occasions like this that one realised the vastness of this sparsely populated land.

It was pleasant to rest in the warm October sunshine, which would be very hot in a few weeks' time. We lay there, talking desultorily.

Gertie was saying she was wondering what she would do, now that she had left school.

"There's plenty for you to do at home," James pointed out. "Ma needs you around."

"If I can get some money together, I'd like to pay a visit to Aunt Beatrice."

"Go home!" cried James.

"Just that," replied Gertie.

"Just for a visit," I said.

Gertie hesitated.

"She hankers," said James. "I've always known it. You can tell by the way she talks about it. What about you, Carmel? What do you want to do?"

"It would depend on who was there," I said.

They knew, of course, that I was referring to Toby. They had learned that he was my father and not my uncle, which they had been led to believe when we were on *The Lady of the Seas*. Neither James nor Gertie interested themselves very much in such matters. They were quite different from me. I always wanted to know details.

"James is enamoured of Australia, aren't you, James?" said Gertie.

"It's our home now. That's how I see it. We came out here and started again."

"And you want to spend all your life here, looking after a property," I said.

"No," said James emphatically, "I do not! I've made up my mind what I'm going to do. I'm going to find . . . opals . . . We're in the right spot for it. There have been some discoveries at a place called Lightning Ridge. Opals are there for the finding."

There was another of those flashes of memory. I was in the drawing-room, we were having tea, and Lucian Crompton was talking about opals.

"Why do all those people who are hunting for them not get them then?" said Gertie.

"Don't be an idiot, Gertie. You've got to *find* them. And that's what I intend to do. I've made up my mind."

"Well, according to your reckoning, if everybody found them, there'd be nothing but millionaires all over Australia."

"*I'm* going to find them," said James.

"What about you, then, Carmel?" asked Gertie.

"I want to go to sea with my father."

"They don't have women sailors."

"There are stewardesses," I said.

"You wouldn't want to do that. It would be *infra dig,* with your father a captain. You'll just have to go on voyages with him. That would be fun."

"Well, I shall be off just after Christmas," said James. "Father says I'll have to get it out of my system. There was a man who came to the property once. He talked about it. It was while you were away at school. We stayed up almost all night talking. He told us how they go into the old gullies and work on the creek—how they go fossicking—how careful you have to be, raking round in the dirt—and how some of the finest black opals in the world come from Australia. You all live in shantytowns near where they're working. Of course, on Saturday night, it's like one big party. They dance, and sing the old songs they sang at home. And sometimes they roast a pig and everyone joins in. It's a grand life, with always the hope . . ."

He was looking at me as he was speaking, and I said, "That sounds exciting."

"You'd love it," said James, "I know you would, Carmel. It must be the most exciting thing imaginable in the middle of all that potch—that's what they call the rubbish—to find one of those gorgeous, brilliant stones. There's a famous one—like a sunset. Fancy finding something like that!"

"Listen to him," mocked Gertie. "He's getting poetical. He does that when he talks about opals."

"That old sundowner who talked to you about it," said Gertie, "was he the one who walked off with Ma's gold watch?"

"No," retorted James fiercely. "He was not."

"Tell Carmel about the thieving sundowner. He beguiled you all with his tales. Then he took what he could and went off."

"That only happened once," said James. He turned to me. "You know there's a tradition here. Swagmen walk the bush trails and, when they can, they take shelter, get food and a good night's rest. If a swagman wants a night's lodging, he shouldn't turn up till the sun is almost on the horizon, just before it goes down. Then it would be bad manners not to take him in—just as it would be bad manners for him to come before."

"I didn't know there was protocol on these matters," I said.

"Decidedly so. That's why they are called the sundowners," explained Gertie.

"Well, this one arrived. Dad was away for the night. I wonder if he would have seen through him."

"No one could have," said James indignantly. "He seemed ordinary enough."

"Except that he'd had such wonderful adventures in the gold fields that he should have become a millionaire. James couldn't do enough for him. He had his meal. He was given a bed, and next morning, before the household was awake, he went off with the leg of lamb we were to have for dinner that day when Father returned, plus Ma's gold watch."

"I've never known it happen before," said James. "There's usually honour among sundowners."

Gertie shrugged and turned to me.

She said, "I should like to go home and see Aunt Beatrice."

Two days later, Mr. Forman suggested that James go over and make sure that Jack Jensen was progressing well and find out if he wanted anything more done for him.

James asked if I would like to go with him for the ride, and I said I would.

So we set out. Jack Jensen was getting better and said he could manage very well. We were given lunch and in the late afternoon set out for home.

We had a pleasant ride back. I was liking James more and more and he was very attentive to me, showing very clearly how much he enjoyed my visits to his home.

I encouraged him to talk about his ambition, because I knew how much he liked to, and as he extolled the beauty of opals my thoughts were back again to Commonwood House, and it was Lucian whom I heard speaking, for, on that strange day, Lucian had talked as enthusiastically about them as James was doing now.

I brought myself back to the present with an effort. James was saying he had several books on opals. I tried to listen, but I could not draw myself completely away from the past.

Then I heard James say that it was time we started to ride a bit faster.

As we went along, he sang the songs which he told me they sang on those Saturday nights when the miners were all together. Most of them were Christmas carols! Ringing the old year out and the new year in was the one I remembered.

James had a good tenor voice, which was very pleasant, and, as he sang the song, I fancied I caught a tone of nostalgia in his voice:

"I saw the old homestead, the places I loved,
I saw England's valleys and hills.
I listen with joy, as I did when a boy,
To the sound of the old village bells.
The moon was shining brightly,
It was a night that could banish all sin,
For the bells were ringing the old year out,
And the new year in."

"One day," went on James, "when I have found the finest opal in Australia, when I have made my fortune, I shall go home. I shall find a beautiful house—an old one—a manor, I think—in the country. I should love that. Wouldn't you, Carmel?"

"I think it sounds very exciting," I agreed.

I could see myself in such a house, not with James, but with Toby, who would have given up the sea. He would be sitting with me in the twilight, telling me stories of his adventures on board ship.

James jerked me out of my reverie. I heard him say, "I suppose it's there in most of us—that feeling for home. Gertie's got it badly. She never lost it. Yes, I think that would be right in the end —when one has done all one has set out to do."

He was certainly solemn, gazing ahead.

We had loitered quite a while, and the property came into view just as the sun was about to go down. Mrs. Forman would be pleased. She never liked us to be out after sundown.

We galloped across the stretch of land which led to the house. As we approached, James pulled up sharply.

Mr. Forman had come down from the porch and was talking to someone in an open shirt and trousers the worse for wear. I noticed the stranger was carrying his billycan, without which few swagmen were ever seen.

James gave an exclamation and said, "No! It can't be."

His father and the man turned to look at us.

"It is!" cried James, and his face was suddenly distorted with anger.

"What do you want here?" he demanded.

The man and Mr. Forman stared at him in amazement.

"This is the one," cried James. "This is the thief. Have you brought back the watch you stole?"

"James!" began Mr. Forman.

"I tell you, it is the thief. What insolence! To come back after . . ."

James slid down from his horse and approached the man menacingly.

"You may have shaved off your beard, but I'd know you anywhere."

The swagman continued to look blank.

"Look here," said James, "get going, and look quick about it."

"James," said Mr. Forman, "are you sure? This is a sundowner . . . and . . ."

"I tell you, I know. He's tried to disguise himself, but there's something about him I'd recognise anywhere. He's come back to scrounge a meal and a bed, and he'll be off with what he's managed to steal before daybreak."

"Look here, young man," spluttered the swagman, "never seen you before in me life. I ain't got a notion what you're talking about."

James moved menacingly towards him and Mr. Forman made an attempt to restrain him.

One of the aborigines who lived on the property came up, and James said, "Do you know this man?"

"Lost hair," was the reply.

"Same man without hair, eh?" said James.

The aborigine nodded. "Man thief," he said. "Take Missus watch."

"Here, you dirty little abo," shouted the man.

"Get out," hissed James, "before I get rough. You might like to return the watch you stole first."

The man's face was ugly. "Turn me out, would you? All right. I'll spread it. Go back to where you belong. And a curse on your land."

With that he started to walk away.

James would have gone after him, but his father held him back.

"It's best," he said. "No point in getting into a fight."

"He had the watch."

"You wouldn't get it back. I don't suppose there could have been a mistake?"

"No, there was not. He had a way with him. Besides, the aborigine recognised him. There's only one way to treat his sort. Never give him a chance to cheat again. He'll know better than to pay a return visit to this property."

"I just don't like turning a sundowner away," said Mr. Forman. "It's the unwritten law here. Sundowners are supposed to be sure of food and a night's lodging."

"Not thieves," said James. "How could you let a man like that into the place when he's already shown what he is?"

"You're right, son, but I can't help wishing it hadn't happened."

"Forget him," said James.

Mr. Forman turned to me.

"Well, what did you think of that, Carmel?"

"I thought James was going to knock him down."

"Came pretty near to it," said James. "Come on, let's get the horses in. I'm starving, if you're not."

There was a certain gloom over the house that evening. The encounter with the dishonest man had created an unpleasantness. Mr. Forman could not forget it was the custom of the country to treat such travellers as guests.

I was very tired when I went to bed, as I usually was after hours spent in the fresh air. It must have been about three o'clock in the morning when I was awakened by the sound of voices. There was a red glow in the room.

I leaped out of bed and went to the window. I saw that some of the outbuildings were ablaze. They were fortunately a little distance from the house. People were running across the grass and shouting to each other. I could not distinguish who they were, but I thought James and his father were among them.

I hastily put on some clothes and dashed to the stairs. The entire household was awake. I saw Gertie, white and frightened.

"Some of the buildings are on fire!" she shouted.

And we dashed out.

For a few seconds, I stared in horror. The outbuildings were a mass of flames. Fortunately, the fire had not yet reached the stables.

"Come on," said Gertie, and we ran towards the blaze.

———

It was dawn before the fire was under control.

We sat in the kitchen and Mrs. Forman made cups of tea. The men were talking about the damage that had been done. Mr. and Mrs. Forman looked stricken, and I had never seen such deep and frustrated anger as I saw in James. I knew that the work of years had been destroyed in one short night.

They were too stunned to talk very much. That would come later. Mrs. Forman seemed glad to busy herself with the tea, and Mr. Forman sat silent, with a perplexed frown on his brow.

As soon as it was daylight, Mr. Forman and James went out to assess the damage, but we already knew how devastating it would be, and were not surprised by the verdict.

When Mr. Forman came back into the house with James, he said, "Ruined. I don't know what we shall do."

"We'll get by, you'll see," said James. "We'll be held back a bit, but we'll manage."

I felt inadequate, and that—not being one of the family—I must be in the way. Perhaps I ought to leave, for there was nothing I could do to help.

"You're not in the way," said Gertie, "but it's not going to be much fun here. Why don't you go back to Sydney and come again when we've sorted things out a bit?"

It was agreed that that was what I should do, and James rode with me.

As we went back, he seemed more ready to talk about the disaster than he had when he was with his family.

"You know who did it, of course," he said.

"You think the sundowner . . ."

"If I could get my hands on him . . ."

"Don't, James," I said. "It will be for the law to punish him. But you can't be absolutely sure that he was the one."

"Who else? He knew where to start it so that it could get well under way before we were aware of it. He had a grudge. He was there, wasn't he? He's a villain, that one. I think my father wished that we'd let him stay. He's asking himself what is the loss of a gold watch compared with all that damage."

"You couldn't have let him stay."

"I don't know. Imagine how I feel! It's my fault, in a way."

"No, James," I said. "You know that's nonsense. You worry too much. I believe you go on blaming yourself for what happened in Suez that time."

"That was a pretty awful thing to have done too. Heaven knows what might have happened to you two girls."

"Well, we came through it, and you'll come through this."

"We'll manage somehow, yes. But it has made a difference. We shall have to sort things out. We've lost such a lot. I reckon it will take us a year—maybe two—to get back to where we were before the fire."

"Oh, it was so wicked!"

"If I had him here . . ."

"I'm glad you haven't, James. It's bad luck. You'll get over it. You and your sister and family. You aren't the sort to let it defeat you."

"I hope so. You know, I had set my heart on going to Lightning Ridge. I can't go now. You see that."

I nodded.

"I was going to leave in the New Year."

"Oh, James, I'm so sorry. I know it meant a lot to you."

"I don't want to farm, Carmel. I don't think I ever did. I suppose I don't see myself getting old in a place like this. I thought I could settle at first, and leaving England and going off . . . well, it all seems so exciting when you are young. Then, when I heard what could be done here . . . gold . . . opals. It was gold that I thought of first, and then I got set on these opals. You see, it became a dream. I knew it could be. And now . . . now . . ."

"It's only a temporary setback, James. In a year or so you'll be back to normal, and then you will be able to go and try your luck."

"You're a comfort, Carmel."

"I'm glad to be that."

We rode on in silence for a while, and when we came in sight of the harbour, he said, "Carmel, you'll come again soon?"

"Yes. As soon as this has settled down. Don't forget, Christmas is coming. You must not disappoint Elsie. She has set her heart on this party she's giving for Gertie and me."

And so we parted.

Elsie wanted to hear all the details about the tragedy at the Formans'.

"James was right," she said. "Certainly they should not let that man into the place. What a terrible thing to happen! I hope that fellow gets what's coming to him. He certainly deserves something pretty bad."

"Mr. Forman was very worried, because he knows the unwritten law about sundowners. Gertie thought it might be unlucky to turn one away, however wicked they are."

Elsie laughed derisively. "That's a lot of nonsense. Unwritten laws here don't apply to scoundrels, I can tell you. Why, people here would be ready to lynch that man for what he did. There's certainly no need for the Formans to worry about turning him off the property. It's what he did to them that would be the trouble. I am sorry for the Formans. To have worked so hard and then to have that done to them overnight! We'll have to see if there's anything we can do. We'll ask Gertie over, if they can spare her. She's not going to be much use putting up new buildings and such like. She might be glad to come here for a while."

Elsie could see how shocked I had been, and she felt I needed something to stop me from brooding too much on that terrible night. No doubt she thought the best thing was to concentrate on the party. Everyone was going to be cheered up with that. It was going to be such a party as they had never seen in these parts before.

There was a great deal to do, she said. She wanted to have everything just right. The food . . . the dance floor . . . all the young people she could muster.

And Toby would be home. The party should not be until then.

"We'll cheer them up a bit. Poor James. I'm sorry for him." I had told her about his plans to mine for opals.

"He's a good lad," she continued. "I like James."

"He has such a conscience," I said. "You know, he still thinks about Suez. Now he is going to worry about this. He says it would have been better if that man had stayed, even if he had robbed them, rather than do all this damage. Because of it James can't go to Lightning Ridge and make his fortune."

"The chances are that there will be no fortune. For every person who comes out of those places with one, there's a thousand who are disappointed. So, perhaps it's all to the good in the long run. Life has a way of laughing at people, and bad can often turn out to be good and be what they call a blessing in disguise, and good luck can be disaster."

"You couldn't very well expect the Formans to believe that now."

"No, I don't. The realisation of that sort of thing always comes later. If there's anything we can do to help them, we must do it. Nothing must stand in the way of that. Let's think of the good things. This party is going to take a lot of planning, with Tobe descending on us at the same time. I thought we'd have it the day after Boxing Day. I'd have said before Christmas, but we're going to wait for Tobe. How does that strike you?"

I was not thinking so much of the party as the fact that Toby would be with us. Whatever happened, I could not be unhappy when I considered that.

The Treacherous Sea

ELSIE AND I saw the ship come in, and I thought nothing would ever again fill me with such joy. He was home.

We went down to the quay. We always had to wait a while before we could see Toby because, on the ship's arrival, he was very busy with all the formalities of arrival. As soon as possible he would be with us.

At last the moment came, and there he was, looking just as he always had, his eyes searching for me, as mine were for him.

Then there was the clinging embrace—the assurance that both knew the other was there; then the laughter and the suppressed emotion which was too precious to be shown.

Arm in arm, we would walk off the ship. Elsie always watched us with an amused glint in her eyes, waiting patiently for her share of his attention. She never showed the slightest resentment in taking second place.

I believed she loved him very much in a certain way. Their relationship had always been something of a mystery to me—a lot of bantering—but there was no doubt of the affection between them.

We went back to the house where, according to Elsie, the fatted calf had already been killed and Mabe would be hopping mad if everyone was not in the right place to do justice to it.

It was a wonderful Christmas because Toby was there.

I never ceased to marvel at those Australian Christmases—so

different from the ones in the past at Commonwood House. The heat could be excessive at this time of the year, but, in spite of that, hot roast goose was served with Christmas pudding alight with brandy flames—all eaten in brilliant sunshine!

Toby said to Elsie, "You still do it as they do at home, even though you have never been there."

"Christmas wouldn't be Christmas without all the trappings," she admitted.

Christmas and Boxing Day were quiet in comparison with the great occasion fixed for the following day, which I enjoyed thoroughly. The only guests were Joe Lester and his nephew, William, and for me they were like members of the family. Toby entertained us with tales of life at sea. He seemed to have a great number of such stories and, when he told them in his inimitable way, he was very entertaining.

He had told us that his stay would be brief. On New Year's Day he would be taking a load of copra from one island to another and that would occupy him for a month. Then he would be back to Sydney for a day or so before going off on a cruise to some other islands.

He smiled at me and said, "Now that you are a young lady of leisure, it did occur to me that you might deign to accompany me on this particular cruise."

I stared at him for a moment. I was so excited, I leaped to my feet. He did the same, and we hugged each other.

"I thought you might be pleased, and I intended to announce it over the Christmas pudding, but I couldn't wait."

"How could you be so cruel as to withhold it so long?"

"He can be a sadistic wretch on occasion!" said Elsie. "Come, Joe. Fill up the glasses. We are going to drink to this cruise to the islands."

That was a wonderful Christmas Day—the best I had ever known—and that was because Toby was there and soon I should be sailing on the high seas with him.

The house was in turmoil the next day. The morning was given over to preparations. The drawing-room, denuded of much of its furniture, would give us the space we needed for the guests to dance. Elsie was very proud of what she called her "orchestra," which consisted of a piano and two violins set up between the potted plants at one end of the room. The glass doors opened onto the lawn where, I imagined, because of the warmth, most of the guests would be dancing. The party was certain to be a success, for everyone was determined to enjoy it.

As I had predicted, though we began by dancing in the sitting-room, we were soon out on the lawn.

I had a long talk with James that evening. I was very sorry for him. He had worked very hard on the family property, and I knew how bitterly disappointed he was that his venture on the opal fields had had to be postponed. My own happiness made me feel particularly sorry for him.

I broached the subject, for I knew it filled his mind and he wanted to talk about it.

"I'm determined to go sometime," he said. "I know most people think nothing will come of it. I know a lot of people are disappointed, but I know I'm not going to be, Carmel. Do you think I'm a fool?"

"Of course not. I think that, as you feel as you do, you must certainly give it a try."

"I have a theory that if you are determined to succeed in life, you will."

"I think that's a very good one."

"I knew you would agree with me. Gertie, of course, thinks I'm a fool. So do the rest of the family, but I know . . ."

"Well, then, James, you have to try it and prove they are wrong."

"It's good talking to you, Carmel. How would you like to go to the opal fields?"

"Me? I've never thought of it."

"It's the greatest fun."

"Oh, I can imagine how exciting it could be."

"Suppose we went together."

"What?"

"Don't sound so surprised. Why not? Suppose we got married."
I was aghast.

He went on quickly: "Well, we are not children anymore. And here we are together. We get on very well. I've always been fond of you. Oh, don't remind me of Suez."

"I wasn't going to."

"Do you know, I have never forgiven myself for that."

"Please don't go over all that again. We were children then."

"It was a dreadful thing to do. You should have heard the lecture I got from the Captain. I have never forgotten it."

I laughed. "It doesn't mean you have to offer me marriage as compensation. I think you are rushing things, James. Just because I understand how you feel about those opals and we happen to be here, and there aren't many people for you to choose from. We get on well together and most people marry sometime. Well, perhaps all that is not a good-enough reason for forming a life partnership."

"But I am very fond of you, Carmel, and it is true we get on very well together."

"And you think it would be very convenient. You've had all this upset over the property and you are not really thinking clearly about all this. Let's leave it for a while."

He brightened a little.

"You always understand, Carmel," he said. "Perhaps you're right. All that did hit me pretty hard. I had it all planned. In a few weeks' time, I should have been on my way. Now I shall not be there for months and months."

"It will all pass, James."

"So. We stay good friends?"

"Of course," I said.

We sat on in the dim light, listening to the sound of the piano and violins coming from the house.

It was a wonderful party, and when it was over Elsie was glowing with triumph. Then Toby left and I could think of little else but the coming trip, though now and then I was reminded of that conversation with James.

It had been unexpected, and I believed he must have spoken on the spur of the moment. *I* go to the opal fields with him! Marry him! Poor James. He had had such a bitter disappointment when his journey was postponed, and I had been sympathetic—more so than his sister. Hardly a foundation on which to build a marriage! When he had recovered from his disappointment and was working in the opal fields, he would be grateful to me for not being as impulsive as he was.

In any case, we said no more of the matter, and I guessed he was beginning to realise that he had been a little rash.

With joy, in due course, I boarded *The Lady of the Seas*.

Toby said, "She should be called *The Old Lady of the Seas*. Do you know, she is thirty-five years old? Most would have been thinking of retiring. But there is life in the old lady yet. She is the finest ship I ever sailed in. I love her dearly. I have my sentimental moments, as you know."

I determined to make the most of the trip and enjoy it all. Elsie came to see us off and stood on the dock waving to us as we sailed out—or rather to me. Toby was always on the bridge during arrivals and departures and never visible to any but the officers, who were involved with him in the ship's business.

And then, there I was, in the familiar cabin, and Toby was showing me the map and explaining what course we should take, and I was completely happy.

The days slipped past quickly. Every morning I awoke to the joyous realisation of where I was. I would lie in my berth and contemplate the pleasures of the day to come.

I particularly remember that evening—in fact, I know I shall throughout my life. It was perfect. The heat of the day was over and the air was soft and balmy. I sat on deck with Toby, and I looked up at the Southern Cross in utter contentment.

Toby said suddenly, "The time will come when I shall leave the sea."

"That will be wonderful, because you won't be going away anymore."

"What shall we do? Have a little house together? Will you look after me in my old age?"

"Of course I shall look after you."

"I daresay you will spoil me. I shall want to be spoiled. So please do that, Carmel."

"I am not sure. Everything I do will be for your own good."

"Oh dear, I am always afraid when people act for one's own good. It usually means something unpleasant. I want six grandchildren, by the way."

"That's rather a lot."

"I can be very greedy. You see, we're not young anymore. Even you are no longer a little girl. One looks to the future. I suppose one day you will marry."

I immediately thought of James's suggestion.

I said, "Well, oddly enough, it was recently suggested to me."

He was alert at once.

"You mean someone asked you? Who?"

"James Forman."

He sat back and smiled. "Well," he said, "I'm not altogether surprised. Elsie was saying she thought there was something brewing there."

"Really? I was taken completely by surprise."

"That is because you are unaware of your seductive charms."

"I think it just occurred to him on the spur of the moment. It seemed to fit in with his plans."

"Well, he is determined to find opals. He's quite obsessive about it."

"I think he wanted someone to go off with him."

"I can understand that. Half the men in Australia are dreaming of making a fortune from something dug out of the ground. It's a quick way of making a fortune, if it works, and it does sometimes. How do you feel about James?"

"I find it difficult to take the idea of marriage seriously."

"I see. Poor James is going to be a disappointed lover. That party of Elsie's set me thinking. At home they would be considering your 'coming out.' We should be doing something like that."

"But there isn't anywhere to come out to here," I said. "There can't be balls and that sort of thing, except Elsie's parties."

"Well, we shall have to see. You ought to meet people. I want you to have the best, Carmel."

"I know. You have always done so much for me, you and Elsie."

"I like to think that I wasn't such a bad father."

"And I have told you often that you are the best anyone could ever have."

"First of all, I want you to be happy."

"I'd like always to be as happy as I am now."

We were silent for a while. Then he said, "We'll do something. You and I must always be together."

"That is just what I want," I told him.

Then he started to plan in the way I knew so well. Whenever it was possible, I must sail with him. Now I had left school, there would be opportunities. When he returned, we would live together. Sydney was a beautiful place. Did I not think so? Elsie would like to have us close so that she could keep an eye on us. We could get a place of our own.

He was frowning. Then he said suddenly, "What do you think about going home? You were dragged away rather suddenly."

My mind went back in time. I was seeing Commonwood House again. Adeline, looking through the window of the station fly, looking for Miss Carson; Estella, with that air of "I am not afraid," which betrayed so clearly that she was. It was all hazy, part of a vague, unreal period. Everything would be very different now.

He did not wait for me to answer but went on: "No, perhaps it would not be a good idea to go back now. We could get a place in Sydney. Right on the harbour, where we could watch the ships come in. That would be best."

"It sounds wonderful."

"As for home—well, that was a long time ago, wasn't it?"

"It would be strange to go back to Commonwood."

"Oh, not Commonwood! It would be quite different there." He was frowning. "No, no. It will be that place on the harbour. Or . . . if we did go home—because home always has a certain pull, you know—I fancy a little place in Devon. On the coast . . . the home of the great Drake. Somewhere near the Hoe. Or perhaps Cornwall. Well, the choice will be ours . . . from Land's End to John o'Groats."

"It will be wonderful to plan."

"Carmel, I'm sorry. It could have been different. In the beginning, I mean. A nice home . . . with parents."

"I have my parent."

"I was thinking of your mother. She would have liked to have you with her. Well, it happened the way it did. She thought it was the best for you."

"That was what Miss Carson said."

"Miss . . . ? Oh, you mean . . ."

"She said that, soon after she came to the house. I wonder what happened to her? She was a lovely person."

"How can we know?" he said. "Anyway, it was all a long time ago."

He was silent for a few seconds, frowning and staring ahead.

Then he said, "I saw your mother not very long ago. She wanted to hear all about you."

"You saw her in England?"

"Yes. It would be good if you could see each other. Perhaps you will one day. I don't see why not."

"I remember her so well in Rosie Perrin's caravan."

"Yes. She told me about the meeting. She was most taken with you."

"It must be strange to meet one's own daughter for the first time when she is grown up."

"Strange things happen in the world. We've got the whole world before us now, Carmel."

I nodded dreamily.

No, I shall never forget the perfection of that night. I have often felt that it is perhaps dangerous to be as happy as I was then, and it may be that such perfect happiness is doomed not to last.

It was two days later. We lay off the island of Mahoo. I had awakened early and looked through my porthole window, and there it was—the perfect desert island, lush and green in that pellucid sea, palm trees swaying in the breeze, native huts scattered around the shore, and little boats rather like canoes coming out to the ship.

Toby had said that we should be too big to get close in to the island, and it would mean anchoring just about half a mile offshore and going in on the launches. First the cargo for the island would be unloaded and taken ashore, and then we ourselves could follow.

While I was on deck watching the unloading of the cargo, Toby joined me for a moment.

"You and I will go ashore together. There'll be something of a ceremony. I shall rub noses with the Chief and I shall introduce you to him. You will be amused."

"How interesting!" I cried. "I often think how lucky I am to have a sea captain for a father. How many people can travel the world, and in such a way?"

He kissed the tip of my nose.

"You haven't seen anything yet," he said. "Now, I must leave you. I just thought I'd have a quick word."

Yes, I was indeed perfectly happy.

Toby and I were taken ashore with the Chief Officer and two of his men. As the launch scraped on the sand, we embarked in about a foot of water and were immediately surrounded by naked children, all shrieking at the top of their voices.

They were welcoming us to their island.

Two formidable-looking men stepped forward and threw flowers, made into necklaces, about our necks. Toby saluted in acknowledgement, which made the children rock about with mirth.

Then the two men who had presented us with the flowers walked on either side of us. They were naked from the waist up, and the garments they wore were made of animal skins and feathers. The feathers had been dyed red and blue. The men had frizzy hair which stood out round their heads, and in it they wore bone ornaments. They carried spears, and, but for the flowers and the giggling children, I should have felt like a captive.

Toby glanced at me and gave me a reassuring wink.

"The usual welcome," he said. "I've done it all before. They know me for a friend. The next step in the proceedings is presentation to the Great Chief."

We walked up the gentle incline, the children surrounding us, laughing and shouting to each other, and there, in the clearing, the ceremonial greeting took place.

I saw the Chief at once. He was seated on what might be called a throne. It was indeed ornate. It looked most imposing, decorated with flowers and the skins of animals. Above it had been fixed a very fierce-looking mask. The mouth was a snarl and the expression menacing. It was bigger than the Chief's face, and he was a very big man. He wore about his shoulders a cloak of feathers—blue, green and red in colour. On either side of him stood two very large men with spears.

Toby stepped up to the Chief and bowed. The Chief inclined his head but did not rise.

Toby said something and the man who had taken us up to him spoke too. The Chief listened. Then he stood up. The feather cloak fell from his shoulders, exposing bare flesh like shining ebony. Toby went close to the Chief, who seized him by the shoulders and brought their faces close together. This was what Toby called rubbing noses. Some words were spoken. Then Toby turned to me and held out his hand.

I found myself looking into the large black eyes of the Chief. He had to stoop low to be on a level with me. His hands pressed on my shoulders and, for a moment, I felt as though I were being drawn away from all that was familiar into a different world as I stared into those pools of darkness. It was an uncanny sensation. I felt his nose touch mine. For a few seconds it moved gently. Then I was released.

I said to myself, so they really do touch noses, and felt normal again.

We were seated beside the Chief, and Toby summoned the sailors to come forward. They carried boxes which they had brought ashore. These were opened and revealed certain gifts for the Chief. The children crept closer, and there were gasps of pleasure and excitement. There were trinkets of all kinds, and all the spectators, including the Chief, regarded them with wonder. The object which aroused the most excitement and appreciation was a mouth organ. Toby played a tune on it, which sent the watching crowd wild with delight.

The gifts were, of course, a token of our friendship, and there must be a return of similar tokens. A ceremonial presentation followed when the Chief placed a necklace of bone about Toby's neck. Then I realised that I was to have one too, for I was the Captain's daughter, and to honour me was to honour the Captain.

The Chief himself placed it round my neck, and again those dark eyes looked deep into mine, as though to read my thoughts. I hoped he could not. I was merely hoping that he would not touch my nose with his. He did, however, and then, holding my shoulders, looked deep into my eyes before releasing me.

We sat down and several of the warriors were presented to my father. Others came forward to perform some of their native dances, which were mainly stamping on the ground with their feet in what appeared to be a warlike manner, and uttering what I presumed to be battle cries. I was relieved that we were friends, not enemies.

This went on for what seemed to me a very long time. The heat was intense and the sun was setting by the time we returned to the ship.

That evening we sat on deck, looking over the sea to the island. We could hear the sound of drums in the distance.

"Rather exhausting," said Toby.

"It was so hot and everything was strange."

"These islands are very much of a pattern. The ceremonies are a little different, but not much. We naturally have to be a little wary in our dealings with the islanders. They could so easily be misunderstanding. We are as strange to them as they are to us. The mouth organ was an immense success, wasn't it?"

I laughed at the memory. "I liked the children best," I said. "They were so amused by us and didn't attempt to hide it."

He smiled at the memory. "Well, we shall sail at midnight tomorrow. The tide will be right and we shall have completed our business by then."

"It has been a wonderful trip. I hate to think of its coming to an end."

"There'll be others. By the way, it will be rather an important occasion tomorrow. We shall be honoured by the ceremony of the Kerewee Cup. That's the native drink. There is something sacred about it, and the fact that we are allowed to watch its preparation means that we are accepted as friends. They make a ceremony of proclaiming friendship."

"I suppose, when you can be set on by an enemy at any time—which is what must have happened to them in the past—you want to make sure of your friends."

"That's right. It's why the dances are like displays of their war-like prowess. They'll make this Kerewee Cup, and it will be done with the utmost ceremony under the eyes of the Chief. Then the cup, which is in fact a large bowl, will be handed round and we have to partake."

"You mean actually drink it?"

"Afraid so. Don't look alarmed. You need take only a sip, but don't let them see you don't drink it. I am sure that would be a deadly insult and bring down all sorts of curses—the vengeance of their gods or something like that."

"What sort of vengeance?"

"I don't know because no one to my knowledge has ever dared to provoke it. Don't look alarmed. It's easy enough. Only don't let them see that you are not eager to drink."

"What strange sights you must have seen in all your travels!"

"Well, I suppose I have been around a bit."

I smiled and thought once more how lucky I was to have a share in his life.

The heat was intense. I had sat on one side of the Chief, Toby on the other, for about an hour. We had witnessed ritual dances and had come to that part of the ceremony where one of the men crouched down and made fire by rubbing two stones together. The pot was placed over the fire and many ingredients were put into it. While it was stirred, the company uttered mournful incantations; and at last the mixture was ready.

It was poured into a smaller bowl which would be handed round. The pot was then placed in front of the Chief. There was a sudden shout from the assembly. The children all began to whimper and in terror ran to their mothers and hid their faces. I caught Toby's eyes, and he nodded almost imperceptibly. I thought he was assuring me that the terror was all part of the playacting and that they were not really in the least afraid.

A newcomer—tall as the Chief and wearing a mask which was huge and horrific—came forward and stood before the Chief. He gesticulated wildly and contorted his body into odd shapes; his teeth were bared. He turned from the Chief to glare at Toby, who looked suitably impressed, even cowering away from the wrath of the man.

It occurred to me that he must be the witch doctor, a breed of which I had heard a good deal. Toby had once told me that they appeared to have power over life and death and if they told a man he was to die, that man did die.

"I don't understand it," Toby had said, "but I know it has happened. Some say it is autosuggestion. 'There are more things in heaven and earth than are dreamed of in your philosophy.' There may be something in that."

I remembered the conversation for a long time. There was certainly something unearthly about this man.

Prancing about in a strange manner, he was telling the Chief something. A silence had fallen over the crowd and I suddenly felt they were no longer playacting. He went on twisting his body into strange contortions, pointing to the sky and making moaning noises. To my horror, he turned to Toby. He moved close to him, still moaning and swaying and pointing to the sky.

Then he turned and stood before the bowl of Kerewee. Suddenly he picked it up and drank. He lifted the bowl, shaking his head back and forth, and I saw the liquid glistening on his chin. Then he laid the bowl reverently at the Chief's feet and sat down beside Toby.

The drinking ceremony had begun. Two men carried the bowl to the Chief, who raised his hands to the sky in what appeared to be a blessing. He bent and drank, after which the bowl was passed to Toby, who managed it very well. There was a deep sigh throughout the crowd as the bowl was handed back to the Chief, who took another drink before passing it to me.

I took the bowl and, as I did so, I almost dropped it. A little of the liquid slipped onto my dress. There was an awed silence. Hastily I lifted the bowl and put it to my lips. I held it so that no one would be able to see how much I drank. My lips were wet with the liquid and I made a show of swallowing. The bowl was taken from me and the ceremony proceeded.

It was not until the bowl was empty and set down at the feet of the Chief and the dancing began that I felt at ease.

Suddenly the witch doctor—if that was what he was—rose and began to gyrate in front of the Chief. He kept gazing up to the sky, and he danced round Toby. He was shaking his head. Then he began to shout, moving his body in strange contortions. Toby had risen; he shook his head and lifted his shoulders. I could not understand what he was trying to convey.

The Chief seemed to be remonstrating with him, and the people began murmuring as they shook their heads to and fro.

I wished I understood what was going on. I had a sudden notion that they were going to prevent our return to the ship, and I sensed that some of the officers were uneasy too.

The sun was beginning to set, and I knew that Toby was eager to get back to the ship to prepare for the midnight sailing.

He rose and, taking my arm, the officers with us, started to walk down to the shore. The Chief walked beside us, shaking his head all the time, as though in some protest. Toby kept a firm grip on my arm.

Finally we reached the boat. Toby helped me in and sprang in beside me. The others followed. There were not many of them who had accompanied us to the ceremony—probably half a dozen officers at most.

The natives could have stopped us with the greatest of ease, but they just stood, watching us leave, sadly shaking their heads.

"What was that all about?" I asked Toby as we moved away.

"They were trying to prevent our leaving," he answered.

"They could easily have done that. They didn't seem to be hostile."

"Far from it. They wanted us to know that they were our friends. It was something to do with the wise old man."

"The witch doctor, you mean?"

"He's something like that. He thought we shouldn't go. He's seen something . . . some message in the sky. We should stay until tomorrow night. They don't understand anything about the importance of time. They see omens and such everywhere."

"It was kind of them to be so concerned."

"They're our friends. Didn't I give them a mouth organ? It may be they were just being especially hospitable . . . just telling us how sorry they were our stay was not longer, so why didn't we extend it a bit? Or perhaps it was just something they got into their heads. It may have been something to do with your nearly dropping the stirrup cup."

"It gave me such a fright."

"I'm not surprised. I don't suppose anyone ever came near to dropping it before. My dear girl, you ought to have realised you were holding a sacred emblem."

"I did. That was why I was so nervous."

"Well, that little jaunt is over. No more sacred drinking for a while."

"It was all very interesting, but I was scared at one point that they were not going to allow us to get away."

"And now, here we are, safe with *The Lady of the Seas*. Doesn't she look a beauty?"

"You love the old ship, don't you?"

"I do. But I love my daughter more."

And at midnight we sailed.

During the early hours of the morning, a strong wind blew up. I was awakened once or twice by the rocking of the ship and lay for some time listening to the creaking of her timbers. At times it seemed as though *The Lady* was protesting quite strongly.

During the late morning, it abated a little, but there was a strong swell and it was too windy to go on deck. As night fell it worsened and I did not see Toby. I was experienced enough to know now that when the weather was bad it was necessary for him to be in charge in person and there could be no delegating to his deputies.

I retired fairly early. Sleep was not easy and I dozed fitfully. The movement of the ship was increasing. Tropical storms could be fierce and it was certain that we were close to one now. I wondered whether Toby would attempt to take the ship into some harbour, if it were possible to find one.

I was fast asleep when I was awakened by the clanging of bells. I knew what this meant. The ship was in difficulties. We had been instructed as to what to do in such cases. One put on warm clothing, took one's lifebelt and made one's way to the nearest deck.

I fumbled with my clothes. I was thinking: If I can get to Toby . . . I must get to Toby.

But Toby would be at his post, and there was no place for me there. But he would want me to be with him. I must find my way there.

Trembling, I buttoned up my coat and tied a scarf over my head. It was difficult to stand up and keep my balance.

I pulled open the door of my cabin and stumbled out into the alleyway. The noise was deafening. It sounded as though everything was breaking up. I staggered along to the companionway. The ship seemed different. It was hard to recognise familiar places. Furniture was lying broken here and there. I could hear people shouting.

I must find my way to Toby.

I mounted the companionway. I felt a rush of air. I was now in a violent wind. I was close to the deck. There had been a door, but it seemed not to be there now. Then I found I was staggering along the deck. I was unprepared for the force of the wind. It caught me and dragged me forward and then threw me back. I fell, and with great difficulty scrambled to my feet. It was impossible to stand upright. I gripped a rail and stood, bent over, clinging to it. Where was I? Nothing looked as it had before.

I was bewildered and very frightened. There was one thought which would not be dismissed: I must find Toby. We must be together.

I tried to be calm. This must be the way, although it looked different. I must find my way to the bridge. He would certainly be there. He had to look after the ship and I must be near him.

I managed to move along the deck. Now there were people everywhere. They were letting down the lifeboats, those which such a short time before had taken us to the island.

The ship gave a sudden tilt. I was falling . . . sliding . . . I heard shouting. I tried to get up but could not move.

There was deafening noise everywhere. I heard a scream. Someone was lifting me up.

"Toby," I said. "Toby."

I was in a boat. It was uncomfortable. My leg was hurting. I was sitting on one side of the Chief, Toby on the other. Toby was winking at me and saying, "Don't let them see you are not drinking."

Rock, rock, rock went the boat. Someone was putting something to my lips. I drank. It was fiery.

"Commonwood wouldn't be the same now," I heard Toby saying.

Then the rocking and oblivion . . .

I was on a ship. I could feel the familiar movement. It was quiet. I remembered. There had been a storm, but it was all right now. I was in bed and someone was bending over me, but I was too tired to open my eyes.

The time came when I did open them. I knew for certain that I was on a ship, but it was not *The Lady of the Seas*. My leg hurt. I tried to move it but I couldn't. I could feel that it was bandaged.

A woman came by. She was in the uniform of a nurse. I called to her.

She said, "Hello. So you've surfaced, have you?"

"Where am I?" I asked.

"On *The Island Queen*."

"But . . ."

"We picked you up. You're all right now. Leg came to grief, but it's getting better."

"What . . . happened?"

"You get some rest and we'll have a long talk about it later."

"But . . ."

She was gone.

How had I come to be here? I was too tired to think. I had been on *The Lady of the Seas*. What had she said? *The Island Queen*? No . . . it was too much . . . and I was too tired.

I floated into oblivion. I was in the garden at Commonwood House. Mrs. Marline was shouting at Adeline and Miss Carson was comforting her. Then I was in the woods. Zingara was sitting on the steps of the caravan.

"I am your mother," she was saying.

I was struggling to get out, to come back to what I vaguely knew was real. I was on a ship which was not *The Lady of the Seas*. Then where was Toby's ship? And where was Toby?

"Hello," said the nurse. "Feeling better?"

I nodded.

"That's the spirit. Leg's not badly hurt. It'll right itself in time. You've had a nasty shock."

I said, "What happened?"

"The weather was very bad. It can be like that in these seas. We picked you up. We're taking you to Sydney. You've got people there, haven't you?"

I said, "The ship . . . *The Lady of the Seas* . . . ?"

"It seems she was on her last legs. Been around a bit. Could be an enquiry."

I could not grasp what she was talking about.

"Don't you fret," she went on. "You're safe now. You were one of the lucky ones."

"The lucky ones." I was floundering for words which would not come, perhaps because I was afraid to say them.

"What . . . what happened . . . ?"

"She was lost . . . and quite a number of poor souls with her."

"The Captain . . . ?"

"Well, dear, the Captain is always the last to leave the ship, isn't he?"

It was the ship's doctor who told me.

He had discovered that Toby was my father, and he was very gentle.

He took my hands and said, "You see, it was a violent storm. They get them now and then in these waters. The ship couldn't stand up to it. Quite a number of people went down with her. I'm going to give you something to make you sleep. That's what you need."

I had lost him. All my happiness, all my dreams of the future, gone. An ageing vessel and a merciless sea had taken that away from me.

I had lost the one I loved above all others. I was aware of nothing but complete desolation.

Echoes from the Past

ELSIE WAS WAITING FOR ME when I arrived in Sydney. We clung together in our misery. We hardly spoke at all as we drove to the house. She asked a few questions about my leg. The bones were not broken, but there were deep cuts and bruises. I had suffered mainly from shock and concussion.

Mabel, Adelaide and Jane were waiting, but the air of well-being had completely disappeared. It was a house in mourning.

Neither Elsie nor I could speak of Toby on the first night. The great comfort was that our grief was understood and shared. Something had gone from our lives which could never be regained.

I lay sleepless that night. I kept going over scenes from the past. He had filled my life, and now he had gone there was nothing left.

If only we had not been in that spot on that night. Many people had said, "If only," at some time in their lives. If only this . . . if only that . . . It was the well-worn cry of those in despair. I thought of that ceremony on the island and the way in which they had tried to hold us back. That wise old man had known that Toby was going into danger. Perhaps he did indeed have special powers. Perhaps he could see into the future. He had lived all his life on that island; he would be weather-wise. He could have seen the signs of the coming storm. He had been warning us, urging us to delay our journey. Oh, if only we had taken heed! If only . . . if only . . .

And so I went on.

Daylight came at last. A dreary day lay ahead because he was not there and we were weighed down by the dreadful knowledge that we should never see him again.

A few days passed, and suddenly we found that we could talk of him.

Elsie recalled stories of him. I would listen and then tell my own.

Then one day she said to me, "Carmel, this won't do, you know. Think how he would laugh at us if he were here. We had the joy of knowing him, and he brightened our lives. But when something's over, and you know that all the wishing in the world won't bring it back, you've got to accept it as it is. We've got to bestir ourselves."

I said, "You're right. But how?"

"That's what we've got to find out. We've got our friends, and we've got some good ones."

She was right. The Formans were always trying to cheer us up. I saw a great deal of James and Gertie. Joe Lester was around, and everyone we knew did all they could to help us. We were constantly invited out to dine, and there were a great many callers.

One day Gertie said to me, "I've heard from Aunt Beatrice. She's ever so keen for me to go and see her."

"You mean, the aunt in England?"

She nodded. "We always got on when I was little. She didn't have any children and I think she liked to think of me as hers. We write regularly. Now they're getting things into shape here, I don't think they'd mind if I went over to stay with her for a bit."

"It sounds exciting."

"Doesn't it? You ought to come."

I looked at her in amazement.

"Why not? You can't mope all your life."

"Mope . . . ?" I said.

"You're not like you used to be. I know it was awful and how fond you were of each other . . . but you can't go on mourning forever."

"Go home," I murmured.

"My father says if I'm so set on it, I'd better do it. He'll pay my fare and run to a small allowance while I'm there. *You* wouldn't have to bother about that. You're an independent woman now."

She was right. Toby had left the bulk of his fortune to me, and it was not inconsiderable. Elsie had been taken care of too. It suddenly occurred to me that, if I wished to, I could travel. Gertie was watching me closely.

"Well?"

"I hadn't thought about going home."

"Think about it now. My mother suggested you might like to go with me. She said it would do you good. Get you out of yourself. You're never going to get any better while you sit around remembering. What do you think about my going home?"

"I hadn't thought about it, really."

"You haven't thought about anything but yourself for the last months."

Gertie had kept the frankness of our younger days when she had never disguised the truth, however brutal. She went on: "The trouble with you is that you are shut in with yourself. Something awful happened to you and you won't let yourself—or anyone else— forget it."

Then suddenly she laid her hand on my arm.

"I'm sorry," she went on. "I shouldn't have said that."

"Yes," I said, "you should. It's true."

"It's that thing I've heard about—taking your troubles out and teaching them to swim—rather than drowning them."

I was thoughtful and, after a pause, she went on: "Well, you could consider it."

I went home and told Elsie what she had said. I knew that Elsie would not want me to go away, and she was very thoughtful as she listened.

"To her aunt," she said. "Well, we have heard a great deal about Gertie's aunt. I guessed Gertie would go sometime. She'd made up her mind. I think . . . perhaps . . . it would do you good to go with her."

"Do you!"

"There's nothing like a complete change when these things happen. I rather think you have accepted grief as a permanency. It was such a terrible blow. It was the worst of tragedies. He was so lovable and meant so much to you. We can't forget him, but he's gone, and we can't let him dominate our lives. I am sure, if he were here, he would say the same. You don't have to decide right away. You should think about it, though."

"Elsie," I said, "I should hate to leave you."

"You mustn't feel that. I love to have you here, of course.

You've been my daughter. But you have your life, and here . . . it's hard to forget. You ought to be meeting people—fresh people. You could at home. I have something to tell you. Then you will see that I should not be so lone and lorn that you have to stay and look after me. I am thinking of getting married."

"Elsie!"

"Yes. Joe and I have been friends for a long time. Toby used to say, 'You would have done better to have married Joe. He'd have made a better husband than I ever would.' In a way he was right. It wouldn't have been the same, though. It's all over now, so Joe and I can marry and it's what he's wanted for a long time. And I want it too, so I shouldn't be alone."

I was amazed, but when I thought of it, I wondered why I should have been. Perhaps Gertie was right when she said I had been absorbed in my own life. Joe was such a steady friend. There was no doubt of his love for Elsie. I thought how amused Toby would have been by the situation, and I found myself smiling for the first time in months.

Elsie put her arms round me and hugged me.

"You've got to break away from it too," she said.

And after that I began to think seriously about going home.

I had broken out of that depression in which I had been living for so long, and Gertie carried me along on her enthusiasm. It would be some little time before we could go, and Elsie thought we should leave in the New Year. Then we should reach England when spring was on the way, which would be a very good time to arrive.

There was much correspondence with Aunt Beatrice, who lived with her husband, Uncle Harold, in Kensington Square. Gertie remembered staying there.

"It's what they call a family house," she explained. "When they married they thought they'd have a big family. They were still hoping when we left. They were very upset about our going. James and I often stayed with them and they looked forward to having children in the house."

"Do you think they will want me?"

"Of course! And if you don't like it, you can go somewhere else. You don't have to worry about money and all that."

"It seems very convenient."

"Convenient! It's perfect. You'll love Aunt Bee."

"I hope she likes me."

"She will. That's if you come out of mourning. Nobody will like you if you stick to that. You've got to remember there are other people in the world."

There was no doubt that Gertie was good for me.

The Formans were a little sad at the prospect of Gertie's going. I had an idea that her roots were so firmly set in England that she might not want to come back. Moreover, James would be leaving home for the opal grounds very soon, for it seemed that the property was in good order now and he could go with a good conscience.

I saw James frequently. He was not very pleased about my going.

He said, "You *will* come back, won't you?"

"I don't plan to stay," I said.

"You might change your mind once you are there."

"It doesn't seem likely."

"Are you sure you wouldn't like to forget it all and come with me instead?"

"I don't think that would be right for either of us, James."

"The offer is still on."

"Thank you."

"It's fun, you know. It would be a complete change."

"As Gertie is always saying this will be."

"If you don't come back I may come for you when I have a fortune to offer."

"I don't want a fortune."

"I know. But it would be nice to have it all the same. Don't forget me, will you?"

"No. I never would. And thank you for all your understanding."

"Oh, I'm the understanding kind. Remember that too."

"I will."

Gertie and I were constantly together. We shopped; we made plans; and in due course booked our passages on *The Ocean Star*.

Elsie wondered how I would feel about going to sea again. She thought the trauma of shipwreck might have had such an effect on me that I would not be able to bring myself to go again.

I had no qualms. I did mention to Gertie that I should feel closer to Toby at sea, to which she retorted, quite rightly, "What maudlin nonsense! Don't say that to anyone else or they'll think you've got bats in the belfry. I am going to sea with you, and I don't want Toby to be with us all the time."

It was brutal, but it was for my own good, I knew. She went on gently: "I've got the plan of *The Ocean Star*. My word, she's a beautiful ship. Look, we can see exactly where our cabin is."

It was late January when Gertie and I set sail. Joe and Elsie had married just after Christmas.

It had been a quiet ceremony and Joe had taken up residence at Elsie's house. I was delighted, because I knew it was what he had wanted for a long time. Elsie too was contented.

Joe's nephew, William, who had long wanted a property of his own, had taken over the management of Joe's. Joe kept an interest in it and would always be close at hand to advise. He and Elsie would pay periodic visits to William, and the arrangements were to the utmost satisfaction of both William and Joe, as well as Elsie.

The Formans with Elsie and Joe came to see us off. It was a moving farewell, and even Gertie seemed a little tearful and looked as though she were wondering whether she was wise to make the journey—but only very briefly.

James held my hands tightly and reminded me that I must come back, and added, "Before long, or I shall come for you."

I nodded, and we kissed.

Gertie and I stood on the deck, waving to them as the ship slipped away, and I could not help thinking of the day I had first come here on *The Lady of the Seas,* how Toby had been with me and how happy we were.

Aware of my thoughts, Gertie hustled me off to our cabin and in her practical way sorted out who should have which berth and which wardrobe space should be allotted to me.

Though there would be much to remind me, I knew I must stop harking back to the old life. I had to go forward and start afresh.

I was familiar with ship life, but every ship is different and, although the general rules apply, they are varied slightly to fit in to each particular vessel.

The Captain was very pleasant. He had known Toby, and when he realised who I was, and that I had actually been on *The Lady of the Seas* when she had sunk, he was particularly kind.

I realised quickly that I had been right to come, for, looking forward to going home, I could feel myself moving away from my tragedy, and I knew I was getting nearer to adjusting myself to life without Toby. I even convinced myself that he was looking after me, applauding me, urging me along the path I was taking. It helped. But it was inevitable that there must be comments which brought back poignant memories.

It would have been easier if we had not taken almost the same route back to England as that of my first journey out, but I did my best not to think of it, and Gertie was a great help to me. I was always aware of her watchful eyes on me, and I was deeply touched because she did so much want me to enjoy the visit.

I think I managed very well. We had pleasant travelling companions; the weather was benign. Gertie and I usually went ashore with a party from the ship. The story of our getting lost in Suez was related with much hilarity, and it struck me afresh how time turns disastrous happenings into comic adventures. However, there was a great deal of laughter about the two little girls who had climbed a rope ladder to board the ship.

Suez, it seemed, was a place where things happened to us, commented Gertie, for, as we were about to board the launch which was to take us back to the ship, I saw a man who seemed familiar to me.

I stared. Then I recognised him.

"Dr. Emmerson!" I cried.

Gertie was beside me.

"It is!" she exclaimed. "Really, here of all places!"

He was a little disconcerted. During the passage of time, girls of eleven change more than men in their twenties or thirties. He stood looking at us, faintly puzzled. Then enlightenment dawned.

He laughed. "Is it really . . . Carmel . . . and Gertie?"

"Yes, it is," we cried together.

"Lost in Suez," he said. "What a business, getting you on board."

"With that rope ladder," gurgled Gertie.

"Still, we did it. And you are travelling on this ship?"

"Yes. Home."

"What a coincidence. So am I."

We chattered as the launch took us out. He told us he had been in Suez for the last two weeks talking to the doctors there. He had a practice in Harley Street and was attached to a London hospital.

"When we last met," he said, "I was going out to Suez to study at a hospital there. Well, I did all that, came home and settled, as it were."

"Do you often go to Suez?" I asked.

"No. Not now. I just happened to pay this flying visit, doing a talk on some new development."

"How strange that you should be on the same ship as we are, going home."

"Things happen that way sometimes."

The voyage changed after that. We saw a great deal of Dr. Emmerson. He seemed to seek me out. At first Gertie was with us, but one of the new arrivals at Suez was Bernard Ragland, and he and Gertie liked each other from the start. He was interested in medieval architecture and was attached to one of the London museums —hardly the kind of subject to attract Gertie, but she suddenly became interested in it.

Dr. Emmerson knew about the shipwreck and he understood what the loss of Toby meant to me, so I was able to talk frankly to him. I found that a relief and would sit on deck and chat for long stretches at a time. He told me of his life and career, how he had worked for a time in Suez. He spoke of the suffering he had seen there among the poor. Somehow he drew me away from my personal tragedy as no one had before, and he made me see that Gertie was right when she had said that I had indulged too much in brooding on my own misfortunes.

Looking back on that voyage, I see that a great deal happened during it. No one could have said it was uneventful.

The sea had been especially kind to us, even in those areas where it could be notoriously unpredictable. We had sailed smoothly; we had met pleasant acquaintances—with some of whom we had made tentative arrangements to see again which would most likely never materialise; in fact, it had been a trip like many others, superficially, but it was to be important, not only to me, but to Gertie.

As soon as I stepped ashore in the company of Dr. Emmerson, Gertie and Bernard Ragland knew that I had passed an important barrier. I had set a distance between myself and the past.

Aunt Beatrice and Uncle Harold were waiting to greet us. Gertie rushed into Aunt Beatrice's arms.

"You're here, you're here!" cried Aunt Beatrice. She was plump and rosy and rather large. Uncle Harold was thin and slightly shorter. He stood looking on, faintly embarrassed, but pleased and as welcoming in his way as Aunt Beatrice was in hers.

"This is Carmel," Gertie announced. "You've heard about her. And this is Mr. Bernard Ragland," she went on with pride, and Aunt Beatrice seized his hand and shook it warmly. Then Uncle Harold did the same.

"And this is Dr. Emmerson."

"So pleased to meet you," said Aunt Beatrice.

"It's wonderful to be home," said Gertie.

Aunt Beatrice and Uncle Harold exchanged glances of gratification, which implied that Gertie should never have gone and how wise she was to come back.

And soon after, Gertie and I went off with her family and Dr. Emmerson and Bernard Ragland their separate ways. They had already made promises to see us again.

And there we were, on our way to Kensington, while Gertie and Aunt Beatrice chattered all the time and Uncle Harold and I sat listening and smiling.

Those first weeks in London were full of experiences and time passed quickly. There were long periods when I did not think of Toby and I realised that, if I allowed myself, I could be very interested in what was going on around me.

Aunt Beatrice and Uncle Harold—Mr. and Mrs. Hyson—were completely hospitable. The family house was comfortable. I was sure they would have made the most loving parents. They were devoted to Gertie and clearly enjoyed having her with them. And they welcomed me, too.

The house was in a square in the centre of which was a large and well-kept garden for the use of residents of the square. The key to the gates of this garden was kept hanging just inside the back door and I took the opportunity of going there to sit now and then. It was very peaceful to be shut in among the trees, through which one could just get a glimpse of those tall houses, standing like sentinels guarding the peace of the square.

The house was roomy. At the top was that part which had been intended for the children who never arrived. Those apartments were now given over to Gertie and me. Gertie was familiar with them from the days when she and James used to visit. There had been their playroom, and in the large cupboard were games—draughts, chess, jigsaws, snakes and ladders and ludo.

It would have been rather sad to contemplate the dreams of these two pleasant people which had never materialised, but somehow one could not, for they had not become in the least embittered, and now that Gertie and I were here, they seemed entirely reconciled.

"They are a wonderful pair," Gertie told me. "It was a blow to them when my people decided to go to Australia. Now, here I am and it's good to be back. They're a lesson to us, those two. Don't you agree?" she added pointedly, and I laughed, because I knew she meant that the lesson was chiefly for me. I thought then that it is indeed a boon to get a glimpse of ourselves as others see us.

The Hysons liked to entertain, and having Gertie with them gave them excuses to do so.

They had some spacious rooms which were suitable for this and they determined to make good use of them. Within a week of our arrival, Dr. Emmerson and Bernard Ragland had been asked to dinner.

We had a very pleasant evening together and the episode of our rescue in Suez was related once more, although I am sure Gertie had told them all about it in her letters.

Gertie listened as though enraptured to some details about the differences between Gothic and Norman architecture and how, in the early fourteenth century, builders were not content with the simple styles and sought something more decorative. I was amazed to see her so earnest.

I thought then: This is Gertie in love.

Lawrence—I was beginning to think of Dr. Emmerson as Lawrence by this time—did not talk intimately of his profession. I supposed diseases of the skin would be a less welcome subject at the dinner table.

I was becoming very interested in Gertie's relationship with Bernard Ragland, and so were her aunt and uncle.

Aunt Beatrice said to me one day when Gertie was out: "What do you think, Carmel? Gertie seems to be getting very friendly indeed with that nice Bernard."

I agreed.

"Well?" said Aunt Beatrice.

"She hasn't known him very long."

"Ships are different from ordinary life," said Aunt Beatrice sagely, although I believed she had never sailed on one.

She paused. "Romantic, somehow. I wonder . . ." She lifted her shoulders. I guessed she was seeing a wedding, organised by herself . . . the young couple settling into a nice little house not far off. And then the nursery . . . Aunt Beatrice being at hand to help . . . taking over the duties of a mother.

It startled me a little, but it did seem to me that Gertie was in love. I could imagine the scorn she ordinarily would have poured on a conversation about linenfold and the advantages of stone over brick, which she now seemed to find entrancing.

Lawrence had become a frequent visitor too, and I wondered whether Aunt Beatrice speculated on our relationship as she did on that of Gertie and Bernard. Surely not. Lawrence was a good deal older than I. He must be over thirty, whereas Bernard would be in his mid-twenties, perhaps a little more but not much.

Sometimes I took Lawrence over to the gardens and we would sit there and talk. On one occasion he mentioned the shipwreck.

"I often think about it, Carmel," he said. "It stunned you, didn't it? You were so devoted to him."

I agreed.

"You'd rather not talk about it, perhaps," he said.

"No . . . no, I don't mind with you."

"You've got to start living, Carmel."

"That's what Gertie tells me. She has been so good for me."

"You are just preserving your grief. He wouldn't have wanted you to do that. He was so lighthearted by nature. He would have wanted you to be the same."

"When you go on grieving, you spoil things not only for yourself . . . but also for others, as Gertie tells me. What I have to do is learn how to stop."

"You've been better since you've been here."

"Yes, I know."

"It's over, Carmel. In no way can you change it. You've got to forget."

"I know. But how?"

"By making a new life for yourself."

"I'm trying."

"If I can help . . ."

I smiled. "I know you are a wonderful helper. There was that other occasion."

"Never to be forgotten," he said with a little grimace.

"You were the gallant rescuer. Poor James, he never forgets the part he played."

"Oh, poor casual James who deserted you!"

"I told you about his dreams of making a fortune in the opal fields."

So we talked of Australia and the life there, and again I was surprised that I forgot my unhappiness for a while.

Gertie had become engaged to Bernard Ragland. It was a month since we had arrived in London.

"It's quick," I said.

"Quick! What do you mean? There was all that time on the ship and now we've been home all these weeks. To you it may seem quick. To me it is just romantic."

"Are you happy?"

"Blissfully."

"Oh, Gertie, how wonderful!"

"It is, isn't it? There must be something about Suez. Fateful for us."

"For you, you mean."

"What a good thing that we were on that ship. Just imagine, if we had not been, I should not have met Bernard."

"Wonderful. Think what a lot you are going to learn about architecture, ancient and modern."

We laughed and she said, "You shall be my bridesmaid. But perhaps you're a bit old for that. I think they call them Matrons of Honour. Matron sounds a bit solemn. Perhaps it's Maid of Honour. I like that—it sounds royal."

"Oh, Gertie, I can't wait."

"Oddly enough, nor can I."

She came into my room that night to talk. She told me about the splendid qualities of Bernard, how he was respected throughout the country for his work, and what a wonderful future lay before her.

"I'm so proud of him, Carmel."

"You're going to be absolutely unbearable, I can see," I told her. And we giggled together as we had all those years ago on *The Lady of the Seas*.

Aunt Beatrice and Uncle Harold were wildly excited and talked continuously of the engagement. Where would the young couple live? Kensington was a desirable area. There were some lovely little houses in Marbrock Square just round the corner. I could see that Aunt Beatrice was already planning that house—the nurseries in particular. Her lost dream was hovering close, in another form perhaps, but near enough. There would be a little garden—a garden was really necessary with children.

Bernard wanted to take Gertie to meet his family. They lived in Kent and she was duly asked for the weekend. Aunt Beatrice thought it would be "nice" if I went with them. I think she had an idea that I would act as chaperone. She had some rather old-fashioned notions which came out occasionally. To my surprise, for I had thought Gertie would scorn the idea, she was in favour of it.

"It will be comforting to have you there," she said. "I might want your advice."

I was astounded, but Gertie in love was not quite the self-assured young lady she had been before. She was faintly nervous and very anxious to make a good impression on her family-to-be.

"I suppose you feel they must be paragons to have produced the god-like Bernard," I said.

"I do want them to like me," she admitted.

It was gratifying to have our roles reversed. I was now the one who had to advise and look after Gertie.

We were to leave London on the Friday afternoon and take the train from Charing Cross into Kent where the Ragland residence was situated. Bernard would escort us. There had been a great deal of discussion as to what we should wear. Gertie had packed and unpacked her suitcase three times. I told her not to be so nervous. Of course they would like her and, if they did not, well, what did it matter? Bernard did, or he would not have asked her to marry him.

At length we were in the train which would take us down to Maidstone. Bernard told us there would be a fly at the station to take us to the house. The parents were very much looking forward to meeting us.

I sat back in my corner seat, watching them and thinking how wonderful it must be to be as happy as they were, and now and then glancing out at the countryside.

Then suddenly it happened.

The train had run into a small station. I glanced out at the bold letters proclaiming its name and I was immediately jolted back into the past.

Easentree.

It was familiar. I had been here before. I remembered it clearly.

Nanny Gilroy had said, "Now, come on, Estella. Have you got everything? Don't you dare leave anything behind. I wonder if Tom Yardley will have brought the trap."

It had been a rare event. It was not often we went on the train. We had gone to London to buy boots which we could not get in the local shoe shop. Easentree was the nearest station to Commonwood House.

As the train pulled out of the station I sat in a daze. I was right back in the past. Commonwood House. Mrs. Marline making everyone unhappy. The doctor's trying to pretend everything was all right. Miss Carson . . . what had become of Miss Carson?

"Wake up!" said Gertie. "You're half-asleep. We're nearly there."

Gertie was drawing me out of my dream of the past.

The weekend was a success. The Raglands were by no means formidable, and seemed as ready to like their future daughter-in-law as she was to like them. In such circumstances, they could hardly fail to do so.

Members of the Ragland family were all eager to meet Bernard's choice, and there were some pleasant family gatherings.

As for myself, my thoughts kept returning to the past. Memories of Commonwood House persisted in coming back, and I was filled with a desire to see the house again. I wondered who was living there now. Suppose I went back?

There would be strangers. The family would have left when Dr. Marline died and the girls and Henry went to live with their Aunt Florence. She was my aunt too, of course. I wished that Toby had told me more. I realised that he had been very reticent about his family . . . which was, after all, mine.

I saw myself walking along the path approaching the familiar door, reaching up to the knocker. But I should not have to reach now that I was grown up.

I rehearsed what it would be like.

"I hope you don't mind. I happened to be passing and I used to live here once. I wondered . . ."

Why not? People did such things now and then. It was not so very unusual.

I pondered it over the weekend while Gertie was revelling in the approval of her in-laws-to-be, and before it was over I had decided that I was going down to Easentree. I could take the fly as we did with Nanny Gilroy. I could hardly let it drop me at Commonwood House as though I had come specially. No. I would go into the little town. There was a hotel. What was it called? The Bald-faced Stag. Estella and I had jeered at the name. What did they expect? A stag to have a beard? I could hear her voice distinctly.

That was how it was during that weekend. Voices kept coming back to me from the past.

I could take the fly and alight at the inn. Then I could walk down the hill to Commonwood House.

I had made up my mind.

Aunt Beatrice and Uncle Harold wanted to hear all about the visit.

"We must invite Bernard and his parents here for a weekend," she said. "We ought to be looking at houses. These things take longer than one thinks to find. For one thing, we have to get the right place."

And, as the happy couple planned to have a short engagement, there was no reason why they should not start looking now.

Gertie was too happy to notice that I was somewhat preoccupied with a matter outside her concerns. She talked constantly about herself and she wrote to her parents.

"They won't like it," she said, "because it means I shall be here and they'll be there. Bernard says we'll be able to pay them the occasional visit. He gets long leaves and he can save them up. Mother and Dad might be able to come and see us . . . if they can get away. Then it won't be quite so bad.

"As for you, Carmel, you don't want to go back yet. You'll have to stay and see me married."

"I can't stay here with your aunt and uncle forever."

"They love having you. Besides, what are you worrying about?

You could go and stay anywhere you liked. Perhaps you'll get married."

"You are like lots of people. Having put your head in the noose, you want to see everyone else doing the same."

"Don't be cynical. It does not become you. There is no question of nooses. You don't know what it means, obviously. It's the best thing that can happen to you."

"I hope you continue to believe that."

"Now let's talk sense. Aunt Bee is mad about my seeing this house in Brier Road. She's made an appointment for next Tuesday. Want to come?"

"Well, as a matter of fact, I thought of visiting."

"You mean, someone you knew in the past?"

"Y . . . yes."

"You mean next Tuesday?"

"Yes, I did, really."

"Make it another day and I'll come with you."

"I think I ought to go alone. Just at first . . . you understand?"

"Of course."

I was glad.

Gertie had never been greatly interested in other people's affairs and, of course, she was now completely immersed in her own.

So I arranged on the following Tuesday to put my plan into action.

I arrived at Easentree. I was lucky. The fly was in service and it was not long before I reached The Bald-faced Stag.

I began to walk down to the common. I noticed the shops in the street which comprised the town. Miss Patten, who kept the haberdasher's, was still there, as were the post office, the butcher's, and the baker. I went swiftly down the hill. When I had been walking for about fifteen minutes, I saw the wood and the common.

My heart was beating fast. I was rehearsing what I would say. It sounded false.

"I was just passing and I thought you wouldn't mind. Natural curiosity. You see, I lived here until I was eleven years old. Then I went to Australia. I have only just returned."

No one was on the common. There was the pond and the seat.

And there was the house . . . hidden by the shrubs, which were overgrown. In my day they had been neater than that.

As I approached, I was amazed that it appeared to be so unkempt.

There was the gate. I opened it and walked towards the house. I stopped and gasped. It was Commonwood, of course, but how different! Some of the windows were cracked . . . one or two actually broken. The brickwork was chipped in places. It looked as though part of the roof had fallen in.

Commonwood was a ruin. I stared at it in dismay. It looked grim and forbidding.

My first impulse was to turn and run away, but I could not do so. I had to find out what had happened to it. Why, when the doctor had died, had they not sold the house? Why had practical Aunt Florence and her husband—for I imagined she had one—allowed a valuable property to become a worthless ruin?

I felt a sudden sense of revulsion. It was so different from what I had expected. But something was urging me on. I stepped forward towards the house.

I was standing now close to the front door. The windows on the ground floor were all cracked. The lock on the door was broken. I pushed it. It gave a protesting squeak and swung open.

I stepped into the hall with the doors leading from it, to Mrs. Marline's sitting-room and bedroom with the glass doors which opened onto the lawn.

My heart was beating wildly now. I fancied I was being warned not to venture further. There was something eerie about the place. It was not the Commonwood House I had known. Why had it become like this? I must get away, forget it. It belonged to a past which was best forgotten. What good could I do by trying to resurrect the past? It was obvious what had happened. The children had gone away; all those who had once been part of this house were dead or dispersed and, for some reason, the house had been allowed to fall into decay.

Go back to the town, I told myself. Have a meal in The Bald-faced Stag and ask them to arrange for some conveyance to get you back to the station. Then, forget about the past and Commonwood House. It is over forever.

But the impulse to go on was irresistible. Just a step into the hall. Just a few more moments to recapture the ambiance of the old days . . . the feeling of being not as the others, the outsider who was there on sufferance because the doctor had a soft heart, to savour once more the feelings of that unwanted girl, soon to be loved and cherished by the most wonderful of men.

I made my way across the tattered carpet. It had once been brown with a blue pattern on it; now it was damp and torn and the blue was barely visible. An insect scuttling across it startled me.

I opened the door of a room and looked in. My mind flashed back to one of the last occasions when I had seen it. Adeline . . . frantic with fear, and Mrs. Marline shouting at her. Miss Carson coming in.

I had not realised how vividly those scenes had impressed themselves on my memory.

The door to the garden was shut. Through the glass panels I could see how neglected it was. I remembered how I had listened to conversations and tried to piece together what was happening in the grim household.

I turned away and looked up at the staircase and, before I could warn myself that a house in such condition might be unsafe, I started to ascend them. I was on the landing, close to that room which had been shared by Dr. and Mrs. Marline before her accident. Empty now. I glanced up the stairs. How quiet it was. How different. I kept thinking I heard whispering voices. Nanny Gilroy, Mrs. Barton and the district nurse . . . shutting the kitchen door, drinking tea and talking secrets.

Then suddenly I heard a sound. I could hear my heart beating. A sibilant whisper. It was coming from the room below. Voices down there. Ghostly voices in an empty house.

I do not think I was particularly fanciful, but from the moment I had come into the house I had thought there was something eerie about it. Perhaps there is about most derelict houses. They seem to preserve something, some character of the people who had lived in them over the years; and when one has known them, and has been aware of some mysterious happenings, it was not surprising that one's imagination stirred.

When I heard a light footfall I was no longer in doubt. I was not alone in the house.

There it was again . . . that sibilant whisper.

I was in the room which had been the Marlines' bedroom. I

stood very still, waiting. I was not sure what I expected. Did I think the ghost of Mrs. Marline was going to appear and ask me what I was doing there? What right had I to be here . . . of ever having been here? Yes, I was her brother's child, and that was the reason why I had been allowed to stay. But Mrs. Marline would say that people had no right to beget children out of wedlock and the children had to suffer for that.

It was a light step on the stairs. There was no doubt now. I was not alone in this house.

I stood cowering in the room as the steps came nearer. I had pushed the door to so that it was half-closed. Whoever was there was very close now. There was a pause. I could hear the sound of light breathing, and then the door was slowly pushed open.

I caught my breath. I was not sure what I had been expecting, but the sight of a small boy was reassuring. He was not alone. There was another, slightly smaller boy behind him.

We stared at each other. I gathered he was as astonished to see me as I was to see him.

He said in a frightened voice, "Are you a ghost?"

"No," I said. "Are you?"

He lifted his shoulders in silent mirth and the other boy came to stand beside him and stare at me.

Then he went on: "What are you doing here?"

"What are you?" I retaliated.

"Looking."

"So am I."

"It's haunted, you know."

"This house . . . ?"

"All of it. The garden as well. It's a real haunted house, en't it, Will?"

Will nodded.

"Do you live near here?" I asked.

He nodded and pointed vaguely in the direction of the common.

"Why is this house falling down like this?" I asked him.

"'Cos it's haunted."

"Why is it haunted?"

"'Cos there's a ghost. That's why."

"Why are there ghosts here?"

"They came to do the haunting, of course."

I calculated how old they were. The elder looked about eight, the other a year or so younger. They would have been babies or as yet unborn when I had left here.

"Did you know the people who lived here?" I asked.

"Only ghosts."

I could see I was not going to learn much from them.

"We're not supposed to come here," volunteered the younger one.

"He dared me to," said the elder.

"My mother says the house could fall down on you. Then you'd be buried with the ghosts."

"It's unsafe," said the other. "They're always saying they're going to pull it down."

"And build another house?" I asked.

"Who'd want to live here?"

"Why not?"

The boys looked at me in amazement, and the elder said, "It's haunted, that's why."

I felt I owed them a reason for my being here, and I said, "I was passing . . . and it looked interesting."

"We've got to go home now. It's dinner time and our mum don't half go off if we're late." He gave me a disappointed look. "I thought you'd be a ghost, not just an ordinary person."

"You're not sorry," said the other. "You're glad. You wasn't half-frightened."

"I wasn't!"

"Yes, you were."

They started downstairs, their voices echoing through the house.

"I wasn't."

"Yes, you were."

I looked out of the window and saw them running across the lawn.

Then slowly I made my way downstairs and out of the house.

I stood looking over the common. No one was about. The experience had disturbed me. I could not rid myself of the feeling that there was something eerie and menacing about the place. I was glad to be out of it. I did not want to go there again. I wanted to get right away and forget it all.

I should probe no more. I expected The Grange was still there but I was not going to look.

I made my way back down the hill into the town. I would have a light meal at The Bald-faced Stag and then go to the station and back to London.

I was about to cross the road to the inn when a rider came along. His horse was rather frisky and, as I was about to step out into the road, it reared up on its hind legs, whinnying. A man, who was also about to cross, halted and stood beside me. We both watched the horse and rider.

"Rather tricky," said the man to me. There was something familiar about his voice.

I turned to look at him and I knew at once. It was Lucian Crompton.

"Lucian!" I cried.

He stared at me in surprise and then I saw recognition in his eyes.

"Why . . . it's Carmel!"

We stood gazing at each other for a few moments. Then he said, "Well, this is a surprise. Where have you sprung from, after all this time?"

"I'm here for the day . . . from London. In fact, from Australia."

"Really! And we meet like this! What luck!"

It came flooding back again. This was the pleasant part of the memory. I was remembering how he had found my pendant and had it repaired, how he had always been kind to the outsider.

Our pleasure in the encounter was undoubtedly mutual.

"We must have a talk," he said. "What are your plans? You are here for the day, you said." He looked at his watch. "It's just about lunch time for me. What about you?"

"I was going to have something light and then get the train back."

"Why don't we have lunch together? I want to hear what you've been doing all this time."

The man with the horse had gone on now and we crossed the road. Lucian led the way to The Bald-faced Stag.

He was well known there and a table for two was found for us.

Now that I was seated opposite him I could see that he had changed. He was no longer the lighthearted boy I had known. When he was not smiling, there was a vaguely strained look about him. I calculated he must be about twenty-five or -six years old. He looked older. He had certainly changed. I supposed I had too.

As though to follow my thoughts, he said, "You haven't changed much, Carmel. Just grown taller. It was only for the first moment that I did not know you."

"Tell me what has been happening to you."

"My father died three years ago . . . unexpectedly. He had a heart attack. That meant I had to take over the estate."

"I suppose that keeps you occupied."

He nodded.

"I'm sorry about your father," I said. "It must have been a great shock. And your mother?"

"She's well. Camilla married and went to live in the Midlands. She has a little boy now." He paused and hurried on. "I have a daughter. She is two years old."

"Oh, so you are married."

"Was," he said.

"Oh . . . I'm sorry."

"My wife died. It was when the child was born."

I thought: No wonder he has changed, with the death of his father . . . the death of his wife.

"And you . . . are you married?" he asked.

"Oh no. I left school not very long ago."

"Tell me about yourself. You went away so suddenly. Everything broke up, didn't it?"

"Did you know my father was Captain Sinclair?"

"I did hear a rumour of it."

"I went away with him. His ship was based mainly in Australia and he thought it best, in the circumstances, for me to stay there."

"Yes, I suppose it was."

"So I stayed . . . and then . . . he was drowned. He went down with his ship."

He did not know this and I told him as briefly as I could, but it was impossible to hide my emotion.

"You were very fond of him, I remember. It must have been terrible for you." He smiled at me with a tenderness that was touching. "These things happen. One has to accept them. There is nothing else to do, is there?"

He reminded me then so much of those days when he had understood how I felt as the one who did not belong.

"Everything happened so suddenly," I said. "It seems unreal

now. I went to Australia with my father and on the way he told me I was his daughter. It was like a dream come true."

"You were happy in Australia?"

"Oh yes . . . very."

"And you have been there all these years? And now you've come to visit the old home."

"I was horrified when I saw Commonwood House. It really was such a pleasant place. I thought they would have sold it."

"They tried to, but nobody would buy it."

"Why not?"

"A house where a murder has been committed?"

"A murder?"

He looked at me incredulously. "Didn't you know? The papers were full of it. People could talk of little else at the time. Even now, you hear an occasional reference to it."

"Murder?" I repeated.

"Of course, you went away before it started to come out. Perhaps that was why your father . . . Oh yes, I expect that was the idea. It wouldn't have been reported in the Australian papers."

"Tell me what happened."

"Well, there was the trial and things were revealed. Then they couldn't sell the house. Everyone knew what had happened there. People get superstitious. I'm not surprised they couldn't sell it. Who wants to buy a house which belongs to a man who has been hanged for murder?"

I felt numb with shock.

Lucian went on: "So you did not know that Dr. Marline was found guilty? The governess was deeply involved, but she got off. She was going to have a child. Some people thought that helped her. But there wasn't enough evidence against her. There was some person . . . a writer or something . . . who took it up and campaigned for her release."

I murmured, "Dr. Marline. Miss Carson. It's hard to believe. Dr. Marline would never have murdered anyone . . . not even Mrs. Marline."

"He had his supporters. He had a reputation for caring and great concern for his patients, and many of them thought highly of him." He looked at me with an odd expression, and I thought for a moment he wanted me to accept the doctor's guilt.

"He had a motive," he went on. "His wife was giving him a bad time and he wanted to marry Miss Carson who was to have his child. There couldn't have been a stronger motive."

"I still don't believe it. Miss Carson was such a good person. We all loved her. She did more for Adeline than anyone. People like that can't commit murder."

"People can be goaded too far. That must have happened in the Marlines' case. It must."

"I wish I hadn't discovered all this. I just thought the doctor died and the family dispersed. All these years, I have known nothing about this."

"Your father obviously thought it better that you did not know."

"You must have been here when it was all happening."

"I was away at school. Henry left and went to his aunt. I didn't know anything about it until it was all over. Then the doctor was dead, the house empty and the rest of them gone."

We were silent for a while, after which he said, "I think it was wise of your father to do what he did. If you had not come back, you need never have known about it. I can see it has upset you. I am sure he would have realised how you would feel."

"I really belong to the family," I said. "Mrs. Marline was my father's sister . . . my aunt, in fact."

"I am sorry this has depressed you. This should have been a pleasant reunion of old friends."

"I am so pleased to see you again, Lucian."

"And I you. Tell me about Australia."

Over sherry trifle and coffee we talked, but my thoughts were really with the Marline tragedy. I felt sure it was on Lucian's mind too.

I told him about Elsie and her goodness to me, and how Toby had died and she had married her good friend Joe Lester, and how relieved that had made me, because it had enabled me to leave her with a good conscience.

"You don't plan to go back then?" he said.

"Well, not at the moment. Later, perhaps."

"Is there anything . . . anyone . . . you want to go back for?"

"My friend Gertie is here. I suppose we are rather like sisters. We went to school together. I'm quite friendly with her brother.

Well, with all the family, really. We all came out to Australia together. They were emigrating."

I told him something about the life out there and how the Formans had bought a property not far from Sydney, and included an account of the sundowner's visit and its consequences.

He was very interested and wanted to hear more about James.

"He's ambitious. He plans on making a fortune out of opals . . . or perhaps he'll turn to gold. But I think opals seem to fascinate him. There's some place called Lightning Ridge, where there have been some exciting finds. According to James, the best black opals in the world are to be found there."

Lucian was staring into his coffee cup.

He said slowly, "A fascinating stone . . . the opal. They interested me at one time. The colours are so beautiful."

"There is a certain superstition about them, I believe. They are said to be unlucky."

"That grew up because they break easily," said Lucian.

"It's absurd to think a stone can be unlucky."

"Of course," he said vehemently.

I was suddenly transported back to Commonwood House in my thoughts. That was not surprising. Scenes from the past had so often intruded, and now, here I was, not far from the place where it all happened. I was seeing poor Adeline sitting on the floor in her mother's bedroom, with the contents of the drawer which she had pulled out all around her. "I wanted to show Lucian the opal ring . . ."

"What's the matter?" said Lucian.

"Oh . . . I was just thinking. I have never really forgotten what happened at Commonwood House. It keeps coming back to me. There was a scene in the house . . . just before Mrs. Marline died. You were there. You had been talking about opals. You and Henry went off somewhere and Adeline . . . poor Adeline . . . went to her mother's bedroom to look for the opal she had. She wanted to show it to you. She pulled out the drawer. There was this scene."

Lucian was sitting back in his chair, his eyes cast down.

"Poor Adeline," he said.

"Mrs. Marline was very angry and Adeline was terrified of her. Miss Carson comforted her, and then she fainted. I suppose a great deal was clear to some of them. I was in a sort of mist. I knew certain things without realising their significance."

"It's no use going back over it," said Lucian. "It's finished. Nothing we can do can alter anything."

"I know. And I didn't mean to talk of it. It was all because of the opals and thinking they were unlucky . . . and it was just after that when Mrs. Marline died."

"I told you everything pointed to Dr. Marline. It's horrible and it's all in the past. Tell me what happened to James."

"Well, he hadn't begun to search when I left. He will go soon, I believe. He would have gone long ago if it hadn't been for the sundowner."

"Would you like a liqueur to drink to James's success?"

I declined and we sat there talking, though I could not forget the tragedy at Commonwood House. There was something else I wanted to know about. That was Lucian's marriage, but I sensed his unwillingness to talk of it.

I was a little puzzled about him. There were moments when he seemed genuinely delighted to see me, and others when he seemed to find the encounter slightly disconcerting. Had that been when we talked of the happenings at Commonwood House?

I mentioned Gertie's coming wedding.

He said, "You will obviously be here for some time. I get to London occasionally. Perhaps we could meet again. Give me your address. I suppose you will be there for a little time yet."

"I am rather vague at the moment about what I shall do. Gertie's people are most hospitable, but obviously I can't encroach on them forever. I think they are certain to want me to stay until the wedding. However, I shall see."

I wrote out my address and he carefully put it away in his wallet.

He ordered a fly and took me to the station. As the train moved slowly out of the station, he stood, hat in hand, looking after me, rather wistfully, I imagined.

I sat back in my seat, thinking about this strange day. The derelict house, the shocking revelations, and my thoughts then turned to Lucian. Of course, he had known great tragedy. He seemed like a man with a secret. I wondered if that were so.

The Warning

"THE HOUSE IN BRIER ROAD doesn't please Aunt Bee," said Gertie. "I think it is because the nursery is too small. It will only accommodate two infants and she is looking for at least ten. How was your visit? Was it a success?"

I hesitated.

"So it wasn't," she said. "It's often a mistake to expect to find old acquaintances just as you left them. I know you vow eternal friendship when you part, but naturally you forget . . . and there's nothing left, really. Dear old Aunt Bee is going house hunting with a vengeance."

I could not stop thinking of that visit. Would it have been better if I had not gone? I was not sure. The revelation had been upsetting, but I should not have wanted to remain in ignorance, and it had certainly been exciting meeting Lucian.

I had been very fond of him in the past; he had been one of my heroes. But I had always had an exaggerated fondness in those days for people who showed me any kindness. That was because Nanny Gilroy had always—and Estella sometimes—impressed on me that I was of no importance.

I wondered if I should see him again. He had taken my address and seemed eager to, but when one was no longer at hand, people forgot such lightly-given invitations.

When I thought back to the time when we had been together, I could not get out of my mind that, though in a way he had been pleased to see me, my visit had upset him. I guessed it was something to do with what had happened at Commonwood. It had recalled things which were best forgotten.

Lawrence Emmerson was asked to dinner. Aunt Beatrice was a little transparent. Her delight in Gertie's engagement was so obvious, and it was clear, too, that she would like to see me happily settled. Dr. Emmerson was a good friend and, as she saw it, interested in me. He was perhaps a little old, but in every other way he was highly suitable—and everyone could not be expected to do as well as Gertie had.

I hoped Dr. Emmerson was not aware of her thoughts.

We did not have much chance to talk together at the dinner party, but he did ask me to lunch with him a few days later, and, as soon as we were seated, he said, "Something has upset you."

I realised, of course, that he was referring to what I had discovered at Easentree and I was surprised that the effect on me was noticeable.

I told him about my visit.

He knew of the murder, although he had been abroad when it had taken place.

"The Captain's sister was the victim," he said, "and I had known your father for some years, often working on the same ship. I was naturally interested because of the family connection. It seemed a straightforward case."

"I can't think it was. Dr. Marline could never have committed murder."

"You knew him well, of course. It is always difficult to believe these things of people we know. According to the evidence, there did not seem to be a doubt."

"No . . . there must have been something . . . Miss Carson too."

He shrugged his shoulders. "It seems to have disturbed you. It's a long time ago and . . ."

"The thought of his being hanged . . . nice, kind Dr. Marline. It upset me."

"Try to stop thinking of it. It's over."

"But I knew these people so well. My life was with them . . . in that house."

"I think it was very wise of your father to act as he did. If you had heard the evidence, you would understand that there was really no shadow of doubt, however hard it is to accept it now."

"It made a great impression on me. I was there in the house in those last months before . . . before . . . And I knew something was happening, but I wasn't sure what. I was groping in the dark."

"There are emotions and passions which a child could not possibly understand. It is all over. You must not be upset about it."

"I have never really been able to forget Commonwood. It has always come back to me in flashes . . . and I would be back there. It was vivid and disturbing."

"It was a disturbing situation and you were an innocent child right in the midst of it. It was not such an unusual situation, really. Unhappy marriage . . . invalid wife becoming more and more difficult to live with . . . attractive governess. It was the classic setting for this sort of thing. My sister calls it the stock situation. She is interested in criminology. She has written a book about criminals and what makes the most ordinary people commit murder. You must meet her. In fact, I have been meaning to ask you to dinner one evening. I shall ask your friend Gertie, and the Hysons too. I have been their guest and owe them hospitality."

"I am sure they will be delighted."

"Dorothy was asking me only yesterday when I was going to invite you. She's looking forward to meeting you."

The outcome was dinner at Lawrence's house in Chelsea. It was one of those terrace houses on four floors, not far from the river.

Dorothy greeted me with interest.

"I've heard such a lot about you from Lawrence," she said.

"That surely included the dramatic rescue at Suez," I replied.

"Oh yes. What excitement!"

She was small and rather frail-looking, which was misleading. I discovered her to be one of the most energetic people I had ever known. She was very interested in everything that was going on, and it soon became clear that her brother was at the centre of that interest. She was very talkative. In a short time I knew that she had looked after their invalid mother for several years. There had been just the three of them, the father having died when she was sixteen. She herself was some eight years older than Lawrence.

They had lived in the country and Lawrence had had a small place in London because of his profession, but when their mother died they had settled in London and Dorothy had given all her attention to her brother.

"I was a country girl," she said. "I do love the country." She lifted her shoulders. "It is necessary for Lawrence to be in London, so here we are, but we do have a little place in Surrey. I call it the cottage. It is not very far out, which makes it convenient for Lawrence to be there and within call of London. It is only a short journey on the train. Sometimes we get down for weekends. We have friends to stay. It's a respite from Town and Lawrence works so hard. I've got Tess here. She's a marvel. She was with us in my mother's day. We've got a couple down there. There's a cottage in the grounds. Well, grounds is a bit grand. Better say, at the end of the garden. It works out very well."

"You seem to have everything very cleverly arranged," I said.

"It's my job. You see, Lawrence's work occupies him completely. His sort of work is so demanding. He needs relaxation. I just see that he gets it."

"He's lucky."

She looked a little wistful. "One day I expect he'll settle down. He'll make a good husband."

"He told me you are very interested in criminology."

"Oh yes. In an amateur's way, of course."

"He said you had written a book."

"About criminals through the ages. I'm particularly interested in those who had led quite normal lives and suddenly commit murder."

"He may have told you about my connection with the Marline family."

"Oh yes, Lawrence tells me most things. That case created a lot of attention at the time, but the outcome was clear right from the start."

"Lawrence said you called it a stock situation."

"It was. That dreadful woman. Well, by all accounts she was dreadful. No one seemed to have a good word to say for her . . . even the nurse . . . who was so much against the governess. More against her than against the doctor. It was absorbing while it was going on, but, as I say, there have been many others like it."

"Which made it 'stock,' " I said.

"Yes. Then I knew that Lawrence's friend Captain Sinclair was connected with the Marlines. He and Lawrence were often on the same ship, and I suppose that gave an added interest. What a charming man he was! I met him once." She put her hand over mine. "It was terrible for you. The connection, of course, made it doubly interesting to me. I shouldn't have taken so much notice otherwise, I suppose, for it was really a case of the classic murder."

"I was brought up there and I just cannot believe that Dr. Marline was a murderer."

She smiled at me. "People often feel like that. Murderers are not necessarily the ordinary criminal. Something happens . . . and it is more than they can endure. If you saw the evidence you would realise . . ." She hesitated. "I've just remembered. I kept cuttings from the papers to show Lawrence when he came home. I'll find them for you sometime."

She looked guiltily in the direction of the Hysons, her other guests. I could see that she was wondering if she had neglected them.

After dinner, when we were drinking coffee and in the drawing-room, Lawrence said to me, "You seem to get on well with Dorothy."

"I like her very much."

"I'm glad. She's always looked after me."

"Yes, she has been telling me about it. You two seem to have everything satisfactorily planned."

"That's Dorothy. She's a great manager. It makes life comfortable. I can see she likes you. She takes strong likes and dislikes."

She came over to us and Lawrence went to talk to the Hysons and Gertie. I heard them speaking of Australia.

Dorothy said to me, "Now that we have met, you must come again. It would be rather nice if you could have a weekend with us at the cottage."

"I should very much enjoy that."

"Do you think your friends would mind?"

"Oh no, no. As a matter of fact, I sometimes feel that I'm encroaching on their hospitality. You see, I'm there because I'm Gertie's friend. I sometimes think I ought to be making other arrangements."

"You are not planning to go back to Australia yet?"

"No . . . not yet. But I think, perhaps I have been letting things drift. I feel rather uncertain. When my father died . . ."

She patted my hand. "We must talk," she said. "Let's have this weekend. That will give us more time. I tell you what I'll do. I'll look out those cuttings . . . about the Marline case, you know. But you'll find the case was more or less 'shut' as soon as it was 'open.' You'll see what I mean."

"I shall look forward to that."

"Good. I'll check with Lawrence." She gave a little roguish smile. "I think it will fit in with his plans if we make it fairly soon."

The invitation came next day. Gertie was amused.

"I say, you have made a hit. Lawrence is a darling. What you had to do was conquer Sister Dorothy. A hard nut to crack, that one—as the saying goes. But you managed it . . . first go. I'd say Lawrence will have her approval. So, it is full steam ahead."

"What are you talking about?"

"Why ask when you know? Lawrence is no longer young, and Sister Dorothy has come to the conclusion that it might be a good idea for him to settle down, providing he can find the 'right girl'— and that means one of whom Sister Dorothy approves. Well, it seems she approves of you. And I do not think there is any doubt that Lawrence does too. How could he resist Sister Dorothy's choice?"

"How ridiculous!" I said.

"I must write and tell James that he must do something quickly. He has a rival."

"Please do nothing of the sort."

She burst out laughing. "I was just joking. But you are beginning to see the daylight . . . coming out of the dark tunnel. I think he's too old for you and you don't want Sister Dorothy managing you forever after, so don't rush it. But it's nice that there's someone."

"I wish you'd concern yourself with your own matrimonial affairs."

She opened her eyes wide. "Don't you think I do? I had the idea that you thought I was concerned with nothing else."

She flung her arms round me.

"Only teasing. I'm glad you've got your Lawrence, even with 'Big Sister' in control. He's nice. I like him. In fact, I wouldn't be averse to the match. It would keep you here, and I am rather fond of you. I'd hate you to go back down under, even if you would in time be my sister-in-law. I'd rather have you as a friend here than a sister-in-law on the other side of the world."

"You are ridiculous," I said.

And she gave me another hug.

But she did make me think about Lawrence. I believed that he was fond of me, and it was true what she had said about Dorothy. It was all very interesting, and I suppose everyone likes to feel wanted.

However, it was with pleasurable anticipation that I set out for that weekend at the Emmersons' cottage.

The cottage was something of a misnomer. It was a house in grounds—not exactly large, but with spacious airy rooms, and the gardens were a delight. There was a small cottage more or less adjoining the house. In this lived Tom and Mary Burke, who looked after the house. It was of two storeys, and I guessed it had been built at the beginning of the century, for it had a certain Georgian elegance and charm.

I thought it was very pleasant, and I was not surprised by Dorothy's fondness for it. It was run with the efficiency I expected from Dorothy. I thought once more how fortunate Lawrence was to be in her care, for, even if she were perhaps a little forceful at times, everything was done for his good.

I was sure Lawrence appreciated her.

The house was just outside the small town of Cranston. Dorothy had gone on ahead to make sure everything was in order for my visit. I was given a charming bedroom overlooking the garden, and I prepared to enjoy a very pleasant weekend, telling myself how fortunate I was to have renewed my friendship with Lawrence Emmerson.

I was shown round the house and garden with great pride by the brother and sister, and we had spent a pleasant evening gossiping in the garden after dinner. The following morning, I was taken into the village by Dorothy and introduced to some of her acquaintances in the little shops, where she was well known. It had all been very friendly, very homely, a glimpse into the ideal country life.

Lawrence had an engagement with a friend nearby which had been arranged before my weekend had been settled upon, and

Dorothy whispered to me that it would be a good time for her to show me the cuttings she had told me about.

We found a shady spot in the garden, well away from the little stream which ran through it.

"The insects can be a little troublesome," she told me.

She settled me in a comfortable chair under an oak tree on the lawn with the newspaper cuttings.

"Tea at four, my dear," she said. "We'll have it just here on the lawn. Plenty of shade there. I shall disappear until then."

The cuttings had been pasted into a scrapbook and were easy to read, and, as I did so, the past came back to me so vividly that I was there in that house and I felt again the atmosphere of mounting tension and impending danger. Only now I understood it and what it was leading to.

There was an account of the inquest. How vividly I remembered the whispering about that. I could hear Nanny Gilroy's voice: "I shall hold nothing back. You can't at times like this."

And it had been after that inquest that Dr. Marline and Miss Carson had been arrested.

Three weeks after the inquest, the trial had begun.

There were extracts from the opening speech of a Mr. Lamson, Q.C., in which he outlined what had happened, a great deal of which I was familiar with. Mrs. Marline had suffered a bad accident on the hunting field, through which she had become an invalid consigned to a wheelchair. Miss Kitty Carson had come to the house to act as governess to the three girls of the household. A relationship had begun between the doctor and the governess. This had been discovered by Mrs. Marline when it was revealed that the governess was pregnant. Almost immediately after that had become known, Mrs. Marline had died of an overdose of a pain-killing pill which had been prescribed to her by Dr. Everest.

It all seemed, as Dorothy had said, "a clear case of murder."

I studied the evidence. Nanny Gilroy's was the most damning, as I had guessed it would be.

Yes, she was aware that there was "carrying on" between the doctor and Miss Carson. So were others; Mrs. Barton and Annie Logan knew it.

"Thank you, Nurse Gilroy. They will give their evidence themselves."

I pictured her nodding her head, self-righteously, glad because wickedness had been exposed and justice was being done.

"Let us go back to that day, Nurse Gilroy. Tell the court exactly what happened."

And Nanny Gilroy told her story, how there had been the scene because Miss Adeline had been caught in Mrs. Marline's bedroom and Mrs. Marline was scolding the girl when Miss Carson came in and said she shouldn't, and Mrs. Marline was angry and was going to dismiss her. Then Miss Carson had fainted clean away. Annie Logan had examined her and it was clear what was wrong with her. That was, of course, no surprise. They all knew what was going on.

Annie Logan was called.

Yes, she had examined Miss Carson. There was no doubt that she was pregnant.

Then it was the turn of Mrs. Barton, the cook. She confirmed everything that Nanny Gilroy had said, though less venomously.

There was no doubt that Dr. Marline had been involved with Miss Carson and the whole household knew it.

Tom Yardley was called. He had found Mrs. Marline dead.

Shaken all of a heap, he was. Yes, he had known how things were.

Because of what he had seen or what he had heard from Nanny Gilroy or Mrs. Barton?

Tom Yardley looked surprised, the paper commented. I could imagine his scratching his head, as though it would help him find the answer.

"I knew her," he told them. "She was a bit of a tartar and led him a life . . ."

He was stopped and told to answer the question.

I could see that Nanny Gilroy and the others had helped Dr. Marline on the way to execution; but I had to admit what they had said had truth in it, even if it were reported in the most damning way.

Medical evidence at the postmortem revealed without doubt that Mrs. Marline had died through an overdose of the drug which was being supplied to her by Dr. Everest.

There it was . . . all the evidence needed to convict the doctor. Even if Nanny Gilroy had given the impression that Dr. Marline was a hypocritical seducer, Miss Carson a scarlet woman and Mrs.

Marline a poor betrayed wife, nothing she had said could be proved to be an actual untruth. It was merely Nanny Gilroy's version of what had happened.

Then there were the letters.

Miss Carson had left Commonwood House and was away for a week.

She had said "visiting friends," but it appeared that she had gone to a hotel in the town of Manley, some twenty miles away, and had stayed there for five days at The Bunch of Grapes. While there, she had visited a doctor and pregnancy was confirmed, and she had received two letters from Dr. Marline, which she had kept. The letters had been discovered when she was arrested and her belongings searched.

If any confirmation of Dr. Marline's guilt had been needed, it could be found in those letters.

They were read in court. One said:

My dearest Kitty,

How I long for your return. It is so dismal here without you. Don't fret, my darling, I'll work something out. Whatever happens, we shall be together and, if there is indeed a child, how blessed we shall be.

You must not blame yourself. You say you should never have come here. Well, my dearest, that would have been the worst of calamities, for, since you came, I have known such happiness as I had never thought would come my way. I am determined not to give up. Whatever has to be done, we will do it.

Trust me, my darling.

Yours forever,
EDWARD

The other letter was on the same lines, vowing his eternal devotion, stressing the happiness she had brought him and his determination that nothing, nothing should stand in their way of keeping it.

I thought of what their feelings must have been when the letters were read in court, and the agony they must have suffered when they were on trial for their lives.

They were damning, those letters, and I was deeply moved. Oh, poor Dr. Marline. Oh, poor, poor Miss Carson. He had died ignobly in his misery, but she had had to live with hers.

I looked at my watch. It was half past three. I sat for a while, thinking of it all. There was a brief account of what happened afterwards. There had not been enough evidence to condemn Kitty Carson, and the fact that she was to have a child, as the press implied, meant that she could not be sent to the gallows.

What had happened to her? I wondered.

Dorothy came out and joined me.

"Well," she said, "you've read it."

"Yes."

"Obvious, isn't it?"

"I suppose people would say so."

"Wouldn't you?"

"It would seem it must be. But, you see, I knew him."

"I know how you feel. You can't bring yourself to believe he's a murderer. Jefferson Craig wrote about that. His book is fascinating. I wrote to him when I read it. I told him how much I had enjoyed it. I had a nice letter back."

"What happened to Miss Carson?"

"I think he looked after her. He did that with some people he was interested in. Rehabilitated them. That's what they call it. I did hear that he had helped her."

"I wonder so much about her."

"Well, we shall never know, but you see, don't you, that there really couldn't have been any doubt."

"I suppose most people would say so."

She laughed and patted my hand.

"You don't like that verdict, do you? It was a pity that woman couldn't have died by natural causes, and then the lovers could have married and lived happily ever after. They would have been an ordinary couple then. Oh yes, it's a pity life didn't work out like that. It does sometimes.

"Oh, look, Lawrence is coming in. I expect he wants his tea."

There were stables nearby where horses could be hired, and later Lawrence and I went riding together. I had improved considerably and he commented on my skill.

"One rode everywhere over in Australia," I told him.

"You are not thinking of returning, are you?"

"Not immediately."

"Sometime?"

"Who is to say? Everything is so uncertain just now."

"I can't help thinking what a piece of luck it was that we both happened to be on that ship. If we hadn't been there at precisely that time, we might never have met again."

"That's true. But that is the way of life, isn't it? So much is based on chance."

He showed me the local beauty spots—the vale, for which the place was famous, and the ancient ruined castle. We tethered our horses and climbed to the ramparts. We leaned over them, admiring the countryside.

"It would be difficult to find a more pleasant spot," said Lawrence. "Dorothy discovered it. She thought we must have this country retreat. She was right, of course."

I thought how right Dorothy always was.

"You and she get on very well together," he said, smiling. "She doesn't usually take to people quite so quickly."

"I'm glad," I said.

"So am I," replied Lawrence, smiling happily. And then: "You'll come again soon, won't you?"

"If you . . . and Dorothy . . . ask me," I replied.

Lawrence brought me back to Kensington on Sunday evening.

Gertie was waiting for me in some excitement.

"How was it? Successful, I am sure."

"Yes, very."

"And you passed all Dorothy's tests?"

"There weren't any. I expect I passed them before I went."

"Of course. You wouldn't have been asked otherwise. Now, listen. You are in demand. I think you must have been a *femme fatale* all these years and kept it hidden."

"Just because I was invited for the weekend."

"Oh no. You're rushing on too fast. Since you have been away, there have been new developments."

"What do you mean?"

"Others have been seeking you," she said mysteriously.

"Others?"

"Well, one. Isn't that enough? Tall, handsome. One of those strong, forceful men. He left his card. Title as well. My word, Carmel, you are a dark horse."

"What is all this about?"

"Well, what should happen on Saturday morning, while you were far off, charming the gallant Lawrence and his sister? There was a ring at the doorbell, and there stood the most intriguing man. Annie was all of a fluster, and you should have seen Aunt Bee! You can imagine how her mind started working. 'I believe Miss Carmel Sinclair is staying here.' 'Well, yes,' replied Aunt Bee, falling immediate victim to his charm. 'I'm a friend of hers,' says the gentleman. 'I wonder if I might see her?' 'I'm sure you could, if she were here,' responds Aunt Bee. 'But she happens to have gone off for the weekend with friends.' Aunt Bee said he looked very disappointed. She was really taken with him. She said there was something really romantic about this one, and when she saw the name on the card, she almost fainted in ecstasy. Now, you must tell me, who is this Sir Lucian Crompton? I can see recognition dawning on your face, so don't deny all knowledge of the fascinating stranger."

"I wasn't going to. Of course I know him. I'd forgotten he'd got the title when his father died."

"You've never mentioned him."

"Why should I? I knew him long ago, before I went to Australia. And, as a matter of fact, I saw him recently."

"Was he the one you looked up on the way to Maidstone?"

"Not exactly, but I did happen to meet him."

"You didn't tell me!" cried Gertie, outraged.

"There wasn't anything to tell."

"But you implied the visit was not successful. Then, only a little while after, he turns up. I call that very successful."

"Well," I said, "perhaps it was."

"The outcome is that he's left a note for you. He wrote it here. It's waiting for you. I'll get it now."

Gertie brought the note and I took it to my room to read. She was laughing secretly and did not attempt to follow me.

I read:

Dear Carmel,

It was so interesting meeting you again. I am in Town today and I was wondering whether we could have lunch together, but your friends told me that you were away for the weekend. I was very disappointed not to be able to see you.

I shall be coming up again on Wednesday. There is a pleasant little place I go to now and then. It's Logan's in Talbrook Street, off Piccadilly. If you could meet me there at one o'clock I should be delighted. I shall be there in any case and do hope you will be able to join me.

LUCIAN

I was smiling as I folded the letter. I felt excited. It was wonderful to be able to feel interested again.

I sat opposite him in Logan's restaurant. I could see why Aunt Beatrice had been so impressed. Although he might not be as handsome as Gertie had said, he was certainly distinguished, and looked more like the boy I had known long ago than the man I had met recently in Easentree. He was obviously pleased to see me.

"I should have been very disappointed if you hadn't come," he told me.

"It's fun to renew old acquaintances."

"There is so much to catch up with. Now, what are you going to eat?"

When that had been decided and the food brought, he said once more how lucky it was that we had met when about to cross the road at Easentree.

"It was much the same with the friend with whom I have been staying. He happened to be coming back from Egypt on our ship. I had met him on the first voyage, when I went out with my father. Life is full of such incidents."

"The consolation is that, if they didn't happen, we shouldn't know what we had missed. Tell me about your weekend."

I told him. "It is a very pleasant spot. Lawrence Emmerson has a wonderfully efficient sister who looks after everything."

He showed a great interest in the Emmersons, and the story of the Suez rescue came out.

"It still seems extraordinary to me," I finished. "Do you believe in miracles? In simple faith, I mean."

He looked puzzled, and I told him how Gertie and I had stood in the middle of the road and prayed, and almost immediately it seemed Dr. Emmerson had appeared and got us to the ship in time, although we had had to climb the rope ladder.

"Well," he said, "I have heard that faith can move mountains and, compared with that, the doctor's gallant rescue seems rather a minor feat."

"It was miraculous to us. There are moments in one's life which I suppose one never forgets. That is one of them for me."

He looked serious for a moment. Then he said, "Yes, I am sure that will be so."

I thought for a moment that he was going to tell me of some memorable moment in his life, but he did not.

"I suppose," he went on, "he seemed a hero to you. St. George slaying your particular dragon. Galahad, Parsival . . . someone like that."

"Gertie and I spoke of him with reverence for a long time after."

"And still do?"

"Gertie wouldn't feel reverent towards anyone—not even Bernard, her fiancé."

"What about you?"

"I shall always be grateful for what he did on that day."

"Tell me more about that visit to the country and the clever sister."

I talked of them with enthusiasm, and he listened intently.

He said, "You must come to The Grange and stay a weekend with us. We'll see if we can rival the Emmersons."

I thought of the visits to tea with Estella, Adeline and Henry, and the idea of going to The Grange was rather disconcerting.

"You must come. My mother would like to meet you. She remembers you. I told her about our meeting in Easentree. Camilla would be interested too. Perhaps I could get her to come for the weekend. What about that?"

"It would be most interesting."

He said quickly, "I promise you, we won't go near Commonwood. Actually, you can ride by without seeing the house. Everything's so overgrown."

"I wasn't thinking of that. I was just wondering if your family would . . . er . . . want to see me."

He looked puzzled.

"After what happened at Commonwood House."

"What happened there had nothing to do with you. And what if it had?"

"The doctor was my uncle. It might be considered better to avoid people connected with such unsavoury happenings."

"My dear Carmel, as if we should feel like that! In any case, the whole business is over. It's years back."

"Do you think people would know me? People living around, I mean?"

"I shouldn't think so. You were only a child when it happened. Oh, we are back to this miserable subject again. Listen. It's over. It's best forgotten. You're letting this affair obsess you. It's all over. It's in the past." He spoke vehemently. "There is nothing anyone can do to change what happened."

"Of course you are right, Lucian. I should love to come. It would be so nice to see Camilla again."

"What about the week after next?"

"That would suit me very well."

"We'll say then. I'll write to you and confirm."

And so it was settled.

I went back in a state of pleasurable excitement. I remembered how I had lost my pendant and Lucian had had it repaired. I still had the pendant. When I arrived back at the house I took it from its box and held it in my hands, while my thoughts went back over the years to that day which was really when I had first met Lucian.

I was smiling as I put it back into the box, which was playing "God Save the Queen."

The Grange looked less formidable than it had in my childhood. It was very impressive, nonetheless, with its grey stone towers and battlemented gateway.

Lucian, who had been at the station with a pony and trap, greeted me warmly.

"I have been ridiculously scared that something would happen to prevent your coming."

"Oh no. I was determined to."

"It's good to see you. Camilla was delighted when she heard you were coming."

It was certainly a warm welcome. We went under the gateway. I could see the lawn where we had had tea on that first occasion; and there was Camilla, hardly recognisable as the girl I had known. She was rather plump and obviously pleased with the way life had gone for her.

She gripped both my hands.

"I couldn't believe it when Lucian said he'd found you. Isn't it exciting that you've come back!"

I was taken into the hall. I remembered it so well—arriving for tea, feeling rather nervous, the outsider until Lucian appeared and made me feel I wasn't. How I had adored him in those days!

"Better come straight up to my mother," said Lucian. "She is so eager to see you."

I could scarcely believe it. Lady Crompton had shown no interest in me in the old days.

I was taken into a room which they called the solarium because it had numerous windows which caught all the available sun. Lady Crompton was seated in a chair near the windows and, with Lucian on one side and Camilla on the other, I was taken over to her.

She held out a hand and I took it.

"How nice to see you, my dear," she said. "I have heard about your meeting with Lucian. I was most interested. I hear you have come from Australia. You must tell us all about it. Camilla, bring a chair so that Carmel can sit near me. My hearing is not very good nowadays and my rheumatism is crippling. And how are you? You look well."

I noticed that she had aged more than the years warranted. She had lost her husband and then there had been the death of her daughter-in-law, Lucian's wife. That must have been a sorrow to her.

"Shall I ring for tea now, Mother?" asked Camilla.

"Please do, dear." She turned to me. "And you are on a visit from Australia?"

We talked about Australia and how, coming over on the ship, the friend with whom I had been travelling had met her fiancé and was shortly to be married.

Then the tea came and was served.

"There have been so many changes," said Lady Crompton. "I was so sorry to hear about your father. Lucian told me. Your father was a charming man. He came here on one occasion. I remember him well. So sad. I suppose Camilla has told you that she has now left us, and of her adorable little Jeremy?"

"We've hardly had time yet, Mother," said Camilla. "Lucian said you were so eager to meet Carmel that we brought her straight up to you."

Lady Crompton talked dotingly of her grandson Jeremy and expressed her regrets that Camilla had not brought him with her.

"It's only for the weekend, Mother," said Camilla. "And Nanny is so capable and she doesn't like Jeremy travelling too much. She says it's upsetting, and it *is* only for the weekend. I came just to see Carmel."

I was expecting Lady Crompton to mention her granddaughter at this stage but, to my surprise, nothing was said of the child. I supposed that I should make her acquaintance during the weekend.

After tea, Camilla showed me to my room.

"It's on the second floor," she said. "Quite a nice view."

She opened a door and I saw a large room in which was a four-poster bed with heavy drapes matching the bed coverings.

"It's charming," I said.

"A touch of other times," said Camilla. "I'm afraid that's how things are at The Grange."

"Well, it's an ancient house with all its traditions," I said. "I think this is delightful."

"As long as the past doesn't intrude too much. My house is modern. It's in the Midlands. Geoff is in pottery . . . rather a sore point with my mother. She would have liked a duke, of course. But she adores Jeremy and, as soon as he put in an appearance, my mother was reconciled."

"It must be a great joy to her to have grandchildren. And you both have given her one."

"Oh yes," she said. "My Jeremy is quite adorable."

"And the little girl?" I asked.

"Bridget . . . of course. She will be more than two now."

"It must have been terrible when . . ."

"You mean her mother? Well, yes, of course." She glanced out of the window. "Look. That's where we used to have tea on the lawn. You were there sometimes. Do you ever hear of Estella and Henry . . . and the other one . . . the one who was rather simple?"

"Adeline. No, I have never heard of them since."

She looked at me gravely. "It was an awful business," she said. "They just disappeared . . . you with the others. Oh well, it's all so long ago. I'll leave you to hang up your things. What would you like to do before dinner? We dine at eight. I expect Lucian has something in view for you. He's ever so pleased that you agreed to come."

It was an unforgettable weekend I spent at The Grange. I was very gratified to be accepted so hospitably by Lady Crompton. Camilla was very friendly, and I could not have had a more attentive host than Lucian.

He and I rode a good deal together, and I saw more of the country than I ever had when I lived there.

On Saturday we lunched at a quaint old inn he had discovered. We laughed a great deal and I began to feel that I had imagined that melancholy I thought I had detected in him when we met at Easentree. He was the Lucian I would have expected him to be. He talked about the Grange estate and some of the people who worked on it, and I had stories of my own to tell of Australia, Elsie and the Formans.

This was catching up with the past.

I had not yet seen his daughter, although I had heard a great deal about Camilla's son, who was not even here. I began to think there was something odd about this reticence, but I did learn something during my stay.

It was late in the afternoon. I had returned to The Grange after a very pleasant time with Lucian. I was looking out of my window when I saw Camilla coming across the lawn. She saw me and waved.

"It's pleasant out here," she called. "Why don't you come down, if you're not doing anything special?"

I went down and we sat on one of the seats which had been placed under a tree.

"Did you have a good day?" she asked.

"Very pleasant. We went to The Bluff King Hal. Do you know it?"

"Oh yes. It's one of Lucian's favourites. I guessed he'd want to show you that."

"Camilla," I said, "what about little Bridget? That is her name, isn't it?"

"Oh, she's up in the nursery with Jemima Cray."

"Is that the nurse?"

"Well, yes. She looks after her."

"I haven't seen her. I wondered . . ."

"Do you want to see her?"

"I'd like to."

"We didn't think . . . you see, Jemima Cray . . . she's a bit of a martinet."

"Oh?"

"It's rather difficult to explain. Lucian's marriage . . . it wasn't very successful. I think it might have been better without Jemima Cray."

"Who is Jemima Cray?"

"She was a maid . . . onetime nurse to Laura. Laura was Lucian's wife. It was a hasty marriage. I was already married myself at that time, so I wasn't here much. It was about three years ago. I never got to know Laura very well. And almost immediately she was going to have Bridget. She was often ailing, I think. I always had the impression that Lucian had rushed into it. And then she died. Jemima seems to blame Lucian for that. Anyway, if you would like to see Bridget, I'll take you up. I think Jemima often goes out at this time. There's a nursery maid . . . a girl from the village. She will be there."

Camilla's rather casual treatment of the matter somehow made me feel that it was more mysterious than ever.

We climbed to the top of the house and entered what was a very traditional nursery. There was the usual big cupboard and a rocking horse in one corner and a board and easel in another. The young nursery maid was seated in a chair, and on the floor, surrounded by bricks which were a sort of jigsaw puzzle, was a little girl.

"Oh, you're here," said Camilla. "I thought you would be. Miss Cray not back yet?"

"No, Miss Camilla, not yet."

"How is Miss Bridget?"

The child looked up at the sound of her name.

"Me," she said, smiling. "Me, me!"

"Hello, Bridget," said Camilla. "I've brought someone to see you."

Camilla picked her up and sat down with the child on her knee.

"Getting a big girl now, aren't you, Bridget?" said Camilla.

Bridget nodded.

"What time does Miss Cray return?" asked Camilla.

"Oh, I reckon she'll be another half hour, Miss. She usually is."

Camilla relaxed visibly. She glanced down at the floor.

"You haven't finished your picture yet, Bridget," she said.

The picture when completed, I saw, would be one of a horse. The head and the tail at the moment had yet to be placed in position. Bridget slipped from Camilla's lap and knelt by the bricks. She picked up the one with the tail and tried to fix it where the head should be.

I knelt beside her and took up the brick with the head and put it in.

Bridget crowed with delight when she saw it fitted. She put the tail in the proper place and then surveyed the finished picture with delight. Turning to me, she smiled and rocked on her heels and clapped her hands. I did the same, as she hunched her shoulders, laughing.

Then she stood up. Taking my hand, she led me over to the rocking horse, indicating that she wanted to mount. I lifted her up and settled her there. Then I gave the horse a little push. She laughed with delight as it began to rock.

"More, more!" she cried. So I stood there, pushing the rocking horse, looking at her fine silky hair and thinking: This is Lucian's child. She is delightful. Why does he never speak of her?

And, as I stood there, pushing the horse, I sensed that something had happened. Turning, I saw that a woman had come into the room.

She was regarding me with intense disapproval. She was tall and thin, with small, closely-set eyes. There was something repellent about her, which was not only due to the annoyance that was directed against me.

The nursery maid seemed to have shrunk. She looked as though she had been caught in an act of treachery.

Then Bridget called out, "Look, Mima, look. More, more."

The woman strode to the rocking horse.

"Too high, pet," she said. "You must only go high when Jemima is here."

"It was all right," I said, rather piqued. "I was watching her."

Camilla said to me, "This is Jemima Cray. She looks after Bridget."

"How do you do?" I said coolly.

"Jemima," said Camilla, "Miss Sinclair wanted to meet Bridget. They seem to get on very well together."

"It's just that I don't like her excited before bedtime. There'll be nightmares."

"I don't think there'll be any trouble," I could not help saying. "I think she enjoyed the ride."

"And I think we should be going," said Camilla.

When we were downstairs, I said to Camilla, "What an extraordinary woman! She was very unpleasant."

"That's Jemima Cray. She is like that where Bridget is concerned."

"She seemed to take a lot on herself. What sort of position does she have here?"

"She's a sort of nanny, I suppose."

"She behaves as though she is mistress of the house."

"She would reckon she is of the nursery quarters."

"But surely Lady Crompton doesn't allow that?"

"My mother doesn't have anything to do with the nursery."

"But Bridget is her grandchild!"

Camilla was silent for a moment or two. Then she said, "It is all rather unusual . . . the whole setup. It was a great pity. I cannot understand Lucian. It was so unlike him. He's usually so . . . well . . . in command of everything."

"It certainly seems strange," I said. "Bridget is a lovely little girl, and yet it seems as though she is shut away . . . with that rather disagreeable woman."

"She is not disagreeable to Bridget. She dotes on her and the child loves Jemima." She hesitated again. "The fact is, it was not a very satisfactory marriage. No one was more aware of that than Lucian . . . it changed him. You know how full of life he used to be when he was young. And then . . . this happened. It was so sudden. He married her and she was going to have a child. She didn't want it. Actually, I think she was badly scared. She brought Jemima Cray with her when she came. She was one of those nannies who, when they are too old to nanny, become a sort of confidante/maid. They make themselves into guardian angels. They're jealous and they hate anyone who comes near their little darling. When Laura died, she transferred her fixation to Bridget. She hates us all, particularly Lucian. She behaves as though she thinks we murdered the girl."

"Why on earth do you keep her?"

"That's what I've said to my mother a hundred times. She said

that Laura promised Jemima that she should look after the child
and be to her what she had been to her mother. Deathbed scene,
that sort of dramatic stuff. She was a rather hysterical person,
Laura. One of those weak, clinging people who have to be obeyed
because if they are not they faint or die and come back to haunt
you for the rest of your life."

"But surely Lucian . . . ?"

"There's nothing Lucian wants so much as to forget what a fool
he was to marry the woman. I suppose Bridget reminds him of
that. So Jemima is up there, and we don't see very much of them."

"How very odd!"

"Lots of people are odd, you know. Sometimes it seems to me
that it is natural to be so. But this works. Jemima is very efficient
and no one could look after Bridget more carefully. She's a dragon
breathing fire if anyone tries to harm her little one. I expect it will
all sort itself out in due course."

I lay sleepless in my four-poster that night, wondering about the
marriage of Lucian and Laura. Camilla had implied that she had
been a poor creature in the hands of the fire-breathing Jemima.
Then why had he married her? One could not imagine Lucian's
being a weakling, drawn into a situation against his will.

That woman Jemima had given me an uneasy feeling. What had
Camilla said? "She acts as though she thinks we murdered the
girl." Who? Lucian?

There was something mysterious about the whole affair. I may
have been right when, on our first meeting at the roadside, I had
sensed that there was something which disturbed him. He had
changed. Well, a marriage like that was enough to change anyone.
I longed to know his true feelings about his marriage, about the
child. This engendered a certain tenderness in me. In the past, he
had seemed so strong and, in my childish mind, invincible. Now he
was vulnerable and I had been right when I thought something had
happened to change him.

I longed to know his true feelings.

Perhaps that was why I kept him constantly in my thoughts.

The weeks were passing and I was still with the Hysons. I could
not help feeling guilty for staying so long, but when I suggested
leaving, there were protests from Gertie in which Aunt Beatrice
and Uncle Harold joined.

"It wouldn't be the same without you, dear," said Aunt Beatrice, and Gertie added, "I need you. There is the house to think of and then there'll be all the preparations for the wedding. Of course you can't go into some hateful little hotel."

I had no wish to go. I found I was feeling much better than I had thought ever possible. However great one's grief, it must fade with time, and what was happening in the present must impress itself over the past. And a great deal was happening. Life was becoming interesting. Even Gertie, absorbed as she was in her exciting prospects, had time to consider mine. She was very amused and talked about two strings to my bow . . . no, three, when you considered poor old James, digging for opals in the Outback.

She had wanted to hear all about the visit to The Grange. I told her something, omitting the existence of Bridget and the strange Jemima Cray. That would have titillated her imagination too far, and I could imagine the wild melodrama she would have indulged in.

She was particularly interested in Lucian, who, to her, represented the romantic hero. The noble doctor Lawrence Emmerson, though, was not forgotten. He would make a good, though unexciting husband, she decided, and I should be well looked after by Miss Dorothy; everything would be done for my own good whether I liked it or not, but it would be the "right thing" for me.

There was another alternative. I could go back to Australia and marry James, with the choice of being an opal millionairess or spending the rest of my life in a tent in the opal fields, which Gertie feared might be the more likely.

"Look what could be yours!" she cried. "Take your pick."

I laughed at her. "The only one which could be open to me is the opal fields. And it would not surprise me if James had found himself a wife by now."

She sighed and put on one of her worldly-wise expressions—the experienced woman advising the innocent.

Whatever happened, I should hate to lose Gertie. We had been friends so long.

I paid several visits to the Emmerson cottage. I was becoming more and more friendly with Dorothy. She was a lively companion, interested in most subjects, and especially in art and music. Now and then she had tickets for some concert or art exhibition and, if Lawrence was working, she and I would go together.

Then there were visits to The Grange, and I was finding my time fully occupied.

Gertie and Aunt Beatrice had found the house, and furnishings and wedding plans had to be discussed. Gertie had written to her parents, telling them that she and Bernard would try to get out to Australia in two years' time.

"Perhaps you would come with us," she said to me.

With so much innuendo in the Kensington house, it would be impossible for me not to wonder what were the intentions of my two men friends towards me.

Dorothy's conversation rather led me to believe that she thought it was time Lawrence married and, if that were so, I was sure that she considered me as likely to be as worthy of him as anyone she could find. And if she thought it was right, Lawrence would be made to think so too.

Perhaps that was not fair to Lawrence. Lawrence was absorbed in his work and he naturally left certain decisions to Dorothy. But marriage would be too important for that, and he himself would be the one to decide. His sister might choose his food and the material for a suit, but his wife was a different matter.

He was always rather tender to me. I think he still saw me as the little girl lost in an alien city. He did enjoy my company, and he liked to talk to me about his work and his aspirations. He was entirely dedicated. Life with him would be predictable, although, of course, one could never be sure what would happen to anyone. Marriage to Lawrence Emmerson and a *ménage à trois* including my very good friend his sister could be as comfortable a life as one could hope for.

Perhaps I should have been ready to accept it—if it were not for Lucian.

I was almost certain of Lucian's feelings towards me, and I believed that one day, at the appropriate moment, when he had had a little more time to consider the matter, he would ask me to marry him. I knew he was fond of me. Sometimes his hand would linger on my shoulder with a certain longing. Yes, he was attracted to me. But I could not understand him as I did Lawrence. He could be very lighthearted. During those weekends at The Grange I grew to know him very well. He could be witty, amusing and fun to be with. I liked to ride round the estate with him and see the respect shown to him by the tenants. I could not imagine Lucian's being dependent upon a sister. Camilla, of course, was not the type to domineer. For one thing, she was too busy with her own life.

So I thought often of Lawrence, but Lucian was constantly in my mind.

I had received two letters from Australia—one from Elsie, the other from James. Elsie wrote:

My dear Carmel,

How are you getting on over there? You should have seen the excitement here when we heard of Gertie's engagement! Her mother says she sounds very happy in her letters. I read yours to them and all round it seems as though Gertie has done very well.

Poor Mr. and Mrs. Forman! Happy as they are for Gertie, they're a little sad. Well, naturally. This was supposed to be a holiday, and it looks as though she has gone for good. She does say that she and her husband will make a trip over to see the family, and that's a bit of a comfort to them. And now James has gone off prospecting, or whatever they call it. Well, that's how life goes, and thank goodness they've got over that terrible disaster.

Fancy that Dr. Emmerson being on the ship! He sounds very nice, and it's good that his sister and you have become such good friends. Well, I must say, it all seems to have turned out very well for you two girls. You sound so much better, dear. No sense in being downhearted. I knew a complete change was what you wanted. Gertie says that you are really having a good time.

Things here are much the same. It is grand having Joe around. He fits in here so well. He's sitting out in the garden now, waiting for me to join him. The harbour looks just the same as it did the day you came in . . . that very first time. I shall always remember that day. You can picture it all. The kookaburras have been noisy today. You always liked them, didn't you? You wondered whatever they were laughing about when you first heard them.

Well, dear, go on enjoying yourself. It's what you need. We miss you, and when you come back, there'll be a big welcome

for you. *You* must decide, and remember first of all, be happy!
It's what Toby would have wanted and it's what I want too.

With lots and lots of love from Joe and me,
ELSIE

I sat for a few minutes, thinking of her and how fortunate I was
when Toby took me to her.

Then I opened James's letter:

My dear Carmel,

How are you getting on? There's a lot of excitement here
about Gertie's wedding. Too bad the family won't be there. This
fellow she is marrying seems to me a gift from Heaven,
according to her. Hope it's true.

Well, I went off as I said I would. We got things in order on
the property and my father knew I would never be satisfied until
I'd had my try, and he said it would be all right for me to go.

So here I am. I can't tell you how exciting it is! You would
like it. There's something in the air. All these men, some with
their families. They talk of nothing but opals. That's on the rare
occasions when they are not working, which they are doing
most of the time.

It can be pretty hot here. It's low gullies and bush and the
mosquitoes can be a pest—and as for the flies! Well, you can
imagine. There's lots of fossicking going on but that's the
amateurs. It's fascinating and can be cruelly disappointing.
Sometimes you think you've found something really fine and it
turns out to be pure potch. That means rubbish.

It's jolly hard work. We live in a sort of shanty town—tents,
huts—and water is hard to come by. Some say it's as precious as
opals. That'll give you an idea. Saturday nights are fun. That's
when we dance, sing and swap yarns—the stories of our lives—
all highly dramatised, as you can imagine. Last Saturday we
roasted a pig and made dampers to go with it. It's a hard life
but worth it, especially for those moments when you hit on the
real stuff.

I've had two reasonably good finds, and I'm a beginner as yet,
so it is not bad.

By the way, you'll be interested to hear this. Do you
remember that old sundowner? He turned up again. Not to
work. That's not his line. But just to do a bit of fossicking and

prowl round and see if there was anything he could lay his hands on. He was found dead outside the camp, looking as if he'd been in a fight.

It was a bit awkward for a time. You see, some of them had heard what he had done to our property, and they all looked to me. That seemed natural enough. They reckoned I wouldn't have let him get away with what he did to my family.

It's a bit of a mystery. I reckon one of the men found him stealing and finished him off. We've got some here, as you can imagine, who wouldn't think twice about it. However, there he was, just outside the camp—dead.

A lot of questions were asked, and of course I knew they were looking at me. But the fellow had made himself unpopular in other quarters. They haven't found out who did it, but they've dropped enquiries now. They found something on him—little bits of opal—but nobody's claimed them. It was obvious that the rogue had stolen them. Well, he got what was coming to him. Rough justice, really.

Well, that's life out here. In the raw, you might say. But just imagine the joy of finding that stone tucked away in some crack or cavity. Isn't it a marvel that a mixture of sand and water— and a few other elements—can crystallise into a thing of such beauty? Forgive me. I'm apt to run on when I get onto this subject.

Now to the serious business. Carmel, I am waiting for you to come back. I'm going to find that precious stone and it's going to make our future—yours and mine. We'll have a wonderful life. I shall expiate my sin of leaving you forlorn in wicked Suez and expunge myself of guilt forevermore. How's that for a dramatic declaration?

I know that you and I were meant for each other. I only have to find that stone, the one which will astonish the world and make our fortune. Then I shall wait no longer. I shall pack up my tools and board the first ship for home.

Write to me soon.

Your loving millionaire-to-be,

JAMES

I let the letter fall from my hands. It brought him back so vividly. Dear James! I wondered if he would find his dream. And if he came back . . . ? There was something about James which suggested that, once he had made up his mind, he would not lightly relinquish his desire. He was obviously enduring a life of hardship now.

Then I thought of the sundowner, of James's anger when he discovered that the man had returned to the property, and with what rage he had ordered him off. And then the outcome.

Suppose when that man came to the camp James had discovered him there? And the man had died. He had an evil reputation. I knew how great James's wrath would have been.

Could it be possible? Could he have fought with the man?

Had James told me all?

And, for some reason, I found I was thinking of Lucian.

I was spending the weekend at the Emmersons' cottage. Dorothy and I had travelled down together on the Friday afternoon.

"How I look forward to these weekends," she said. "Sometimes I think I enjoy the place more because I don't see it as often as I should like."

"You couldn't possibly be here all the time, I suppose?"

"There's Lawrence's work."

"He'd be well-looked-after in Town. I suppose you could spend a little more time here."

"I know that he's well-looked-after, but I like to be there to make sure."

I smiled at her affectionately. "And Lawrence certainly appreciates that."

She was a little thoughtful. "He is the best man in the world. Well, there is no need for me to tell *you* that."

Sometimes I wondered what she would have felt if Lawrence married. It would change her position considerably. On the other hand, if she considered it was for his good, she would waive all other considerations, I was sure. But I did believe that she had considered me for the role and I fancied I detected an expectancy in her that weekend. I even wondered whether there was a certain telepathy between the brother and sister, or even whether they had discussed the matter—though I thought that hardly likely.

We had said we would go for a ride and have lunch out.

"I expect he wants to show you another of his pet inns," said Dorothy.

She was asked to accompany us but said she had not the time. She had promised to look out some jumble for the church sale, and she wanted to take it over to Mrs. Wantage and with her put a price on some of the goods they already had.

So Lawrence and I set out. We went to our favourite spot—the ruined castle—and there we tethered our horses and climbed the slope to the ruined battlements.

Lawrence did not hesitate and, when we had seated ourselves, came straight to the point.

"Carmel, I know I am some years older than you, but I think you are quite fond of me—and Dorothy as well, of course."

He pulled up a blade of grass and, studying it, went on: "Well, we get along, don't we, the three of us? These weekends have been very happy for me. I don't think I have ever been so happy before. I love you. I know that it is not very long since we caught up with each other, but there was that incident."

I was not surprised, of course, but I was a little at a loss.

I should have been prepared. I hesitated, and he continued: "We could be married soon . . . just as soon as you are ready. We have the London place and this to step into."

"Lawrence," I said quickly, "I don't think I want to be married . . . not just yet. Everything seems to have happened so quickly since I came home."

"Of course. I understand that. You need time. Of course you do. Well, there is no great hurry. I don't want you to go back to Australia and forget all about us."

"I shan't do that, I assure you. It is just that I should like to go on as we are . . . for a time."

"Then we shall. Why not? It's very pleasant. Then the idea is not too absurd to you? My age . . . ?"

"Oh, Lawrence," I cried, "that would not matter in the least. It's not so much, after all. It is just that I am . . . unready."

"I understand. I feel that I have known you for a long time. Your father and I were good friends . . . long before I met you. He talked about you a great deal. He was very proud of his daughter. Then we met and we had our little adventure. You see, it doesn't seem such a short acquaintance to me."

"You and Dorothy have been so good to me. I can't tell you how much you have both done for me. I was very wretched, and you were a comfort on the ship. Then, having me here so often and being my very good friends. . . ."

He took my hand and pressed it. "You are getting over it gradually. I know you never will . . . quite . . . but it has faded a little, hasn't it? The grief is not quite so intense. . . ."

"I have been so fortunate in my friends: Elsie, Gertie, the Hysons . . . you and Dorothy."

"It is a great joy to us that we have been able to help. We both love you dearly, Carmel."

"Thank you, Lawrence," I said. "And I love you both. But you see . . . marriage . . . it's such an undertaking. It is something I should have to think about. I am so unsure . . ."

"Of course, of course. Let us put it aside for the moment. I shall ask you again when you have had time to discover how you really feel."

He took my hand and helped me to rise and, as I stood beside him, he kissed my cheek.

"Oh, Lawrence," I said, "thank you. You are so good and kind. I know I could be happy with you . . . and Dorothy . . . but . . ."

"Of course, I understand."

He took my arm and we went to the horses.

We lunched in a quaint old inn, the origins of which he described enthusiastically, and then we rode back.

Dorothy was home, waiting for us, and I was sure she knew that he had asked me. I had the impression that she was waiting for an announcement and was disappointed when it was not made.

Gertie's wedding preparations were going on apace.

Between them, she and Aunt Beatrice had found the house and were now in the process of furnishing it. It was about ten minutes' walk from the Hyson establishment, situated in a tree-lined street, and had a small but pleasant garden and that essential nursery.

I was often called upon to help choose some piece of furniture or to give my opinion on some new plan, and, I must say, I was caught up in the general excitement.

I had thought a great deal about Lawrence's proposal. I smiled to recall it. I could remember every word. It was just what I would have expected it to be—dignified, gallant—not exactly what one would call passionate. It was characteristic of Lawrence.

I did think about it very seriously. I was sure that I did not want to go back to Australia. My life was not there among the opal fields of Lightning Ridge or some such place. Much as I loved Elsie, I had always subconsciously felt that England was home. If Toby had been there, it would not have mattered where I was. That would have been where I wanted to be. Perhaps that was an indication. I wanted to be where the people I loved most were. If I had loved James enough to marry him, it would not have mattered where I lived.

There came an invitation to The Grange, and I felt that excitement which this never failed to bring.

Lucian continued to puzzle me, although I saw less of that strange, brooding mood which came to him very briefly from time to time. There was an added interest now. I had made a habit of going to see Bridget when I was there. She always seemed pleased to see me. Jemima Cray did not, however, share the child's enthusiasm. But sometimes I would find Bridget in the garden, alone with Mary, the nursery maid. Then I would spend some time with her. Mary seemed almost conspiratorial at such times, which bothered me a little. It seemed such an odd situation. Why had I not met the child, as I surely should have done, in normal circumstances? Bridget herself was normal enough. Mary was always watchful during these sessions in the grounds, and I knew it was because she was afraid that Jemima Cray would suddenly descend upon us.

So I happily packed my bag and set forth, full of that expectation which I always felt at the prospect of a visit to The Grange.

Lucian met me at the station as usual, and we set off in high spirits.

Lady Crompton now greeted me with even more friendliness than she had shown when I first appeared. I think she was rather pleased to have a visitor whom she did not have to treat with too much ceremony. She told me at great length about her rheumatism and how it prevented her from doing as much as she had in the past. She enjoyed that topic, and I was a good listener. Then she liked to hear about Australia and the various places round the world which I had visited.

Lucian was pleased and amused by her pleasure in my company.

"My mother does not get on so well with everybody," he commented with a grin.

Camilla had been there once or twice, and she and I had become friends. She told me how life at The Grange had changed in the last years.

"There used to be a great deal of entertaining when my father was alive," she said. "Lucian doesn't seem to have the same taste for it. In fact, everything seemed to change when he married."

On the Saturday, Lucian and I went riding. He had several calls to make round the estate and I fancied he liked me to go with him. I was beginning to know some of the workers and tenants, which I found interesting.

I was not sure whether I imagined it or whether I really did intercept some significant looks. People often began speculating when they saw a man and a woman together enjoying each other's company. Did some of these people wonder whether I should be the next Lady Crompton, or was I thinking that, because of James and Lawrence, every man who showed me friendship was thinking of asking me to marry him? People are inclined to imagine that when a young man is unmarried he must be in need of a wife. That was by no means a certainty, and when one has had an unsatisfactory experience, there would be a certain wariness at the prospect of repeating it.

I had a notion that that was how Lucian felt, and I must confess that I found those sly looks a little disconcerting.

We had returned to The Grange. Lucian leapt down from his horse to assist me to dismount. He looked up at me and smiled as he took both my hands.

There was a decided pause, and I could not quite interpret the expression in his eyes, but it was very warm.

He said, "I can't tell you how glad I am that you came back, Carmel."

"So am I," I answered.

I heard a footstep close at hand and, looking beyond Lucian, I saw Jemima Cray walking close to the stable on her way to the house.

Just before I went to dinner that evening, I paid a visit to the nursery to see Bridget.

When I entered the room she ran to me and clasped my knees. It was an endearing habit she had. Then she wanted me to sit on the floor with her and form the bricks to make a picture. There were pigs and oxen, sheep and cows; she was very fond of these picture puzzles. She was an enchanting child. I wondered afresh why Lucian never mentioned her. Well, she had the enigmatic Jemima Cray, whom she obviously loved, and there was no doubt of Jemima's devotion to her.

While we sat there, Jemima appeared. I knew she would find some excuse to separate me from Bridget. She definitely did not like my friendship with the child.

To my surprise, she said quite affably, "Good afternoon, Miss Sinclair. I wonder if I could have a word with you?"

"But of course," I replied.

"Mary, take Miss Bridget into her bedroom. She can have her milk there. You can get it for her. Not too hot, mind."

Mary looked at the clock on the wall. Like her, I knew the nursery ritual. It was too soon for Bridget's milk.

"Do as you are told," said Jemima in a voice which must be obeyed, and Mary prepared to carry out the order.

Bridget protested. "No," she said. "No, no."

"Now, pet," said Jemima in gentler tones, "you go with Mary. You're going to have some nice milk."

Bridget was taken out, still protesting, and I was flattered by her reluctance to leave, but all the same eager to hear what Jemima had to say.

"Well, Miss Sinclair," she said as soon as we were alone, "I'd like a word in your ear. I only speak because I think it's right and proper that you should not be in the dark."

"What is it?" I asked.

"Things are not always what they seem, you know."

"Indeed, I know that."

She put her face close to mine, assuming an air of wisdom. Her eyes were small and too closely set together. I thought she looked like a witch.

"I think you are a good, respectable young lady and you should not be deceived."

"It is the last thing I want," I said. "I should like to be enlightened in whatever way you think."

She nodded. "There is one who should be here now, and would be . . . but for what others did to her. If anyone was thinking of taking her place, I reckon they ought to think twice before they took that step."

I felt myself flushing, and I said, "I don't understand what you are implying, Miss Cray."

"I think you do," she said severely. "All I am trying to do is drop a word in your ear. It's for your good. She married into this place and, before a year was out, she was dead—and before she came here she was a merry, lighthearted little thing."

"You are referring to . . . ?"

"My Miss Laura, that's who."

"I understood she died giving birth to Bridget."

"Poor mite. She never ought to have been put through it. He knew that . . . and yet he made her. There had to be a child . . . a son, I suppose. The family and all that nonsense. She knew it was dangerous. I knew . . . but it had to be. It was pitiful to see her. Frightened, she was. She said to me, 'Jemima, you'll always stay and look after my baby when I'm gone? You'll look after my baby, just as you've looked after me.' And I swore I would. Oh, it was wicked. It was cruel."

I said, "It was very sad that she died, but it does happen sometimes."

Her face hardened. "There's some as would say it was murder," she said.

"Miss Cray!" I said. "You must not make such insinuations. It's quite wrong. It is natural for people to have children when they marry."

"He knew, just as she knew . . . but it had to be. Oh, he knew well enough . . . and I reckon that's the same sort of thing as murder. And nothing will make me change my mind. That's the sort he is. And people should know it."

She rose and in a matter-of-fact voice went on: "Well, I must go and see to Bridget. You can't trust that Mary with much."

She turned away. I called after her.

"Come back, Miss Cray. I want to talk to you."

She was at the door. She turned and said, "I've said my piece. I know what happened. I saw it all. I know just how it was."

Her face was distorted with venom and hatred, and I knew it was directed against Lucian.

I said to myself: She's mad. But I was very shaken.

———

The memory of Jemima stayed with me. I found it hard to stop thinking of what she had said and the expression in her face when she had talked of murder.

She was warning me. She had seen me with Lucian in the stables. Murder, she had said. She was accusing Lucian of that because his wife had died in childbirth. She meant, do not become involved with him. He knew Laura was unfit to bear a child and yet he insisted. Such a man is capable of anything . . . murder of any kind . . . to achieve his ends.

I thought again: The woman must be mad. Indeed, there was a hint of fanaticism in her eyes when she talked of Laura's death.

Why did she stay? Because of this vow she had made to Laura . . . the wife who had known she faced death. It all seemed very melodramatic, and I did not believe a word of it. Jemima was a highly emotional woman. She had given all her devotion to the girl whom she had looked after, and when that girl had died, she had to blame someone, so she blamed Lucian. I was almost a stranger to her, but she thought that Lucian might ask me to marry him, and she was warning me, or pretending to. And now she was jealous of my friendship with her charge. She did not want me here.

I suppose there was a certain amount of reason in that.

Murder, she had said. It was pure nonsense. But she had used the word and that was very upsetting.

I decided to take the first opportunity of talking to Lucian. It came next morning as he was showing me something in the garden.

I said, "Lucian, you never talk much about Bridget. She's such a dear little girl. I have made her acquaintance and we get on quite well."

"I don't know much about children."

"She seems to spend most of her time with that nurse."

"Most children spend a lot of time with their nurses."

"But it seems as though you . . . and Lady Crompton . . . are hardly aware of her existence."

"Does it?" he said. "I expect I have been remiss. One doesn't talk about one's failures. It was all rather hasty. That marriage, I mean. A mistake from the first. The child was born and Laura died. That's really all there is to it. It wouldn't have been very satisfactory, even if that hadn't happened."

"If Bridget had been a boy . . ." I began.

His face darkened slightly. "Perhaps it is as well . . . It's all over now. It was a mistake. I have made a few in my life, but that was the greatest. I meant to tell you about it, but somehow I could not bring myself to. It's a depressing subject."

"She was very young to die."

"She was eighteen. It all happened so quickly. She did not like The Grange. She said it was old and full of ghosts and shadows and the ghosts didn't want her. It was so different from everything she was used to. Her father made a great deal of money out of coal. She couldn't understand the customs of a family like mine. And then there was the child. She was terrified of having it. She seemed to know she was going to die. She lived in fear of death, and that woman never left her."

"You mean Jemima Cray?"

He nodded. "She was the only one who could calm her. It was a wretched time for us all."

"The little girl is charming. I should have thought she would be a comfort to you and Lady Crompton."

"That woman was always there."

"She is certainly rather odd."

"She is good with the child. She would do anything for her."

"Have you ever thought of replacing her?"

He lifted his shoulders. "We've wanted to, of course. But there's some promise. In the circumstances, the easiest thing is to let her remain here. So it seems Jemima Cray is a fixture. Oh, let's talk about something pleasant! You must come down again soon."

I said, "This visit is not yet over."

"No, but I can't tell you how much I enjoy them. My mother is saying that we must entertain more. She is not well enough to do a great deal, but she did enjoy it in the old days. We have some interesting characters round about—the usual mixture of traditional country types and the occasional eccentric. I can't tell you how we look forward to your coming—my mother as well as myself."

"And you will come up to Town for the wedding, won't you?"

"I must, of course."

And I went on thinking of Jemima Cray.

Castle Folly

GERTIE WANTED Aunt Beatrice and Uncle Harold to give a dinner party.

"We'll have the Rowlands, Lawrence Emmerson and his *alter ego* Dorothy, you, myself and the romantic Lucian. I think it will be fun. You've had so much hospitality . . . all those weekends . . . and you're our responsibility. Soon we shall be cluttered with wedding obligations, so we'd better do it soon."

Aunt Beatrice was delighted, and then she was a little apprehensive.

"Shall we be grand enough?" she asked. "The Emmersons are all right, but what about that *Sir* Lucian?"

I assured her there was nothing to fear on that score.

It would have to be dinner, not lunch, said Gertie. Lunch was not quite the same. The Emmersons would be all right—they had their place close by—but what about Lucian? He lived in the country. They couldn't put him up for the night.

I said he would stay in a hotel. He did when he came to London for a brief period. We would invite him to the dinner party in any case.

The invitations were given and accepted. Lucian said he would stay at Walden's in Mayfair, as he had done on previous occasions. He had some business in London and he would arrange to do it at the same time. So it was all satisfactorily arranged.

Gertie was in ecstasy; she was over almost everything at this time. She was so delighted with life. It would not be long now before she was Mrs. Ragland. The house was almost ready and the future looked rosy. All she needed now was to see me in a similar state. Dear Gertie. She had been such a wonderful friend.

She and Aunt Beatrice talked constantly of the coming dinner party. What flowers should they have? The best china, used only on special occasions, was brought out; there was a higher gloss on the furniture than usual.

"Dorothy might notice," I said. "The others certainly won't."

The great day arrived. We had an aperitif in the drawing-room before dinner and in due course assembled at the dinner table.

Conversation was lively and ran smoothly. Lawrence told a few anecdotes about life in the hospital to which he was attached. Lucian talked animatedly of the estate and country life and the rest of us joined in. Even Uncle Harold had something to contribute, while Aunt Beatrice kept an alert eye on the food, so anxious was she that nothing should go wrong.

She need have had no qualms. Everything went according to plan, and I think the guests were so interested in the conversation that they would not have been aware of it if it had not.

We had left the table and had gone to the drawing-room for coffee when Dorothy started to talk about a book she had read.

"You would not suspect Dorothy of being interested in such gruesome subjects, would you?" said Lawrence. "But crime has always fascinated her. She wrote a book on the subject."

"It was inspired by the Jameson case," said Dorothy. "Do you remember it? It took place years ago. Martin Jameson married women for their money and then, when he had arranged for it all to come to him, he just disposed of them. The interesting thing was that he was such a charmer. No one believed he could commit such crimes, and he was able to operate with success for some time."

"The charm would equip him for the work he had decided to do, I imagine," said Lucian.

"But it was not exactly a pose. The man *was* kind. It turned out that he had helped lots of people. They came forward to testify for him. He was highly respected wherever he went. And all the time, he was seeking out these women with money, going through a form of marriage with them, then murdering them. Right up to the moment of his death, he was gentle and charming."

"There must have been some violence in him," said Lawrence. "And don't forget, he did it for the money."

"A murderer deserves to hang," said Bernard.

"I think Dorothy wanted to understand the man," explained Lawrence. "To discover what his thoughts were as he put aside his gentler instincts and became a killer."

"That's clear enough," put in Uncle Harold. "He wanted the money."

"And so he was hanged," said Gertie. "Anyone who kills someone deserves to hang." She looked at Bernard. "Especially husbands who kill their wives."

"I'm listening," said Bernard.

"I don't think you'd think what I've got would be worthwhile," retorted Gertie.

"Well," replied Bernard, "I shall have to look into it!"

Dorothy had no intention of allowing this kind of lovers' banter to intrude on a serious subject.

"It's interesting to study these cases," she said. "It gives one a certain understanding of people, and people are fascinating. There is this case I have just been reading about. A young girl was shot in a place called Cranley Wood. It is in Yorkshire. This was some years ago. There is a possibility that they hanged the wrong man."

Lucian leaned forward, listening. "I don't remember this case," he said.

"There was not a great deal of publicity about it. I think people thought the man who confessed sometime after was mad."

"Do tell us," said Lucian.

"I am sure Dorothy will," replied Lawrence. "She's on her favourite hobbyhorse."

"Murder is so interesting," said Gertie.

"Briefly, this is the case," began Dorothy. "Marion Jackson was the daughter of a farmer. She was engaged to marry Tom Eccles, also a farmer living in the neighbourhood. A small landowner, also in the district and known to be something of a lady's man, had been abroad, and when he came back a number of the local girls were fascinated by him, and it seems that Marion was one of those who fell under his spell. It is not a very unusual story. Marion was seduced by the philanderer and became pregnant. She made an attempt to pass off the child as Tom Eccles's. There was a scene in the woods between Marion and Tom which was overheard. Tom had discovered that the child was not his and made Marion confess who was in fact the father. That afternoon Marion was found in the woods, shot through the heart."

"The farmer fiancé did it," said Gertie. "I expect he was furious."

"Understandably," said Bernard.

"So it was thought," went on Dorothy. "There was an enquiry. There was nothing special about the shot. It was fired from an ordinary sort of gun. Tom Eccles had one, so did Marion's father and countless other people around the district."

"What about the philanderer?" asked Aunt Beatrice.

"He too, I daresay. Several people had heard the shot. Tom Eccles could not account for his whereabouts at that time. He had, however, been heard to say, 'I'll kill you for this' during the scene with Marion earlier on; and he was in a rather hysterical state at the time. The trial did not last long. It seemed certain that, overcome by an excess of jealousy, Tom Eccles had killed Marion Jackson. He was found guilty and hanged. That happened more than twenty years ago. You might say it was a perfectly commonplace crime, the sort of thing that has happened again and again."

"No crime is ordinary," suggested Uncle Harold.

Dorothy turned to him.

"You are right. That is why it is so fascinating to study these things. As I said, this happened a long time ago. A crime was committed and a man was hanged. Has it ever occurred to you that there might be other occasions when a person can be hanged for a crime he or she did not commit, although all the evidence may point to that person's guilt?"

Lucian said quietly, "It has."

Dorothy nodded at him approvingly. "This is what has interested me about this case. Five years ago . . . that is, fifteen years after Tom Eccles was hanged, a man wrote a letter to the press. He was on his deathbed, and for a long time, it seemed, he had been troubled by his conscience. It was just possible that he had been the murderer of Marion Jackson, although he had never known her—had never even seen her."

"Then how could he have been the murderer?" cried Gertie.

"It is very strange and yet . . . plausible. His name was David Crane. He was in those woods that day when Marion died. His hobby was pigeon shooting. His home was in Devonshire and he was on a walking holiday in Yorkshire, going wherever the fancy took him. Sometimes he'd stop at an inn; sometimes he would sleep out of doors if the weather was good enough. He'd fire a shot at a rabbit, pigeon or a hare when the fancy took him. It was a pigeon at this time. He missed and did not think much more about it, but when he realised that it was at that very spot where Marion had been killed, he began to consider.

"Some years later, he returned to the woods. He discovered that exact spot where Marion's body had been found, and it occurred to him that his shot may well have been the one which killed her. Tom Eccles's last words were: 'I swear to God I did not kill Marion.' David Crane could not forget it. He went back again to those woods. He encountered Tom Eccles's father and talked to him about the case. The old man was sure Tom had not committed the crime. He swore he was not in the woods at that time—but alas, he could not prove it. True, Tom possessed the kind of gun from which the shot had been fired, but so did hundreds of others. 'Tom would never have died with a lie on his lips,' declared the old man fervently, and that was when David Crane's conscience began to trouble him."

We were all listening intently now. Dorothy was on her favourite topic and she knew how to hold an audience.

Lucian said, "And this old man . . . what did he do about it?"

"He wrote the letter on his deathbed."

"He waited till then!"

"He would have reasoned that, if he had come forward, he could not have saved Tom Eccles."

"No," said Lucian firmly. "There was nothing he could have done."

"What a thing to have on one's conscience!" said Lawrence.

"I can understand his feelings," added Lucian. "I understand absolutely."

"Imagine," said Dorothy, "a normal sort of person having to ask himself, 'Did I kill someone?' "

"It must have worried him for years," said Lucian. "An innocent man hanged for what he had done."

"Exactly," went on Dorothy. "Poor man, he did not know how to act. He was afraid to come forward and accuse himself, and he would reason there was nothing he could do to save Tom Eccles."

"He was right. There was no point in bringing up the matter," suggested Lucian.

"Except, of course, that he would clear Tom Eccles's name," reasoned Dorothy.

"He was dead," said Lucian.

"There was his family," Lawrence put in. "For instance, the old father. People don't like to have murderers in the family, particularly one who has been hanged. People talk about these things. There's a slur."

"Well," said Dorothy, "he did nothing until he was on the point of death. Then he wrote that letter to the press. No doubt it cleared his conscience."

"After all," said Lawrence, "he couldn't be sure that he *had* fired the fatal shot."

"No. That was the point. It was just that he *might* have. No one will ever know."

"I suppose that sort of thing has happened before?" asked Lucian.

"It must have," replied Dorothy, "though I have never come across it."

"If it were so, it is a case of accidental killing."

"All very intriguing," added Lawrence. "You can see why Dorothy has this passion."

The discussion had sobered everyone and the mood had changed. I guessed we were all thinking about that poor young man who had been hanged for a murder he probably had not committed.

After the guests had gone, I sat in the drawing-room with Gertie and the Hysons.

"Well, Aunt Bee," Gertie was saying, "I think you can congratulate yourself on being a very successful hostess."

"I was rather dreading that Sir Lucian," replied Aunt Beatrice with a giggle, "but he turned out to be ever so easy."

"You had the right assortment of guests, you clever old thing," said Gertie. "Dorothy was good, wasn't she? She's a real entertainer."

"My word, wasn't that Sir Lucian interested in all that about the murder?" said Aunt Beatrice. "As much as any of us, I'd say."

A week after the dinner party, I was surprised to receive a letter from Lady Crompton:

Dear Carmel,

Lucian has to go away for a few days next week and I should be so pleased if you could come and stay with me. It is always pleasant to talk to you, and when Lucian is here, he does tend to monopolise you. I thought, if you were agreeable, we might have a quiet time together. I have so enjoyed your visits and, now that I am incapacitated, I do feel a little lonely. I should be so pleased if you could come.

Do not hesitate to say if it is inconvenient.

ISABEL CROMPTON

I was rather intrigued by the idea and wrote back at once, accepting.

Gertie was amused.

"This could mean one of two things," she prophesied. "Either you are going to be granted parental approval, or you will be told some ghastly secret which is designed to warn you to keep off the grass."

"Don't be so absurdly melodramatic," I retorted. "This is just a lonely old lady seeking a little diversion."

"Oh, isn't it fun! Life is so amusing."

"Particularly to people whose wedding day is looming!"

"Or for those who have a trio of suitors."

I was met at the station by one of the grooms and taken to The Grange, where I was warmly welcomed.

"Lucian was so pleased when he heard you were coming. He's very sorry not to be here. He was telling me about the delightful dinner party your friends gave. How I wished I could have been there!"

"It was interesting, and so good of the Hysons to give it for my friends."

"He was telling me about the doctor and his lively sister. They are very good friends of yours, I gather."

"Oh yes. The doctor was a friend of my father's, and then I met him on the ship again when I was coming over."

"Yes, Lucian has told me."

Later in the evening, she talked a little about Lucian's marriage.

"It was unfortunate. So unlike Lucian. This girl . . . she was not right for him at all. Of course, she was very pretty. I suppose he must have been carried away. Young men do such foolish things. I knew from the moment she came into the house that it would not be a good thing. I wish he could make a sensible marriage now. The name has been in the family for three hundred years. In a family like ours, one feels there are obligations."

"If Bridget had been a boy . . ." I said.

"I'm rather glad she's not. With a mother like that . . ."

"She seems a very bright and delightful child."

"Children can be delightful. No, I am glad she is a girl. I wouldn't have wanted that woman's child to have inherited. I did wonder whether she was Lucian's child, you know."

"What makes you think that?"

"I don't know. It was all so hurried and wrong from the start. I don't think he really cared for her. I imagined he was caught up in some way. It was a horrible time. I was most unhappy."

"Does it distress you to talk of it, Lady Crompton?"

"No, my dear child. I want you to know. He never really cared for her. There are some things I do not understand. There is something rather secretive about Lucian at times. He used not to be like that. He was such a frank sort of boy . . . if you know what I mean. So serene. He took everything in his stride. Now he has changed. All of a sudden he became . . . well . . . moody. I think introspective is the word . . . reflective . . . as though something worried him. I am so glad he enjoys your company."

"I'm glad to hear it. I enjoy his."

"And that friend of yours . . . the doctor . . . ?"

"Lawrence Emmerson?"

"The one with the clever sister. Lucian wondered about them. I'm not sure whether he likes them or not. The doctor is a bachelor, isn't he?"

"Yes."

"Attractive, presentable . . . dominated by his sister. Is that so?"

"Well, not really dominated. They are very fond of each other, and she looks after him. She gives herself entirely up to the task. She is a very strong-minded person. She would tell you what she thought ought to be done, and you'd find that she was right most of the time. She is very practical and really is a wonderful person."

"And they are obviously great friends of yours."

"Yes, very good friends."

"As friendly as Lucian and myself, I suppose?"

"Yes, I suppose so. It's difficult to make comparisons."

"Lucian is a good man, you know. That marriage was so wrong. That sort of thing has an effect on people. Nothing would please me more than to see him happy. He ought to be. He has a great capacity for happiness. But that wretched affair hangs over him. I'd like to see a complete break from the past. It is difficult, because there are always . . . consequences."

"Do you mean Bridget?"

"Not so much Bridget . . . that woman in the nursery."

"Jemima Cray."

She nodded. "While she's here, we shall never be able to put the past behind us. She's a constant reminder."

"I understand that, but this is your house. I suppose if you told her to go, she would have to do so."

"I would send her straight away and tell her to go, but Lucian won't hear of it."

"Why not?"

"Some promise she gave to Laura to stay. She holds that over us, though it isn't mentioned often. I have said to Lucian, 'Laura is dead. We care for the child. Why do we have to keep that woman here?' But she says it was Laura's wish, so the creature stays. I don't like her at all, but I suppose, because of this deathbed promise . . ."

"She is very fond of the child, and the child of her."

"I don't doubt that. All the same . . ." She put her hand over mine. "I think, my dear, that between us, you and I might do something about all this."

I was astonished, but she smiled at me serenely.

I knew then that, if Lucian asked me to marry him, I should have the wholehearted approval of Lady Crompton.

I spent the next morning in her company, but she made no further reference to Lucian's marriage. Instead, she showed me some of the tapestry work which she did before it became such a strain on her eyes.

In the afternoon her rheumatism was very painful and, apologising profusely, she told me she would have to retire to bed and rest. Could I amuse myself?

I said I could quite happily, and decided to take a walk.

It was inevitable that my footsteps should turn towards Commonwood House. It was the first time since my visits to The Grange that I had been out alone. Had I been, I should probably have found the impulse irresistible to take another look at the house. Now was my chance.

There it was—sad and derelict, yet so familiar. Mingling emotions rose in me at the sight of it.

Walk past it, I advised myself. What good will be achieved by going closer? It only saddened me. But when I approached, I found myself turning in at the gate. Just a quick look, I promised myself, and then I would hurry away.

As I walked up the drive, I could imagine that eyes watched me from the cracked windows of the old ruined house. Eyes of those who had once lived there in the past—Mrs. Marline, Miss Carson, the poor, sad doctor.

Go back, I told myself. What point is there? But I went on.

I approached the door. I saw the broken hinge. I stopped myself from pushing the door open and instead walked round the house. I noticed the damp on the walls, the smudges of dust on the windows. I wondered to whom it belonged now. Henry? Why did he leave it like this? Where was Henry now? Lucian did not know. They had lost touch when Henry had gone to Aunt Florence with his sisters.

I was in the garden where Tom Yardley had found me under the azalea bush. It was withered now, smothered by the weeds. There was the spot where Tom Yardley used to wheel the chair. I looked back to the french windows of the room in which she had died.

It was too depressing. It was foolish of me to have come. What was I achieving by this?

I looked towards the woods and saw a column of smoke rising to the sky.

The gypsies, I thought. They must be there now.

My spirits lifted at the thought. I had to see if it was the same clan who had come before. I wanted to escape from this feeling of desolation which the house had set upon me. I wanted to see the children playing round the caravans.

A hedge separated the garden from the edge of the wood. I remembered there had been a spot where I had scrambled through as a child. I found it. I did the same and walked through the trees until I came to the clearing.

There were the caravans. The children were playing on the grass; women were squatting around, chipping wood for their clothes pegs. Nothing had changed.

Could it really be that they were the same band? I had heard that gypsies returned to the same spots all over the country. If this were so, and I could see Rosie Perrin and Jake, it would be most interesting.

As I approached, I saw a caravan on the steps of which sat a woman. She looked remarkably like Rosie Perrin, but then there was a similarity among these gypsy women.

The children were watching me. I knew that because of the silence which had fallen on them. The women looked up from their chipping.

Then a voice I remembered well cried out, "Well, if it isn't Carmel come back to see us!"

I ran forward. The woman sitting on the steps was indeed Rosie Perrin.

She came down, and we stood smiling at each other.

"Where have you been, Carmel?" she said.

"To Australia," I answered.

She gave that hearty laugh which I remembered so well.

"Come up. Come up and tell me all about it."

I followed her up the steps and into the caravan. It was just as I remembered. She bade me sit down, her eyes gleaming with pleasure and excitement.

"You went away when the trouble started. I heard all about it. It was big trouble. Commonwood is a house haunted by tragedy."

I told her about Toby who was my father and how we had gone to Australia.

She nodded. "He did not want you mixed up in that. You, a child. And the other children went away too."

I told her everything that had happened to me, that I knew that Zingara was my mother, and how I had come to visit The Grange.

"And you have been coming here ever since?" I asked.

She nodded. "We have seen the house falling into decay. What good is it now? It is a ruin. Nobody will live there. It will fall right away . . . into nothing."

"Why? Why?"

"Because houses have lives of their own. Something happened there and the memory lives on. I feel it when I go near. Sometimes I look that way and a sighing comes to me."

"Sighing?"

"It is in the wind . . . in the air. It is an unhappy house."

"It is only bricks and mortar, Rosie."

She shook her head. "We gypsies feel these things. It will be like that until . . ."

"Until what?"

"Until it can be made happy again."

"It would have to be razed to the ground and another house built there . . . a new Commonwood."

"And made into a happy house."

"It was never a really happy house, Rosie. Mrs. Marline would not let it be."

"She is dead now," said Rosie, "rest her soul. She made unhappiness in her life and in her death. There was more pity for the poor doctor than for her."

"I cannot bear to think of him. Even before I knew what had happened to him . . . all through the years, when I have been so far away, even now and then I would remember."

"Ah, my child, what happened yesterday can at times decide what will happen today. There are never-to-be-forgotten yesterdays in all our lives. But this is a happy meeting between us. Let us enjoy it. Tell me what has been happening to you."

So I told her in detail about the trips with Toby, and of Elsie, who had been a surrogate mother to me; how Elsie was, in fact, Toby's wife and how, though they were fond of each other, they were not contented to live together as husband and wife.

She nodded wisely.

"He was that sort of man. I know that from Zingara. Many loved him. He was a man who gave much and received love in return. You had a wonderful father, Carmel, and you have a wonderful mother. I say that, though perhaps all would not agree."

"Where is Zingara now?"

"She is no longer on the stage. She gave that up. I shall tell her that I have seen you again. Tell me where you are living and I will let her know. Then she will write to you. She is clever. She can write. A gentleman taught her, the gentleman who came here to study us at first hand."

Rosie paused and smiled into the distance.

"He taught her to read and write. She loved that. She always liked to know that bit more than anyone else."

She paused again. "You will write down where you are staying and I will have it sent to her. She will then do what she thinks is best to do."

"I think that is a good idea."

I took a pencil from the little receptacle I carried and tore a sheet from a small notebook.

"I'm Carmel Sinclair, not March, now," I said. "My father thought I should have the same name as his."

I wrote down the Hysons' address and gave it to her.

She nodded and put the paper in her pocket.

Then she made some fragrant tea like that which I had had before in this caravan, and we sat drinking and talking. There was so much I had to tell her still and she asked many questions.

Then I realised that I had been absent for a long time and Lady Crompton would be wondering what had become of me.

Gertie was married the following week. There was breathless excitement throughout the house. It had all been planned, down to the smallest detail. The reception was to be at the house after the ceremony, and then Gertie and Bernard were going to Florence for three weeks' honeymoon. When they returned they would settle into the house which was waiting for them.

Lucian, Lawrence and Dorothy were present, and the Hysons had invited numerous friends, and then there were Bernard's connections. Aunt Beatrice was worried as to how they were all going to get into the house.

Gertie was in a state of ecstasy and Bernard was clearly a very contented man.

It was two days before the great event when I received a letter in an unknown handwriting. My heart beat fast as I looked at it, for something told me it was from Zingara.

I was right.

My dear Carmel,

I was delighted to have your address from Rosie. For so long I have wondered about you. You will see from the address above that I am living at a place called Castle Folly in

Yorkshire. It is not a real castle, but you will see it when you come to visit it—which you will soon, I hope.

You would have to stay a while, for you could not make the journey there and back in a day. Send me a note <u>please</u> and say when you will come.

          ZINGARA

          (I am Mrs. Blakemore now)

I reread the letter and I thought: I will write to her at once. I will go just as soon as I can. I should have to wait until after the wedding, of course, and then perhaps I could hardly leave Aunt Beatrice immediately. She would miss Gertie, although it would only be for a short while. But I would write and fix a date . . . perhaps a week ahead. That would give time for the wedding and a little interval.

So that was what I did.

There was an enthusiastic reply from Zingara. She was greatly looking forward to seeing me. As for myself, I could hardly wait to go.

The wedding was over. There had been none of those hitches which Aunt Beatrice had greatly feared. The married couple had left for Florence, and we all missed Gertie very much. I had always known what a difference her coming had made to Aunt Beatrice, but now I saw it was even more than I had realised.

She admitted to me that she was a selfish old woman, because good fortune had given her Gertie while robbing her own mother of her, and she could not help rejoicing in that.

"Gertie and I were always such pals in the old days," she said, "but now, to have her here so close . . . like my own daughter, really. It's my gain . . . but I do think of my poor sister."

"She has James," I said.

"I never thought they would go gallivanting off to Australia. Now I'm going to stock their house with everything they'll want when they come home. You must help me, Carmel."

"I will, but I have to pay this visit to Yorkshire. It is someone I have to see."

I did not say it was my mother. I had told no one that. I should have to wait until I had understood Zingara's reactions before I imparted that information.

Lucian thanked me for visiting his mother.

"She said she so much enjoyed having you there. It was good of you to go."

"I enjoyed it. She was charming to me."

He looked at me thoughtfully. "There's a good deal I want to talk about," he said. "We must meet . . . sometime . . . soon."

I thought: Weddings have an effect on some people. There was some purpose behind that remark. Perhaps it was because of all the hints I had received from Gertie that I wondered if he really did care enough about me to want to marry me. I was unsure of myself and of him. There was something that held me back . . . something I did not understand. When I remembered the boy he had been and how I had adored him then, I wanted him to be just like that now. He had changed. Something had happened . . . there was his marriage, of course. What was it Rosie had said? Our yesterdays must leave their mark upon today.

How different it was with Lawrence! I felt I knew exactly what he was thinking, exactly how he would react to any situation. There was no mystery about Lawrence.

Dorothy was saying, "There is something so affecting about weddings. How happy they both seem!"

She looked at me wistfully. She did not expect marriage for herself, but she wanted it for Lawrence, and I felt that she was hoping that I would grant her wish.

It was a bright autumn day when I arrived in Yorkshire.

Zingara was at the station to meet me. She had changed a little from the last time I had seen her. That must have been about ten years ago. She was more serene. Her hair was still magnificent— black and glistening coils piled up on her head. Heavy creole earrings swung from her ears, and her dark eyes were as bright and beautiful as before. She was dressed in a midnight blue cloak under which was a scarlet dress. One would have noticed her immediately in any crowd.

She came to me with arms outstretched. We were both too emotional to speak. Suddenly she murmured, "Carmel, my child," and, drawing me to her, held me as though she would never let me go.

"My darling!" she said, "I am so happy that you have come."

Then she held me at arm's length and looked at me.

"You have grown up," she said. "You are no longer a little girl. And I . . . I have become the old lady."

I laughed. "What nonsense! Nobody could call you an old lady."

"My life is changed. I no longer sing, no longer dance. But that is for later. Now, here is the trap. I drive this myself and I shall take you to my home at Castle Folly."

"It is so exciting to be here."

"We have much to tell each other. But first I will prepare you. I am Mrs. Blakemore now. I have a husband. He is very old and he owns Castle Folly. It is not a real castle. He wanted a castle, so he built one . . . a ruin of a castle in his own grounds. We have the battlemented towers . . . scattered here and there . . . the remains of the old banqueting hall. I can tell you, it is a most wonderful ruin of a castle, and it suits Harriman very well because he always wanted a castle and now he has one all of his own."

"He sounds as though he is a very interesting man."

"He is indeed. And he has been good to me, and when the time came I let him carry me off to his castle. You will like him and he will like you."

"How do you know?"

"Because it is what I want, and he always does what I want. But we will save our talks for the right time. Now, this is your luggage? Come."

I sat beside her and we started off.

"We are close to the moors," she said. "Have you ever seen the Yorkshire moors? They are the best moors in the world. The wind is fresher here and to let it buffet you is as exciting as an audience clapping and shouting bravo. To me, that is, but then I am a gypsy. Give me the feel of the wind in my hair! Sometimes I take out the pins and let it blow about me. I tell you, my darling, this conventional attire is to come to that station and collect you. You will see me change."

I laughed with pleasure. I had not expected a visit to Zingara to be a conventional one, and this was certainly going to be unusual.

We drove on for about fifteen minutes before I saw the beginning of the moor—wild open country with boulders rising here and there and little streams glistening on their rocky surface. It was awe-inspiring.

"We're on the moor now," she said. "There are one or two

houses round us . . . but not many. Look over there. Do you see that grand building? When you get closer, you will see that it is a ruin. Castle Folly!"

I could see it clearly now—remains of towers and turrets. It certainly had the appearance of a once magnificent edifice now in ruins.

Zingara laughed. "Well, if you can't inherit one, build your own! What's wrong with that?"

"Nothing at all, I'm sure."

"The house is in the grounds. It is rather insignificant after the castle . . . but comfortable. We have a couple looking after it. Then there are just Harriman and myself. Life is queer. I never thought this could be my destiny."

I saw the house then. It appeared to have been built in the mid-century, when Georgian elegance had been replaced by the heavy style of the industrial era. It looked solid, built to withstand the weather, which I imagined could be bleak on the moors in winter. There was an air of strength about it.

"This is the house, known as Castle Folly. Doesn't fit somehow, does it, until you look round and see what it's all about."

She drove the trap up to the house and, as she did so, a man and a woman came out.

"This is Tom Arkwright, and here's Daisy. Hello, Daisy. This is Miss Carmel Sinclair. You know she's staying with us for a while. And this is Tom and Daisy, Carmel. They're my mainstay."

Tom, rather dour by nature, I imagined, twisted his mouth into a grin, rather reluctantly.

"And how are you, Miss?" said Daisy, who was small and energetic-looking and had an air of strength and immense capability. "Welcome to Yorkshire."

"These two keep the whole show going," said Zingara, beaming on them. "I just don't know what I would do without them."

"There's hot coffee and buns waiting for you, Mrs. B.," said Daisy. "Happen the young lady will want a bite after that train journey."

"That's wonderful. Come along and taste Daisy's buns and have the coffee while it's hot. Then I'll whisk you up and introduce you to Harriman. Daisy makes the best buns in Yorkshire."

"You get along with you, Mrs. B.," said Daisy.

I was taken into a room where there was a large pile of buns set out on a table with cups, saucers, plates and a coffeepot with jugs of hot milk.

"Tom will take your bag up while we eat the buns. Then I'll show you your room and you can meet Harriman after."

As the door shut on us, she lowered her voice and said, "Tom and Daisy are wonderful, but they have to be obeyed. They're gruff. They stand no nonsense, and you have to remember they are as good as anyone if you want to get along with them. And by the way, they expect you to eat. Good food and plenty of it is the way they show their welcome. Daisy is a wonderful cook, and you could trust her and Tom with everything you have. Now, you must do justice to her buns."

They were hot, spicy and delicious.

"Not too much of an ordeal," said Zingara with a grin.

The coffee was hot and good. "They think I'm a little mad," said Zingara, "but they make excuses for me."

She went on to tell me how she came to be here.

"The last place in the world I should have thought I'd land up in. You see, I'm getting old. You're going to contradict that, but I *am* getting old, for a dancer. And it was a dancer I really was. The singing . . . well, that went along with it, but on its own it wasn't quite good enough. I wanted to leave at the height of my glory. You understand?"

"Yes, of course."

"Harriman was always a good friend to me. I have many friends, but Harriman has always been the one I relied on and trusted. And when you are no longer young, it is reliance that you want. I have known him since I was a child. He came to the camp to study us. That was when we formed this great friendship."

"Rosie told me."

"There was one night . . . on the stage . . . I felt a pain in my leg. I knew I could not stretch far enough. I hid it, of course. It was not so much then . . . only a sign. I went to the doctor. He said I was straining my muscles. If I stopped doing that, all would be well. I must slow down. That was enough. I said to Harriman, 'I cannot wait until they shoo me off.' He said, 'Rosaleen, you must marry me.' He always called me Rosaleen. That is my true name. Zingara is for the stage. This was sudden. I had not thought of it. But Harriman makes quick decisions. 'I want a castle,' he said, 'and the only way I shall ever get one is to build one.' 'Rosaleen must leave the stage,' he says, 'so she will marry me.' "

"And so you married him?"

"At last I saw that it was a good thing to do. I needed Harriman. I was downcast. I had lived the life of excitement in the theatre for so long. How could I give it up? I had some money, yes. But what should I do? Go back to the gypsies? That had always attracted me. All through my life, I had never forgotten them. Harriman said, 'No, you will not be content. You will think of the old life in the theatre, just as before you thought of life with the gypsies. You must marry me and come to my castle in Yorkshire. You can walk on the moors and feel the joy of the gypsy's life and at the same time enjoy the comfort you have come to expect.' "

"And so you did."

"You will see how it works. Now . . . you have eaten two buns. Well, that is something. They will not be too disappointed. Now I shall show you your room. You can unpack, wash your hands and then I will introduce you to Harriman."

My room was large, with big windows overlooking the moor. I was delighted with the view and filled with exhilaration. I was completely fascinated by my mother, and I longed for more revelations.

Harriman was the next surprise. He was indeed old. He told me later that he was seventy. He was tall and thin, with a craggy face rather like an eagle's.

He held out his hand, grasped mine and studied me intently.

"Can't rise," he said. "I am something of an old crock these days. Rosaleen will tell you."

"He's not in the least," said my mother. "Just a little bit weak in the knees."

It was obvious that Harriman Blakemore was a most unusual man. The folly in itself was evidence of that, and the more I saw of this unusual household, the more eager I became to discover more.

Harriman and my mother were two of the most lively-minded people I had ever met. They talked continuously. My mother astonished me by her knowledge of various subjects. I guessed that this stemmed from her relationship with Harriman. He said once that he had gone to discover the true gypsy and had found Rosaleen, who was unlike any other. It was he, of course, who had tutored her, moulded her character, made her the woman she was.

He was a man of means. He had been involved in several business concerns; he had travelled widely and, in his fifties, had retired from business life and devoted himself to his hobbies. Studying the gypsies and writing a treatise on them was evidently one of these; building Castle Folly was another. Now his body was inactive but his mind was as lively as ever.

He told me that he had had a good life and that he was as content now as he had ever been.

"That, my dear Carmel," he said, "is a successful life. Success is contentment. Is that not what we are all striving for? It is not fame and fortune, it is not the pleasure of the moment. Of what use is something so ephemeral? What every human being wants is happiness. The mistake most make is that they seek those things which can only bring a fleeting satisfaction. I have had a good life and now I have come to my old age I have my castle, which I can see from my window. My folly, they call it. I think it sums up my achievement, my success. You see me, Carmel, a happy man."

It was not that he talked a great deal about himself. His interest in others was great. My mother told me he was interested in everyone he met. He wanted to know all about them. He could tell you details of the lives of Daisy and Tom Arkwright which he had extracted from them to their own amazement, she was sure, for neither Daisy nor Tom was noted for loquacity.

He wanted to hear about my life in Australia, and I found myself going into details about the Formans, including the episode of the sundowner and James's search for opals.

I was so completely fascinated by everything I found at Castle Folly that I believed, for the first time since Toby's death, I had not thought of him once.

My mother took me to see her caravan. Harriman had arranged for it to be installed.

"He says there is so much of the gypsy in me that I'll never lose it. I'll never forget that I was born in a caravan and I lived my early life in one. I have gypsy blood in me. And that means, my darling, that you, who are part of me, must have too. Sometimes I want to be alone. I come here and sit on the steps. I feel the silence all round me. I am quite alone with nature. Then I go back to the house, and Harriman is there, my guide, my guardian, as he has always been. And then I know that he was right. I belong to two worlds . . . and he has made it possible for me to live in both, for he knew that I could not be completely happy with one alone."

"And you are completely happy?" I said. "It must be a great contrast to the days in the theatre when you were the toast of the town."

She laughed. "I was never that. Mine was a success of a moderate nature. But I have heard the applause in London, Paris and Madrid. It was intoxicating. But Harriman has always made me aware of the danger of caring too much for ephemeral success. He reminded me that public approbation is fickle. Favourites come and go, and it is demoralising to become a fallen idol. Better never to have been an idol at all. He taught me how to regard that kind of success."

"What a wonderful teacher he must have been!"

"I bless the day when he decided to come to our encampment."

"I think he does too."

"But you think it is strange, do you not? This old man and this woman . . . such as you can guess I must have been. Well, Harriman is not old. He never could be. He has the most lively of minds, and he can never fail to enchant me. As for myself, I have lived what would be called an adventurous life, and at forty-five I have settled down to what would be called retirement from the world. Is that not amazing? Oh, Carmel! There is so much for us to tell."

Each day was full of interest. Rosaleen—I thought of her by that name now, for Zingara was the dancer—and I belonged together. We were mother and daughter, and we desperately wanted to make up for all the years we had lost.

We walked a great deal. She wanted me to know the magic of the moors. She unbound her hair and let it flow loose in the wind. We found a boulder which made a rest for our backs, and we sat and talked. She talked of Toby. I was surprised that I could join in without that overwhelming sorrow which I had felt before.

"He was a wonderful man," she said. "I loved him and he loved me in his way. He was a man who could love many people at the same time. The great love of his life was for his daughter. I was not so very young when we met—twenty-three, in fact. That is older than you are now. I was making my way on the stage. Although Harriman was in the background of my life, we were not as we became later. He was interested in me, but he had many interests. He was out of the country at the time. All my life there have been

times when I have hankered for the gypsy way . . . wandering
from place to place . . . the open road . . . the fresh air . . .
the freedom. I went back. Rosie always understood. She was so
proud of what I had done. I think she believes it was a great deal
more than it really was. She was always happy when I visited her."

"And it was when you were visiting her that you met Toby."

She nodded. "I met him in the woods. We talked. There was an
immediate attraction between us. I was lighthearted, so was he.
We were young. We were both the sort who would slip into a
relationship carried along by the desire of the moment. He was not
my first lover. There had been several. But he was different. We
met again and again. For people like us it was natural. Toby did
not know about you until sometime later. By then you were safe in
Commonwood House. He said he would have married me if he
had not already had a wife in Australia. He often told me how it
was at Commonwood. He was very sorry for the doctor. His sister
was a termagant, he said. The women of his family were like that
. . . efficient, practical, but hard to live with. I loved to hear
about Commonwood. I knew it was the place for you . . . and,
after all, you belonged in a way. I used to see the good doctor
going out in his carriage, visiting his patients, and occasionally his
wife, very formal, very proper; and the children with their nanny.
They were all especially interesting to me because of Toby's connection with them. One day he gave me a pendant. It was a Romany pendant, and it had 'good fortune' on it in our language."

"I have it still," I said.

"I knew the doctor would recognise it, and I put it round your
neck. Toby told me of the time when he had bought it. The doctor
had seen it and had warned him to be careful. He knew how it was
between us, of course, Toby and me. When I was going to have a
child, I went back to Rosie and I wanted you to be brought up as
Toby's child should be. I knew they would give you that sort of life
at Commonwood, and, well, you know the rest."

"You left me under the azalea bush and Tom Yardley found me
there."

"I watched. I saw that you were taken in. I knew then that I had
done the right thing. And when Toby came back, I would tell him.
I wondered what he would feel to learn he had a child. As you
know, he was overcome with pride and joy."

"How did you feel when you left me?"

"Heartbroken. Do you believe that?"

"I do."

"I want you to know that I watched you . . . from outside. I knew you would have the right sort of home. If it had not turned out as it did, I should have taken you away. With Harriman's help I would have looked after you. But it was better that you should be brought up conventionally . . . as you would be at Commonwood House. And there you were . . . with Toby's nephew and nieces. You were one of them. I thought that was the easiest way. I said to myself, 'There she will be as the doctor's daughter, and she will grow up as a lady.' "

The tears were falling down her cheeks as she talked. Tears and laughter came easily to her, but I knew she was deeply affected.

She went on: "I knew that Toby was watching over you. I saw him when we came to Commonwood. He was so happy. He said you were the most enchanting child. He was proud of his daughter and he said too that he was glad I was your mother. He always knew how to say those things that people wanted to hear. I said it must not be known that your mother was a gypsy, and he said that if you knew me you would be proud of me."

She was choking with emotion, and I put my arm round her and dried her tears. Soon she was smiling.

"And here we are, talking of the past which can never be changed, and we are together and what is important to me is you. There is much I have to know."

It was not long before we were talking of James, his search for opals and his rather nonchalant offer of marriage.

"He is the good, practical man," she said. "He will cherish his wife but not excite her. It is good . . . in a way."

Then I told her of Lawrence Emmerson, who had saved Gertie and me from disaster all those years ago, and how he happened to be on the ship which was returning to England.

She cried, "It is fate. When fate takes a hand, we must take notice."

There were times when she became the gypsy, her eyes alight with an assurance of her special powers, and she seemed to be probing the future.

I laughed. "So, dear Gypsy Rosaleen, it was fate, was it?"

"Tell me more of him. I like this man. I like him very much. And the sister? She is good too. She will see that the servants are kept in order and that the household is run as a house should be. Why do you smile? I am not laughing at this. It is important."

"I am smiling because you have assumed the manner of the seer. Tell me, did you learn to tell fortunes from Rosie?"

"Of course. It is part of a gypsy girl's upbringing."

"But you do not believe in it, really?"

She was thoughtful. "It can be . . . and it cannot. You must know all you can of your subject. You must find out, and it must be done quickly. Sometimes it is shut against you, but not always. Then you think, 'What does this one want? What will she do?' And sometimes you guess. But there are moments . . . wonderful moments . . . when something passes between you . . . a flash of understanding. It is there and you believe you know what is to come. I cannot say how it happens, and it is rare. Perhaps it is what they call telepathy. But it could be something. There are wonderful things here all around us . . . of which we know nothing. You must talk to Harriman about this. He will talk of the unknown universe of which our earth is but a fragment. He has many theories, and he will remind you that with nature all things are possible. Perhaps, now and then, it may be that the gypsy sees into the future. 'There are more things in heaven and earth than are dreamed of in your philosophy.' But tell me more of this Lawrence, because I like him."

"Perhaps I should bring him to see you."

"That would be very enjoyable. And the sister too."

"They would naturally expect to come together."

"And you think that the sister wants you to marry her brother?"

"I am sure she does."

"She will not be a little jealous of her brother's affection for you?"

"I am equally sure she is not."

"But *you* are not sure . . . about him . . . although it would be such good sense. He would be a good husband . . . and reliable in every way. But there would not be this . . . what shall I say? . . . this enchantment."

I thought of Gertie's ecstasy, and how excited she had been about the most trivial things, simply because she was so happy.

She watched me closely, and I told her about Gertie.

"I know," she said. "That is love. It will not stay like that. How could it? But love will stay if they cherish it. So there are this James and this Lawrence."

"And," I said, "there is Lucian. Lucian Crompton of The Grange."

"The Grange near Commonwood?"

"Yes."

"And he too wants to marry you?"

"He has not said so. It is just that Gertie and her aunt cannot see a man and woman friendly together without assuming that there is some romantic attachment."

"And they see it with you and Lucian?"

"They would see it with anyone."

"And what of you? Do you see it?"

I was silent for a moment while she watched me intently.

"He is very friendly. I met him when I returned to England. He was very kind to me in the old days. He has changed somewhat."

I explained how my desire to see Commonwood House had been irresistible, and I told her in detail about my visit to Easentree, how I had gone into the house and been startled by the two boys, how, in the town, I had met Lucian at the roadside and we had lunched together.

"It is interesting," she said, "and once again we cannot ignore fate. You could so easily not have met. Then you would not have met Rosie again, and we should not be sitting here, reunited. You see, it is indeed the hand of fate, and look what it has given us! Now, tell me more of Lucian."

It was so easy to talk to her. She seemed to understand every nuance of my mood. I told her of the boy Lucian had been, how he had always been kind to me, how he had drawn me into the circle and become a hero to me.

"You were in love with him then . . . in your child's way," she said.

"How could I not be? The boy from The Grange! The Grange family was very important in Mrs. Marline's eyes. Lucian seemed tall, handsome, strong and powerful. Even Henry was in awe of him. And he was so kind to me. Toby had given me a pendant. I lost it and Lucian not only found it but had the clasp repaired for me, and he insisted on my joining them for tea—which Nanny Gilroy had thought I was not worthy to do. After that, he always made sure that I was all right. It was no wonder that I adored him."

"And then you did not see him again until you were about to cross the road and the frisky horse appeared. Undoubtedly Fate! I am getting excited about Lucian . . . and now you are less enchanted with him."

I was silent, and she added quietly, "Yes, still a little, I believe. But he has changed, you say?"

"He was so lighthearted in those days. He seemed invincible."

"The perfect hero, yes. And now . . . ?"

"There seems to be something. You see, he was married and his wife died. There is a child. The wife died when she was born. She is looked after by a ghoulish old nurse. It is all rather melodramatic. On her deathbed the wife made the nurse swear to stay to look after the child, so she stayed, although both Lucian and his mother would like to be rid of her. The nurse spoke to me. Do you know, she accused Lucian of murdering his wife . . . or at least she hinted at it."

Rosaleen was alert. "I see," she said. "No wonder you're unsure. Do *you* think he was responsible for his wife's death?"

"No . . . no! I would not believe that of him, any more than I can believe Dr. Marline was guilty of murder."

"The Commonwood affair, you mean. My darling, what dramas you have . . . well . . . not exactly been involved in . . . but been on the fringe of! This is very interesting. You like Lucian. I can see that there is something rather special about him. Then there is this hint of suspicion. Now, Lawrence would always be above reproach. It is interesting because you wonder whether Australian James did have a hand in despatching the sundowner, but you do not feel the same about him as you do about Lucian."

"Perhaps James would have said if he had been responsible for the death of the man. But maybe not. He might feel that if one is caught up in something like that it is better to remain quiet. I suppose people sometimes commit murders and remain undiscovered. Do you think this venomous old woman is throwing out hints because she does not want me there? Perhaps she is looking at it as Gertie and her aunt do . . . I mean, that Lucian is contemplating asking me to marry him."

"Why should she go to such lengths?"

"Because she might fancy her position would be threatened. A new wife might not be impressed by that deathbed promise. Besides, the child, Bridget, has already shown a liking for me."

"And you are telling yourself that you do not believe this woman. She is lying, you say. You find reasons for her to lie. There is a difference in you when you speak of Lucian. I do not see this for James, or even Lawrence. It is very interesting. I have learned so much . . . and I shall learn more."

Lucian had caught her imagination, and I think she was telling me, as well as herself, that he was the man for me.

We used to sit long over dinner. Harriman was a great talker, but he liked to listen, too. He was obviously very interested in me, as Rosaleen's daughter, and that I had been brought up in that house which had figured in a murder case.

"You were there," he said, "when the drama was building up."

"And I knew nothing of the outcome until a short time ago."

"That is amazing."

"Toby thought it wouldn't be good for her to know what had happened there," said Rosaleen, "so she was whisked away before the trial took place. Carmel is convinced that Dr. Marline did not commit the murder."

"I have often said so," I told them, "but people tell me that the most unexpected people will commit murder in certain circumstances."

"That is true, of course. And you have this strong conviction?"

"I do. I knew him. He was a man of kindness and extreme gentleness. I know he was very unhappy and there was a relationship with Miss Carson. But I still believe he did not do it."

"There was the motive and the evidence," Harriman pointed out.

"Mistakes can be made," said Rosaleen. "And Carmel has this strong conviction."

"You were only a child, Carmel," said Harriman.

"Children sometimes see more clearly than their elders," added Rosaleen.

"I should like to know for certain," I told them, "but that is not possible."

"Everything is possible," said Harriman.

"This seems not to be. Dr. Marline is dead. He cannot defend himself. I wonder what happened to Miss Carson."

"That would be interesting to know. She disappeared, as people usually do in these cases."

"Poor girl!" said Rosaleen. "Just imagine what agony she must have endured! Her lover hanged for murder, and she herself at one time in danger of such a fate. And she was to have their child. What must her life have been like?"

"It would be revealing to know," said Harriman.

"Do you think she would have the answer as to whether he was guilty or not?" I asked.

"It is a possibility that she might."

"How I should like to know what became of her!" I said. "We were all very fond of her. I cannot believe she would ever have been involved in murder, any more than I can the doctor. They were both the very last people you would associate with a crime."

"She must be somewhere," said Rosaleen.

"She may have gone abroad," suggested Harriman. "I daresay she would want to get as far away as possible."

"There was someone who was interested in her case," I told them. "Dorothy Emmerson told me about him. It was some criminologist who was sure of Miss Carson's innocence. He campaigned for her acquittal."

"Who was he?"

"I can't remember his name, but Dorothy did mention it."

Harriman was thoughtful. Then he said, "It might well be that Miss Carson would like to hear from you."

I stared at him.

"You were fond of each other, you say. If you could find her, get in touch with her in some way, tell her that you are convinced of the doctor's innocence, you could discover whether she wished to see you, and if she did not . . . well, there is little harm done."

I was excited. I thought of her sweet, kindly face. I remembered how she had looked when she comforted Adeline. The accomplice of a murderer? I would never believe that.

Harriman was saying, "There is this man . . . the man who campaigned for her. He is presumably some person of importance. Suppose you could get into touch with him?"

Rosaleen was watching us, her eyes round with excitement.

She said, "Miss Dorothy would remember who she is. Did Miss Dorothy not once write to him? And he replied, I believe."

"Oh yes, she did."

"Then might it not be that she would have his address?"

"Yes," I repeated. "Oh, it would be wonderful to see Miss Carson again."

We sat over dinner that night talking for a long time. I was deciding I would go to Dorothy. I would explain everything to her. I was sure she would help if she could. It was just possible that she might still have the letter this man had written to her. If she had, I could write to him and ask if it were possible to get in touch with Miss Carson. He could not fail to remember her. Yes, I could see that this was a possibility.

I was feverishly excited by the idea.

We talked of it for the rest of the visit, and it was decided that, as soon as I returned home, I should consult Dorothy.

I should have left Castle Folly with great regret had I not been so eager to pursue my enquiries.

Rosaleen made me promise that I would come again soon and that I should keep them informed as to what happened. I must remember that there would always be a welcome for me at Castle Folly. We had been separated too long. We must make plans, for I could not stay at my good friends', the Hysons', forever, and Castle Folly would be my home for as long as I wanted it.

A Meeting
in the Park

MRS. HYSON welcomed me back with genuine pleasure. It was clear that she was missing Gertie. She wanted to know if I had enjoyed my trip to Yorkshire, but did not ask searching questions, for which I was relieved. Her thoughts were really with the honeymooners.

The next morning, I called at the Emmersons' house. To my joy, Dorothy was home. Lawrence would already have left, as I guessed. I was glad of this, because I felt that he would have been less enthusiastic about my plan. He would feel that it was not good to stir up the unpleasant past and it would be more sensible to leave things as they were.

"Carmel!" cried Dorothy when I arrived. "It's good to see you. When did you get back?"

"Last night."

I had called on her as soon as possible, and her satisfaction was obvious.

"You've missed Lawrence. He went off an hour or so ago."

"Yes, I guessed he would have gone."

"He'll be delighted you're back. You must come round to dinner soon."

"Thanks, Dorothy. I've a lot to tell you."

"Good. I'm all eagerness to hear."

"First, I didn't tell you that I was visiting my mother."

She looked at me in astonishment. "You said . . . a friend."

"Well, she is a friend, too. You see, it was all so unconventional. My father told me who my mother was, and I had met her once when I was a child—only I didn't know she was my mother then."

"Well, I do know something about that, because, after all, Lawrence was a great friend of your father when they were on ships together."

"Yes, of course. My mother was on the stage and she is now married to a most interesting man. They will invite you and Lawrence to Yorkshire. You will enjoy their company."

Dorothy's eyes sparkled. There was nothing she liked more than meeting interesting people.

"I will tell you more about them later, but first of all there is something I want to talk to you about . . . something that is really on my mind. When my mother was living with the gypsies, she came with them to their encampment in the woods near Commonwood House. She had seen something of the household there. She was naturally interested because of my father's connection with the family. We talked about the tragedy . . . Harriman Blakemore, my mother's husband, is the kind of man who has wide interests. He has theories about this and that and it is fascinating listening to him. Briefly, we discussed the Marline case. As you know, I'm convinced there was some mistake, and I will never believe that Dr. Marline was a murderer.

"During the course of the conversation Harriman raised the point that Miss Carson probably knew more about what happened than anyone else. Then we talked about them and wondered what had actually happened to her, and we came to the conclusion that she must be living somewhere, probably under an assumed name. We wondered whether she might like to hear from me. She and I had always been the best of friends."

"Yes, go on," said Dorothy.

"We decided that there would be no harm in my writing to her and telling her how much I should like to see her. If she preferred not to do so, well, then, she could just ignore my letter."

"How will you get a letter to her?"

"That bothered me. Then I thought of you."

She stared at me, her eyes round with excitement.

"There was a man who campaigned for her," I went on.

"Jefferson Craig, the criminologist, yes. I haven't heard anything about him for some time. He seems to have faded quite out of the public eye."

"You wrote to him once."

"Yes. I admired his book and one day had the temerity to write and tell him so."

"And he wrote back."

She nodded.

"Was there an address on his letter?" I asked.

"I'm not sure. I was so thrilled to get an answer that I didn't give a thought to the address."

"I suppose you couldn't remember it then?" I said in disappointment.

She shook her head and laughed at me.

"You don't suppose I'd destroy a letter from Jefferson Craig, do you? Of course it's in my box of treasures. Let me get it and put us out of our suspense. But don't get too excited. It's some years ago. He was very prominent at the time of the case, and that made him more so. But after that he seemed to fade out. If there is an address, he might not be there now."

"Dorothy, please get the letter."

She went off and in a few minutes reappeared, waving it in her hand. She gave it to me. I read:

Dear Miss Emmerson,

Thank you for your letter. I am so pleased that you enjoyed my book and it was good of you to write and tell me so.

Yours sincerely,
JEFFERSON CRAIG

And there was an address: Campion & James, 105 Transcombe Court, London E.C.4.

"That would be his publishers," said Dorothy. "Don't look downcast. They will probably be in touch with him and will forward it on wherever he is. So write to Jefferson Craig and enclose a letter to Miss Carson. Then put it in an envelope with the one addressed to this Campion & James and ask them to forward it to him. It's simple."

"Oh, Dorothy, what a help you have been."

"Don't get too excited! This could come to nothing. On the other hand, it might work. And don't thank me. I'm as excited as you are. I always wanted to know what became of Kitty Carson."

I immediately wrote to Campion & James. Between us, Dorothy and I had decided what should be said. I had written:

Dear Sirs,

I am anxious to get into touch with Mr. Jefferson Craig, and I wondered if you would kindly forward the enclosed to him. If this is not possible, will you be good enough to return it to me. With many thanks in anticipation of your kindness in this matter, I am,

       Yours sincerely,
          CARMEL SINCLAIR

Inside this letter was the one addressed to Jefferson Craig, explaining that I wished to get in touch with Miss Carson, and in that, the letter to her.

To Kitty Carson herself, I had written:

Dear Miss Carson,

You will remember Carmel. I have never forgotten you and all your kindness to us all. Perhaps you will also remember Captain Sinclair. He was my father and he took me to Australia where I remained until now. I have returned to England only recently and only just heard what happened after I left.

I remember you with such fondness that I wondered if it would be possible to see you. I should be so pleased if it were, but if you do not wish it, I shall understand.

I so much look forward to hearing from you.

    Your onetime pupil,
        CARMEL SINCLAIR
        (I am no longer March. I took my father's name.)

Dorothy read the letters several times. When we thought we could not improve on them, we sent them off.

Then the waiting began.

Almost a week had passed and there was no response. It must be expected, I told myself. Suppose I were in Kitty's place. Suppose I had suffered the agony she must have endured. Suppose I had succeeded in establishing myself in a new life. Should I want to revive the past with its anguish and misery?

Had Campion & James forwarded the letter? That seemed

likely, otherwise they would have sent it back to me. Had Jefferson Craig passed it on?

I had a letter from Lucian. He was coming to London for a day or so. Could we meet for lunch the following Tuesday? What about Logan's? We had been there before, I would remember.

I had not seen him since my visit to Castle Folly. I was sure he would be very interested to hear what had happened, and I wanted to learn what he thought of my trying to get in touch with Miss Carson. I knew that Lawrence would not approve. He would think immediately of how distressing it might be for a woman in her position to be reminded of the past. I tried to make myself believe that he would be wrong and that Miss Carson would be pleased that I remembered her with fondness.

As I entered the restaurant, Lucian rose from the table at which he was seated and greeted me. He looked happy, without what I had come to think of as that haunted look. In fact, he looked very like the boy I had known at those tea parties who had tacitly insisted that I should be treated as the others were.

"It's been a long time since we met," he said.

"You always say that, Lucian."

"That's because it always seems so."

He smiled at me, and, as we sat down, said, "So you have been visiting again."

"It was a particularly interesting visit." I told him about my mother, Harriman Blakemore and Castle Folly.

"What an interesting background you have sprung from!" he said.

"You would like my mother. She is so amusing and so different from everyone else. And Harriman is unique too."

"I hope I shall meet them."

"Oh, you must. They want to meet you. It was wonderful finding her." I explained what had happened. "It was during that time I was staying with your mother. I found Rosie Perrin in the woods and she put me in touch with Rosaleen—Zingara, that was."

"Tell me more."

So I did.

"The wonderful thing is that I have a home there now. I have felt guilty about staying so long at the Hysons'. Not that they have hinted in the slightest way that they don't want me. In fact, there are protests if I speak of leaving. But my mother's home will be mine. And I suppose Harriman is my stepfather. It's a wonderful feeling of security."

"Carmel, I have been wanting to talk to you seriously for some time."

"Yes?"

"When you came back, it was so interesting for me. I felt as though we were young again. I wish we had not lost all those years. We ought to have grown up together."

I laughed. "When we knew each other all those years ago, I was just a little girl. You were far above me. You only condescended to know me because I was a poor little outsider and you had a kind heart. It was like that, you know. I wasn't even as old as Estella or Camilla."

"That's true, I suppose. But I did miss you when you went away."

"As you did Estella and Henry."

"Differently. That is the point. Everything is different. There is something missing at The Grange. It's my fault, of course. It ought to be as it used to be when I was young. I suppose it is because I made the most ghastly mistake that anyone can make. I've changed everything. I've brought a gloom into the place. I want to break out of that, and I want you to help me."

I looked at him steadily and said, "You had better say exactly what you mean."

"I want to marry you."

I felt a lifting of my spirits. I had not felt like this since before that terrible night when they had put me on the lifeboat, leaving Toby behind. I knew that part of me wanted this and that I felt for Lucian what I would never feel for James or Lawrence. I liked them both very much, of course. I enjoyed their society, but my feelings for Lucian were different. There was an excitement for me in his company. With James or Lawrence I knew exactly what to expect, but there was something in Lucian which mystified me. I felt there was something secret he was keeping from me.

Because of this, I hesitated, and he was immediately aware of it.

"You don't like the idea?" he said.

"No, no, no. It is not that I am not very fond of you, Lucian."

"That sounds like the classic refusal. 'I am very fond of you, but . . .' Carmel, tell me quickly. There is a 'but,' isn't there?"

"I will say what I intended. I am very fond of you, but . . ."

"Ah," he said, "there it comes."

"It is just that I am unsure. So much has happened. I do care for you . . . very much. You were the hero of my childhood. You must understand. I hope we shall continue to see each other as we have been doing. They have been very happy times for me, but we have to know more of each other. You see, it was for me a very particular childhood friendship, but we have both changed since this. So much has happened to us . . . both. Important things. They have had their effect on us. That is what I mean. I do care for you, but there are times when I feel I do not know you as I should someone with whom I propose to spend my whole life."

"You are thinking of my marriage."

"I think that might have something to do with it."

"I will tell you exactly what happened. I can understand your feelings, of course. It is the whole setup in the house, isn't it? The wife who died so soon after the marriage, the child, that old ghoul of a nurse. I will tell you everything. I intended to. In fact, I have come near doing so on several occasions, but I am afraid that, like most people, if something is unpleasant, I try to forget it and deceive myself into thinking that it is all past and forgotten. It happened quickly. There was a sort of gathering . . . those of us who had been at university together. It was a grand weekend party. There were several girls with us. Laura was one of them.

"I had met her once or twice before. She was very young and pretty, in a rather artless way which had an appeal. We had all drunk more than we should. I suppose I felt I must be like the rest . . . sophisticated, worldly. You know what young men are like. I make no excuses for myself. I must be like the rest. Later, one realises that in one foolish moment things can happen which will affect one's whole life. Let me hasten over that act of folly. Sometime after, she came to me in great distress. She was pregnant. What was she to do? She said her father would never forgive her. He had given her a London season in the hope that she would make a good marriage. There was only one course open to her. She was going to kill herself."

I looked at him in horror and he went on: "I did not know then that was the way she talked. I believed her. She was so small and helpless." He looked at me steadily. "Imagine what it would be like to be responsible for someone's death. It would be something you would have to live with for the rest of your life. How would you feel about that, Carmel?"

"It would be unendurable."

"It did occur to me that I might not be responsible. In fact, I had a very strong conviction that that might be the case. But she was so certain, so determined that if I did not marry her there was only the one course for her. I could not have that on my conscience as well as . . ."

"So you married her."

He nodded. "It was a speedy wedding. Her father was agreeable. He said that he had the brass, and all Laura needed was a good handle to her name. He would have liked a grand wedding, but he had to be contented with what we could have in such circumstances. Well, the rest was inevitable. I suppose I discovered that the child could not have been mine, and that she had tricked me into marrying her. Her father would never have allowed her to marry her lover, so she had chosen me to help her out of her dilemma. There was only one good piece of luck in the affair. The child was a girl. I should have felt very guilty about foisting someone else's bastard on the family."

"Lucian, I am so sorry for you. You must have suffered a good deal."

"You can imagine it, can't you, Carmel? The wretchedness, the frustration. And she brought Jemima Cray with her, that woman who had been her nurse and, as some nurses do, stayed with her to be her constant companion and confidante. She knew of Laura's secret liaison with the father of the child. He was some distant connection of hers, I discovered. She had hoped her father would relent when he knew there was to be a child, but he had done no such thing. He wanted to be rid of the child, and he would have had it adopted as soon as it was born and the matter kept a secret. Then Laura saw the chance . . . and, like a fool, I was duped. The father was agreeable that she should marry me and all would be forgiven.

"I don't suppose it is the first time this sort of thing has happened. It is in a way funny, like a comedy in which I play the part of the fool who is easily taken in."

"And it was only after you married that you discovered all this."

"Yes. She was going to pass off the child as prematurely born, but I learned the truth. I will tell you how. Laura developed a terrible fear of childbirth. I think her conscience may have troubled her. When people have wronged someone, they often hate them for reminding them, by their very presence, of their own perfidy. At least, I think that was how it may have been with Laura. She was unbalanced, and this fear became an obsession. She was convinced she was going to die. Sometimes she would be overcome by hysteria. It was in one of these moods that she admitted to me that I was not the father of her child, that I had been completely taken in. How clever she had been to plan it, and how foolish I had been. Although by that time I had begun to guess something of this, I was deeply shocked. I hated her and I told her so. Jemima, of course, was close at hand, ear at keyhole. Laura shouted, 'I shall die. I know I shall die.' And I said, 'Well, that will be a good solution to the affair.' Jemima hated me. I am sure she believed that if I had not married her, Laura's father might have relented and she would have been allowed to marry this connection of hers. I am sure she had set her heart on that. She hinted that I had made Laura bear this child, knowing that she was not strong enough to have children, and it was all for the sake of the family. It was absolute nonsense and she knew it. She even hinted that I was responsible for Laura's death."

I said, "There is one thing you should do without delay, and that is get rid of Jemima."

"She looks after the child."

"Bridget is a normal little girl. You can't let that woman bring her up."

"The child would grieve if she went."

I thought she might, as no one in the house seemed to pay much attention to her apart from Jemima.

"You see, I am telling you all this because you thought I had changed. Do you wonder?"

"No. Life leaves its mark. We all suffer in our different ways."

"I can imagine what that shipwreck did to you . . . and losing your father."

"It is something which I shall never forget."

"As I this. Carmel, I have thought more often of it since you have been back. Life seemed to change when we lunched in The Bald-faced Stag after all those years. I saw a way out . . . with you. I thought, Len Cherry is an excellent manager. He could run this estate without me. I'd get a new and experienced man to help him. And I would get away from the place. In Cumberland there is a small estate which belongs to the family, and I could enlarge that and start afresh. I'd like to put everything that happened behind me."

"What of your mother? What would she think? What of Bridget?"

"My mother would come with us."

"She would never leave The Grange."

"I think she would understand."

"It's a wild dream, Lucian. You could never leave The Grange. Think of all the years your family has lived there. There must have been troubles before. People grow away from them. Your wife is dead. I know you were unhappy, but nothing can be changed. She deceived you and she was unhappy. You both were. If she had married her lover and lost her inheritance, she might have been happy. It was her decision . . . not yours. You were the victim. You can't run away. You would despise yourself if you did. Besides, it wouldn't work. You should take an interest in the child. She has no mother. And where is her father? She will ask questions when she grows up. I know what it means to be without parents. I spent the early years of my life believing that I was not wanted. Don't let that happen to Bridget. But I am convinced that Jemima Cray should go."

"I see how you would take care of these things," he said, looking at me appealingly. He had certainly changed from the invincible Lucian of my childhood, and that had been the one I had loved.

"Now you know it all, Carmel," he said. "I hope you don't despise me."

"I could never do that."

"And you don't reject me altogether?"

"Of course I don't."

"Does that mean that there is no hope for me?"

"It means that there is hope for us both."

I was deeply affected by Lucian's confession.

He had seemed so vulnerable, sitting opposite me, making his pitiable confession.

He had been foolish. Who had not been at such a time? I could see exactly how it had all happened, and how he despised himself for being so gullible, and how it had changed him from a young man of pride and confidence into a bitter one with little regard for himself.

The hero had feet of clay, and oddly enough that increased my tenderness for him. I believed I could love the weak man perhaps even more than the all-conquering hero.

I wanted to see more of him. I would take him to Castle Folly. He should know Rosaleen and Harriman and they should know him.

I was sure Rosaleen had chosen him as the man I should marry. And myself? I did love him. I had been convinced of that when he had told me frankly what had happened, and yet I still felt that there was something more I had to learn, that he was holding back even more than he told.

He had talked so earnestly, so sincerely. He had been weak, certainly, but his weakness had grown out of his compassion for Laura, and for a desire to do what was right. He had not loved her, and I fancied that, from the first, there were doubts as to whether the child was his, but when she threatened to kill herself, he could not endure the possibility that he might be responsible for her death.

And now his life was in disorder and he was calling to me to help him.

There were moments when I contemplated going to him and saying, "Yes, Lucian, let us marry. Let us make The Grange a happy house, a home for Bridget, and send Jemima away." And then I would hesitate. I did not know everything. Why did I have this strange feeling that he was not telling me all the truth?

Wait, said caution. And a few days after that meeting with Lucian, there came the letter.

The handwriting was faintly familiar, and it took me right back to the schoolroom at Commonwood House. I knew from whom it came. I took it to my room so that no one should be there when I read it, and my hands were trembling when I slit the envelope.

Dear Carmel,

I was deeply moved when I read your letter—so much so that I could not reply for some time. That is why there is this delay.

Of course I remember you. I wondered how you found me. But perhaps you will tell me that when we meet.

I was not sure at first whether I could do it. You see, I have tried hard to distance myself from what happened and your letter brought it all back. But do not think I was not deeply touched. I should very much like to see you. Perhaps we could meet somewhere quiet . . . just the two of us. I thought out-of-doors where we could be sure not to be disturbed.

I see that you are at an address in Kensington and I thought of the Gardens there. I am living in Kent and it is an easy journey by train to London. I could be there about ten o'clock next Wednesday. Suppose we meet at the Albert Memorial? Then we could find a seat and talk. If that is not convenient for you, we could choose another time.

Write to me at the above address.

Thank you, Carmel, for thinking of me.

> KITTY

> By the way, address me as Mrs. Craig.

I read and reread the letter. Then I wrote to her. I should be at the Albert Memorial next Wednesday.

It was clear that Kitty was anxious that no one should know of this meeting. I could well understand her desire for absolute anonymity. But I had to tell Dorothy—I owed it to her. Had she not been entirely instrumental in making the connection? I knew I could trust her completely.

"How exciting!" she cried when I showed her the letter. "I wish I could come with you."

"That's entirely out of the question," I said at once. "If she saw I was not alone, she might go away."

Dorothy realised that.

"And she is Mrs. Craig," she said. "Could Jefferson Craig have married her? Good Heavens! Who would have thought of that?"

We agreed to say nothing to Lawrence about it, and I was glad that she saw the necessity for that. I was also relieved that Gertie had not yet returned from her honeymoon. I knew she would have guessed something had happened and made an effort to learn what it was.

I was at the Albert Memorial at exactly ten o'clock. It was easy for me. I only had to walk there. She had not arrived, but I was not alarmed, for I knew she would find it difficult to judge exactly the time the journey would take. Eight minutes passed before I saw her hurrying to our rendezvous.

I went towards her and, for a few seconds, we stood looking at each other. Then she held out her hands and I took them both in mine.

She had changed considerably. There were signs of grey in her golden hair; she had lost that air of serenity which had once been a feature of her personality. Even if I had not known her history, I should have realised that she was a woman who had suffered much tragedy.

"Carmel!" she said in that well-remembered voice. "I am so pleased to see you."

"And I you. I have thought about you so much and have wondered where you were."

Her lips trembled, and there were tears in her eyes. She seemed suddenly her old self. But we must not have an emotional scene in public.

"Let us find a seat and sit down," she said.

"I know just where," I said.

We walked away from the Memorial and into the gardens.

She said, "I'm sorry I kept you waiting. It is difficult when one relies on trains."

"Yes," I said.

Then we were silent, for making light conversation seemed banal and we knew that when we were seated there would be so much to say.

I had selected the seat for our purpose some days before. There was a stretch of ground just behind the flower walk and one isolated seat looking over it.

We sat down and she said, "Well, Carmel?"

"Oh, Miss Carson . . ." I began.

"You should call me Kitty now that I am no longer your governess."

"Kitty, tell me what you are doing now."

"I live very quietly."

"You are Mrs. Craig. Have you a husband?"

"Yes."

"Can you bear to talk of it?"

"It is what I have come to do."

I braced myself. I said, "I want you to know that I only recently heard what happened. I went away with my father."

"I know Captain Sinclair took you away when the others went to their aunt."

"I was with him in Australia. He was shipwrecked. That was not very long ago. And then I came to England and that was when I learned . . ."

"So, all those years, you did not know."

"No. I thought you would all have been at Commonwood House."

"It must have been a shock to learn the truth."

"Yes. I was devastated. Perhaps it was impertinent of me to try to find you. It was through a friend who was interested in such cases. I knew that Mr. Craig had helped you, and it was a shot in the dark. She had written to him through his publishers and she thought they might forward a letter to him."

"That explains it. Oh, Carmel, it was . . ."

"Don't. Don't. It must be terrible for you to talk of it, even now."

"I must not be foolish. I have come to talk . . . to tell you. And, Carmel, I *want* you to know. I could not bear that you should believe . . . as so many people believed. I am going to tell you . . . so that you know how it really happened. You already know what they did to Edward . . . to the doctor . . ."

I nodded. She could not speak for a moment.

Then anger burst forth.

"It was false. It was wicked. And they did that to him. He was innocent, Carmel. I know he was."

I took her hand and pressed it.

"It was what I felt," I said. "That is why I was so anxious to hear from you."

"Who could believe such a thing of him? He was the gentlest man who ever lived." Her voice broke again. "I must be calm. We were always friends, you and I, weren't we? I know that he was innocent. You will believe me."

"Yes," I said fervently, "I will."

"There is only his word."

"That is enough," I said.

"Carmel, how glad I am that I came to you! But what use is it? It is done. But I shall not rest until the world knows he was innocent —and all I can say is that I know because he told me. That is all I can say. When he knew they were going to arrest him, he said to me, 'Kitty, my dearest, they are going to accuse me of murdering Grace. Everything points to me, and there is no way of proving that I am innocent of that crime. I was not in her room. I did not touch those pills. I know nothing about them. And I want you to know, and to believe I speak the truth. I shall forget all else.' And the next day we were arrested . . . both of us."

We were silent. I did not know what to say to her, but my own belief in his innocence was confirmed.

It was some time before we could speak. Then I said, "I am glad I came. I have always been sure that he was innocent, and now I am absolutely certain."

"He would have told me," she said. "He would never have lied to me."

She was calmer after that, and I think I conveyed to her the sincerity of my belief.

"I was on trial with him," she said. "Those days are not very clear to me now, for which, I suppose, I must be thankful. Not many people stand on trial for their lives. He had his enemies. That pernicious old woman. How she revelled in it!"

"You mean Nanny Gilroy?" I said. "I always disliked her."

"Mrs. Barton was influenced by her . . . and there was the district nurse, too. They all knew how difficult Grace Marline was to live with. That could not be denied. It was evidence against him. But, of course, it was his feelings for me that convinced them. Oh, Carmel, think of it! Those letters he wrote to me, read in court . . . those intimate, loving, damning letters! What a fool I was to keep them! They searched my room and found them. They had been such a comfort to me . . . and how was I to know? You must not condemn us."

"Condemn you! How I wish there was something I could have done to help you!"

"You must forgive me. I become emotional. I was so angry with that wicked woman . . . with her innuendoes. She hated me from the moment I came into the house. And to think she knew . . . and was tittering about us! I loved the doctor, Carmel. I want you to understand. It wasn't as they made out. It was true love . . . which is never to be laughed at and sneered at . . . as they did. I hope, Carmel, that you will find a love as tender and true as mine for Edward Marline—and his for me. It was worth living for . . . dying for . . . Oh no, not the way he did."

"Please don't distress yourself. Perhaps we had better not talk of it . . ."

"But I have to talk . . . and I want you to know. It does me good to talk to you, because you believe as I do."

"I do. I always knew, within me, that Dr. Marline was innocent. I always wanted proof that I was right . . . and now I have it . . . from you."

"Proof? Only my word."

"That is good enough for me. I wish it were for the rest of the world."

"I will try to talk to you calmly and reasonably," said Kitty. "You know what happened at the trial. Edward was found guilty and they hanged him. They could not come to a decision about me. I was going to have a child and they do not hang pregnant women. There was a great deal of discussion. Jefferson Craig was in court.

"I must tell you about Jefferson. He has written a great deal on crime and the criminal. He believed from the start that Edward was innocent. He felt there had been a miscarriage of justice. He was certain that someone else had given Grace Marline the over-dose. There must have been several in the household who hated her.

"And there was the remote possibility that she had taken it herself, by mistake perhaps. There was another trial for me, and, as a result of Jefferson's articles which had appeared in the papers, a certain amount of public sympathy was engendered for me. I have always believed that it was largely due to this that I was acquitted. I came out of that court a free woman, but with uncertainty hovering over me. But Jefferson was there. He had found a lodging for me. There was a woman there to look after me, and he used to visit me from time to time. This was not a case of romantic love. I was just a 'case' to him. Jefferson's cases were his life. He had been particularly struck by mine. He was at that time in his late sixties.

"I don't know how I should have survived without him. I was in a state of deep depression. I had terrible nightmares. I did not want to live. Jefferson reminded me that I was carrying Edward's child.

He made me feel that, because of the child, I had not lost Edward completely. He told me afterwards that, at that time, he had feared that I might have taken my life. Jefferson thinks in terms of 'cases.' He had studied mine with the single-mindedness which he brought to all—but I do think that mine was of special interest to him. He decided that I needed an occupation. Work was the antidote to boredom and a lacklustre interest in life. I needed work. I thanked him for what he had done for me, told him I could never repay him, and he said that there was a way I could repay him. I could help Mrs. Garfield.

"Mrs. Garfield was his secretary. She had been with him for many years, and she was almost as old as he was. She understood him and his work as few could, but the work was getting too much for her. She needed an assistant. I could be that assistant, and that would be a great help to him.

"He was right, as he always was. Mrs. Garfield showed me what I had to do, and I was soon finding it absorbingly interesting. She had been with Jefferson so long that she had grown a little like him. She was determined to do all she could to help him in this particular 'case.' Well, they pulled me through, those two, and then the baby came. She is beautiful, Carmel. I have called her Edwina. Sometimes I fancy I see something of Edward in her, and I think how happy he would have been if he had known her. Oh, how different it might have been, Carmel!"

I took her hand and pressed it while she smiled sadly.

"It is no use, is it? Life doesn't turn out as we plan it. I was lucky in so many ways. Jefferson has been wonderful to me. He made me talk. He always wanted to know what was in my mind. He discovered that what worried me most was the future of my child. She would be Edwina Carson. I could hear people say, 'Carson? That name strikes a memory. Oh, it was that case, you know. The man was hanged and she got off . . .' I should fear that forever. I could change my name, I supposed. I used to lie awake at night and think of it.

"It was a month before she was born. Jefferson came to me and said, 'I know what you have on your mind. It's the baby to be born without a father. Now, we are going to put a stop to all that. I am going to marry you so that the child will be born in wedlock, and who is to raise questions about Jefferson Craig's child?' It was very noble of him, but he is noble. He is a great man. I know I say that again and again, but I owe so much to him."

She was too emotional to continue for a moment.

I said, "He is indeed a wonderful man, and I am so glad that he was there when you needed him."

"It is often like that in life, Carmel. One is lost and lonely and then the miracle happens. So I became Kitty Craig and my baby was born, and from that time life was no longer so utterly wretched that I longed to escape from it. I had my baby and she enchanted me—as she did Jefferson and Mrs. Garfield.

"Time passed quickly. We watched Edwina grow up . . . a baby, and then a little girl. She is nine years old now. Can it be all that time ago? I went on working with Mrs. Garfield. I found the work more and more exhilarating. Mrs. Garfield had been a wonderful teacher. Two years ago, she retired and Jefferson was doing less work than he had previously, and I was able to take over. So your letter came direct to me from the publisher."

"Oh, Kitty, I am so glad I wrote."

"So am I. And there is something else I have to tell you. Adeline is with me."

I was amazed.

"Yes," she went on. "It was soon after Edwina was born. I had a letter which came through Jefferson's publishers . . . just as yours did. It was from a Mrs. Darrell. She was Adeline's Aunt Florence."

"Oh, I remember her from when she came to collect them from Commonwood."

"She asked, most graciously, if she could come to see me. I was surprised. I had met her only briefly at that time when she had come to collect the children. I had thought her extremely haughty then, and I was surprised that she should be writing in such an ingratiating manner—almost begging me—asking me to see her. Jefferson was most intrigued, and she came to the house.

"She began by telling me that she was relieved that I had come through that distressing business and was now Mrs. Craig. She said she had always believed in my innocence. Then she came to the point. It was Adeline. She was extremely worried about the girl, and so was Mr. Darrell. Adeline had been ill for a long time, but she was better now . . . physically. She was obsessed by one thing: her desire to be with me. At first she had talked of nothing else. They had thought she would get over it but, alas, she had grown worse. There had been one or two violent scenes.

"Mrs. Darrell said, 'We tried to explain to her, but she would not understand why she could not be with you. We have had medical advice. She will have to go away, they said. The idea of sending her into a mental home is dreadful and we know that it would do her no good. There is only one thing that will. That is the only chance for her, if she could be with you. Would you be prepared to give it a trial? You would be well paid. And, of course, if you found it too much, there would be that other alternative. Would you be prepared to give it a trial? The doctors think that, with a child-like mind like hers, there is a chance of her regaining her serenity.'

"Well, of course, I talked it over with Jefferson. Here was another 'case' for him. He was prepared to study Adeline and he was soon eager to know how she would respond to being with me. So we haughtily declined payment."

"And she came to you?"

"Yes, she did. That was about seven years ago. It worked. She is now exactly like the old Adeline—loving and gentle. She adores Edwina. At first I was afraid to leave the child alone with her and contrived never to do so. But now all that is changed. They are the greatest of friends. It is a joy to hear Adeline singing about the house. Do you remember how she used to, when she was happy?"

"I am so glad that she came back to you. I know how distressed she was at that time when you went away and then when she went off with Aunt Florence. She loved you from the beginning. I remember how frightened she was when she heard there was to be a governess, and you became the most wonderful person in the world to her."

"Poor Adeline! They didn't know how to treat her. Her mother particularly frightened her and made her unhappy. She was very easily frightened and very easily made happy."

After a brief pause, she went on: "Jefferson is, of course, very interested in Adeline. He is so good with her. He understands her. She is happy now."

"Jefferson sounds a wonderful person."

"He is indeed. He treats Edwina as his daughter, and she looks on him as her father. They are very contented together. So, you see, Carmel, I have much to be thankful for. There is one thing I

245

ask. Perhaps I shall never have it and must be content with what, miraculously, has been given me."

"What is that?"

"To know what actually happened on that day in Commonwood House. Who killed Grace Marline? All I know is that it was not Edward. Then who? I want to know most of all for my child's sake. I know she has her name and she can go through life as Jefferson's daughter. But there is a chance, fainter now, thanks to Jefferson, but it is there, that someone might discover who her father was . . . they might remember me. Jefferson was very anxious that there should be no publicity about the wedding. Imagine what a field day the press would have had with that! 'Jefferson Craig marries Kitty Carson whom he saved from the gallows.' It would have been unbearable, and you can be sure that, if some of them discovered this information, there would be no hesitation in using it to get a good story which would sell papers."

"That would be dreadful."

"You see, it is hanging over me. If only it could be cleared up. But there it remains. Perhaps one day . . . It seems unlikely, but one can hope. Carmel, you won't lose touch now that we have found each other? It has been good to talk to you. You must come and see us. We have a pleasant house in Kent. We used to be in London, but when we were married, Jefferson bought this house and we retired to the country because he did not want to be too much in the public eye. You see what he did for me."

"I do, but I could not admire him more than I do already."

"So you will come?"

"I should very much like to."

"Soon, please. Jefferson will be so eager to meet you, and he is very impatient. He does not like to wait."

"I promise."

"I want you to meet Edwina . . . and there is Adeline. She will be so excited."

"Do you ever hear of Estella and Henry?"

She shook her head. "No, I think they realised that the past was something best forgotten. Adeline does not seem to care about them. You were the one of whom she was most fond."

"I think all her love was for you."

"Poor child. Life was not very good to her."

"Until you came and it was clear then how much she loved you."

"Well, I was saying how pleased she will be to see you. So, when?"

"I could come at the end of next week."

"Oh, could you?"

"Not too soon?"

She laughed at me. "We shall look forward to it. Let me give you instructions."

She took a piece of paper from her bag and wrote on it.

"I shall be at the station to meet you," she said.

"Friday week," she said, and we settled the time of the train I should catch.

She was smiling. She looked very like the Miss Carson who had come to Commonwood House all those years ago. Our meeting had cheered her. I was glad I had had the courage to step into the past.

Confession

DOROTHY CALLED that afternoon, eager to hear what had happened at the meeting. She was greatly excited, especially when she heard I was to pay a visit.

"How wonderfully it worked out! And he married her! He was always known as an eccentric. I can understand the worry about the child. It would be just the sort of titbit the press likes to get its teeth into. Just imagine if that came out! The object of the marriage would then be completely pointless. And she didn't have any light to throw on the case?"

"Only that she confirmed my conviction that the doctor did not kill his wife."

"Well, I suppose she would believe that, wouldn't she?"

"I am absolutely convinced of it."

"Unfortunately, that wouldn't carry much weight in a court of law. And you are actually going to stay in Jefferson Craig's house! Perhaps you'll get an invitation for me, one day."

"I should think that might be possible."

"What's the next plan of action?"

"I am to go down at the end of next week."

"Wonderful. And in the meantime . . . secrecy."

I looked at her steadily. "At this stage, I think so."

She nodded. She would agree with me that there could be no point in telling Lawrence at this time. We both knew that he would consider it unwise to become involved in something unsavoury that happened a long time ago. Dorothy understood Lawrence absolutely. Had she not been looking after him for so many years?

I wrote to my mother and told her what had happened. I thought she would be interested, and it was Harriman who had suggested what I should do. I had not told the Hysons, and Gertie would not be home until Saturday. So I would wait until after the visit before saying anything specific about it to anyone else. Dorothy knew, of course, but then Dorothy was involved, as my mother and Harriman were.

One thing I must tell them was that Edward Marline had sworn to Kitty that he had not poisoned his wife. I knew they would say it was natural that he should do that, but I knew, and Kitty knew, that Edward would not have sworn that he was innocent if he were not. So I was positive that it was someone else who had administered the fatal dose.

I had a letter from my mother wishing me luck and telling me how much she looked forward to being with me again and hearing the result.

Gertie and Bernard came home the following Saturday. They were in excessively high spirits. Aunt Beatrice, Uncle Harold and I went to the station to meet them. There were hugs and kisses and shrieks of delight. We drove to the house, where everything had been prepared by Aunt Beatrice to give the newly married couple a suitable welcome home.

Bernard had not carried Gertie over the threshold, and she insisted they go out and enter in the correct manner, so Bernard performed his duty to everyone's satisfaction and we all went into the drawing-room, where Uncle Harold produced champagne and we all drank to the return of the happy couple.

And they were happy. Gertie shrieked her pleasure at the well-stocked larder and demanded to know if Aunt Beatrice wanted to make her as fat as she was.

It was a wonderful homecoming, and it was some time before Gertie turned her attention to me.

I told her about my mother, which interested her, and that I had found some other friends from the past whom I was visiting the following weekend.

"What a lot of friends from the past you have!" she cried. "You are really a dark horse, Carmel Sinclair."

Fortunately there was too much to absorb her in her new house for her to be very interested in me.

I had a note from Lucian. He was coming up to London in the middle of the week and suggested we have lunch together at Logan's.

This threw me into a dilemma. I should have to tell him that I was going away again. He had been in my thoughts a great deal since he had asked me to marry him, and there had been many times when I had wanted to say yes. Very much I had wanted it. I thought how unhappy I should be if he had to go away. I felt envious of Gertie, whose life ran so smoothly. That was how I should have felt if I had been certain of Lucian. There was just that barrier which I could not cross. I did not know even if it were a barrier. There was just something I could not understand, and I must know what it was before I could marry him.

I knew now that Lawrence could never be anything but a good friend. Of course, some people married good friends and were very happy. There was my mother and Harriman Blakemore—and now Kitty and Jefferson Craig. A marriage of convenience, if ever there was one. But for what motive? Not financial gain, but genuine desire to help on one side, and on the other an overriding need for support. My mother and Harriman. Kitty and Jefferson Craig. There was no pretence between them.

I was thinking of telling Lucian what I had told Gertie. That I was going to see a friend from the past. Well, I was . . . but there was more to it than that.

Then the thought came to me. If I were not frank with Lucian, why should I expect him to be with me?

I decided then that I must tell him that I had seen Kitty Carson, that I was going to stay with her and that I was becoming more and more caught up in what had happened at Commonwood House during that fatal time when it had become part of a *cause célèbre*.

I met him at our now familiar table at Logan's.

When we had ordered, he said, "Something has happened. Tell me."

I hardly knew where to begin, so I said, "You know I have always been interested in the Marline case."

His face changed. He frowned slightly. "Oh, it is so long ago. It's all over. What good could anyone do now?"

"I don't know. But I have seen Kitty Carson."

"What?"

"Let me explain. You know I stayed with my mother. I told you how she had married Harriman Blakemore and how they would like to see you one day. I am going to arrange that. When I was there, we talked a lot about the Marline case. You see, my mother was interested in Commonwood, for obvious reasons, and we talked about the old days. Harriman suggested that, as a man called Jefferson Craig had campaigned for Kitty, he might know something of her whereabouts."

"What made you go to all this trouble?"

"I suppose it was due to knowing them all so well and my conviction of the doctor's innocence."

"If he were, who killed Mrs. Marline?"

"That is the mystery. Suicide possibly, but I can't believe that. However, Harriman had this idea, and Dorothy Emmerson had once written to Jefferson Craig and had an address. So I wrote to Kitty care of him, and she got the letter right away because she had married him. The outcome of all this was that we met in Kensington Gardens. It was easy to talk there. I had found a quiet spot, and there are not many people about at ten o'clock in the morning."

He stared at me unbelievingly, and I added: "There it is. And that is where I am going."

"I can't see . . ."

"You think I should not have done this?"

"Perhaps, when something like this has happened, it would be better not to become involved. I think it is something you should put out of your mind and forget."

"There are some things one cannot forget, however much one tries."

"What did she tell you?"

"How she suffered. She has a daughter now. Jefferson Craig married Kitty so that the child should have the name of Craig. He seems to be a wonderful man. Harriman is too. How lucky both Kitty and my mother are! Poor Kitty, she suffered so much."

He was staring ahead of him. "Yes. Both of them seem to have found very good men."

"Kitty admits how fortunate she has been in that respect. Her great fear is that, although her little girl has the name of Craig, someday someone might discover that she is the daughter of Edward Marline. She says that will hang over her forever."

"It is very remote," he said.

"Yes, she knows that, but it is there. And, Lucian, it is possible."

"Yes, I suppose so."

"So I am going to her. I shall meet Jefferson Craig. Dorothy Emmerson is most impressed. She says he is a very clever man."

He was silent, and I guessed he was thinking that my preoccupation with this unsavoury event was unhealthy and rather foolish. Yet, at the same time, he had looked rather disturbed when I had spoken of the shadow which Kitty had said would hang over her daughter.

He changed the subject, and we talked of other matters, of Gertie's return and my next visit to The Grange, which would be after my return from seeing Kitty. Then my mother wanted me to go to Castle Folly, and she had said that it would be very pleasant if Lucian accompanied me.

But some pleasure had gone out of this meeting, and I felt the barrier between us was stronger than ever.

I was very surprised that evening to find that a note addressed to me had been delivered at the house. It had been pushed through the letter box, and I was surprised to see that it was in Lucian's handwriting.

I opened it with eagerness and read:

My dear Carmel,

I must see you tomorrow. It is very important. I have something to tell you without delay. We must go somewhere where we can be undisturbed. You told me you had met Kitty Carson in Kensington Gardens and there was hardly anyone there at ten in the mornings. Could you possibly meet me there tomorrow at that time? I will wait for you at the Memorial. I shall be there in any case.

My dearest, this is very important.

I love you.

LUCIAN

I read and reread the note. He had called me dearest and he had said, "I love you." That gladdened me, but the mysterious urgency of it faintly alarmed me.

I scarcely slept that night, and in the morning at ten o'clock I was at the Memorial, to find Lucian already there.

"Lucian!" I cried. "What has happened?"

He took my arm. "Let's sit down in that quiet spot you mentioned."

We hurried there. His face was stern and very solemn.

As soon as we were seated, he said, "It is about the Marline case."

I was astonished. "Yes, yes?" I said eagerly.

"You are convinced that Edward Marline did not commit that murder. I think I know who did."

"Lucian! Who?"

He was staring straight ahead. He hesitated, as though he found it difficult to speak, then he said slowly, "I think . . . I did."

"You! What do you mean?"

"I mean that I fear I may have been responsible for Grace Marline's death."

"That's impossible! You weren't there."

"Carmel, I think I may have been responsible," he repeated. "I mean, her death may have been due to me. It has haunted me for a long time. I try not to think of it, but sometimes I wake in the night with a horrible sense of guilt, and I think of that man who hanged for something which could have been due to me. I think of the governess . . . and now her daughter . . . who have this hanging over them for the rest of their lives . . . because of what I did."

"How could you have had anything to do with it? You hardly saw the woman. You weren't there."

"I was there," he said. "Do you remember the day before she died? I shall never forget it."

"I remember," I said. "You and Camilla came to tea."

"Yes. We were in the drawing-room downstairs because Mrs. Marline was in the garden and it wouldn't matter if we made a noise. We talked of opals. You remember that?"

I nodded.

"Camilla said our mother had had some fine ones, and Estella, or it might have been Henry, replied that their mother had an opal ring. He wanted to show it to me."

It was all coming back to me—that warm afternoon. Tom Yardley had wheeled Mrs. Marline into the garden, and there we were, in the drawing-room, laughing because we did not have to worry that we might make too much noise since she was in the garden and out of the way. I had been disappointed because Lucian had gone off with Henry, leaving us girls together.

Lucian went on: "Henry was determined to show me his mother's opal, because he was sure it was as good as anything my mother had, and I was eager to see it. Henry said, 'Come into her bedroom. It's all right. She's in the garden. I know where she keeps it.' We tiptoed into her room. She was safe in the garden, in the shade of the oak tree. Henry found the opal. 'Look!' he cried. It was then that it happened. I knocked over the table at the side of her bed as I went to take the jewel. There were two bottles of pills on it. The tops were not properly screwed on and they were scattered all over the floor.

"I was dismayed, but Henry said, 'Look, pick them up in a minute. Just look at this. Look how it flashes. I reckon that's a very fine opal . . . one of the best.' I was about to proclaim the superiority of my mother's when I heard Mrs. Marline say something to Tom Yardley and the chair began to move. Henry put the opal quickly back and I started to pick up the pills. There was one idea in our minds. We must not be caught here. I picked them all up. I had put them into the bottles. They were on the table where they had been and we ran giggling from the room just in time. Carmel, I did not think about that incident until later . . . much later. I awoke early one morning. The possibility had dawned on me. I had mixed up the pills. They were two different kinds, I was sure now. Mrs. Marline had taken the wrong ones."

"I can't believe that, Lucian."

"I have been trying to tell myself it couldn't have been like that. I never stop trying to assure myself. But it is a possibility. I should have come forward. I should have told what had happened. But I could not have saved Edward Marline. He was already dead. I was away at school at the time of the trial and the execution and knew nothing of it until it was over. It was not until a long time after that I realised what could have happened. The idea suddenly came to me. It might have been due to my action. Those pills were in different bottles to distinguish them. They might have looked different. In my haste, I had not thought of that. My one purpose was to get the pills back in their place before I was discovered. Mrs.

Marline might have intended to take a small dose and had taken a fatal one."

"Lucian, you are building up a fantasy. How do you know there were two sorts of pills, just because there were two bottles on the table?"

"I saw some newspaper cuttings about the trial once. There was a great deal about the medical evidence and those pills figured largely in it. What the pills contained was described. There was one which was to be taken only if she were in great pain—and no more than one a day. Then there was a milder sort, of which she could take three a day. I supposed they were both at her bedside. You can see how it might have happened—they were spilt. They were hurriedly picked up and put back . . . anyhow. It is almost certain that some would have got into the wrong bottle."

"But suppose you did mix them in your haste? There would be some difference in the pills. One would be larger, or of a different colour. You might not have noticed it, but anyone in the habit of taking them would."

"There was no suggestion at the trial that she had taken the wrong ones by accident. There was no suggestion that they had been put into the wrong bottles. They did not know they had been spilt, of course. All that was said was that she had taken a massive overdose of strong pills which had proved fatal. As it was so long after they hanged that poor doctor that this occurred to me, I tried to convince myself that it was too late to alter anything. There was nothing I could do to save him. But I can't stop thinking of Kitty Carson and her daughter, who have to live their lives, as you say, under a threatening cloud. I can't forget it. It has haunted me for a long time.

"I am glad I have told you, Carmel. I must do . . . whatever has to be done."

"I'm glad you've told me. We'll talk of it. We'll work out what has to be done. We must always share."

He turned to me. We looked at each other for a second and then his arms were round me. He kissed me lingeringly and with a yearning passion. He was asking me to help him. Fleetingly, I thought of him as he had been when I first knew him. The hero who protected me. Now it was his turn to be vulnerable, and I wanted more than anything to care for him.

I knew in that moment that I loved him completely. Understanding was there between us. Barriers had been swept away. I had said it all when I had told him we must share.

"What's to be done?" I said.

He replied, "You are going to Kitty Carson. I am coming with you."

I stared at him in astonishment.

"Yes," he said. "I thought it out last night. There is that man, the expert, Jefferson Craig. He will know what action to take. I will tell them exactly what happened. I have decided on that. It is the only way I can live now. There will be publicity, but I shall face it. Do you agree, Carmel?"

"I think you will not be at peace until you have faced up to this. But to come with me . . . I am not sure. We shall have to think more about that. Kitty will not expect me to arrive with anyone. I think the best thing would be that I should first explain to them and perhaps you could come down the following day. Kitty will probably remember you. You must have seen her now and then when you came to the house."

"Yes, I do remember her—a very pleasant person."

"I will tell her what you have told me and then we can all talk it over."

"I think that is probably the best way of doing it. Oh, Carmel, how glad I am that I told you!"

"You should have told me before."

"I know that now."

"You have to throw off this sense of guilt. Even if it were as you fear—and I cannot believe it happened like that—it is not your fault. A boy's careless act does not make him a murderer."

"No. But it can make him the cause of someone's death. And that is a sobering thought. One can't help its having an effect. Oh, I wish I could be sure that it had not happened that way!"

"We'll ask Jefferson Craig's advice. He will know what could be done."

Lucian smiled suddenly. "Oh, Carmel," he said, "I like the way you say 'we.' "

We were a great deal happier when we left the Gardens. Guilt still hung heavily on Lucian, but now I shared his problem, and we were both aware that through it we had come closer together.

When Kitty met me at the station there was a young girl with her. I knew at once that this was Edwina—a pretty girl with considerable charm—and I was immediately aware of the great affection between her and her mother.

"This is my daughter Edwina, Carmel," said Kitty. "And, Edwina, this is Miss Carmel Sinclair, whom I used to teach."

Edwina smiled and shook my hand.

There was a gentleness about her which reminded me of the doctor, and I could understand why Kitty was proud of and apprehensive for her.

Kitty drove the trap herself. As we passed along through those pleasant lanes, I was trying to work out how soon I could approach the matter which was uppermost in my mind.

We made conventional conversation and in due course arrived at the house. It was very pleasant, of three storeys and painted in white, which gave it a clean, fresh look. The house was made more attractive by the green shrubs which grew around it. There were steps to the front porch, and on the second floor were two balconies, one on either side, which had a charming effect.

As the trap drove up, a young woman appeared on the porch and ran down to greet us. I knew her at once and felt a rush of emotion. Adeline!

She stood still, looking at us. She had aged very little with the years. Her wide, innocent eyes had retained their youth. She must be thirty, but she looked no more than seventeen.

She skipped towards us as a child might. Indeed, I believed Adeline had remained a child at heart. She seemed happy and serene.

A man came out of the stables and took the trap. He touched his forelock to us.

"Thank you, Thomas," said Kitty. And then: "Adeline . . . Well, you two know each other."

Adeline had run to me. She stood there, smiling shyly. I took both her hands and kissed her.

"Adeline," I said, "I am so pleased to see you."

"It's Carmel," she said and laughed.

"Yes," said Kitty. "Carmel is going to stay with us for a few days. Won't that be nice?"

Adeline nodded, and we went into the house.

The hall was spacious. There was an oak chest on which stood a bowl of flowers, arranged, I guessed, by Kitty. A man came into the hall and I knew at once that he was Jefferson Craig. He stooped a little and walked with some difficulty, but the eyes that met mine were among the most alert I had ever seen. They were brown under bushy grey brows and his hair was thick and almost white. He was an old man, but he certainly had a great presence.

He said, "I am so glad you have come to see us. Kitty has been talking of you ever since she came back from your meeting, so you are not exactly a stranger to me. I look forward to getting to know you better."

"Thank you, and I do not think of you as a stranger either . . . for I have heard a great deal about you."

"I shall take her to her room, Jefferson," said Kitty. "We'll get together for lunch. How's that?"

"Excellent. I'm looking forward to it."

"So . . . be with you shortly."

He nodded and went back to the room which I presumed was his study.

Adeline had slipped her arm through mine.

"Kitty," she said, "I want to show Carmel her room first."

"Go ahead then," said Kitty.

With the delight of a child, Adeline took my hand. She whispered, "It's next to mine."

"That's very nice," I replied.

She was leading me on ahead of the others. Kitty was smiling. Life must have been very good for Adeline since she had gone to Kitty. There was no doubt of her happiness. I thought how different it had been for her at Commonwood, when all the time she had been terrified of encounters with her mother.

Adeline turned and said to Kitty, "I want to take her through mine first, Kitty."

"Well," retorted Kitty, "I don't suppose she will mind the extra journey."

I could see that Adeline had not grown up at all. She was still the child she had been all those years ago.

She opened a door and went in, standing aside for me to follow. It was a bright room and I noticed immediately the door which opened onto the balcony. There was a single bed with a blue carpet, a dressing-table and a mirror. On the wall hung many pictures. They were all colourful scenes of happy family life. It was a young girl's room and it was clear from the manner in which she was watching me that she expected me to exclaim in admiration for it.

"It is lovely," I said, and I thought how different it was from her room in Commonwood House, with its lofty ceiling and heavy furniture. This was light and full of colour. Adeline must be very happy now.

She beckoned me to the window.

"Come," she said, and I followed her onto the balcony. There was a pleasant view of the garden. I looked over the railing. Below was a stone patio with tubs of flowering plants.

Then she took my arm and, glowing with pride, showed me that the balcony extended to the next room, which was to be mine.

She went to it and beckoned to me.

"Carmel," she said, "this is your room. You see, we have the same balcony. If you leave your door open and I do the same with mine, we can call on each other this way."

"That's very convenient," I said.

We had stepped into my room. It was very like Adeline's, but there were only two pictures on the wall.

The door opened and Kitty came in with Edwina.

Kitty said, "We are going to leave Carmel to hang up her clothes and wash her hands. Then we shall have lunch." She smiled at me. "Is everything all right, Carmel?"

I assured her that it was, and she went on: "We shall be in the garden when you are ready."

"I'll bring Carmel down," said Adeline.

"I can see you are going to have a guardian angel," commented Kitty.

"I'll be your guardian angel, Carmel," cried Adeline.

"Thank you," I replied.

They left me. There was a basin and ewer in a small alcove and I washed. Then I unpacked and hung up the few things I had brought with me.

I was feeling a little apprehensive, wondering what their reaction would be when they heard what I had to tell them. I was eagerly waiting for an opportunity to do so. It would not be possible, of course, in the presence of Edwina or Adeline.

I suddenly felt as though I were being watched. It was an uncanny feeling.

I swung round. Adeline was standing at the door to the balcony.

"Hello, Carmel," she said, as though we had not seen each other for some time. "I shall take you down," she said.

"I'm not quite ready yet."

She came into the room and sat on the edge of the bed.

"Where have you been?" she asked.

"In Australia."

She wrinkled her brows and repeated, "Australia?"

"It's on the other side of the world."

"Why?"

"Why is it there or why was I there?"

"You," she said.

"Well, I was taken there a long time ago."

"When we went."

"Yes, about that time."

"It was horrible. I hated it." Her face suddenly distorted in fury. "Then I came to Kitty." In half a second, she had changed from hatred to sheer joy.

"It's very good now," I said. "I am so glad you came to Kitty, Adeline. That must have been wonderful."

She nodded. Then she said, "Why did you come here?"

"I met Kitty and she asked me."

She nodded again, as though she were satisfied about something which had troubled her.

"Shall we go down?" I suggested. "I am ready now."

Kitty and Jefferson Craig were in the garden. Edwina was with them. We sat and talked for a time about the journey and my friends in London and Australia. I was getting impatient. I think Kitty was aware of this, for she smiled at me, as though to say there would be plenty of opportunity to talk later.

We had an enjoyable lunch. There was a maid, Annie, who waited at table, and I discovered that the cook-housekeeper had been in Jefferson's employ for many years. So they lived comfortably but not ostentatiously.

It was not until after the meal that the opportunity came to talk to Kitty and Jefferson. Edwina had taken Adeline off somewhere and the three of us sat under the oak tree, looking across the lawn to the house. That was the moment, and I lost no time in telling them about Lucian's confession.

Jefferson was very interested.

"Poor young man!" he said. "What a dilemma! And he has carried the burden of guilt for a long time. One can see exactly how it happened. He jolted the table, the pills were scattered over the floor, the fearsome Mrs. Marline would be wheeled in at any moment when she would discover him in her bedroom. He falls into a panic. His one aim is to get the pills back and escape. Well, I would say it is just possible, but highly improbable that he was responsible for the woman's death."

"Improbable!" I cried. "Oh, if only he could see that!"

"Let us consider it all. There must have been some difference in the pills. They would probably be of a different colour . . . a different size. Lucian was in a panic. He did not notice these differences. His one aim was to get them into the bottles and escape. Mrs. Marline took the pills regularly. She would be well aware of the difference between the strong ones and the others. I could not think she would have taken the stronger ones unless she intended to."

"So you think Lucian could not have been responsible?" I cried.

"It is, of course, a possibility, but by no means a certainty."

"Lucian thinks he has been wrong in not letting it be known. He fears that a man may have been hanged because of his carelessness."

"But Lucian could do nothing about it before," put in Kitty. "He was away at school, wasn't he, and he did not know what was happening until it was too late for him to intervene."

"There are you and Edwina to consider," I reminded her, and we talked of the effect it could have on Edwina if it was discovered who her father was.

"I have often thought of that," said Kitty. "If Edward's name could be cleared, it would be a great blessing."

I said to Jefferson, "Lucian and I thought you would know what action ought to be taken in a case like this. I don't think Lucian will be at peace with himself until he has told what happened."

"I see what you mean," said Jefferson. "And it is true that there are Kitty and Edwina to consider. If this came out, there would be more publicity to contend with, and the case would be brought before the public. Attention would be focused on Kitty, which would be the worst possible thing for Edwina. If we could come up definitely with the one who had killed Grace Marline . . . someone who confessed . . . there would, of course, be a great deal of notice then, but it would be well worth it. We should have a conclusion to the case, and Edward Marline's name would be cleared. Kitty would be beyond suspicion and she need have no fear for Edwina. That would be quite a different matter from a flimsy possibility."

I told them that I had arranged for Lucian to call the next day.

"I should have asked your permission first, but there was no time, and, believe me, please, he is very distressed. He thinks Jefferson could tell him what has to be done."

"It will be good to see him," said Kitty. "I remember him. He was such a nice boy. You were very fond of him in those days, Carmel."

"He was always kind to me and a little attention meant a great deal to me at that time."

"Yes, I know."

"We shall look forward to seeing him very much."

"He will arrive in the afternoon on the two o'clock train. Is that all right?"

"Of course," said Kitty.

Jefferson said, "This is very interesting. I shall enjoy talking to him. In the meantime, I shall brood on this. There may be something we can do. I just feel at the moment that it is all rather suppositious, and I'm wondering whether, if he did reveal what he fears to be his guilt, he might not do more harm than good. However, I always like to think over these matters. We'll have a long talk tomorrow. That's always useful. My word, this is getting interesting."

"What a big part those opals play, don't they?" went on Kitty. "You remember, Carmel. Adeline was looking for them when she pulled out the drawer which resulted in that dreadful scene."

"Yes, I remember vividly."

There was a rustle in the bushes. We all turned in that direction from whence it came.

"Some animal," said Jefferson.

"Perhaps a fox?" suggested Kitty.

"I hardly think so," said Jefferson.

"We were talking of those opals," continued Kitty. "Some people say they are unlucky. I've never liked them since. They certainly brought bad luck to Lucian and poor Adeline."

There was a sudden movement from the bushes and Adeline was running across the lawn to the house.

"It must have been Adeline, not a fox, we heard in the bushes," said Kitty.

We watched her go into the house.

"She is a strange child," went on Kitty. "So absolutely childish at times. Then she will astonish you with her knowledge. Her memory is prodigious. Sometimes she will make a remark about the past which astonishes me. Of course, she did live through that terrible time like the rest of us. It must have left its mark on her."

"She is so happy to be with you."

"Oh yes. There is no doubt of that. At first, when she came here, she was really disturbed. All she needs is understanding."

Then we went back to talking about the great problem, and I was longing for the time when Lucian would join us.

He arrived in the early afternoon of the next day. Both Kitty and Jefferson greeted him warmly and told him how pleased they were that he had come. Jefferson said right away that I had explained his problem to them and he was looking forward to discussing it.

Adeline cried out when she saw him, "It's Lucian! Lucian, I'm Adeline. Do you remember me?"

Lucian said that he did and was gratified that she remembered him.

"You're bigger," she said. "A lot bigger."

"You haven't changed much."

She smiled to herself.

It was not long before Kitty contrived for the four of us to be alone together. We sat under the same tree where we were yesterday, and we were soon in deep discussion.

Jefferson listened intently to Lucian's version of the incident. When he came to the conclusion, Lucian told them that he had made up his mind that he must confess and he wanted Jefferson to tell him how it should be done.

Jefferson waved his hand, then said he was not sure that it would be wise. He set forth his reasons and brought forth the points he had made to Kitty and me yesterday. It was not good enough, he said, to say that Grace Marline had died because the pills had been mixed. We had to think of the publicity there would be if this new theory was put forth, and it was by no means conclusive.

Lucian listened with great attention. There might have been a difference in the pills. He could not remember. His one objective had been to get them back into the bottles.

"The more I think of it, the less I like of this idea of making it known," said Jefferson.

"Then I must go through my life not knowing whether I was responsible for that woman's death," said Lucian. "A crime for which her husband went to the gallows."

"You would do that in any case," Jefferson pointed out. "For how does your confession alter the facts that it can only be a possibility? If fact, it is only just remotely possible that she died because the pills were mixed. You must not blame yourself. You had no intention of doing anyone any harm."

I was watching Lucian closely. I should have to make sure he did not go on blaming himself. But I knew it would always be there . . . to haunt us until the end of our lives.

He thanked Kitty and Jefferson for taking such an interest in what Jefferson called his dilemma.

"It is ours too," said Kitty.

She was right. How strange it was that we were all caught up in this tragedy. It had affected the lives of every one of us and it seemed as though it could go on doing so for the rest of our lives. We could not escape from the tragic consequences of the events of yesterday.

Kitty said that Lucian must stay the night. The train service was not ideal and they had another spare room which Annie could easily make up. It was no trouble at all. They enjoyed his company. There was so much to talk of, and talking helped in cases like this. That was when ideas came, and they could be studied from all points of view. That, said Jefferson, was the way to arrive at the right solution.

So Lucian stayed.

He and I went for a walk in the evening. It had been Kitty's suggestion. She was aware of our feelings for each other and she guessed we should like to be alone.

Lucian and I walked down to the village and then beyond. I slipped my arm through his and he pressed it against him.

"It is good to be here with you," he said. "I couldn't wait to get here. What delightful, interesting people they are."

"You look better already," I told him.

"I should have talked to you before."

"It is they who have lifted your spirits. You do feel better now, I know. You realise that it is as Jefferson says—just a possibility. There was nothing you could have done."

"I'm not sure."

"But you can see what they mean about the publicity it would raise."

"It might clear his name."

"Only if it proved to be true, and how could anyone ever be sure of that? Jefferson is right. It would only bring the case to the fore again. Most people will have forgotten the Marline case by now. Oh, Lucian, don't you see? We have to leave it. It would only revive it all and then not many would believe that it was because the pills were mixed. Don't you see? We can do nothing. We have to forget. In any case, it was an accident. If you could have told what had happened before Dr. Marline died, it would have been different. But you can't bring back yesterday. It has to be forgotten. You will forget, Lucian, because I am going to make you."

"You will take that on then?"

"Most joyfully."

"A little while ago you were so uncertain."

"I am no longer so."

"You have changed suddenly."

"I don't altogether understand myself. You were the one I always loved since you found my pendant, took me to tea with the others and repaired the clasp of the chain. I remember every minute of that day."

"It was nothing much. What about Lawrence Emmerson's gallant rescue at Suez?"

"It must have been something more than the lost pendant. Of course it was. You have changed everything for me. When my father died, I thought I should never be happy again. You showed me that I can be. Perhaps that's it. You ask me why I changed so suddenly. I think it was when I saw you so unhappy with this great burden. You seemed young then—not the grand fellow I used to think you. You needed help. Oh, I suppose there are a hundred reasons why one suddenly knows one is in love."

"Carmel, I know too that I can be happy. I believe I can forget this thing. In any case, I can convince myself that it was an accident and there is nothing I can do about it now. It was the best thing that could have happened when you decided to get into touch with Kitty. I suppose I shall have my dark moments when the sense of guilt overcomes me, but you will be there, Carmel. I have to keep reminding myself of that. You will be there."

"I shall be there," I repeated. "We shall be together."

"Then we should plan to marry . . . soon."

"What will your mother say?"

"She will say, 'Glory be!' For some time she has wanted me to marry. She is the sort of woman who would like to have a hand in choosing her son's bride, and I have been receiving hints for some time that she has chosen you for that questionable honour."

"Don't laugh at it. It is an honour, and I want it more than anything."

"When then?"

"I think we should discuss that with your mother."

"I shall talk to her as soon as I return, and next weekend you must come down so that plans can go ahead."

I was happy, as I had thought I should never be again. I would go on mourning Toby all my life, and Lucian would remember that, because of an accident, he might have been responsible for the death of two people. That could not be changed. But we had each other. He would comfort me for my loss and I would be beside him when his fears were with him.

We should be happy. We would build our lives together. We knew what we wanted and we were going to do all in our power to attain it.

When we returned, there was some consternation in the house. Adeline was agitated. She was saying, "It is dangerous. People could fall over. You know what happened to that lady at Garston Towers."

"That was different," soothed Kitty. "That was the castle ramparts."

She turned to me. "It's nothing much. One of the stakes on the balcony has worked loose. Adeline has only just noticed it."

She smiled at me, her eyebrows raised to imply that Adeline could be unnecessarily excited over such things.

She went on: "Tom from the stables will be coming over at any minute. He'll soon fix it."

"Shall I look at it?" asked Lucian.

"No need to bother," replied Kitty.

"Oh, I'll have a look."

We went up to my room. The balcony in question was the one shared by Adeline and me.

"Where is it?" said Lucian. "Oh, I see." He knelt and examined the faulty stake. It moved as he touched it.

"Tom can usually fix these things," said Kitty.

"It's dangerous," cried Adeline. "People could fall over. There was that lady at Garston Towers."

I heard Edwina calling Adeline, who seemed to forget the stake and went off to her.

Kitty said, "Adeline gets disturbed about things that make an impression on her. The Garston Towers affair really caught her imagination. She often refers to it. Tom will soon mend that thing. The best thing in the meantime is to keep well away from it."

Tom arrived. He examined the balcony and agreed with Lucian. He said the best thing to do would be to put a new stake in. He'd get Blacksmith Healy to make one. He would have it shipshape in a few days. Meanwhile, he'd patch it up a bit.

While I was dressing for dinner that evening, I again had that feeling of being watched. This time I was not surprised to see Adeline at the balcony door.

"Hello," she said. "Are you having a nice time here?"

"Yes, thank you, Adeline."

"You were away a long time."

"Yes, I was."

"Why did you come now? Was it to tell Kitty something?"

"Well, just to be with her again. We were always good friends. Don't you remember?"

"Yes. I remember it all. Do you know about Lady Garston?"

"Only what I heard you say."

"It was at Garston. Garston is a castle . . . very big. She used to walk along the battlements. Do you know what battlements are?"

"Yes."

"It was dangerous there and they had put up a railing. People used to stand up there and throw boiling oil down on invaders."

"My goodness! That must have been a long time ago!"

"One day Lady Garston went up there. She leaned over the railing and it broke. She fell down . . . down . . . and then she was dead."

"Poor Lady Garston!"

"She didn't know the railing was loose."

"Well, we know ours is, so we have to be careful until it is mended."

"It would kill us just the same."

"Oh, let's be more cheerful. That's a pretty dress you are wearing."

Her expression changed to one of pleasure. "Kitty chose it for me."

"It suits you."

"Kitty says I ought to wear pretty clothes."

I smiled at her. "You love Kitty dearly, don't you?"

"I love Kitty more than anything else in the world . . . more than anyone ever loved anyone. I love Kitty." She looked at me very steadily. "No one must ever take Kitty away from me."

"I am sure no one would want to. Oh, look, it's time we went down to dinner."

After dinner, when Lucian and I were alone with Kitty and Jefferson, we returned to the subject which was uppermost in the minds of us all. Jefferson had not changed his opinion. He still believed that at this stage the mixing of the pills should be kept to ourselves.

"I'd like to go on mulling it over," he said. "You don't need to go tomorrow, do you?" he asked Lucian. "Could you stay another day? There is nothing like talking something over, even if you do go over the same ground again and again. It helps one to come to a conclusion."

Lucian said, "The offer is very tempting."

"Sometimes it is good to give way to temptation," said Kitty, "and I am sure this is one of them."

"Well, then, thank you for your hospitality and your interest in my problem."

"It is also ours," replied Kitty.

I lay in bed. Sleep was evasive. I was not surprised. I was thinking of Lucian and how much I loved him, and how wonderful it was to have made contact with Jefferson, who was so positive in his thinking and had already done a great deal to ease Lucian's mind.

I heard a faint sound and opened my eyes. Adeline was at the door which opened onto the balcony.

"Carmel," she cried in alarm, "come . . . quick . . . please hurry."

I leaped out of bed. "What is it?"

"Please . . . please come."

I followed her onto the balcony. She stopped suddenly.

"It's here," she said.

She held my arm and was gripping it very firmly. She took me to the balcony railing. There was a wildness in her eyes.

I cried out, "Adeline! Be careful! Remember . . ."

She held me firmly by both my arms. Her face was distorted. She looked quite different from the Adeline I knew. She was forcing me against the balcony, and I knew then what she was trying to do. The balcony was faulty. The stake was loose. And she was trying to push me over! I felt the railing move and then give way. It fell. I heard it clatter to the stone patio below.

Now, I thought. Now! And with all my strength I tried to free myself. But she was strong and her grip was firm. There was a menacing look in her face.

I was saying, "Why . . . why?"

She was still gripping me firmly, and began to sob.

We swayed a little. In vain, I made every effort to free myself. Then suddenly she was pulling me away from the balcony.

She was still holding me in that vise-like grip while she went on sobbing bitterly.

"I can't do it," she was whimpering. "I can't kill Carmel. Not Carmel . . ."

I felt this must be a bad dream. It could not be real. But she had meant to kill me. Why? It was for this reason that she had been obsessed by the faulty balcony. She had meant to push me over, and if she had . . . well, that would have been the end for me. What was in her poor troubled mind? Why had she turned against me?

She went on sobbing.

"Adeline," I said, "what does this mean? What are you trying to do?"

269

"I couldn't do it," she said. "I couldn't kill you, Carmel. But I won't let anyone take Kitty away from me."

I managed to get her into my bedroom. We sat side by side on the bed and I put my arm round her.

"Adeline," I said, "please tell me what is troubling you. I daresay it can be explained."

"You hate me now," she said. "You know, don't you?"

"I don't hate you. I never could. I'm very fond of you. We were always good friends in the past, weren't we?"

She nodded. "You came to tell her," she said. "You know. I heard you talking. I know what it's all about. It's about her . . . my mother . . . my wicked mother. She was going to send Kitty away. She wouldn't have let me see her anymore."

"Adeline," I said, "suppose you tell me exactly what this is all about."

"They'll take me away from Kitty," she said.

"They won't. Kitty loves you. You'll always be with her."

"I won't let them take me away from her. I won't."

"No, of course. But why did you want to hurt *me?*"

"You were going to find out. You brought Lucian down here. I heard you talking about it. You were going to tell Kitty to prove it all. You were going to tell them all . . . the newspaper men . . . the police . . . and all of them."

"Tell them what, Adeline?"

"That I did it. I killed her. You came down to tell them."

"You killed your mother?"

"She was going to send Kitty away. She was cruel. Nobody loved her. It was better without her. She frightened me. She caught me in her room. I only wanted to show Lucian the opal when the drawer came out . . . and then Kitty came for me, and my mother was so angry she said Kitty was to go. I went into her room when she was lying in her bed. She was gasping and couldn't breathe very well. She said, 'Pills . . . pills.' Just that. So I put a lot of them in a glass and gave them to her. She drank it. And then she was dead. But they took us off to Aunt Florence, and I wouldn't stay there, and after a time they sent me to Kitty. Then I thought you had come to spoil it all."

"Oh, Adeline, my poor, poor Adeline."

She leaned against me, sobbing.

"I came back to Kitty," she said. "It was lovely here. It's the best place in the world. I can't go away from Kitty. And you came here, and I listened and you were always talking to them about . . . what you knew and you were going to tell them . . . and when they knew they would take me away from Kitty. I can't go away from Kitty. It's safe here. It's my home. I didn't really want to hurt you . . . but I had to . . . and then I couldn't do it, because I like you too much."

"Adeline, I did not know what you thought I did. You didn't get it right. I came to see Kitty and we did talk about that. Now, you must stop crying. I am going to call Kitty now. She will know what to do. I'll be back in a moment."

She was quiet suddenly.

"Kitty," she said. "She'll know . . . but now I've told . . . Kitty will know what to do."

I left her. I ran to Kitty's room. She was asleep and I roused her hastily. I told her she must come at once. There had been a scene with Adeline.

She was out of bed in seconds.

"What's happened?" she said.

"She's been talking about the past. Please come quickly. She frightened me."

We ran to the bedroom. She was not there. Her balcony door was open, but she was not in her room.

Then I went to the edge of the balcony where the faulty stake had been.

I looked over. Adeline was lying on the patio below.

She was taken to the hospital and Kitty was with her all the time and she was happy.

She felt little pain, the doctor told us. Her spine was irrevocably injured. She was quite lucid at times and she talked of the past.

She told us all again and again—including the doctor and nurses —how she administered the pills which had killed her mother and why she had felt it was necessary to do so. She knew about the pills because she had heard the district nurse talking about them to Nanny Gilroy and Mrs. Barton. She had listened a great deal. People thought she couldn't understand, so they talked in front of her.

She knew that her mother was going to send Kitty away, and for that reason she, Adeline, had killed her. She had been sent to Aunt

Florence, and had made them hate her so much that they begged Kitty to take her. Then everything was right and she was happy for a long time. But now they knew she had killed her mother they would take her away from Kitty. She did not think they would hang her because they would say she was silly, but she would rather that than live away from Kitty. But this was the best way and Kitty would be with her till she died, which she knew would be soon.

She had told me she was going to kill me because she thought I knew she had killed her mother. But I had been her friend and she couldn't do it after all, so she had tried to kill herself. Lady Garston had fallen from the battlements, so she fell from the balcony.

She lived for two days. She had made her confession—not only to me but in the presence of several people and in doing so had banished the cloud which hung over so many of us.

As Jefferson had predicted, there was a great deal of publicity. Adeline's confession of guilt, the fact that an innocent man had been hanged for a crime he had not committed, had aroused public interest, and for a few weeks there was comment throughout the press. Kitty, with Jefferson and Edwina, went abroad for a few months to escape attention. The case was closed, solved without a doubt. Adeline's last dramatic act had settled that.

I felt sad when I thought of poor Adeline's life, but I remembered the joy she had displayed when she and Kitty were together. Surely she had been happy then. I think her conscience had not worried her a great deal. Her mother was wicked, she would reason, causing unhappiness to many people. She had deserved to die. And her father? How had she thought of him? She had not known him well, but he had never been unkind to her. She had probably been able to put him from her mind.

Lucian and I were married three months later. Lady Crompton had insisted on making it a more grand affair than either Lucian or I wanted, but that was of small importance.

We were too happy to care.

And After

FIVE YEARS HAVE PASSED since Adeline's death. They have been five happy years.

A new century has come, and I think that the whole of Britain knows that this is the beginning of a new era. The Queen has died and the Court is plunged into mourning on this cold and wintry day. They have buried her beside the husband she adored in her "dear mausoleum" at Windsor.

I stood at the window, looking over the lawn where so long ago I had had tea with Camilla and Lucian, Estella, Henry and Adeline, and I thought, this is my home. Lucian is my husband, and all that happened has brought me to my present happiness.

Lady Crompton is an invalid these days, but her life has considerably brightened. I have a son, Jonathan, aged four, and a two-year-old daughter, Catherine, who is equally dear to her. There is also Bridget. Jemima Cray is no longer with us. I was greatly relieved when we were finally rid of her. I had steeled myself for the ordeal. I offered her an annuity, implying that she should have it only if she left without fuss and stopped her ridiculous fabrications. I also hinted that such monstrous untruths amounted to slander and she had better take care. I was delighted when she decided to go quietly.

My mother and Harriman are frequent visitors to The Grange, and the children greatly enjoy Castle Folly. Gertie continues happily married, and there are two little Raglands in that nursery which Aunt Beatrice prepared with such high hopes.

Two pieces of news from Australia cheered me. They concerned James Forman. Elsie wrote:

I think he was a bit cut up when he heard of your marriage. James was never one to talk about his emotions. But Mrs. Forman says he is interested in a very nice girl, and they are hoping something will come of it. He has had a few finds, nothing much so far to boast about, but comforting, I suppose. Poor James! He is as determined as ever.

Oh, one good thing has happened. They found the one who killed the old sundowner. It was one of the miners. It was what we expected, but I think James felt he was a bit under suspicion. So he's relieved that that little matter is settled.

I thought of Lucian's ordeal, and I rejoiced for James.

I was delighted a few months after my wedding to hear from him. With his letter came a gift, and when I opened the small box I was amazed to see lying there a black opal. James had written:

This, my dear Carmel, is a belated wedding present to remind you of the time you spent in the Outback. I am still slogging away, rewarded now and then by the occasional find, but I wouldn't be doing anything else. I hear news of you now and then from Gertie. I wish you all the best life can give you. That's why I thought this would do for you.

I was reading the other day about one of those old Roman historians. He had a good word to say for opals. In those days the word opal meant "magic eye" or "seer of good fortune" and was supposed to bring the gifts of foresight and prophecy to its owner. There was a proviso. They must only be used to bring happiness to people, and then they would bring luck to its owner. The stone was then known as the lucky opal. I said to myself, "That shall be for Carmel."

I took out the stone and, studying it, thought of what a big part opals had played in our lives. If Adeline had not searched for her mother's opal on that fatal day, she would not have been goaded to do what she did; Dr. Marline and Kitty Carson would not have been accused of murder; and Lucian would not have suffered those years of guilt.

I had the opal made into a ring. I wear it constantly.

And then there is Kitty. When I heard what was in her mind, I must say I was very surprised, but now it is done, I think I understand how she feels.

Jefferson died three years ago, leaving Kitty and Edwina very well provided for. There was a certain amount in the papers about his life and his work and it was recalled that he had married Kitty Carson, and there was further reference to the Marline case of course.

After his death, she and Edwina often came to stay with us, and she had a habit of going to Commonwood House.

One day she asked me to go there with her. As we stood among the ruins, she said, "Carmel, I am coming back."

I did not understand what she meant at first. Then she went on: "In my dreams, long ago, I used to think of living here. I loved this house. I used to think of how it might have been. I should like to be near you, Carmel. Edwina loves you all, and so do I. I think she is happier here than anywhere. She grows more like Edward every day. I want to be here. I am going to buy this ground. You know Jefferson left me very comfortably off and I can do it easily. The ruins shall be cleared away. I shall build a new house here . . . a new Commonwood."

At first I thought she could not be serious, and I was surprised to discover she was in earnest.

And that is what she has done.

She came down to the new Commonwood during the first week of the new era, and, as I stepped over the threshold, I knew this was right for her.

She has her daughter, her memories of Edward, and his name has been cleared forever.

Now, as I look across at the lawn, I see that the snowflakes are beginning to fall. The children are coming across the grass. Jonathan is holding up his hands to catch the snowflakes, laughing with delight. He loves the snow.

Lucian is there. Catherine runs to him and he lifts her in his arms.

They are coming into the house.

I look at my black opal and think of its promise. That good fortune has been mine.

I am happy. This is my world now, and it is good.